Frankenstein's Witch:
St. Lizzie, Pray For Us

Frankenstein's Witch: St. Lizzie, Pray For Us

A
Porter Down
Hollywood
Mystery

by
Gregory William Mank

BearManor Media

2022

Frankenstein's Witch: Saint Lizzie, Pray For Us
A Porter Down Hollywood Mystery

© 2022 by Gregory William Mank

Published in the United States of America by:

BearManor Media
1317 Edgewater Dr #110
Orlando FL 32804

bearmanormedia.com

Printed in the United States.

Typesetting and layout by John Teehan
Cover design by Kerry Gammill
Cover painting: *Lilith* (1887) by John Collier (1850–1934)

ISBN—978-1-62933-946-7

Table of Contents

PART FOUR—VALERIE (SEPTEMBER 25 TO DECEMBER 24, 1931)

Dedication:

To my beautiful Barbara
Who believed this book would happen
And makes all my dreams come true.

Dedication:

To my beautiful Barbara
Who believed this book would happen
And makes all my dreams come true.

PART ONE – LIZZIE
May 15 to May 29, 1967

Saint Dymphna, young and beautiful... Help me to imitate your love of purity... Give me strength and courage in fighting off the temptations of the world and evil desires.

– From *The Novena to Saint Dymphna*,
patron saint of lunatics, epileptics,
and rape and incest victims.

1

The Feast Day of
Saint Dymphna

MONDAY, MAY 15, 1967

Frankenstein's Monster's ass itched.

The blast furnace costume, the stifling rubber mask, the friggin' giant boots—they were all part of the actor's torturous, $120-per-week Gothic gig as the legendary, bolt-necked creature, haunting the Universal Studios Tour.

Yeah, so much for a Masters from Yale Drama School, moped the "Monster."

On this blue, smog-free Monday, the "Monster" woefully sat behind an archway of a decaying, back lot Tyrolean village set, with a tall rickety steeple and crooked gabled houses. The Santa Ana winds shrieked fiercely through the cobbled streets as he stretched his 6'5" frame, wishing fervently that he were anywhere else, doing anything else.

Christ, it's hot, he cursed.

The pale green mask covered his whole damned head. The suit—a tawny brown rather than the traditional black, so he'd appear more "tourist-friendly"—was roasting him alive. Sweat trickled sinuously down his back, butt, and crotch, and the costume's padding made it impossible for him to scratch. The romper-stomper boots were a bitch, making it a challenge to balance himself. He stank.

How'd Boris Karloff ever deal with this bullshit? pondered the Monster.

* * *

3

Once upon a time, Universal City had been a pastoral film studio, founded in 1915 on the frontier of the San Fernando Valley. During Hollywood's Golden Age, coyotes howled at night on Universal's mountain, high above the giant carcasses of old film sets. There'd even been a shepherdess, leading her flock over the studio's hills and past its lakes.

However, over the decades, fires had destroyed most of the historic sets. Coyotes had long ago slaughtered the lambs. And the studio, although still producing films and TV shows, had glutinously morphed into a voracious tourist-trap... hence, the Universal Tour.

When in Southern California, pimped the '67 world-wide ads, *Visit Universal Studios*

The Monster relaxed behind the archway, his Motorola transistor radio playing Strawberry Alarm Clock's *Incense and Peppermints*. He took a deep drag on his Mary Jane as he studied his lines for *Hamlet*, in which he'd be starring with the Sepulveda Little Theatre, for friggin' free, of course, in two weekends. He tried again to scratch his ass. No luck.

Then came the "Glamor Tram" car, packed with gawking tourists, snaking its merry pink-and-white way through the village. The Tram guide, a blonde Barbie doll wanna-be, had been breathlessly cooing about such studio sites as the pond from *McHale's Navy* and the mansion from *The Munsters*. Now and then she'd plug Universal's new feature-in-production: *The Shakiest Gun in the West*, starring Don Knotts.

"This is our 'European Village,'" she now recited, "where, way back in 1931, Universal filmed the all-time-great horror classic, *Frankenstein*. And sometimes, after all these years, on these all-hallowed streets... ."

It was his cue, and the Monster came a-roaring through the archway, running and waving his arms over his head like Robert Preston performing "Ya' Got Trouble" in *The Music Man*.

"AARGGH!" growled the Monster.

"WOOO!" squealed the blonde guide.

The Monster lumbered alongside the tram, the tourists aimed their cameras, the tram resumed moving, the Monster chased the tram, and the guide grinned "Wave to the Monster!" The Monster waved back... and then he tripped in his boots and fell flat on his face.

Shit, thought the Monster.

The tourists howled. The guide tee-heed through her microphone. The Monster awkwardly got to his humongous feet and, after the tram turned, gave them all the finger.

There'd be another tram in fifteen minutes. It was the only way the tourists saw the back lot—no one was allowed off the tram, so the Monster had the next quarter-hour free on the ghostly, ramshackle set. He headed back to the archway to study Hamlet's "Now I am alone" soliloquy. The hot wind howled in falsetto again… and then he heard a woman singing. The song was *As Tears Go By*, and her soprano voice was so flat, so lousy, it was almost eerie. He turned, looked up through his rubber mask eyelids, and saw her.

What the…? thought the Monster

She was tall, had long red hair, was standing on a little balcony high on the village's steeple, was holding a lily… and was stark naked. Actually, she was wearing a large black hat like the hippie chicks wore, the brim up in the front, and a crystal amulet was hanging from a chain around her neck, catching the sunlight. She smiled slyly, and her bright, yellow, darkly made-up eyes stared down at him.

Holy Hell, thought the Monster.

Was he hallucinating? The heat? The Mary Jane? The fall on his face? No… the balcony's broken railing provided him a clear, head-to-toe view. Perky nipples. Auburn beaver. He could smell her scent—honeysuckle—all the way down in the street. She stopped singing, giggled, and pointed at him with a long, red, fake fingernail.

"Boo!" she said.

She cackled, high-kicking one leg like a spastic Rockette, nearly losing her balance, almost falling from the balcony, her psycho laughter virtually a goddamn scream.

Fucking stoned, the Monster thought.

Suddenly he realized—this was a joke. Vic and Ron, who supervised the tour and knew he despised his job, had set up this prank, to "give him a lift," so to speak. The gal was so high up on the balcony that the security camera couldn't see her. And the fact that she'd made her appearance just after a tram had driven away, and almost fifteen minutes before another one arrived, made the Monster figure Vic and Ron had timed this gag to the minute. He wondered… how much did those two horndogs pay a Hollywood hooker to come to the back lot, strip in the steeple, and climb all the way up on that gonna-fall-any-minute balcony? He expected Vic and Ron to emerge from their hiding places any second, and there'd be gales of laughter from them, and maybe the wacky whore herself.

"Vic?" he shouted. "Ron?" Silence.

She was singing *As Tears Go By* again, and in his rising anxiety, the Monster noticed specifics about her. She was gawky, gangly. Her nose was witchy, pointy. He figured the cascading red hair was a wig and imagined she looked scalped without it. He guessed her honeysuckle perfume was so heavy because she stank like an anteater under it. And there were those spooky yellow eyes, staring at him under spidery false eyelashes.

Then he noticed something else... a thin but livid purple scar, snaking up her abdomen out of her pussy hair.

Yeah... Vic and Ron must have gone far east on the Boulevard after midnight to find this witchy bitch. Or did they? The Monster decided he better follow protocol and report the trespasser, but as he turned to go, the freak began to speak.

"Let us pray," she said, almost chanting. "To Dymphna, my guardian angel in Heaven... Patron Saint of Lunatics, Epileptics, and Rape Victims... whose father cut off her head because she wouldn't let him fuck her..."

The Monster stared up at her. She ritualistically raised the lily above her head, and touched the amulet that hung from her neck.

"Don't let me go crazier, or let me have a seizure, or let anyone rape me today..."

And now, as in a mockery of the Sign of the Cross, she touched the lily to her left nipple, then her right, and sinuously slid it against her vagina.

"Amen!" she sighed, tossing the profaned lily to the Monster. It landed at his giant boots. She giggled again.

"Jesus," mumbled the Monster, turning and righteously stomping off. This freak was no joke. She was fucking crazy. Yeah, the Monster thought wryly... All Universal needed, competing with Disneyland in the big arena of Southern California family fun, was a naked, scarred, wild-eyed bitch on the loose, tickling her pussy with a lily.

A loyalty to his employer had conventionally kicked in, and the Monster knew they had to get her down and out of here before the next tram arrived in about ten minutes. He stalked to the archway, walkie-talkied the studio police, and looked back across the square at the steeple.

She was gone, but the lily was there, the hot wind blowing it across the cobbled street.

"We have an emergency," he informed security, giving details. These guys were fascists when it came to trespassers, and the Monster figured they'd surely find the freak and kick her rancid tail right out onto Lankershim Boulevard. Meanwhile, they temporarily closed the tour and ordered the Monster to leave the set. He picked up his radio, which was playing *California Dreamin.*' Yeah, maybe the woman, was a dream, a goddamn nightmare, yet that damned lily was still there. He grabbed his *Hamlet* script and glanced at these words:

> *The spirit that I have seen*
> *May be the devil...*

"Son-of-a-bitch," he said, feeling a wet, creeping sense of danger as he sprinted from the set as fast as his boots could carry him.

Minutes later, with security *en route*, the *Frankenstein* village exploded into flames.

* * *

It burst like a volcano, the flames towering 300-feet. Burning debris flew on the Santa Ana winds like witches on broomsticks. The fiery steeple collapsed and the old bell crashed and clanged into the street. Hundreds of screaming tourists, beholding the conflagration, wildly stampeded for the exits.

"This way! This way!" shouted the "Barbie" tour guide, surprisingly fearless, directing the hysterical crowd toward the gates, even as the mob came perilously close to stomping and trampling her.

Sirens wailed all over L.A. as fire engines raced toward the gigantic plume of smoke ascending over the Valley. TV news helicopters waged virtual dogfights for footage. The blaze hungrily devoured 12 acres, destroying the village, the Western street from TV's *Laramie*, and part of the square built for 1960's *Spartacus*. Miraculously, there were no deaths, but several firemen narrowly escaped injury.

The estimated damage: $1,000,000.

After the firefighters contained the blaze, assuring the safety of the main lot, several Universal starlets posed for the press, smiling flirtatiously and suggestively holding fire hoses.

* * *

"*Hollywood History Inferno!*" proclaimed the May 15th 11:00 P.M. news.

As smoke rose from the ruins into the night sky and the Santa Ana winds still shrieked, a stocky, semi-retired, semi-grizzled P.I., who'd driven in from Twentynine Palms, joined the all-night investigation. The P.I. learned that a studio employee had eye-witnessed a suspicious female trespasser, naked no less, moments before the fire erupted. The employee had even helped a police artist develop a composite sketch of her face.

The P.I asked to see it.

In 1931, the P.I. had been a troubleshooter on the filming of *Frankenstein*. He retained a crystal-clear image of a woman who, at that time, had claimed she was a witch, committed a gruesome murder, and nearly sabotaged the production. He was aware that today had been the Roman Catholic Church's feast day of Saint Dymphna, and knew how this date related to the 36-years-ago case.

A cop handed him the composite sketch. The P.I. stared at it for a moment, grinned, and shook his head.

"Well, I'll be damned," said Porter Down. "Look who's back!"

2 The Witch Burner

At 7 A.M., the tower chimes rang.

The 95-foot-tall tower, crowned by a 25-foot gold-leaf statue of the Virgin Mary, stood on the mountain above the National Shrine of the Grotto of Lourdes near Emmitsburg, Maryland. Below in the foothills was the campus of Mount Saint Mary's College and Seminary, a year away from its 160th anniversary.

The college's student body had an irreverent nickname for the sacred statue: "Lady Goldfinger."

Meanwhile, the bell in the campus church's steeple announced morning Mass. A freshman opened his dormitory window, his record player blasting Jefferson Airplane's *Somebody to Love,* Grace Slick blaring a lusty reveille for the all-male campus. The tower chimes, the church bell, and Slick's voice all battled for dominance, the cacophony ascending above what the college called "Mary's Mountain."

* * *

A few miles north of Mount Saint Mary's, over the Pennsylvania line, were the Gettysburg battlefields. Several miles south, guarded in the Catoctin Mountains, was Camp David, President Johnson's retreat.

As Mass ended at the Mount this morning, a tall, lanky man came jogging in front of the church. His full gray hair made him look older than his 37 years.

9

"Dr. Wyngate? Will you autograph this for me?"

Dr. Anthony Wyngate turned to see a stocky man with a thin, trimmed mustache. He was dressed in a navy blue shirt, slacks, and battered yachting cap and was holding a copy of Wyngate's recently published novel, *Boudicca: An Historic Fiction*. Wyngate had based the novel on the legendary female Celtic queen who'd defied the invading Romans in 60 or 61 A.D., suffered glorious defeat, and possibly committed suicide. The jacket cover presented a full-length color portrait of Boudicca, resplendent in her helmet, flowing hair, and gown.

"Sure," said Wyngate, and the man handed him the book and a pen.

"That Boudicca was quite a gal," said the man.

"Yes, she was," said Wyngate.

"You really poured it on in that chapter where the Romans flogged her and raped her daughters," said the man.

"Glad you liked it," said Wyngate wryly.

"Nice shirt you're wearing," said the man. "Did you get it in Egypt last summer?"

For a moment, Wyngate, whose black T-shirt pictured a gold Sphinx, thought that he might have his own groupie. The visitor hardly looked the type. He had cold pale eyes, his face was tanned and intimidating, and his age tough to guess—maybe a hard-living 50, perhaps a well-preserved 70. The 6'2"-tall Wyngate loomed over the barrel-chested man, who was about 5'8" and built like a tank.

"Yes, I bought it in Cairo. So... to whom should I sign this?"

"Me," said the man. "Porter Down."

"Where are you from, Mr. Down?" asked Wyngate, inscribing the title page.

"California," said Down. "I'm investigating the fire at Universal Studios last week. You probably read about it in the papers."

"Oh," said Wyngate, wondering why the man was 3,000 miles from the scene of the fire. "Well... welcome to the Mount." He handed him the book.

"That's my pen," said Down. Wyngate handed him the pen.

"Can I offer you anything else?" asked Wyngate.

"Yeah," said Down. "Breakfast."

* * *

They headed for breakfast. Wyngate's guest walked with a jaunty, marching strut, and his blue cap, clothes and white canvas shoes gave him the look of a sailor. His shirt was short-sleeved, his arms thick and still muscular.

"Were you a military man, Mr. Down?"

"Lafayette Escadrille, 1918."

"You must have been a very young pilot."

"17."

"Did you remain in the military?"

"U.S. Naval Academy, Class of '25. Kicked out in '22."

The man kept marching. *He reminds me of a puffin*, thought Wyngate.

* * *

Wyngate, free today after having graded senior exams, ate with the visitor in the cafeteria. He figured the man, based on his World War I service, must be 66 or so. He had remnants of a matinee-idol profile, yet his physique was short, thick, almost squat.

It's like somebody put the wrong head on the wrong body, thought Wyngate.

"I hear the Grotto's jim-dandy," said Down, enjoying his rubbery bacon. "And that you used to be its custodian. Will you take me up there?"

"'Do not neglect to show hospitality,'" recited Wyngate, "'for by that means some have entertained angels.'"

"*Hebrews*," replied Down. "Chapter 13, verse 2."

* * *

Wyngate offered to drive Down to the Grotto but the man wanted to walk. Down tossed his signed book into his rental car parked near the church and he and Tony began climbing the steep steps up the mountainside. Interspersing the woods were the black, twisted Judas trees, having recently dropped their small, deep-pink flowers.

"These are Judas trees," said Wyngate. "They're called that…"

"Because Judas Iscariot hanged himself from one," said Down.

They reached the top of the hill, approaching the tower and the large iron gates of the Grotto. It was a replica of the Grotto of Lourdes, where the Blessed Mother had appeared to Bernadette. The old mountain cemetery was off to the left. The tower started banging out 9:00.

"So that's Lady Goldfinger," said Down, gazing up at the statue.

"Yes," said Wyngate. "Consecrated three years ago. Illuminated all night."

Down turned, whistling at the view of farms and fields. A marker at the viewpoint featured words by Mother Elizabeth Seton:

We are half in the sky;
the height of our situation is almost incredible.

"Peace, love and dope," said Down, looking out at the horizon. "All blowin' in the wind and heading this way." He indicated the Grotto. "Shall we?"

As they entered the gates, the tower chimes were playing *Immaculate Mary*, an old hymn sung by pilgrims to Lourdes. Tony thought the melody strangely sad. They walked into the garden, under the tall oak trees, passing bronze tablets of the 14 Stations of the Cross. Blue, white and pink wildflowers grew along the path. The scent of boxwood was fragrant and blue-jays called in the trees.

"The Grotto's been restored the past few years," said Tony. "The shrine ahead, where Mother Seton prayed, was locked up and off-limits when I came here."

"1954… right, professor?" asked Porter Down.

"Call me Tony. And how'd you know that?"

"Call me Porter," said the visitor, but didn't answer Tony's question. "So, Tony, I hear that you're quite a guy. Only novelist on campus."

"So far."

"Still teach Classics here, despite your success as a writer."

"I'm probably not as successful as you think."

"A night shift volunteer at Gettysburg Hospital. Awarded for your service."

"The award should have gone to a volunteer who doesn't have insomnia."

"I also hear you're piss-poor at taking a compliment."

"Sorry."

"They said I'd find you jogging this morning," said Porter.

"And you did," said Tony.

"My first wife," said Porter, regarding the Grotto's iconography, "was a rosary-carrying Catholic. She died 40 years ago next month."

"I'm sorry," said Tony. "We'll light a candle for her at the altar."

"Thanks," said Porter. "By the way, what do you say to students who ask why an intellectual such as yourself believes in God?"

"I say that if Michelangelo, Shakespeare, Beethoven, Poe, and JFK, my personal heroes, all had room in their minds for faith, I have room in mine."

"Damn good answer, Tony."

Tony thought so too. He wished he believed it as firmly as he'd stated it.

* * *

They'd reached the end of the path. There was a small chapel and the mountain stream ran under a short bridge that led to the Holy Grotto. A statue of the Blessed Virgin, her robes painted in the traditional blue and white, stood in a niche in the stone wall above the altar. Votive candles burned day and night inside its recess and two nuns knelt in silent prayer below the statue.

Tony lit a candle for Porter's wife. For a moment, Porter watched the candle burn, then led Tony away from the nuns at the altar, back over the bridge and to the front of the chapel. He stood by a Judas tree and Tony noticed the man's gold medallion, worn on a chain around his neck.

"So, Tony," said Porter. "You're probably wondering why I'm really here?"

"You could say that," said Tony.

"Ready to make 'Lady Goldfinger' proud of you?" asked Porter.

"How so?" asked Tony.

"You're coming to L.A., Professor. I'm gonna burn a witch who's risen from the dead—the witch who set the Universal fire—and you're going to write a book about it."

"You're actively serious?" asked Tony.

"I'm by-God serious," said Porter. "And I promise you a swell time!"

3 The Funeral of Big Leonard Brodey

Big Leonard Brodey, once upon a time, had been a daredevil movie stunt man.

Starting in 1930, he'd tumbled off stallions, fallen off cliffs, and come-a-crashing through second floor saloon windows. Occasionally, he'd ventured out of Westerns, as when he leaped and bounded for Lon Chaney, Jr. in a Wolf Man movie. Then came 15 fetid years of alcoholism, leading to a summer night in 1957 when Big Leonard had cashed his Motion Picture Relief Fund check, picked up a hooker, savagely beat her to a pulp, and threw the still-alive woman through a closed window on the 6th floor of Hollywood's Knickerbocker Hotel.

"The whore laughed at me," he'd growled when arrested.

It had been the dazzling courtroom combat of Alfred Pinkerton, Esq., that had spared Big Leonard execution, sending him to San Quentin on a 20-year sentence. He'd been released after doctors diagnosed a tag-team of fatal ailments and had moved into a deserted, decaying ranch in Lone Pine, near Mount Whitney, where he'd worked in 1939's *Gunga Din* and many westerns. Then, two nights ago, Big Leonard, always aggressive, had decided to confront a bear that had wandered onto his property.

The funeral was today... at high noon.

* * *

"A most beautiful morning, sir," said the driver of the red, top-down, 1966 Jaguar. The man seated beside him lit a cigarette and said nothing.

14

The tall hills beyond Olancha, about 170 miles north of Los Angeles, were turning vividly green and only a vestige of snow capped the Sierra-Nevadas. Gerald Mahugu, the driver, wore an African robe from his motherland tribe and a warlord scarf. He saw his clothes as a "black power" statement.

The muscular Mahugu, having fled Apartheid South Africa, loved L.A., especially the art museums. Twenty years ago, he would have been "houseboy" to Alfred Pinkerton, but now he was his chauffeur/bodyguard. Gerald had arrived in L.A. during the "Burn Baby Burn" Watts riots of '65. Some black brothers felt he was no better than a houseboy now, and he knew Mr. Pinkerton wanted him mainly for show. But Gerald had ambition. One day, he would be a lawyer too. Gerald already return-addressed his weekly letters to his father in Africa *Gerald Mahugu, Esq.*

* * *

Alfred Pinkerton's pearl-white suit was immaculate and his Panama hat and wire-framed sunglasses shielded his eyes. He carelessly tossed his nearly spent cigarette from the car, lighting a fresh one. He felt smug—rumors were raging all over L.A. as to what the real story was behind the Universal Studios fire, and he was one of only half-a-dozen people who knew.

In fact, the perpetrator was his client.

A one-time legal superstar in eclipse, Pinkerton, 55, was still dashingly if bizarrely handsome—a large, leonine head, thinning tawny hair combed forward Julius Caesar style, and huge, blue/gray cat eyes. In the Coliseum arena of L.A. courtrooms, Pinkerton, in his prime, had always drawn blood, his belief or disbelief in his clients' innocence completely irrelevant.

"I militantly believe in nothing," Pinkerton said often, privately but proudly, "that I can't buy, consume… or penetrate."

Apropos of penetration, he thought of Felicia Shayne, his former lover, protégée, and junior by over 25 years, who expected to learn today if she'd passed her BAR exam. Tobacco indulgence had left Pinkerton with a loud, alarming smoker's cough of a laugh, and it erupted as he imagined brunette, soft-lipped Felicia summating in the courtroom rather than sucking in the bedroom. Yet her ambition, in light of his recent setbacks, intimidated him… despite his being on the eve of a comeback.

He needed self-exaltation. He was about to get it.

* * *

Gerald Mahugu drove the Jaguar into the grove and past the cedarwood chapel, stirring up the tumbleweed. Outside were the sheriff of Lone Pine, the preacher, the undertaker, and a half-dozen morbidly curious mourners, looking like ancient extras from a *Gunsmoke* episode.

"Lord a'mighty," gummed a geezer, staring at the car's color and Mahugu's.

Also watching was Big Leonard's long-suffering hunting dog, "Mike." A rancher had thought it a fine idea to bring the old beast to its master's funeral, and had hitched the hound to the rail by the chapel steps. "Mike" epically panted and drooled in the morning heat.

As Mahugu stood vigilantly beside the Jaguar, Pinkerton marched into the chapel, up to the pine coffin at the altar. Yes, there was Big Leonard, all 250 pounds of him, laid out in a flannel shirt and overalls, as if ready to embark on a hunting junket into the Great Beyond. *Sic Transit Gloria Big Leonard*, thought Pinkerton who, as the man's legal guardian, had now and then looked in on him at the ranch.

No more of Big Leonard referring to Mahugu as "the Zulu" with Mahugu in earshot. No more waddling around the ranch like he had a load in his pants.

Probably because he had *a load in his pants*, thought Pinkerton.

No more throwing tantrums if Pinkerton failed to deliver the latest issue of Leonard's favorite underground magazine, *La Muff*. No more taking trips down Hollywood's memory lane as he bragged to Pinkerton about his career.

"I once doubled... *the Wolf Man!*" Big Leonard would boast.

"Hardly a stretch," Pinkerton would say.

And no more chatter about his Goddamned liver... Big Leonard's pride and joy after decades of rampant alcoholism. "Looka' here!" he'd leer, opening his shirt, showing off the grotesquely distended liver, bulging perkily like a misplaced erection.

"Impressive," Pinkerton would mumble.

From his briefcase, Pinkerton removed a stack of his press releases:

Alfred Pinkerton, Esq., attends the funeral of "Big Leonard" Brodey, veteran Hollywood stuntman, today in Lone Pine. Mr. Pinkerton was Brodey's attorney in a sensational murder case in 1957.

The problem was that at noon, when the funeral was set to begin, not a single reporter had shown up. Nor were there any in evidence at 12:20. Or 12:25. Pinkerton, outraged and humiliated, stormed outside. The preacher, glad to be free of him, tolled the bell in the tower and the mourners filed into the chapel for the delayed obsequies. Alfie Pinkerton and Gerald Mahugu drove off in the Jaguar, in a cloud of dust and a scattering of tumbleweed.

"Mike," watching the car speed away, lifted his leg and pissed against a cactus.

* * *

The Alfred Pinkerton estate was in Pacific Palisades, a ranch house hacienda with canyon-and-ocean views and an Olympic-size pool. It was after ten that night when they arrived, having stopped at Pinkerton's club, where he'd dined and played several hands of poker.

Lightning flashed as brief but intense storms blew in off the ocean. The roof up on the Jaguar, Gerald opened the large oak gate, draped by wet bougainvillea, and drove his boss to the front door. Pinkerton was surly. Debts were swamping him. His ex-wife, Alexandra, was no longer absorbing most of the bills since their recent divorce. Only Mahugu had stayed with Pinkerton as a point of honor; all other servants had followed Alexandra back to the Hamptons.

Fat bitch, thought Pinkerton.

Mahugu closed the gate, parked the car and checked the grounds. Pinkerton entered the living room, skulked to the bar, poured a Scotch, lit a cigarette, and called his message service. There was one message, from Felicia, and the operator read it to Pinkerton:

"*I passed! Isn't it wonderful?*"

"Shit," said Pinkerton, throwing his Panama hat in a corner.

The rain was falling heavily again. Pinkerton sat on the living room couch, staring at the empty fireplace and the painting above it of a Wild West brothel. He sipped his Scotch, brooding about Alexandra, his debts, and that presumptuous cocksucker Felicia.

"Mr. Pinkerton." It was Mahugu. "Miss Hirsig is here to see you. By the pool…in the rain. Shall I invite her inside?"

"No. Tell her to wait where she is. You're done for the night."

"Thank you, Mr. Pinkerton. Good night, sir."

Mahugu left the house, heading for the garage at the rear of the property, where he lived in the upper quarters. Pinkerton thought of his visitor and the fire last week at Universal. He'd told her to "lay low" for a while, yet here she was. He listened to the rain, smugly waiting for it to stop.

I've never fucked a goat, thought Pinkerton, a proud sybarite, *but I have fucked Lizzie Hirsig.*

The rain ended, but there was still lightning. He finished his Scotch, lit a cigarette and came out the back door. Mahugu had turned on a lamp-post by the pool. The Pacific wind carried a scent he recognized... the honeysuckle perfume.

Then he heard her, softly, badly singing. The song was *As Tears Go By*, which he knew was her favorite. He saw her in a flash of lightning, under the old Eucalyptus tree.

"Boo!" she said, pointing a long, red-nailed finger at him.

Her head was almost in the lower branches, and for a moment she appeared to be a gangly, freakish giantess. The lightning flashed over the ocean and Pinkerton saw she was standing in her spiked heels on the marble bench under the tree. He moved toward her.

"Why are you here tonight, Lizzie?" asked Pinkerton sternly.

She giggled, drenched by having waited in the rain, looking like a rag doll in her short black dress and long red hair, which he knew was a wig. The wig was soaking wet, tangled under her large black hat, its wide brim up in the front, and her eye makeup ran down her long, thin face. Her pointy witchy nose looked to him as if she could peck out his eyes with it.

Hippie whore, he thought.

Yet... she was crazy and dangerous enough, he knew, to be, if all played out, his entrée back into prominence. And despite this, and maybe because of it, she drove him wild with desire. He could tell she was stoned, her almost yellow eyes unnaturally bright in the shadow, and he saw another pair of eyes, also yellow, that seemed to be where her tits belonged. He looked more closely and saw she was cradling a black cat.

"I brought my pussy," she giggled again, dropping the cat to the ground, coyly lifting her dress, exposing her red pelt of pubic hair. That hair, Pinkerton knew, was natural.

He tossed his cigarette and approached her, trying to put his nose against her vagina. He wasn't a tall man, and since she was standing on the bench and in her heels, he was too short to do so. Pinkerton stood on his toes but she was still out of reach.

"You're funny... Pinky!" she laughed teasingly.

He suddenly grabbed her around her long legs and she squealed as he lost balance and fell backward, both of them landing in the wet grass. Her hat came off, she pinned him to the ground, and he looked directly at the crystal angel, hanging from a chain around her neck. One of the wings was broken, and its tiny red jewel eyes seemingly stared into Pinkerton's gray cat eyes.

"Jesus Christ," he said.

"No," she grinned, touching the angel. "*Saint Dymphna.*"

Her long red nails were clawing him, her honeysuckle scent was all around him now, and she slid so her eyes looked directly into his.

"Bleeding Christ Almighty," Lizzie whispered, "fuck me."

He gave his nicotine laugh and she stuck her tongue in his mouth. As the lightning flashed and the rain came again, the cat climbed up the Eucalyptus tree, watching the two people in the grass enjoying their ritual and getting very wet.

4 Gettysburg After Midnight

TUESDAY, MAY 23, 1967

Charnita was a ski resort in the mountains near Mount Saint Mary's. Off season the chalets went cheaply. Tony Wyngate lived there year-round, so his rent was modest.

It was 1:10 A.M. Tony sat by the unlit fireplace while his Judy Collin's *In My Life* album played *Suzanne* on the stereo. The oddly haunting song by Leonard Cohen was his favorite on the album.

Then he thought again about Porter Down's medallion.

The day had taken several twists. After leaving the Grotto, Porter had asked Tony to drive him to Saint Joseph College, the Mount's all-female neighbor, just outside Emmitsburg and under the auspices of the Daughters of Charity. Tony didn't know why Porter would want to come here. Porter provided no explanation. Tony had listened to his '65 Mercury Comet's radio as Porter marched off to see the college's president, Sister Mary Luke Harper. He'd been back within ten minutes.

"Swell gal," said Porter. "Too bad about the rod up her ass."

Porter had announced his intention to visit the Gettysburg battlefields. Tony had driven him back to his car at the Mount, and as Porter prepared to go, Tony had noticed again the man's medallion, dangling from his shirt on a chain.

"You like that, don't you?" Porter had asked. "I've worn it every day since 1918." He held it so that Tony could see it closely. The image was of Saint George battling the Dragon. To Tony's historian's eyes, the medallion appeared ancient. Despite its small size, there was remarkable detail in the knight's face and savagery in the Dragon's.

20

Porter said he'd call Tony tonight from his room at the Gettysburg Hotel, and arrange to meet him for supper. The call had never come. Now, Tony sat by the fireplace, thinking again about the visitor and his mystical medallion. Was the man unhinged? Should Tony contact authorities?

When the phone finally rang at 1:25 A.M., it startled Tony. It was Porter. He said he had important matter to discuss that couldn't wait until morning.

* * *

Wolfe's Pub, on the square in historic Gettysburg, offered weeknight service until 2:00 A.M. for the college crowd. Tony entered Wolfe's at precisely 1:45 A.M. in blue jeans and his tan windbreaker. A young, stout, dark-eyed waitress, clearly tired after her graveyard shift, looked at Tony as if she wanted to bite him. Her name tag read *Joy*.

"I'm here to meet somebody… ," said Tony.

Joy sullenly led him to a corner booth and the restaurant's only other patron. There sat Porter Down, his cap pushed back on his head. He looked like an old Nantucketer who'd spent the day harpooning whales.

"My treat," said Porter. "Give this sassy wench your order."

Joy glared. "Just a beer, please," said Tony, sitting. Joy skulked away. Porter contentedly chewed his cheeseburger. Tony again noticed Porter's medallion, dangling outside his shirt. "You have something you need to tell me?" asked Tony.

Porter nodded and took his time chewing. "I've been thinking," he said. "If you sell your novel to the movies, I know who should play Boudicca."

"Who?" asked Tony.

"Ann-Margret." said Porter.

"Maybe," said Tony. "She was pretty intense in *Kitten With a Whip*."

Joy delivered Tony's beer, sighed mightily and retreated. "So," said Tony wearily. "You got me here at this hour to announce this incisive casting choice?"

Porter, raised his Coke bottle. "No. I want to toast my collaborator. Cheers."

They clinked bottles. "You mean your fellow 'witch burner'?" asked Tony.

"You know, Tony, Shakespeare believed in witches. And Sir Thomas Browne said that those who *don't* aren't only infidels but, by implication, atheists. Still, I wager that Professor Anthony Francis Wyngate, novelist, professor and 1967 sophisticate, is too cool to believe in witches."

"Well," said Tony, "'There are more things in Heaven and Earth, Horatio...'"

"Yeah," growled Porter, "'than are dreamt of in your philosophy', *Hamlet*, Act One, scene five, drink up."

They both drank. Porter signaled the waitress, holding up his empty Coke bottle. She brought another. "We close in three minutes," said Joy.

"Then before it's too late," said Porter, "I want a hot fudge sundae."

Joy rolled her eyes and stormed off. "Joy's a cutie," said Porter. "Why don't you ask her out? I hear you're a heartbreaker."

"Hardly," said Tony.

Porter ate and drank for a moment. "So. You ready to write a book about my burning her up?"

"Who? Joy?" asked Tony.

"No, smart ass, the witch," said Porter.

"Alright," said Tony. "Porter, you need to make sense. If you don't, I'm warning you—I'll have to contact somebody about what you're threatening to do."

"You got me all-a-tremble," said Porter. "Okay. After the May 15th fire at Universal last week, rumor leaked of a letter to LAPD, claiming this was a terrorist act by a Satanist. It promised another one in southern California on June 25th. May 15th is the feast day of Saint Dymphna. If you've never heard of her, look her up."

"What's June 25th?" asked Tony.

"I'll tell you later," said Porter. "LAPD hasn't publicly confirmed the letter, but it's for real. It says the Universal fire 'sacrament' was the 'offering' of a disciple of the Church of the Light Bearer, based in San Francisco. The Light Bearers deny any involvement and swear—at least for now—they aren't aware of any renegade member looney."

"Any idea of her target?" asked Tony.

"Who knows?" said Porter. "Maybe she'll blow up Sleeping Beauty's Castle at Disneyland. But I doubt it. I've got her number... .and know about her little pet fascinations."

Joy marched to the table, brandishing the sundae, placing it in front of Porter. "We close in *one* minute," she said, and stormed off.

Porter picked up a file beside his seat. "There've been incidents long before the Universal fire," he said handing the file to Tony. "Read this.

Yours to keep. For now, just take a peek at the top picture." Tony opened the thick folder and was shocked to see a crime scene photograph of the Grotto statue of the Blessed Virgin, garishly and profanely defiled. He remembered the desecration 13 years ago.

Porter leaned in toward Tony, his voice hushed. "On the night of December 15, 1954, a 20-year-old slashed his wrists in the Mount's Grotto. A seminarian, like you were, Dr. Wyngate, once upon a time. It was your first year as a teacher at the Mount and you were also the Grotto custodian. You found him early the next morning."

Tony was silent.

"Only it was more than suicide," said Porter. "Someone had mutilated the seminarian's genitalia with a knife shortly after his death. If you need to refresh your memory, dig a little deeper into the file. There are photos of the body."

Tony didn't look for them.

"Two nights later, just before Christmas break, somebody defiled that Virgin statue... just the way you see her in that top picture. Remember?"

Tony sipped his beer before responding. "Evidently, you connect the seminarian's murder in 1954 and the desecration with the fire at Universal last week. Well, as you've probably read in the reports, I only saw movement that morning in the trees behind the altar. I couldn't identify anyone."

Porter contentedly and silently finished his sundae. "Porter," Tony asked, "why the hell do you really want *me* in L.A.?"

"Because I like your books," said Porter. "You're a good Catholic fella. And you and I need to warn the world about the Devil. After all, you and I have seen her... even if you only saw her moving in those trees behind the altar."

Tony felt a chill. He drained his beer, looking out the window at Gettysburg Square, the American flag spotlighted on its pole. He wasn't the solid Catholic that Porter thought he was. In fact, he'd lost his faith years ago, despite what he presented in his books and his teaching. He despised his hypocrisy.

"Last summer I did research in Egypt," said Tony. "This summer I'm putting it into manuscript form. I'm already busy with a new novel."

"That'll wait a year," said Porter. "Or ten."

Tony had lost patience. "Porter... you say that you want to 'burn a witch.' The expression's historically reprehensible. From the late 1400s to the late 1700s, almost 50,000 women were burned, hanged, or tortured to death in Europe as witches. And as I tell my students, those were just the redheads."

"Well, guess what, prof? They missed this one... and she's a redhead. Sort of."

"And you're saying she's been around since the Middle Ages?"

"I know that she was full of piss and vinegar as far back as 1931."

"36 years ago? And why do you believe that?"

"Because in 1931," said Porter Down, "I was the man who killed her."

* * *

A long silence had followed. "It wasn't murder," Porter said finally. "I was across the country the night she died. It was Manslaughter. *Woman*-slaughter, actually..."

"Thanks for the beer," said Tony, standing to leave.

"Not so fast," said Porter, staying seated, his voice low and confidential. "1954 was a tough year for you, Tony. I mean, besides the corpse at the Grotto."

Tony, beside the table, looked down at Porter and reddened. "Stop," he said.

"A nun and a seminarian," said Porter. "Very tragic. You must have only been 23. Ever visit her grave, Tony? It's not that far a drive from here."

Tony turned and walked out of Wolfe's. Porter took Tony's forgotten folder, approached the counter and gallantly handed the weary Joy a $50.00 bill.

"Here, honey," he said, winking. "Keep the change and keep smiling."

* * *

Tony was almost across the square when he heard Porter call him.

"No blackmail, I promise," said Porter, approaching, handing Tony the folder. The two men stood under the flag, the spotlight throwing their shadows up on the old buildings under the bright moon.

"I'll pay airfare and basic expenses for four weeks of your time in June," said Porter. "You get the book rights and royalties. I'm flying home in the morning and my number's in the folder. See ya' soon... maybe." He started away, walking his puffin strut toward the hotel across the square.

"What's all this really about?" called Tony, and Porter turned and faced him.

"We'll go ask Alice," he said. "When she's ten feet tall."

Tony watched him go, wondering why Porter was quoting from *Alice in Wonderland*.

5 Pacific Coast Highway

TUESDAY, MAY 23, 1967

It was after 2:00 A.M. Pacific time. A cold, sharp wind blew off the ocean, wafting the stench of two star-crossed California octopi who'd washed up on shore, died in each other's tentacles, and were stinking up the beach.

There were only pilot lights on Santa Monica Pier. The storm had moved up the coast, the moon was breaking through the clouds and the surf was boisterous. A pair of hitchhikers walked north on Pacific Coast Highway. It was their favorite time to travel because there weren't many cops. They were silently strolling along what Hollywood used to call "the Gold Coast," the strip of beach homes that once upon a time housed movie land aristocracy. On the east side of the highway were the Palisades cliffs, the palm trees forming a weird conga line in the starlight.

"Keep up, Margo," the man said to the woman. She carried a guitar case with one hand and a sack with the other, and walked behind him. Inside her sack was a transistor radio. An all-night DJ was taking requests and the Mamas and the Papas were wailing *Monday, Monday.*

"Today is *Tuesday, Tuesday!*" said the man.

"Who gives a shit?" said the woman.

The male hitchhiker, a tall, gaunt 31-year-old, looked up at those dancing palm trees. He'd have smiled but he was smiling already. He wore his large, horse-toothed smile as if it were part of his clothing, along with his long linen duster coat and the old brown fedora, cocked rakishly over his black, flowing, Buffalo Bill-style hair. It was his John Barrymore fedora. Barrymore...The Great Profile... "Mad Jack," as they'd called him. Always seemed to be crazy in those old movies Lizzie made them watch on TV, and he liked that. In his duster and fedora, he felt he looked like a Wild West Barrymore, although other people had a different impression.

"Get lost, *Dracula!*" a gas station manager had shouted at him in San Clemente, where he'd been loitering by the Pepsi machine. But he called himself "Mad Jack," and tonight he faced the traffic, raising his thumb, long and defined like his artistic sculptor's fingers. A car drove speedily by.

"*YAAAAHHH!*" Mad Jack roared.

At his best, his voice, speaking and singing, had a dynamic in it—*like a circus ringmaster*, Lizzie had once said. But when he was stoned, his voice was slowed and slurred, like a warped record. It was very warped tonight.

Mad Jack and his companion, 26-year-old Margo, both felt the joy, the tingle of being tonight in the great state of California, with all its conflicting sensations. Governor Reagan and Janis Joplin. Disneyland and Haight-Ashbury. The protestors at USC Berkeley, hoping to end the Vietnam War, and the ensemble cast of *Gilligan's Island,* hoping for a fourth season. Beach, mountains, and desert, all tight-rope walking on the San Andreas Fault, daring the "Big One" Earthquake to send the whole fucking coastline on a one-way joyride to the bottom of the Pacific.

"Still behind me, Margo?" asked Mad Jack.

"Shut up," said Margo.

Short, wispy thin, and also stoned, the pop-eyed, prim-mouthed Margo hefted the sack and guitar case. She wore a red mini-dress, white Keds tennis shoes, and no underwear. Her blonde hair, once running all the way down her back, was short now and parted on the right. Lizzie had cut it, claiming the new hairdo made Margo look like Bela Lugosi's leading lady in *Dracula,* but Margo suspected the jealous bitch had *really* hacked it off because Lizzie, the hag, wore a wig. Lizzie's scalp showed through her sparse hair, and she'd fed them some crock story that she'd sacrificed her hair in honor of prostitutes of olden times, who'd cut off their hair to avoid lice, and wore wigs.

A cool story—but it smelled like a pile of steaming bullshit to Margo. Anyway, the thought of Lizzie's wig story made Margo laugh, or actually snort. The more she tried to control the porcine sound, the more she snorted.

"Oink-oink," smiled Mad Jack.

"Eat me," said Margo.

Yes, "Saint Lizzie" was crazy, and Mad Jack and Margo were her "acolytes," as she'd called them. Lizzie was lots of laughs …and fuckin' *scary*. She claimed she was a witch and had the loudest, most bloodcurdling goddamn scream that two of them had ever heard. Lizzie called it her "Fay Wray" scream, and said she let it loose in bed when she came, or even if she faked it.

"It makes the fucker feel like he's King Kong," Lizzie had giggled, "and sometimes it makes him forget that *he* hasn't even *come* yet!"

Mad Jack's smile beamed as he thought of Lizzie… crazier than ever. Screaming in her sleep, having nightmares about a "snake lady." Singing while stoned, crying while she sang *As Tears Go By*. Smelling like a honeysuckle vine when freshly perfumed, smelling like a honeysuckle vine somebody had pissed on when she was dirty. Always wearing her red-eyed crystal angel around her neck, even when naked and dancing alone to her favorite Stones' songs. Always telling fucked-up stories. One of his favorites was her tale of living with "the Devil" in San Francisco—"the Devil" a fat old pervert who, Lizzie claimed, had done all kinds of nasty things to her. One night, to the hilarity of Mad Jack and Margo, she bitched, seriously, that "the Devil" had made her have a nose job. Not only was that funny, but as Mad Jack and Margo often snickered, Lizzie's long, thin witchy nose looked like somebody had stuck it into a pencil sharpener.

"Saint Lizzie" … swearing she was out to "avenge" somebody, although she was never clear as to who or why. And there was Lizzie's scar, shaped like a cross, that rose up her abdomen out of her curly red pussy hair.

Yeah, thought Margo, Lizzie was scary. And the way the bitch put herself together, the wig, the makeup, the falsies, the fingernails… it was like Dr. Frankenstein, stitching together his Monster. Only Lizzie was Dr. Frankenstein *and* the Monster… or whatever. What the fuck.

Tonight, Mad Jack and Margo were heading for Lizzie's "abbey," an abandoned ranch out at Malibou Lake. From what Lizzie had told them, "God," who'd owned the property, had given it to her. "God's" lawyer, on whose face Lizzie had been sitting, was protecting her. So, after a virtual all-dope-all-the-time week in sunny Tijuana, where the two of them had hightailed it after assisting Lizzie in last week's fire at Universal, they were back in L.A., watching cars constantly speed by them on the highway. "Mad Jack" kept raising his thumb, the drivers just kept ripping by, and he was getting really tired of this shit. Finally, he jumped out into the highway, raising his arms out scarecrow-style while making a face at the headlights.

"FUCK YOOOOOOU!" he cried.

The car blared its horn, its brakes screaming as it pulled into the next lane, somehow missing Mad Jack and a truck heading south, weaving almost out of control back into the northbound traffic. Horns sounded and Mad Jack laughed—his stoned laugh. It *rrr-rr-rrred*, like an old car engine trying to turn over on a cold morning.

"Asshole," murmured Margo.

They continued up Pacific Coast Highway. Mad Jack looked down at his dusty shoes, his feet so big they almost looked like clown shoes. They hurt, Goddamnit. "Your turn, Margo," he said, sprawling on the ground and resting. "Try *It Happened One Night*."

It was another of those corny old black-and-white movies Lizzie had made them watch—Claudette Colbert had hitched a ride by hiking up her skirt and showing off her leg. Margo had her own variation. She put down the sack and guitar case, looked down the highway, bent over, pulled up her dress, and mooned the passing car. The car blared its horn and roared on by. From its open windows they heard raucous male laughter.

"They are laughing 'cause your ass is *ugly*, Margo," smiled Mad Jack.

"Fuck you, you creature from the deep," said Margo.

Now an 18-wheeler approached. Margo hung another moon. The truck slowed, and almost 100 yards ahead pulled off to the side. Mad Jack touched his linen duster, felt the bags of dope from Tijuana sewn inside the lining, and stroked his butcher knife. The trucker might want to fight. Nevertheless, he and Margo trotted to the truck.

"Hop aboard!" called the down-south voice of the driver.

* * *

The trucker was maybe early 40s, his gut wedged against the steering wheel. Part of his load was fruit and an opened box of grapefruit was on the cab floor, along with the peels of several grapefruit the driver had eaten. Still, there was plenty of room in the spacious cab for the guitar case and sack, Margo, who sat beside the driver, and Mad Jack, who sat by the passenger window. The driver turned off his radio. Margo's transistor still played, muffled in her sack.

"My name's Bob!" said the trucker nervously, playfully touching the brim of his baseball cap. "From Tennessee."

"I am Jack," said the passenger. "And she is Margo."

"Just Jack? Just Margo?" the trucker smiled broadly.

"Just Jack, just Margo," said Mad Jack. Margo said nothing. She stared at Bob.

"So!" said the trucker as he pulled out into traffic. "Here we are, sittin' in this fine truck, all headin' north together!"

He laughed. They smiled at him. Silence. "So, what do you folks do?" asked Bob.

"I paint," said Mad Jack, hearing how warped his voice sounded "Write and play music."

"I knew it!" said the trucker, nodding his head energetically. "Could tell lookin' at ya'. What kinda painting, what kinda music?"

"Religious… in a way."

"And the lady?"

"She's a technician…in a way."

"A technician," repeated Bob, eyeing Margo and her slender legs. She knew he was checking her out. So did Mad Jack.

"Well, I want to tell you young folks," said Bob, suddenly somber. "I'm on *your* side. I might not look like a hippie on the *outside* but, believe you me… I'm 100% hippie on the *inside*."

Actually, he seemed 100% asshole outside *and* inside to Mad Jack, who was leaning around Margo, smiling at Bob.

"This country's goin' to the dogs," said Bob, shaking his head sadly and solemnly. "And look what we're doin' in Vietnam. Roastin' babies."

"Mmm. Delicious," said Mad Jack.

Bob looked over curiously at the man and noticed both Mad Jack and Margo smiling at him. "Oh!" he laughed good-naturedly, as if he got the joke he didn't get. As he laughed, Mad Jack began his tired engine *rrr-rrr* laugh, which started Margo snorting. Mad Jack's laugh rose in volume. Margo seemed on the verge of hysteria. Her nose was running.

"It's good to laugh," said Bob solemnly. "Especially in these times." The trucker thought he smelled b.o. He raised one arm on the window ledge and tried to check if it were he. It didn't seem to be.

The radio in the bag was playing *Feelin' Groovy*. Margo, wiping her nose with her finger, began wriggling on the seat to the music. Risking that she might be stoned and susceptible and her smilin' freak of a companion friendly and accommodating, Bob shyly patted Margo's thigh. She stopped wriggling. Mad Jack saw the pat and smiled even more broadly.

"Up here is Malibu Canyon Road," said Mad Jack. "That is our stop."

"Oh?" said Bob, clearly disappointed, fearing he'd gone too far. "Gee… sorry. I hoped I might have the company of you good folks all night long… all 400 miles to Frisco."

"You have been kind to us," said Mad Jack. "We want to thank you. *Margo* wants to thank you."

The trucker looked at her. She smiled, raised her eyebrows, and nodded.

* * *

The truck had chugged up the canyon road, into the hills, onto a gravel pull-off. Bob was almost disbelieving that the fantasy he'd concocted when he saw the hitchhiker's hangin'-in-the-breeze tail was coming true.

"I'll give you privacy!" leered Mad Jack, sticking out his tongue and winking. He wandered off into the shadows with the guitar case. A moment later, the couple heard him playing, very well, a Spanish flamenco. Margo casually pulled her red dress over her head and tossed it in the gravel. Bob, nervous, watched the girl, naked except for her Keds, kneel in the dirt and aim her ass at him, matter-of-factly assuming the doggy-style position. She reached back and extracted a tiny bag of top-of-the-line poppy grass from her rectum, hidden just the way Lizzie had taught her to hide it. Bob assumed it was some feminine hygiene product.

"Well," he chuckled, "here we are!" It was the skinny creep who had b.o., thought Bob, and probably this gal had it too, badly. But hell, she was a hot, young, blonde, and it'd be one helluva story to tell at the diners. He undid his belt buckle, trying to appear as brazenly cool as she was, dropping his pants and shorts, looking over his bulging stomach and seeing he wasn't at all excited. She turned and looked and saw it too. He knew it.

"Hell, I'm sorry," he sighed. "Just give me a minute." He turned, walked a few feet away, gave himself a few desperate tugs, and shook his head in frustration as the romantic Flamenco serenade tauntingly continued.

"Aw, shit!" Bob whispered to himself.

Then he realized the guitar music had stopped. Bob looked up. Mad

Jack was standing on a rock above, smiling at him. He was holding something long and rattling by its tail.

"Surprise!" smiled Mad Jack.

Bob knew right away what it was that Mad Jack viciously slung at him. It hit right below his face and he shrieked as it bit his neck. He staggered, his pants around his ankles, and fell backwards into the gravel. The rattlesnake slowly uncoiled and crawled away.

"Rattle-he-go," said Mad Jack, watching the reptile.

Margo was back on her feet. "I was gonna stick him," Mad Jack said to her, patting the knife inside his duster. "Then I saw the rattler as we drove up. Warmin' himself on the road right back there. Picked him up the way Lizzie showed me that night... remember?"

Margo nodded. Mad Jack bent over Bob's corpse, removing the man's baseball cap. He put it on Margo, who otherwise still wore only her Keds. Mad Jack then took out his knife, lifted the dead man's head and sliced off his ear.

"A present for Lizzie," said Mad Jack.

"She'd probably rather have *that*," said Margo, pointing to the man's penis.

"His ear's bigger," said Mad Jack.

They found Bob's wallet in his back pocket, took the cash, pulled off his wedding band and stuck the wallet back in his pocket. Margo yanked on her dress. They found more cash and change in the truck, then loaded Bob into the cab.

"Looks like nobody gets it up for you," mocked Mad Jack.

"Fuck you and the lagoon you crawled out of," said Margo.

She turned her attention to revving up and turning around the eighteen-wheeler. It was no challenge for a woman who'd built the bomb Lizzie had detonated last week at Universal, and who'd had a 4.0 academic average before M.I.T. had expelled her.

* * *

A short time later, the truck careened down the canyon road, the body propped up in the cab, smashing through a fence, plunging nearly 100-feet off a cliff edge, the explosion echoing through the canyon, the flames soaring in the field hundreds of yards from the ocean. Up in the hills, coyotes smelled the burning flesh and kept vigil for the fire to subside.

"Lizzie likes fires," said Mad Jack, always devoted.

"Lizzie's a douche bag," said Margo.

She pulled her new baseball cap over her eyes. After a moment they heard the sirens. Mad Jack began walking. Margo picked up the guitar case and sack and followed him, neither looking back as they silently made their way up the moonlit road of Malibu Canyon.

6 Joshua Tree National Monument

The Jeep's headlights lit the yellow rock arches as the young driver sped over the dark, twisted road, the cycles close behind her.

Joshua Tree National Monument, 160 miles east of L.A., looked like another planet by day. At night, it took on an even starker sci-fi non-reality as the shadows fell over its gnarled trees and black rubble mountains. Its peaks, mines, and desolation made it a favored locale not only for adventurers, but for cults and acid droppers.

It was after 3:00 A.M. She drove over 65 miles per hour, her unconscious passenger crumpled beside her. "Hold on, Dottie," she said, grabbing the teenager's arm, trying to keep her from falling to the floor or maybe tumbling out of the open Jeep.

She couldn't slow down. She'd seen the headlights of the motorcycles behind her. And over the roar of the Jeep's engine, she believed she'd heard shots.

The bikes could outrace the Jeep and she only hoped her pursuers were too stoned, drunk, or both to manage maximum speed. Suddenly a jack rabbit bounded in front of her and she instinctively swerved, the Jeep almost sailing airborne before she regained control, navigating back onto the road.

"Almost there, Dottie," she said.

The rendezvous point was just ahead. Yes, there were the lights of the ambulance. She skidded to a stop. A male nurse named Matt hurriedly opened the ambulance's rear doors.

"Janice Lynnbrooke," grinned Matt. "We meet again."

"They're close behind us," said Janice. "Move your ass."

She and Matt quickly loaded the unconscious girl into the ambulance. Janice grabbed her knapsack and jumped inside as they heard the bikes approaching, hardly 300 yards away. Tom, the driver, sounded the siren and at top speed, raced the ambulance toward San Bernardino.

Matt tended to the moaning teenager on the stretcher. There'd been no evidence of further pursuit by the bikers and he glanced at Janice, seated across from him, her long, dark brown hair tied in a ponytail, her denim jacket and jeans speckled with sand and dust. She sipped water from a canteen as she wiped the patient's face with a handkerchief.

"We have to stop meeting like this," said Matt jocularly.

Janice took another sip of water. Matt checked Dottie's vital signs.

"That Jeep you were driving belong to the cult?" asked Matt.

"Yeah."

"Why don't the police do what you do?"

"Too much legal horseshit."

"I hear the F.B.I.'s out here," said Matt, "investigating the cults."

"Do you see the F.B.I. out here tonight?" asked Janice, her very blue eyes angry. "They're too busy tapping phones and getting laid. They're a joke."

"You know what I think?" asked Matt. "I think the Army should come in here and blow up every damn dope-addict hippie they can find."

"That's cause you're a fascist," said Janice.

Matt made no reply. She was a hero tonight, no doubt about it, and deserved respect. He looked at the patient. "She's dehydrated," he said. "And obviously stoned."

"She has been most of the past week."

"Sexually abused?"

"Yes. That's why we had to get her out."

"We'll check everything at the hospital," he said, looking again at Janice. "How long were you in there?"

"About two weeks."

"They'd have killed you if they caught you," said Matt. "You know that, right?"

Janice Lynnbrooke said nothing and wiped the face of the patient.

7

The Faye MacConnell Show

The Faye MacConnell Show was both of its time and ahead of its time.

The half-hour talk show aired at 10:30 P.M. weeknights in San Francisco. Advertised as "Live, Uncensored, and Wildly Unpredictable," it attracted guests from the 1967 fulcrum of art, politics, and show business. Candor reigned at this hour and members of the studio audience could enter the "docket" and question the guests. The atmosphere often became heated and security stood by. They'd moved too late on a recent night where a Vietnam veteran charged the stage and, with his surviving arm, slugged a Black Panther.

Faye MacConnell resembled a glamorized version of Mary Travers of Peter, Paul, and Mary. She sat in her stage-left hostess chair, attractive in her short skirt and laced-up black boots, relaxing during a commercial break, reviewing her notes. Despite her rather "mod" aura, Faye actually ran a tight ship, working from a basic script with pre-arranged questions.

During the mid-show break the stage was dark, a directive of Faye, who minded the hot lights. Her third and final guest of the evening, seated in the stage right chair, was a large, corpulent man, perspiring heavily. He held a cane, which he'd used since a recent mild heart attack and now kept as a prop, pointing it with a flourish to punctuate his points. He sipped a glass of ice water as the stage manager began the 10-9-8 count down to resume the telecast. A makeup woman quickly mopped the guest's brow and retreated offstage.

Lights up. Applause. "Welcome back," said Faye, looking into the camera that exalted her rather plain face. "All of Los Angeles was shocked and frightened last week when an anonymous source sent police a letter, claiming credit for the devastating fire at Universal Studios. The letter claimed the fire was the work of the Church of the Light Bearer, a satanic congregation based here in San Francisco. We have with us tonight the high priest of the Church of the Light Bearer. He's also the author of the recent best seller, *Demonizing the Devil: 2,000 Years of Intolerance*. Please welcome Mr. Simon Bone."

Applause. "A delight to be with you, Faye," smiled Bone.

In the bright light, Simon Bone evoked a jovial classical actor whose signature role was Falstaff. His full gray hair was combed straight back, his Van Dyke beard well-groomed, and his impeccably tailored blue double-breasted suit flatteringly cloaked his 300-plus-pound-girth. There was a rococo flamboyance about the man that appealed to the audience.

"It's strange," said Faye, indulging herself an ad-lib, "but you remind me of someone..."

"Perhaps," chuckled Bone, his voice almost melodious. "In my younger days, many thought I resembled Laird Cregar, who played Jack the Ripper in the 1944 film, *The Lodger*."

"Maybe you remind me of Jack the Ripper," deadpanned Faye.

"Maybe!" laughed Bone. "At any rate, our late-lamented Mr. Cregar has been dead for over twenty years now. The poor soul dieted himself to death. I'll *never* repeat *his* fatal mistake!"

Laughter. Faye returned to the script. "So, first of all... What *is* Hell, Mr. Bone?"

"Ah!" said Bone, smiling charmingly. "Hell. It's the land of the *Thou shalt*, not the prison of the *Thou shalt not*. It's whatever you wish it to be—a football game on Thanksgiving Day, a Wild West rodeo on the Fourth of July, the Folies Bergère on New Year's Eve. It's not the dungeon of a dogmatic God who condemned all humankind due to one little apple. It's the playground of the Fallen Angel who truly understands us and offers genuine compassion. One isn't sentenced to Hell for daring to sin. One is *awarded* Hell for daring to *live*."

Applause. "No one's been demonized like the Devil," said Bone, taking his book from the table so it faced the camera. "God might be dead, as *Time* magazine pondered in its cover story in the spring of last year. But I assure you, Satan is alive. And... he *cares*."

He winked, pointing his cane at the camera, as if to show he'd intended to have been at least partially humorous. There was some laughter and more applause. "Is your Church of the Light Bearer synonymous with the Church of Satan?" asked Faye.

"No," said Bone, placing the book beside him. "We are the *lunatic fringe* of the Church of Satan."

Laughter, some of it uneasy. "Actually," smiled Bone, "Anton LaVey officially founded the Church of Satan only last year, on April 30. Walpurgis Night, you know... the European night of Evil. The Church of the Light Bearer, however, dates back over 500 years."

"It sounds ominous," said Faye.

"Yes, it does. I'm sure some of our audience expect the Light Bearers to be a coven of caped, hooded fiends, hell-bent on devouring babies and sacrificing virgins. But I'm not the Bogey Man. And our church's history is benign... comparatively. No racist Crusades. No torture-mad Inquisition. No Holocaust-coddling Pope..."

Tentative applause. "Nor do we possess," said Bone loudly, exhilarated by the response, "any Grand Guignol fascination with one man's agony and crucifixion. I've always felt...how shocking for children to grow up in the Catholic Church with so blatantly disturbing a central image. And those same children taught by celibate 'Brides of Christ,' clad in mournful black."

Bone paused for applause. Some followed.

"You claim," asked Faye, springing her pre-rehearsed big question, "that your Church of the Light Bearer is non-violent. Yet only last week, word leaked that your Church took credit for the fire at Universal Studios..."

"Outright defamation," frowned Bone. "Indeed, my reason for being with you tonight, Faye, is not to promote my book, which is selling quite nicely without my promotion, but to protest publicly this libelous accusation. Please be assured that the vast majority of the Church of the Light Bearer are, in fact, social activists who defiantly reject violence, who vigilantly champion peace and love... and who were doing so centuries before our charming friends in Haight-Ashbury embraced such principles. Indeed, we were, in a way, the very first 'hippies.'"

"So, you officially deny accusations about Universal's fire?" asked Faye.

"Unequivocally," said Bone. "The foul letter was a crank. My church endures its persecutions."

"We have some people at the docket," said Faye.

A young man with short-cropped hair stood there. "What you said about the crucifix," he began challengingly. "My mother prayed to the crucifix every day and held it as she died. If she were alive tonight, would you call her stupid?"

"Of course not, my friend," said Bone. "I only hope she did so out of personal *choice*. Not because some dogmatic priest or fanatical nun had terrified her into doing so. Do you understand?"

"I understand," said the man, "that you're a fat sex creep who for years has gotten away..."

"Security!" shouted Faye. "Remove that man!"

Security did. Both applause and boos sounded, drowning out the man at the docket as two burly guards marched him out of the studio.

"No doubt a devout Catholic," sighed Bone of his angry interrogator. "Filled with Christian tolerance for one and all."

Now Faye acknowledged a bespectacled woman in the docket. She had long, straight hair and the ascetic look of an activist.

"Mr. Bone," said the woman, "I see your name on various petitions for anti-war and environmental causes. Yet, although you come from a wealthy family, I happen to know that you've never contributed a single cent to any..."

"Ma'am!" snapped Faye. "Mr. Bone's financial contributions are not our topic tonight! Must you be removed too?"

"No need," said the woman sweetly, returning to her seat with a Cheshire Cat smile.

"I've contributed to many causes, always anonymously," said Bone. He drank some ice water and his hand shook.

"Are you claiming that Satanism is, by its nature, pacifistic?" asked Faye.

"No, no," said Bone sternly, still rattled. "Every church has its factions. So does Satanism. It's the profound difference between 'white witchcraft' and 'dark witchcraft.' Perhaps, Faye, you'll allow me to tell a story... one that will hopefully make my point."

He was deviating from the script. "All right," said Faye reluctantly.

"When Pope Pius XII died in 1958," Bone began somberly, "he had a trusted physician, Dr. Riccardo Galeazzi-Lisi. This physician prepared the pontiff to lie in state, via a formula called 'aromatic osmosis'—a sprinkling of resins, oils, and various chemicals. No surgery, no evisceration, no injections. Galeazzi-Lisi claimed it had been the method of embalming used on the early Christians, Emperor Charlemagne, and Jesus Christ himself. The Vatican laid out Pope Pius XII's corpse in all his papal finery, and a funeral procession began from Castel Gandolfo to Rome. However, the 'aromatic osmosis' ...*reversed.*"

"Yes," said Faye. "I remember accounts that..."

"That the body immediately began decomposing," interrupted Bone. "Mourners filing past the catafalque saw the pontiff virtually rotting before their eyes. His body turned black. His nose and fingers fell off. His chest, filled with gaseous accumulation, exploded. A Swiss Guard at the bier passed out from the stench. It was as if all of the Pope's secret sins, the mortal and the venial, were suddenly pocking his corpse, and he went to his grave as a vile, stinking atrocity."

Bone's face had remained sober, but Faye, seated so close to him, uncomfortably sensed an unnerving pleasure in the way the man told the story.

"The Vatican, naturally, suppressed the truth," said Bone, "but it was reported all the same, world-wide. Although Dr. Galeazzi-Lisi was never blamed for this debacle, the Pope's minions banned him from Vatican City for life, for having released photographs of the dying Pope to the media. As for the 'aromatic osmosis,' Galeazzi-Lisi had an assistant in creating and administering this elixir. And this assistant, it's widely presumed, was a disciple of Satan."

Bone sat back, taking a dramatic pause, gripping his cane. "It was," he said with almost lip-smacking satisfaction, "a magnificent, international embarrassment to Roman Catholicism. Dr. Galeazzi-Lisi is still alive—76 years old—and while he has defended himself over the years, he knows he dare not ever reveal the truth."

The audience was still. "Excuse me," said Faye, looking at Bone with distaste, "but are you gloating? Do you *respect* that action?"

The audience rustled, sensing the same gloating. "Of course not," said Bone, fearful he'd tipped his hand. "Nor am I confirming as a fact, I hasten to add, that any Satanist was responsible for that flamboyantly macabre terrorist act against the Catholic Church. What I *do* say, once again, is that there are degrees of witchcraft... *dark* witchcraft... *white* witchcraft. Do you see?"

"Yes, I *do* see," said Faye coldly. "We have less than a minute and time for one more question."

The young man in the docket wore a Roman collar. "Mr. Bone," he smiled, "I'm one of those terrifying priests you mentioned a while ago, and I'd just like to say one thing. Christ on the cross doesn't represent agony. He represents love... how much love God has that He sent His only Son to suffer and die willingly for us."

Considerable applause. The priest nodded gratefully to Faye and returned to the audience. "I consider myself properly chastised," said Bone, barely concealing his anger. "But..."

"I'm afraid we're out of time," said Faye. "Tomorrow night my guest is..."

"I was about to ask," interrupted Bone hotly, showing his teeth, "regarding Christ on the cross... do you remember what the celebrated writer Ben Hecht said? He said that the mob should never have crucified Jesus. Rather, they should have turned Christ over to Rome, consigned to the arena as a feast for the lions. After all, the early Christians could *never* have exalted a Savior out of seething lumps of *mincemeat!*"

There were gasps. If Hecht had meant it humorously, Bone obviously had not. His vicious contempt had thrown a chill into Faye and the audience. Cold, dead air followed.

"Thank you, Mr. Simon Bone," said Faye, formally. "Goodnight."

There was no final plug for the book, nor any applause. Faye Mac-Connell perfunctorily shook Bone's hand and promptly marched off the stage. The lights dimmed. Simon Bone, seething that he'd lost his credibility and control in the final moments of the show, sat alone on the stage, glistening with sweat and looking strangely unformed in the darkness.

He wondered if Lizzie had been watching tonight. He hoped not.

8

Urns and Shoeboxes

Kevin Silver's friends in Somerset, New Jersey believed he was a rapidly-rising Los Angeles musician. His ex-girlfriend, Marjorie Dunford, passed on the news she read in his letters.

Only recently had it dawned on Kevin that if Marjorie really believed he was hanging out with the Beach Boys and dancing at parties with Michelle Phillips, she just might show up out here and beg him to take her back. Then she'd discover he really survived in L.A. by baby-sitting stiffs in an on-the-skids funeral parlor in danger of having its license revoked by the State of California.

He could just imagine Marjorie giving him one of her Aren't-you-pathetic smiles.

Located at 1000 Venice Boulevard, the Edwards Brothers Colonial Mansion Mortuary really was a mansion, established in the early 1930's and designed like an old Southern domicile, complete with front pillars. It reminded Kevin of *Gone With the Wind.* He knew that, in more prosperous times, the Colonial Mansion had a real guard, trained and ready if some ghoul actually did come a-bursting into the premises one night. From what he heard; some *real* kink shit had gone on in Hollywood in the 1930's. From what he'd seen, the town was in ruins now... mainly whores, hippies, and queers. Yet, even in flagrant decay, Hollywood just wouldn't give him a chance.

It sucked.

Actually, the 11 P.M.to 7 A.M. watchman gig, which Kevin had landed without training or competition, wasn't so bad. His apartment was only two blocks away, so he walked to and from the Mortuary. His work space was in the basement, so he wasn't on the same floor as the stiffs, or in the same section as the undertakers and embalmers. He was expected to patrol the two upstairs floors twice a night. He almost never did. Checking on stiffs, laid out in flower-filled rooms, the lights out... if one of them got up, what the hell was *he* supposed to do about it?

Kevin would sit in the basement, below the dim overhead ceiling light, playing his portable tape recorder, on which he'd taped his favorite songs. Sometimes, he brought his guitar, trying to compose songs, but mainly writing a lot of bullshit letters. The nights crept by, the songs played, and the old grandfather clock upstairs solemnly banged out the hours. All in all, Kevin rationalized, it wasn't as scary as Vietnam... or even his own mailbox, which any day might contain a draft notice. When it did, he was heading for Canada.

There was only one really creepy thing about the basement: the cremains. They sat there, about 300 of them, on floor-to-ceiling shelves, some in urns, some in what looked to Kevin like shoeboxes. The Colonial Mansion had handled the funerals of these folk, cremated at the nearby Chapel of the Pines or Rosedale Cemetery or wherever, and nobody had claimed them. They'd ended up here in the basement, all stacked up on shelves, like canned pineapple in a supermarket. Some had nameplates, others just had ID numbers.

Damn cold, thought Kevin.

An anonymous letter with a Los Angeles P.O. box return address, had come recently to Edwards Brothers'. It asked about Colin Clive, the dude who'd screamed "It's alive!" in *Frankenstein,* which Kevin had seen on TV in Somerset. The question: Were Clive's ashes, as rumor claimed, still at the "Colonial Mansion," having never been returned to his native England after his death in 1937?

Since a fire had destroyed many of the Edwards Brothers' records, including whose cremains were identified by only an ID number, the only thing to do was to look at the urns and boxes on the shelves and hope that Clive's, if it were there, had a nameplate. The manager ordered Kevin to do so. He did. No dice. He was also ordered to write a nice letter to the interested party, claiming he'd made a thorough search and regretfully found nothing.

He never wrote the letter.

* * *

This Wednesday night on Mount Lee, the old HOLLYWOOD sign lay under the full moon, looking like the bones of a dug-up dinosaur. Kevin had learned that the sign once had spelled HOLLYWOOD-LAND, and that it used to light up at night. But the LAND had fallen down years ago, and souvenir-hunting assholes had stolen all the light-bulbs.

11:30 P.M. The Edwards Brothers' grandfather clock was booming upstairs, the night, as usual, crawling along like a dying snake. Kevin, the urns and shoeboxes his audience, strummed his guitar, thinking of all the musicians working in L.A. this night, probably set to get laid later. He hadn't been laid since he got to the west coast. Hell, he'd never been laid on the *east* coast. He'd fantasized his virginity would have sprouted wings and flown right out the window the very night he'd arrived in L.A., with a line of ass-shakin' chicks all waiting for him in white Go-Go boots, but no such luck. Kevin was good-looking enough—slim, dark-haired, 5'10," no more acne—but nothing was happening. It had become a taunting obsession.

Kevin the Virgin, he thought of himself.

At this point, the filthy whores and hippies were even looking good to him, if not the queers. He'd actually decided he'd grab the very first opportunity that came, even if it meant putting a bag over her head and hurrying to a clinic for a VD exam.

He used to get high during the job, smoking weed, as easy to get on his block as a Baby Ruth bar. But then one night a couple weeks ago, while high, he'd imagined the cremains were alive, and the tops of the urns and boxes popped off and the dead people came crawling out, the size of lit-tle dolls, dancing to the Rolling Stones' *Paint It Black*. Colin Clive had crawled out too, in his *Frankenstein* laboratory gown, prancin' around like Mick Jagger and singing the solo.

It had been enough to make Kevin swear off the grass, at least while on the job.

Tonight, however, was so goddamn dull that he dug out the little plastic bag hidden behind a desk drawer, rolled a stale joint, and lit up. He turned on his tape recorder, on which he'd taped the debut album by his favorite new group, The Doors. Kevin idolized their lead singer Jim Mor-rison and loved their dark, sexy sound. He sat back, inhaled deeply, and wondered what Marjorie Dunford was doing tonight as he fast forwarded to his favorite song:

Light My Fire.

Kevin played it, rewound it, played the song a second time, a third, strumming along on his guitar, puffing his joint… and then he heard a crash upstairs. Either a corpse had climbed out of its coffin, or a trespasser had broken into the building.

In his panic, Kevin turned off the tape recorder and the overhead basement light, deciding to hide in the dark. He had no gun—his job was to call the police if anything happened. Stoned, sweating, and suddenly needing to piss, he reached for the phone on the desk in the dark, knocking off the receiver, unable to find it or its cord. Upstairs, he heard a voice, then a giggle.

Then somebody turned on the stairs light.

Kevin froze and looked at the stairs. He eventually saw what looked like black ballet slippers, then long, bare legs, then denim cut-offs, then a pale blue T-shirt, and then…

"Oh!" gasped the visitor, seeing Kevin.

The person on the stairs—a he or a she?—was nearly bald and wearing make-up, false eyelashes, and lipstick. He/she had an Aren't-I-Naughty smile, as if amused that Kevin saw him/her, wore black silk gloves, and pointed his/her long finger at him.

"Boo!" said the freak and giggled.

Kevin, figuring this was a crazy queer who'd broken into Edwards to steal a mortician's makeup kit or God-knows what, frantically grabbed again for the phone. His nervous hands accidentally hit the tape recorder and *Light My Fire* resumed.

"What do you want?" he started to say, heart-pounding, but all that came out was, "Whaaa…?"

Lizzie usually went *sans* wig for such occasions—it added to the risk factor. Also, a casing of Edwards Brothers' last week had occurred on a night Kevin had called in sick, so the supposition had been there was no night guard at all. When Lizzie hadn't gotten an answer to her letter about Clive's ashes, she decided that the only thing to do was to go see for herself if they were there—and to grab them if they were. Dressed for a robbery but hardly a seduction, and sensing Kevin's confusion and fascination, she went into a vamp act, stripping her T-shirt off over her head.

Breasts, Kevin thought to himself. *Definitely not what you see in Playboy, but what the hell.*

"You're… a lady," said Kevin.

She giggled again, tall, balding, bare-breasted, androgynous, and—Christ!—she was giving him the eye. Was she a hallucination, whipped up by the poppy grass? No, he could hear her, *smell* her... like a wet honeysuckle vine.

"You're a pretty boy!" the freaky lady sighed.

Kevin grinned shyly, and then saw the crystal angel dangling on a chain between her breasts. He stared at the angel's red eyes, and then at the freak's yellow eyes, unaware of the man and woman peeking down from the landing of the stairs behind him.

He'd always wondered whether his first lay would be blonde, brunette, or redhead. He'd never fantasized bald-headed. Kevin's semi-stoned brain cautioned... Is this freak a hermaphrodite? Not a *she* or *he*, but an *it?* And after *he* does *it*, does *it* do *him?*

He suddenly noticed the scar snaking up out of her cut-offs, shaped almost like a cross. Spooky, but...

Oh, what the hell, he thought.

It was his night of nights. And as Jim Morrison climaxed *Light My Fire* on the tape recorder, Kevin the Virgin, eager for consummation, reached and squeezed his first-ever two fists-full of tit.

"Honk-honk," said the freak.

* * *

The next morning, the manager of the Edwards Brothers Colonial Mansion Mortuary beheld in horror the 300 urns and boxes, yanked off the shelves, jumbled in a giant pile on the floor. Fortunately, they were sealed, so there was no spillage. The manager called the police and sent them after Kevin.

He was already hours ahead of them. Terrified when Mad Jack and Margo, who'd been spying from the east wing steps, suddenly began heckling his debut sex performance, Kevin had jumped up pre-coitus, run buck-naked out of the mortuary, raced the two blocks home oblivious to the laughter of the passers-by, dressed at his apartment, fled in his car and was now heading for Canada. As he drove, he remembered with awe the scent and gyrations of his demon lover... but realized, mournfully, that he was still Kevin the Virgin.

Meanwhile, Lizzie, strolling by Malibou Lake, felt a bit moody. She'd imagined placing the urn with Clive's cremains on her night table. Nevertheless, there were other ways to indulge her obsession.

June 25th was still a month away.

The Sanctuary

The sky had only a few silver clouds as Bill McDonough steered *The Mariner* over the St. Lawrence River.

As skipper and owner of this handsome yacht, McDonough would earn much of his annual income this summer, taking tourists among the Thousand Islands on fishing trips and twilight cruises. This morning's trip, however, was a personal courtesy.

His only passenger stood in the bow on the starboard side. She wore a pale blue silk dress under a lightweight navy-blue windbreaker jacket and had tied a white scarf around her graying auburn hair. She looked out at the river, not seeming to mind the cold breeze.

* * *

Chimes, hanging from a tall post, rang in the wind as McDonough navigated *The Mariner* beside the island's private dock. He stepped onto the dock, took the woman's overnight bag and reached for her hand, which she offered with characteristic elegance.

"Thanks again, Mrs. Cromwell," he said, "for your generous contribution to the Conservation Guild. We appreciate it."

She handed him an envelope from her purse containing payment for the day's trip. He resisted taking it but she insisted. "Thank you, Bill. You and Kathy have a wonderful summer."

"You too, ma'am," said Bill. Eve Cromwell was a lovely woman. Bill imagined how beautiful she must have been in her youth.

* * *

The door of the three-story stone and timber house opened and a young woman came down the granite steps, followed by a Great Dane, both eager to welcome Eve.

"Hello, Nancy. Hello, Boy."

Nancy was a 20-year-old, working her second summer for Eve as a housekeeper to save money for tuition. Her brunette hair was cut short and she wore a *Boston U.* sweatshirt and jeans—Eve never insisted on dress formality. Boy, the Great Dane, joyfully bounded ahead of Nancy.

"Miss me, Boy?" she asked, rubbing his muzzle as he greeted her.

Nancy took Eve's bag. "How'd the meeting go, Mrs. Cromwell?"

"Fine, Nancy." The public relations and fashion consultation firm Eve had founded in New York City in the late 1940s now basically ran itself, and she trusted totally her executives. Yesterday had been her last business conference before spending the summer at her home in the Thousand Islands. She called her island *The Sanctuary.*

* * *

Eve picked up the past few days' mail from the foyer table and went into the living room, Boy in tow. The house was decorated in Early American style, with a large fireplace. Displayed on the wall were several flintlock rifles, dating to the Revolutionary War. Eve's husband Stephen, who'd died three years ago, had been a skilled marksman and had taught her to shoot early in their marriage. Eve sat on the sofa, looking through the letters.

"Lunch at noon, Mrs. Cromwell?"

"That'll be fine, Nancy."

Nancy took the bag upstairs as Eve saw an envelope's return address:

PD
Twentynine Palms, Calif.

It was his second letter—the first had come last month. For a moment, she felt like an infatuated girl. Then came apprehension. It had been over 35 years since she'd seen the man who'd mailed this letter...the man who'd helped her during the most severe tragedy of her life.

Eve walked quickly from the room, the unopened letter still in her hand.

* * *

To be one of the Thousand Islands—there were actually 1,864 of them—the island had to be above water level all year long, have an area greater than one square foot, and support at least one living tree. Eve's island was over two acres and had several tall trees. After Stephen's death, she'd sold the estate in Connecticut, taken an apartment in Manhattan and spent as much time at The Sanctuary as possible.

Eve had changed to jeans, a buttoned russet shirt and soft boots, and after lunch she and Boy went for a walk. It was a beautiful spring: the color of the wildflowers, the smell of the river, and the songs of the birds. They all seemed mystical, personal discoveries, as they had in her childhood.

Boy, full of canine machismo, ran ahead to bark at the ducks gathered near the rear of the island. Eve sat on a fallen tree. The letter, which she'd yet to open, hadn't been fully out of her mind. His first letter had mentioned the fire at Universal Studios and had referred vaguely to sad events in Los Angeles that seemed macabre echoes of the tragedy he and she had shared there in 1931. She'd written back immediately, offering to help however she could. She hadn't told him that his letter had prompted her to dream again about the woman.

It was always the same dream. Eve was in the mortuary in Hollywood, with its front pillars and gothic extravagances, keeping vigil beside her former lover's body, which lay in state in a large funeral bed. A clock chimed midnight and the woman, tall and all in black, a large hat over her flowing red hair and a veil over her face, entered the room, slightly lifted her veil, and kissed the corpse on the mouth. Then she fully raised the veil, looked at Eve, and smiled.

"Boo!" said the woman, who then screamed... and the dream ended.

Yes, the screaming woman of her nightmares had been real, a monster. She'd killed one of the dearest friends Eve had ever had. She'd also coveted Eve's lover and had attempted to kill him and Eve herself. The monster was long dead... more than 35 years. She'd died years before her lover's death, and the scene she imagined in the mortuary had never really happened. It was only a nightmare, although one she'd suffered off and on for almost 30 years. Yet in Eve's dreams, the screaming woman was so alive that Eve imagined she could smell her.

Her lover dead, 30 years next month. She remembered his intense eyes, and the last time she'd heard his voice...

Suddenly the ducks began a mass taking-off, startling Eve from her thoughts. Boy was barking, prancing as if to take claim for the great duck exodus.

Males, Eve smiled to herself.

She began walking again. Yes, one month from today would be the 30th anniversary of his death. She always remembered, even though she'd only been his lover one summer, even though he and the horrible woman had broken her heart all those years ago.

The man who'd sent today's letter had saved her lover from the monster, but couldn't save him from his own demons and addictions. He'd destroyed the monster, but couldn't destroy Eve's memory of her. Very few ever knew the story. Her husband, proud of his attractive ex-actress wife, used to ask her to tell stories at parties about her Hollywood experiences, although even he knew nothing about her most traumatic one. "Eve had a small part in *Frankenstein*, you know," he'd usually add. Eve would say, "Boris Karloff, the Monster, is actually a charming Englishman," but offered no more.

She looked out at the river, thinking again of the letter, embarrassed by the romantic aspect she was giving it, unable to deny her fascination. Eve would read the letter tonight, before going to bed, perhaps with a glass of wine. It demanded a little ceremony. After all, she'd needed him desperately all those years ago.

Now, perhaps, he needed her.

10 The Santa Monica Pier

THURSDAY, MAY 25, 1967

Gerald Mahugu piloted the sleek, rented limousine down Pacific Coast Highway, looking out at the full moon over the ocean. The Santa Monica Pier was luring the crowds, despite the windy, chilly night. They were mainly teenage couples and college kids at this late hour, although some families with children were still enjoying the rides.

The Summer of '67 was soon to begin.

The chauffeur, in his African headband and tribal robes, tried to ignore the lady in the back seat. He did not like her teasing game. He never turned around but he knew what she did. She would pull up her dress and giggle and do naughty things and say naughty words. The car reeked in her scent. Sometimes she would sing softly, like a little girl, or tell silly riddles.

"Ger-ald," she sighed, in her sing-song voice. "Do you know the difference between an oysterman with epilepsy and a whore with diarrhea?"

"No, Miss."

"Well… the oysterman *shucks* between *fits*… while the whore *fucks* between *shits!*"

She squealed with laughter. No, he had never liked her. Of all he did not like about Mr. Pinkerton, he did not like her most. It was her bright eyes that always bothered him. He could see them now in the rear-view mirror, and she was looking at him, and her yellow eyes in the darkness were like animal eyes.

She giggled again, and he knew she was parting her legs.

51

No, he did not want her at all. Anyone who would put his holy man into *her* sacred hall, thought Gerald, would throw a rock through a Rembrandt.

* * *

10:58 P.M.: The caper had to proceed like clockwork… calculated for a live report. The KTLA Late Night News, which attracted its largest viewing audience on Thursday nights, would switch to Weather and Sports about 11:13. Gerald, nervous, looked at his watch, unloaded his passenger and pulled away. He was to be back at 11:15.

11:01 P.M.: After a quick piss and wig check in the Ladies Room, Lizzie made her entrance on the Pier. She wore a black mini-dress, sashed, cut above the knee, and with a V-shaped neckline. Fishnet stockings, a black hat with a wide brim and a pointed crown that looked almost but not quite like a witch's hat, her highest heels, and of course, her crystal amulet… a foxy hybrid of witch priestess and hippie princess.

"Boo-Wa-Ha-Ha-Ha!"

It was Mad Jack, awaiting her as planned, jumping in front of her. He wore a devil mask with horns, and a red costume complete with cape and tail. He held a packet of flyers and a chain-and-leather leash, which Lizzie now hooked around his neck.

Showtime!

* * *

11:03 P.M.: Lizzie the red-wigged witch began her stroll, walking her leashed pet devil this fine spring night, parading to the Pier loudspeaker's strains of Nat King Cole's *Lazy Hazy Crazy Days of Summer*. In her heels, she was several inches taller than Mad Jack, but he slumped in his bondage nevertheless, as directed, to accentuate her height. The priestess chanted little blessings to those she passed as her hunchbacked devil handed out the flyers:

Saint Lizzie's
Black Mass
Malibou Lake
Starting June 12

The crowd was gawking and whispering. Lizzie was chanting and winking. Mad Jack was lunging and cavorting. He unleashed his basso devil laugh. Lizzie, refusing to be upstaged, yanked his leash, hard.

"Cut the shit," she hissed.

Near the carousel, Lizzie saw her secret contact... Pinkerton's former protégée and, Lizzie knew, his personal all-state blow-jobber, Felicia Shayne. The lovely Felicia stood in all her full-lipped glory, with lustrous brunette hair Lizzie would have killed for, a Melrose Place salon dress that barely covered her ass, and heavy makeup calculated for the TV cameras to come. In fact, it had been Felicia herself, as planned, who'd anonymously tipped off her contact at KTLA to be at the pier shortly after 11.

11:05 P.M.: Felicia bristled a bit as Lizzie passed her—she bristled very well—then made a beeline for the pay phone to call security. As Mad Jack bought a Ferris Wheel ticket, digging into his costume to get change, Lizzie watched the carousel, waving to the kiddies.

11:06 P.M.: Lizzie rode the Ferris Wheel, screaming each time her car crested the top, baying at the moon over the Pacific, attracting attention. Mad Jack, scampering around the pier, pointed up at Lizzie. The ride took precisely three minutes. The TV crew was expected here any moment, and as Lizzie's car topped the last time, she saw the KTLA truck with its antenna at the foot of the pier.

11:09 P.M.: "Miss, please come with me," said a security chief as Lizzie walked down the Ferris wheel ramp. He looked at the antic Devil. "You too... sir."

Meanwhile, a blonde reporter and her camera crew posse came charging up the Pier. A crowd of the curious was gathering too.

"How dare you come here, you *devil worshipper!*" shouted a woman at Lizzie. "This is a place for *decent families!*" It was, in fact, Margo, delivering her carefully pre-rehearsed 15 words, wearing a dress that was actually clean and a pair of phony glasses that gave her the semblance of a prim librarian. There'd been some doubt that Margo would be a credible plant in the caper, but she was doing fine.

"Your presence and hand-out are upsetting some patrons," said the security chief amidst the gawkers. "I'm afraid I must ask you to leave the premises."

"Oh!" gasped Lizzie.

11:11 P.M.: KTLA cut in live from their Hollywood studio, reporting a "civil disturbance" at Santa Monica Pier. The TV crew's lights came up, capturing the casting out of the sexpot witch and her Beelzebub-on-a-leash. Lizzie swayed a bit, as if a little overcome by it all, giving the crew time to get picture and sound.

"Miss," asked the blonde reporter, lunging at her with a microphone, "were you asked to leave Santa Monica Pier tonight, because you profess to being a witch?"

"I… only wanted to ride the Ferris Wheel," said Lizzie, her voice slightly cracking, a sad, broken-hearted little girl, walking her pet devil.

More security cops arrived. Mad Jack whimpered. Lizzie had figured the leash and bondage bit would spark the showmanship. It sure in hell had. The crowd lined both sides of the pier and some college kids razzed the cops.

"Freedom of Expression!" shouted a student, and others took up the chant.

Mad Jack, thrilled at the attention, cranked up his devil dog characterization, rolling on   his back, waving his arms and legs in the air. Lizzie, hell-bent on squelching his scene-stealing, lifted her short dress a bit higher, aimed one leg and scratched his belly with her shoe. The spiked heel came perilously close to his crotch. Several patrons made their kids look away. Felicia Shayne, fearful things were getting out of hand, decided it was time for her own performance and stepped up to the press.

"I'm Felicia Shayne, Esquire," she said, "and this is an abomination of civil rights and religious liberty. I happen to know that Saint Lizzie fortunately has the legal services of Mr. Alfred Pinkerton. He'll undoubtedly attack this woman's shocking persecution."

Many in the crowd cheered, and Lizzie began a martyr's procession down the pier, to the loudspeaker accompaniment of The Happenings' *See You in September*.

11:15 P.M.: As Felicia fielded final questions, mentioning Lizzie's upcoming Black Mass premiere, Mahugu returned in the limo and Lizzie took refuge in the back seat. Mad Jack, unleashing another devil laugh, chased a couple of screaming teenage girls before disappearing under the Pier.

11:16 P.M.: They'd made the KTLA late night news. Keeping an eye on all the excitement, meanwhile, was Janice Lynnbrooke.

* * *

The limo pulled away, heading north on the PCH. Lizzie, in the back seat, told Gerald Mahugu to turn on the car radio, which offered The Association's *Along Comes Mary*.

"Louder!" shouted Lizzie.

She lit a Mary Jane—wasn't that what the song was about anyway?—and clenched the joint in her teeth, singing and wiggling to the music, kicking off her high heels, peeling off her fishnets and, almost acrobatically, her new, black, open-bottom Frederick's of Hollywood girdle.

"Ger-ald… Do you know the difference between a magician and the Radio City Rockettes?"

"No, Miss."

"Well… the magician has a cunning array of *stunts*… while the Rockettes have a stunning array of…!"

Lizzie cackled before hitting the punch line, high from the Mary Jane and the caper. She was silent for a moment, and then Mahugu heard her giggling and sighing in the darkness. He smelled her scent and frowned.

She was playing the game with him again.

11 Alliance

Alfred Pinkerton sat by his illuminated pool in the Palisades, wearing a robe over his swimming trunks. A chilled bottle of wine and two glasses sat on the table in candlelight.

He'd watched the KTLA late night news, delighted by how well the caper had played, how both Lizzie and Felicia had shown star quality. He'd paid Felicia in advance—her first gig since passing the BAR. It had been money well-spent.

Felicia was to drive here from Santa Monica Pier. A few minutes after midnight, Pinkerton heard her 1960 Corvette pull through the gate.

* * *

Felicia Shayne let herself in the house that she knew so well, making an entrance through the back door to the patio. Pinkerton stood and applauded.

"Bravo, Miss Shayne!" he said. "You're ridiculously photogenic."

Felicia took a soignée victory sashay, her long black hair catching a sheen from the candlelight, her high heels clicking on the stone. She stood by the pool's edge. "Perhaps you'll celebrate your triumph with a swim," said Pinkerton, admiring her legs. "Skinny-dipping, you'll recall, is always allowed here ... and encouraged."

"Have you changed the pool water?" asked Felicia.

"Since when?" asked Pinkerton.

"Since that junkie bitch swam in it," said Felicia.

56

Pinkerton chuckled. "Now, Felicia. You're aware that Lizzie's a remarkable lady."

"She's a sack of puss in a red wig," said Felicia.

Pinkerton pulled back a chair at the table. Felicia sat, opened her purse, removed a packet of *Virginia Slims* and lit up. Pinkerton poured two glasses of Madeira wine, her favorite.

"To your splendid work tonight," he toasted, "and to your brilliant future." They both drank. "I missed you," said Pinkerton, "while you were away, preparing for your BAR exam."

"So you consoled yourself," said Felicia, "by fucking that psycho."

"Actually," said Pinkerton, "Lizzie is an opportunity... for both of us."

"No thanks," said Felicia tartly, sipping her wine.

"Not *that* way," grinned Pinkerton. "Please. It's time you learned the truth about my relationship with Lizzie."

He drank his wine and refilled both glasses. "You've probably heard the rumors that both federal and state agencies have been working in California, undercover, to disgrace and destroy the 'Peace' Movement. They've been scouting for a figure who they can apprehend and crucify as epitomizing the most sordid sins of the Drug Culture. They want a monster. I already have a monster—and she's all mine."

"Lizzie?" asked Felicia. "Has she committed any major crime?"

"Yes," said Bone. "The fire at Universal, for one."

"*That* was *her*?" asked Felicia. "Christ, I should have guessed."

"And as the press has reported," said Pinkerton, "she's anonymously promised another crime on June 25th."

Felicia played it frosty. "So, you know she's going to commit an atrocity, but you're doing nothing to stop her?"

"I'm an attorney," said Pinkerton. "Not a cop. I'll be her devoted and outspoken lawyer."

"And go down in flames with her?" asked Felicia.

"You should have learned in Law School, Felicia, that the public admires lawyers who defend the monsters... as long as they don't win."

"And you plan to lose?"

"We'll discuss that later. For now, let's consider how much a talented, glamorous woman would add immeasurably to Lizzie's Defense."

Felicia's face clouded. Pinkerton wondered if her conscience was troubling her. He never thought she had one. "What about Gerald?" she asked. "He knows about her... and me."

"Ingenuous Gerald has become enamored of L.A art museums and Southern California ladies," said Pinkerton. "I'm sure he'll do nothing that would cause him to forsake his access to either of those fascinations."

"And you're confident," asked Felicia, "that Lizzie will perform another crime?"

"I am. So is Simon Bone, her 'discoverer,' who I'm sure you recall from the excitement at last year's Christmas party. He and Lizzie remain deadly enemies."

Felicia crossed her legs. Pinkerton heard her stockings swish against each other. "I was hoping our collaboration might resume, professionally and... intimately," he said, lighting a cigarette. "After all, imagine making your courtroom debut as co-Defender in a trial that promises to be a sensational media event."

Felicia downed her second drink. She wet her lips with her tongue and with one finger, slid her empty glass toward Pinkerton.

"Tell me more," she said softly.

12 Villa Magdalena

It was 3:30 A.M. in Emmitsburg.

Tony Wyngate, unable to sleep, sat by his unlit fireplace, listening to Judy Collins on the stereo. He'd canceled his date last night with Cynthia, a Languages professor at Hood College in Frederick. On their last "sleepover," Cynthia had left her panties in Tony's bed—she claimed she'd forgotten them—and he was supposed to have delivered them to her at her place. Distracted, and not up for her fetishist games, he'd called to arrange a rain date. Cynthia had pouted but agreed.

He'd been unable to get Porter Down out of his mind. He'd done a little research. The Lafayette Escadrille was legendary and many men boasted falsely to have been a part of its lore. At the Gettysburg Library, Tony had found a book on the Escadrille, with a list of the veterans. There was Porter Down, credited with five air victories.

How could the man have learned so much about him, and the tragic events of thirteen years ago? And what did his cryptic words mean?

In 1931, I was the man who killed her... We'll go see Alice, when she's ten feet tall...

He was looking again at the file that Porter had given him, which raised more questions than it answered. It contained names of various churches and hospitals in the U.S. and Europe with Down's mostly-illegible annotations, and various disconnected papers, such as a flyer for a circus with *Mendocino, 8/1930* scribbled on it. There were also pictures of various religious statuary including, of course, the Grotto's obscenely defaced Blessed Virgin.

Also in the file were several morning-after newspaper stories on the Universal fire and a few behind-the-scenes shots from *Frankenstein*. Penciled on the verso of each one was the film's title and a date. An 8" x 10" shot, dated *9/8/31*, showed Boris Karloff in Monster makeup and costume, relaxing on the set in a striped beach chair, smoking a cigarette, raising a cup of tea or coffee. Another was a 3" x 5," dated *9/19/31*, taken during *Frankenstein's* romantic garden scene. It featured Colin Clive, who played Frankenstein the scientist, and Mae Clarke, who played Frankenstein's fiancée, Elizabeth. Clarke, in bonnet and frilly white dress, smiled sweetly. Clive's face was a lightning bolt. Tony thought the man looked almost wild-eyed with rage, anxiety, or both.

Then there was an 8" x 10," dated *9/22/31*, of a woman dressed in a lovely bridesmaid's costume. She was standing outside, in what appeared to be a European village—probably, thought Tony, the *Frankenstein* set that had burned last week. Although no one else was in the picture for comparison, the woman appeared very tall.

Alice, when she's ten feet tall? wondered Tony, remembering Porter's words.

Her eyes, thought Tony… strangely bright, staring directly at the camera. She wore her bridesmaid bonnet with the brim back, tendrils of her hair hung wildly down her cheekbones, and her dress, festooned with ribbons and tiny pearls, was too short for her—her dark hosiery and black high heels showed incongruously at least 6" beneath the hem. Strangest of all, however, was her expression—a sly, almost vicious grin, as if she were enjoying playing a cruel joke.

The word *Discard* was penciled under the date. Yet somehow the picture had survived, ending up in Porter Down's mysterious file. Tony kept hearing Porter's words, including the most disturbing ones:

Ever visit her grave, Tony?

* * *

Approximately 60 miles from the Mount, Villa Magdalena was a home for ill and aged nuns, located in Rushford, a remotely rural section of Baltimore County. The Roman Catholic Sisters of the Notre Dame order had bought the property, formerly a Civil War plantation and breeding ranch for thoroughbred horses, in 1908, creating the sanitarium. The large, five-story main building sat far off the road, and atop the roof was a tower with a 500-pound bell that the sisters had named after Saint Joseph. The sexton rang the Angelus on the "Joseph bell" every day at 6:00 A.M., 12 Noon, and 6:00 P.M. The nearest neighboring buildings were the Villa's own farm, with its barn and outbuildings.

Until recent years, Villa Magdalena had also treated women, nuns or otherwise, diagnosed, for lack of a better expression, as "the religiously insane." It had been one of the Catholic Church's very few hospitals in the country with specific care for this mania, and the Archdiocese of Baltimore had always tried to keep the patients' presence there a guarded secret. Now the old, vacated ward, locked up on the top floor, was a medical anachronism, considering the advances in psychiatry.

After his sleepless night, Tony arrived in his car at the foot of Villa Magdalena's quarter-mile drive entranceway. He drove up the hill, the lane lined with weeping willow trees. He looked out over the view, saw the pond, and glanced up at the 5th floor. There were still bars on the windows.

* * *

He didn't announce his arrival, although the Villa was private property. He knew how to get where he wanted to go and drove around to the left of the main building. An old priest walking the grounds, raised his hand for Tony to stop and looked in the open passenger window. "Know where you're heading?" he asked cordially.

"I'm driving up to the cemetery on the hill," replied Tony.

"You mean the unconsecrated cemetery?" asked the priest, clearly alarmed. "For those who died in the state of Mortal sin?"

"Yes," answered Tony. "They need prayers too, don't they?"

"Those souls are lost to Satan," said the old priest. "Prayers are of no help to them now. No. It's entirely off-limits. It's not even safe… there are snakes up there. No, sir. You can't visit that cemetery."

Tony thanked the old priest but, ignoring his admonition, drove toward the cemetery. The old priest watched and shook his head.

* * *

The hill dead-ended in a circle of gravel and weeds. *No Trespassing,* read a tattered sign on a pole.

Tony got out of the car, walking past the sign and along the ridge of woods. His previous time up here had been in cold, pre-dawn darkness. Now it was bright, the late morning sun hot, the high dry grass bristly. The broken stone wall was tangled with honeysuckle, and the forlorn cemetery had maybe a dozen graves, marked by small marble squares. They bore no names, just Roman numerals. Only one, to the left, had a cross, tall and lashed at the beam, its arm cocked crookedly, resembling a rack for a scarecrow. Tony presumed it had been placed there fairly recently and since neglected.

The cemetery was a disgrace, thought Tony, angry that his church would ever allow anything so coldly lacking in compassion. Then he went to her grave, to the right. Although it had been thirteen years, he walked directly to it. Her marker bore the number XII. It was the grave, he knew, of Bridget Anne Cannady.

Bridget. Twenty-four when she died. After the guilt and nightmares over the years, it felt surreal that he was actually standing here. For a reason he didn't know, he reached in his pocket and removed a small, black pouch with gold lettering:

My Rosary

He carried it every day, a sign of hope that one day he'd have Faith again. His belief, once strong, had evaporated at this very spot all those years ago, and he desperately missed that belief, wishing he could reclaim it. He didn't open the pouch that contained the red, translucent beads.

Then, as Tony stared at the marker, he sensed something nearby. A long, black snake with a white mouth had curled up the tall, cocked cross, sunning itself. Tony watched the reptile flicking its tongue, entwining itself on the cross, and then he looked back at Bridget's marker. He knelt and without any sense of ritual, placed his hand on the stone.

The bell in the tower began ringing. For a moment, Tony imagined the old priest was sounding an alarm for his capture. Then he realized it was noon. Someone was ringing the Angelus, and as the old "Joseph" bell tolled, Tony glanced once again across the yard. The snake was slowly crawling down the cross, slithering away, scaling the wall, moving toward the woods. A moment passed, then another. Tony placed the rosary pouch back in his pocket and took a final look at Bridget's grave.

"Please forgive me," he said aloud.

As he left the graveyard, something compelled Tony to look again at the tall, odd cross on which the snake had wrapped itself. The marble block was marked VII, and he noticed a small, almost faded carving above the crossbeam. He couldn't make out the initials, but he recognized the date, which was coincidental considering what Porter Down had told him:

1931

* * *

Tony drove to Gettysburg, determined not to think about the morning. He went to the hospital and began a volunteer round at 2:00 P.M. He skipped dinner and volunteered for the 10:00 P.M. shift—the graveyard shift, he realized ironically—but wasn't needed. He drove home.

He passed the file on the table, resisting the temptation to look at it again. He went out on the chalet's deck and sat, closing his eyes, and in a limbo between sleep and consciousness, finally allowed the memories to come.

* * *

Thirteen years ago. A seminarian at the time, he'd taken one of Saint Charles Borromeo Seminary's cars after midnight, defying the Bishop's mandate that he not attend the funeral. He'd driven from Philadelphia into Maryland, through the dark countryside, finally seeing the illuminated bell tower of Villa Magdalena far off the road. The Mass was to be at 4:00 A.M., so not to upset residents who felt it wrong. The Baltimore Archbishop had shown compassion in allowing a Mass at all. Tony had learned of the funeral's time by calling the Villa and claiming that he was a relative of Bridget's.

Tony's grief and guilt were almost overwhelming. Bridget had been a nun at Immaculata College in Philadelphia, a first-year teacher of Latin and Greek. She was bright, pretty, fragile and, he soon realized, disturbed. He'd seen it in her eyes.

By the time he tried to control things, it was too late: She spitefully, so it seemed, revealed their relationship to their authorities. There followed a cruel double standard of punishment: Tony went for a month's retreat at St. Augustine's, outside Philadelphia, what the clergy called "the bad boy school" for errant priests and seminarians, while Bridget was exiled to the 5th Floor at Villa Magdalena as an aide. She'd sent Tony letters to the seminary in Philadelphia. Despite the emotion in them, he hadn't replied.

Bridget's physical health was as precarious as her emotional, and less than a month after her arrival, she became ill with pneumonia. During her illness, she shocked her superiors by bitterly denouncing her vows, and shortly afterwards, left her infirmary bed, possibly delirious, wandering outside into a cold, snowy March night. Workmen had found Bridget the next morning, unconscious near the pond. Some suspected she was planning to drown herself. Never regaining consciousness, she died that night.

An old nun admitted him to the Villa shortly before the Mass time, silently leading him to the chapel, where he sat in the back pew. Inside were fewer than a dozen nuns, reciting a Rosary. The only illumination were the candles, casting flickering light on the wooden coffin at the foot of the altar. At precisely four o'clock, the Monsignor who was then Director of the Villa began the Mass, clad in his black vestments. He scowled when he saw Tony. There was no family evident... Bridget's parents were dead. The Monsignor rattled off the Latin prayers. The nuns briskly responded. Tony, feeling unworthy to receive Communion, had received it nevertheless, and hadn't received it since.

Incense, final blessings... burial. Several maintenance men hoisted the coffin outside into a pick-up truck. For her possible mortal sin of suicide, Bridget could not be buried in blessed ground. Tony, to whom nobody had spoken, got in his car, joining the procession. They drove past the main cemetery, through the darkness, up the hill, along the woods, to the unconsecrated graveyard. The maintenance men unloaded the coffin, and as one of them held a flashlight, placed it on wooden planks above its grave. The Monsignor recited the final prayers, sprinkling the dust on the coffin, intoning almost vindictively:

Remember, woman, thou art dust,
And unto dust thou shall return.

Tony had always hated those cold words, never more so than now. There was a final "Amen." Tony had looked once more at the coffin, walked away, and driven back to the seminary. That afternoon, he'd cancelled his plans to pursue the priesthood.

Having already earned his Master's degree, Tony had been hired to join the Mount Saint Mary's faculty. Looking after the Grotto was one of his first-year duties. Then in December, only nine months after Bridget's death, he'd found Jonathan Brooks' body in the Grotto. The throat was cut, the genitalia mutilated, and although the same person couldn't have inflicted both wounds on himself, there was only one knife found, and it had only Brooks' fingerprints on it. Tony never forgot the blood, the agonized face, and the memory that, as he'd prayed over the corpse, all he could think of was Bridget.

* * *

Tony, having fallen asleep on the bench on the deck, had been dreaming. He was back at Villa Magdalena, the bell was ringing in the tower, the snake was crawling up the cross, and he was kneeling by Bridget's grave, head bowed in shame. A sibilant voice behind him spoke:

"Poor Anthony Wyngate. She still hates you...".

He turned, expecting in his nightmare to see a talking snake. Instead, it was the woman whose picture was in the file... the tall woman in the bridesmaid costume. She'd transfigured, appearing an immaculate, wanton angel, her hair and mouth red, her eyes yellow.

"You got a nice fuck from Bridget," said the angel. *"She killed herself and went to Hell because of you. Quite a bargain... Darling Tony."*

Darling Tony... It was how Bridget had referred to him while in his arms. Tony winced, the angel laughed, her amulet miraculously glowing, and he heard himself cry out, waking up on the deck, soaked in sweat.

* * *

The wind was cold, the waning moon bright. He went inside the chalet, washed his face, sat by the hearth, and remembered yet again Porter Down's brief allusion to Bridget:

A nun and a seminarian... Very tragic... Ever visit her grave...?

Strange... as taunting as Porter's words had been, it was the only time anyone had mentioned Bridget to Tony since her wretched funeral. There were still times after all these years that he feared his guilt would either kill him or destroy whatever was left of his life. He had to decide if he deserved such punishment. He had to face his past. Bridget deserved this commitment. Porter Down seemed to be providing a tortuous pathway to it.

After today and tonight, Tony believed he was mysteriously but definitely linked with Down and his invitation. He opened the file and dialed the California phone number.

"Yeah?" answered a terse voice that Tony recognized immediately.

"This is Tony Wyngate," he said. "Where and when do I meet you?"

13 The Flower Game

The sun was rising over the mountains at Malibou Lake.

High on a hillside, she walked barefoot… tall, willowy, naked, her feral eyes yellow and bright, tendrils of red nylon hair cascading down her high cheekbones, flowing under her large black hat. Her makeup was streaky, her witchy nose shiny, her red-eyed angel sparkly, and she carried a baby lamb.

Lizzie had a little lamb…

She sang, holding the sweet little lambie, strolling toward the spring house, feeling like a pre-Raphaelite Angel, or a Nativity shepherdess. She remembered the verse, about the lady in the meads, "full beautiful, a faery's child:"

Her hair was long, her foot was light,
And her eyes were wild.

And her nipples were hard, thought Lizzie, shivering in the morning chill. "I love you, Lambie," she sighed, looking into its black eyes, wanting to kiss its mouth. But the lamb kicked, fell and ran away toward the pen. She never understood why the lambs always seemed so afraid of her.

They think I'm a freak… with "wild eyes" …

67

She needed a kiss. Desperately. She felt like some cursed, horny Disney princess, fated to turn into a newt or frog or some goddamned reptile if she didn't get a kiss. She usually didn't bother with the wig or makeup in the morning, but she'd awakened scared, having suffered her latest nightmare about the skeletal snake lady. Crawling after her, hissing at her. The snake lady had long red hair, or maybe it was a long red wig like hers, and she was rank, as if dead and rotting, and the snake lady's stench made Lizzie think *she* stank too. Defying the nightmare, she'd made herself pretty, splashed on her honeysuckle perfume, and her vanity became arousal.

I need a fucking kiss.

Yes, she realized… even a ripe, balding, gawky girl with a witchy nose and yellow eyes and a scar snaking up above her pussy needed kisses. It didn't have to be true love's kiss, or a French kiss… hell, she'd take a pity kiss. Of course, she could always wake up Mad Jack and Margo…
Sooey.
She wandered by the spring and the wildflowers. There were three marijuana ciggies from the bunch Mad Jack and Margo had brought from Mexico… left on a rock, with a packet of matches. Giving up hope of a kiss, she lit up, took off the hat and the itchy wig and ran a hand over her thin pinkish strands of hair.
The nasty things that happen to a girl, she ruminated.
She looked into the spring and remembered. It was May 29th. The tenth anniversary of James Whale's suicide. Yes, she'd learned all about the *Frankenstein* folk, although she hadn't met any. On this day, a decade ago, James Whale had thrown himself into the pool behind his Pacific Palisades house and drowned.
She had to celebrate.
Lizzie knelt in the grass. A butterfly flew by, flirting with her cold, hard nipples. Her black cat had followed her and now its yellow eyes stared at her as it sat across the spring. She pointed a long, red fake fingernail at the cat.
I am Maria!
Yes, she was Little Maria in *Frankenstein,* and Cat was the Monster, who would drown Little Maria in the lake. It was the "Flower Game" of *Frankenstein,* in tribute to the dearly departed Jimmy Whale. She mimicked a "Little Maria" voice:
Would you like one of my flowers?

The Monster was Cat's part. Karloff's Monster, gawky, towering, eyes like an insane baby lamb, laughing in joy as he and Little Maria tossed flowers into the lake, watching them float. Then the Monster was to imagine *Little Maria* was a flower and toss *her* in the lake. Funny, in a way. Lizzie threw a violet into the spring.

I can make a boat. See how mine float?

Cat ignored the violet. Lizzie, the Mary Jane clenched in her teeth, tossed two more into the spring. It was the Monster's cue to give his weird, baby-like falsetto laugh, reach for Little Maria and drown her, but the damn cat just sat there. Then she realized… it was staring at her scar. The long, snaky scar, almost cross-shaped, that rose from her red pussy hair…

"Bitch," she said to the cat.

Lizzie changed roles. Now *she* was the Monster—she was tall, gawky, had crazy eyes and could do, and now did, a baby-like falsetto laugh. She tossed the Mary Jane, lunged for the cat, lost her balance, splashed into the spring's edge, and the cat ran like hell up the hill.

"Goddamn it!" shrieked Lizzie, but she had to laugh… outfoxed by a freakin' cat.

Then she saw a frog, squatting on a stone. His eyes bulged, his chin wiggled, and she'd have sworn he was eyeballing her. Maybe *he'd* come to kiss her… French her with his fly-catcher tongue, magically transform before her eyes into a tall handsome prince, unbuckle his sword, pull down his tights and do her right here by the spring. She got on her hands and knees, creeping through the water, oh-so-slowly, reaching to trap the frog… and the little bastard dived away.

He thinks I'm a freak too!

Yes, poor Lizzie. Nobody loved her. Not even her "god," in San Francisco, who claimed he'd created her… who'd haunted her so cruelly that, whenever she looked in the sky and imagined "God," He had her god's gray beard, fruity voice, and pudgy fingers.

Screw him. She'd created herself, for better or worse, and very soon, Bleeding Christ Almighty, the whole big round wonderful world would know it. Anyway, when she prayed, it wasn't to God… it was to Saint Dymphna. The crystal angel figure, with the tiny red eyes and the broken wing that hung on a chain around Lizzie's neck, represented Dymphna— the patron saint of lunatics, epileptics, runaways, rape victims, and incest victims. Lizzie qualified, she figured, on four of the five counts, but she included them all in her prayer as she stood, alone, tall, bald, naked, scarred, wet and reptile-still, looking up at the sky:

Saint Dymphna, keep me from going totally crazy today, save me from ever having a seizure, don't let me run away scared, and please don't let anyone rape me, especially a family member... Amen.

It was a simple prayer, but it always moved Lizzie to tears, and her black eyeliner ran in little rivers down her face.

Part Two – Valerie
July 10, 1930 to September 24, 1931

It's Alive!

– Colin Clive, *Frankenstein*, 1931

14 The Voluptuous Viper

The A.E. Croenjagger Circus proclaimed itself "An Alluring Caval-cade of Flesh and Savagery!"

The traveling Big Top was a sexed-up spectacle of wild life menager-ie, Roman Coliseum and Burlesque peep show. Its management boasted, privately, that more women screamed, more men got boners, and more kids pissed their pants at a Croenjagger performance than at any rival circus playing the Pacific northwest circuit.

The lion tamer, "Armando," roared at his caged beasts, lustily exhort-ing them to roar back at him. His ebullience with the beasts had cost him his right arm. He cracked a whip perfectly well with his left one.

The trapeze artist, "Fioretta," lost her scarlet red brassiere at every show in the middle of her daring triple spin. Nobody could see her bare breasts, since she was madly spinning high in mid-air at the time, and she covered herself in a robe as soon as her partner landed her on the platform. Still, the sight of the bra wafting down into the center ring saw-dust—Fioretta used no net—was one of the show's favorite erotic visuals.

The band was shrill and brassy. The showgirls wore skimpy costumes and heavy makeup. And the clowns leered rather than smiled.

* * *

The Croenjagger Circus was playing this full moon night in Bonners Ferry, Idaho, located on the Kootenai River, smack against the Canadian border. The Act I finale was a slapstick riot in which the clowns and a man

73

in a gorilla suit chased each other through all three rings, while the band belted out *Happy Days Are Here Again* in triple tempo.

As the crowd laughed at the hilarity, a very tall showgirl stood by the rear entrance of the tent. Her presence, even in the darkness between two aisles of the audience, was striking. At first glance, she might have been a vainglorious Follies showgirl. Or an alluring Shakespearean tragedian. Or, if not for her alarmingly yellow eyes, her pointed witchy nose, and her 6'1"-height, a movie star.

Her name was Valerie Ivy.

She was adorned in her Act I costume—a black silk cape over a black leotard with black tights and black high heels. Valerie wore a black bonnet, cocked over her right eye, its brim up on the left side, with a red plume. A strand of cascading red hair fell against her left cheekbone. Her face was pale, her lipstick reddish-black, her eyebrows tapered, her eyes ringed delicately by liner, crowned by false eyelashes. Her scent was honeysuckle.

She lit a long Fatima cigarette, watching the eight clowns surrounding the man in the gorilla suit and squirting him with seltzer bottles. Suzy, the wardrobe lady, suddenly ran up to her.

"Valerie! You nearly fell off the moon!" This was in reference to a preceding act called "Heavenly Bodies," in which the showgirls had clung for dear life to cable-strung "stars" and "planets" as the band played an ad-libbed *glissando*. Valerie had stood on a quarter-moon, soaring to the crown of the tent. And yes, she'd nearly fallen.

The wardrobe lady stood on her toes and sniffed near Valerie's mouth. "You haven't been drinking again, have you?" she demanded.

"Oh, don't be so high and mighty," sighed Valerie, pointing her cigarette toward the center ring. "Everyone knows you're fucking the gorilla."

Suzy was shocked—she'd thought she and Albert had kept their fling an airtight secret. "Your costume for your next act is washed and in your wagon," she said to Valerie, then grinned cruelly. "Better hurry. I know you'll want to look nice."

Valerie ignored the jab, took a long drag on her cigarette, blew out a jet of smoke, and silently left the tent, her stride like a panther's.

* * *

Less than an hour later, the Act II finale ended. Nero, the circus's only elephant, flatulently led the climactic parade. Fioretta, reunited with her red brassiere, rode atop him, waving goodnight to the crowd. The curious drifted out of the tent toward a fenced-in corral, where a banner and string of lights hung stretched between two tall posts:

Croenjagger's
FREAK PHANTASMA

At first look and listen, it was a pretty cut-rate phantasma. A fire eater. A sword swallower. A chain-smoking fat lady who laughed a lot and apparently at nothing. A man in a top hat, playing what was supposed to be spooky music on a dilapidated calliope,

In the middle of the arena was a seven-foot pit. A barker in a derby stood on a box, spieling and gesturing toward the pit with his cane.

"Ladies and gentlemen... Dare you behold ... Valerie, the Snake Lady? Peek into her pit! See the 'Voluptuous Viper' and her satanic serpents... and remember: She's at her fiercest on nights of the *full moon!*"

On cue, a wild, harrowing shriek arose from the pit. Deep below, Valerie lie on her back, along with at least two dozen black snakes and garter snakes.

All the world's a stage, mused Valerie ... *and tonight, I'm playing the fucking Snake Lady.*

The pit was so deep and dark that few if any would recognize her as the showgirl who'd ridden the moon. Her hair was wildly teased, her costume was a gold-colored bra and matching skivvies, and she was probably the only snake lady on the carnival/circus circuit who wore false eyelashes and smelled like honeysuckle. Several world-weary snakes indifferently draped her torso. Valerie's unblinking yellow eyes stared up brightly at all beholders, her arms were stretched away from her sides, her long legs quivered slightly, and her mid-drift undulated sinuously in a sort of supine cooch dance.

Very serpentine, she thought, pleased by her performance.

A blonde teenage girl and her boyfriend were among the gawkers. Valerie, holding a snake in one hand, stared up at the girl, flickered her tongue, and winked. The girl screamed, spun around and vomited her popcorn. Her boyfriend laughed.

Cute couple, thought Valerie.

A strapping man and his blowsy wife stepped up to the pit. He tossed the burning butt of cigarette into the hole. It barely missed Valerie and his wife playfully slapped his arm.

Probably have a two-headed kid at home, thought Valerie.

Then came a hatchet-faced woman, her dress starched to her neck and a straw-hat square on her head. Valerie took the gargoyle for a preacher even before she saw the Bible the woman brandished. "I'm Sister Grace," she shouted down into the pit. "It was the Serpent who seduced Eve, and I have a name for each and every one of those snakes with which you foully consort!" She raised the Bible in her right hand and began. "Satan! Lucifer! Beelzebub!"

Oh, for Christ's sake, thought Valerie, rolling her snake eyes.

"Abaddon! Leviathan! The Dragon!" continued Sister Grace.

Kiss my cunny, thought Valerie.

"Ruler of Darkness! Serpent of Old! Angel of the Bottomless Pit!" ... and suddenly, Valerie felt the fit coming, mercilessly striking as it always did, like a bolt of lightning. The jerking, the writhing... and then the full epileptic seizure. Sister Grace crept away as if she'd broken something that belonged to Croenjagger's and would be made to pay for it. A crowd gathered by the pit, gasping at the spectacle. In her short time at the circus, Valerie hadn't revealed her epilepsy to anyone—only her alcohol and drug addiction. The barker, looking into the pit and figuring she was overacting, shouted an ad-lib.

"Behold the Voluptuous Viper!" he cried out. "See her flail away, possessed by all the demons of Hell!"

* * *

In the blackness of the fit, the nightmare came... again.

She herself had become a snake. A giant snake, long, scaly, almost a damn plesiosaur, crawling out of water, over rocks, through briars.

Yes, she was truly Valerie the Snake Lady.

She still had her long red hair, somebody had sewn her tits on her underbelly, and her yellow eyes stared unblinking. In tonight's version of the dream, there was music, *Happy Days Are Here Again*—yes, in triple tempo, just as it had been as the clowns and gorilla chased each other. Now she was doing the chasing, crawling and sidewinding after the screaming clowns and rampaging ape... and ahead was a dark figure, shrouded in shadows and holding a shotgun. Valerie flickered her tongue, bared her fangs, hissing wildly. Then the shadowy form cocked the shotgun, aimed it, pulled the trigger....

... and Valerie's head exploded—flickering tongue, bared fangs and all.

* * *

Valerie the Voluptuous Viper wasn't sure how much time had passed when she came to, drenched in sweat and urine. It was quiet now. Nobody was gaping down at her. The moon was gone, a sharp wind blew from the border, it was cold, and she smelled a storm coming.

My needle... How long till my needle?

Yeah, the "Voluptuous Viper" needed her needle. Funny, in a way. "Viper" was slang for "dope fiend," and she was the freak show's viper. *Voluptuous, no less,* she thought, almost grinning.

There was thunder, a sudden flash of lightning, and rain started falling. Valerie sat up, her back against the pit wall. No more show tonight, which was a blessing... they wouldn't be throwing her the chicken. Up above she heard the foreman whistle sharply for his crew.

"Get the animals under cover," shouted the foreman. "We'll pull the geek out later."

"Careful how you refer to the dainty damsel," called out a burly roustabout. "She ain't a bad lay, after she dopes out and I hose her off." The men laughed.

A witch, she thought proudly. *One day, they'll all know I'm a witch...* and with all the savagery the term suggested. But right now... *All I want is my needle.* Dope was expensive, which was why Croenjagger made her earn her keep by double-dipping as Moon Lady and Voluptuous Viper. The snakes glistened in the rain, and Valerie moved one off her shoulder and two off her thighs as she looked up into the storm. Her eye makeup ran in rivers down her cheekbones and her honeysuckle scent washed away.

My needle... Please get me my fucking goddamn needle... or at least a drink...

Then she touched something that few if any of her beholders tonight had noticed. It was a small crystal amulet of an angel, with two red pinpoint jewel eyes and a broken right wing, hanging around her neck by a silver chain. She held it close to her yellow eyes, viciously looking into its red eyes.

"Saint Dymphna," hissed Valerie... and she screamed.

Her trembling hand dropped the amulet, and as she kept screaming, the little angel fell, hanging from its chain, nestling between Valerie's breasts, as if trying to hide from her livid, twisted face.

* * *

On May 15, 1931, eight months after Valerie Ivy had left the show and apparently faded into booze-and-dope obscurity, Croenjagger's Circus catastrophically burned to the ground near Mendocino. The animals crashed through their pens, with two hysterical horses falling over a cliff to their deaths far below in the Pacific. While no performers were killed, a roustabout died in the blaze. He was found with his genitalia mutilated by the sword swallower's sword, ravaged before the fire had reached his corpse.

Police suspected arson and murder. No one was ever apprehended.

15 The Lorayne

San Francisco was chilly and windy this Friday night. Lt. James J. O'Leary, LAPD, stepped off the cable car and looked at the full moon over the misty bay. A church tower was chiming 11 o'clock as the ringing of the cable car's bells slowly faded down the hill.

The plane ride had been hell. Trapped in a big metal tube, miles in the sky, rocked by the Pacific... mass air travel, O'Leary mused, would never happen. He walked a block, peering through his rimless spectacles at the name carved on a marble slab above the main door:

The Lorayne

The 10-story art deco tower had a bay view and a litigious history. The architect/ bootlegger, who'd named this monument after his Follies dancer mistress, had allegedly used inferior earthquake-proof supports. Since many doubted the building's safety, *The Lorayne* was the only apartment house in San Francisco which regularly swayed in the wind...and where the rooms were cheaper the higher one went.

O'Leary looked up at the top floor, then entered the lobby. The receptionist, a young lady with bleached platinum blonde hair *a la* Jean Harlow, sat mesmerized by a movie magazine. Marlene Dietrich peered seductively from its cover, wearing the same I-know-your-fly's-open grin that all the Hollywood vamps seemed to favor, or so it seemed to O'Leary. The radio at the lobby desk was blaring a jazzy *I've Got Rhythm* as O'Leary announced himself, telling the receptionist whom he'd come to visit. She pointed toward the lobby elevator.

79

"Tell Mr. Down I think he's cute," she cooed, returning to the wonders of her magazine.

Rattling its chains like Marley's Ghost, the caged-door elevator took O'Leary to the top floor, jarring to a stop. At the end of the hallway was a door with a smoked glass window. He gave three friendly taps.

"Yep."

O'Leary opened the unlocked door himself. The room was almost dark, with a small lit lamp to the left. The curtains wafted through the open casement windows, and the shadow of a stocky figure sat at the lamp-lit table, a round sailor's cap on its head, its feet up on the desk.

"Pardon me," said O'Leary. "Is this the Porter Down School of Charm and Etiquette?"

"Kiss my ass," said the figure.

"Yep, this is it," chuckled O'Leary in his Virginia drawl. "So, how ya' doin, fella?"

No answer. He approached the shadow and looked out the window beside the shadow's head. "Look at that full moon hangin' over the Bay! I bet it almost makes you forget this place could fall down any minute."

"You got me all a-tremble," growled the shadow.

The lieutenant slipped off his raincoat but not his hat, and eased into a chair in front of the desk. The wind blew and O'Leary could have sworn he felt the building sway.

"By the way," said O'Leary, "I'm supposed to tell ya' you're cute."

"Says who?"

"The gal at the desk downstairs. With the Jean Harlow hair."

"Tell her to go soak her Jean Harlow hair."

The desk light slightly bled onto the shadow's face. "You do look a little bit baby-faced," said O'Leary. "Maybe you should grow a moustache."

"Maybe I will one day," said the shadow.

O'Leary took his pipe from his pocket but didn't light it. He watched his host, delicately working his penknife in the lamplight. "Whatcha' makin', Porter?"

The man turned and held up a balsa wood model of a fighter biplane. He spun a propeller so to show off its moving parts.

"Why, Porter! A Spad, right? Just like you flew in the Great War. Just like you got now—*Timber Wolf*. Pretty fast bird, right?"

"The fastest. One hundred thirty-one miles per hour at thirty-three hundred feet."

"I never pictured you up here playing with toys."

"I'm just a fun-lovin' guy."

O'Leary laughed. "Good ol' Porter Down!"

"You know," said Porter, "I finally figured out what you sound like with that 'Virginny' accent. Like one of those radio cowboys, all ready to break into song."

"Want me to sing a few bars for you?"

"Like hell. Have a Coke." Porter stood, leaned out the window and grabbed two bottles of Coca-Cola from the windowsill. "Chilled in nature's own icebox," he said. "Cold nights in San Francisco, even in August."

"Saw cold folks tonight," said O'Leary. "A very long soup line. Seems like this Depression's hitting rock bottom, my friend."

Porter opened the bottles with his penknife and handed one to O'Leary, who noted the man's Arrow Collar profile atop a squat, solid body. It reminded O'Leary of the tank he'd driven into battle in France.

"Pearls in your oyster," toasted Porter. They clinked bottles. O'Leary drank, looking at the crammed bookshelves. Porter was the most amazingly well-read man O'Leary had ever met.

"How's the family, Doc?" asked Porter.

"Have I ever asked you why you call me 'Doc'?"

"Yeah, and I've told you. Because you look more like a dentist than a cop."

"Maybe. Anyway, Charlotte's happy in our new house in Westwood. And both girls are doin' great at Marymount."

"Why the hell didn't you stay in Virginia, Doc? And grow peanuts?"

"Well...San Francisco and L.A. sounded exciting... the modern Sodom and Gomorrah."

"Yeah. Or as I call 'em, Sodomy and Gonorrhea."

Both men drank. "Ya know, Porter," O'Leary grinned, "if you'd stayed Hollywood's top troubleshooter, they'd have made a movie about you. *The Adventures of Porter Down.*"

"Sez you."

"Teenage pilot in the Lafayette Escadrille. Wounded twice, right?"

"Yep. Once in the head. Which is why I'm listening to you tonight."

"Came home a War hero, got an appointment to the Naval Academy. Why'd they kick you out, Porter? Bad grades?"

"VD."

"Still wear your plebe uniform and cap, nine or ten years later. How come, Porter?"

"They're comfortable. Will you get the hell to the point, Doc? You still have that bargain basement hat on. And you haven't lit your sweet-smellin' pipe. I know all your little rituals."

O'Leary sat back in his chair, stubbornly keeping his hat on and his pipe unlit. "Fella, how'd ya' like to be able to afford a down payment on that little ranch you want out in the desert? Fly away happily ever after there, maybe by Halloween? Room for *Timber Wolf.* Ya' won't have to keep it at that airfield in Sausalito."

"Throw your pitch, Doc," said Porter, resuming work on his model Spad.

"OK," said O'Leary. He reached into his inside jacket pocket and removed a folded paper. "As you might have heard, Universal Studios has started shooting *Frankenstein.*"

"Mary Wollstonecraft Shelley," said Porter. "Quite a gal."

O'Leary unfolded the paper and passed it to Porter. "Have a gander," he said.

It was a graphic sketch, drawn in purple ink, of Christ Crucified, hanging on the cross. The gaunt, naked figure was wild-eyed and drenched in blood and gore.

"You recognize who that is?" asked O'Leary.

"Sure looks like the Christus to me," said Porter.

"Yeah," said O'Leary. "But the face is a dead-ringer for Colin Clive, the British actor who's playing the scientist in *Frankenstein.* This came in his 'fan mail' this week. He turned it over to studio security. They sent it to LAPD."

"And it has him all upset?" asked Porter.

"Well, he upsets easily," said O'Leary. "Clive's a young man but a severe alcoholic. Back in December of '29—I remember because it was Christmas time—he came to Hollywood from England to star in *Journey's End.* He was so drunk he scared the other actors. He almost ended up an emergency case at Patton."

Porter knew about Patton Hospital. Until recently Patton, located in San Bernardino, had been known as *The Southern California State Asylum for the Insane and Inebriates.*

"Sad," said O'Leary. "In *Journey's End*, Clive played a captain who couldn't face the front lines in the Great War unless he was doped with whiskey. As an actor, he apparently can't face an audience or camera without the same crutch."

The wind blew and a tugboat moaned out in the bay. The room was very still.

"I don't baby-sit drunks," said Porter finally. "Even if they do look like Jesus."

"There's more," said O'Leary. "From our early reports, Clive's been on the wagon but... well, *Frankenstein's* Universal's big picture of the season. If he falls apart and the movie goes with him, the whole damn studio crashes. In this Depression, it'll probably never recover."

"Anybody think about this when they cast him?" asked Porter.

O'Leary shrugged. "Hollywood's goin' to hell, Porter. Paramount makes sex pictures. Warner Brothers makes gangster pictures. And Universal makes *satanic* pictures, like *Dracula*..."

"With Lugosi," said Porter, "that Hungarian who was sackin' Clara Bow."

"Yeah," nodded O'Leary, "and now they're making *Frankenstein*. The Roman Catholic Church is heatin' to fight the Film industry, which is primarily Jews, and the Jews aren't backing down an inch. It's gonna be a Holy War, Porter—the Jews vs. the Catholics. And based on the nuns who taught me in grade school... I'm bettin' on the Catholics."

"You can put me down for ten bucks," said Porter.

O'Leary sipped his Coke. "*Frankenstein's* about sacrilege and blasphemy. It has an alcoholic star who might hit the bottle any night now. And he's getting that sketch in the mail of himself, wearin' nothing but a crown of thorns, drawn and sent by some looney fan who, based on the sketch's analysis at headquarters, is a female and ..."

"A witch?" grinned Porter.

"Maybe," sighed O'Leary. "Anything's possible out here in Sodomy and Gonorrhea."

"Yep," said Porter. "I can imagine Universal's wildest nightmare. 'Frankenstein' and the 'Witch' get together, up in the hills above Universal City, making the beast with two backs while the coyotes howl at the moon. Meanwhile, the newsreel boys film it and premiere it at the Vatican."

"L.A.'s a factory town," said O'Leary. "You know that, Porter. Without the Movies, the city withers and dies, and a lot of decent people wither up with it. Say Universal goes under. There's a domino effect. Paramount, Warner Brothers, RKO... they're all barely breathing. If the studios fall ... well, all of L.A. might have to give up the goddamn ghost."

"What do ya' want, Doc?" asked Porter.

"Troubleshoot *Frankenstein*," said O'Leary. "Make sure Clive stays sober. If there's anything 'demonic' happening, slam down the witch, or whatever the hell she is. Clive's contract expires in late October, and until he heads back to England, Universal will pay you top dollar. Yeah, I'm making a big deal out of that sketch, but I've got a bad feeling about all this."

Almost beseechingly, O'Leary removed his hat and lit his pipe. "Porter... please?"

Porter gave the model Spad's propeller a spin. Dangling from his open collar was a medallion on a chain, showing Saint George slaying the Dragon. It glittered in the dim light. O'Leary knew the medallion's history, as well as the tragedy that haunted his friend. For a moment, he regretted asking this man to investigate what his cop's gut instinctively warned him would lead into deep, tragic darkness.

Porter raised his Coke bottle. "'Angels and ministers of grace defend us!'" he grinned, as if relishing the battle-to-come. "*Hamlet*, Act I, scene four!"

O'Leary smiled, even though the wind was blowing and he was sure he felt the building sway.

16 The Shepherdess

It was three nights before Ilsa's 18th birthday.

Ilsa lived in a frame house on the back lot of Universal City, California. She and her family had sailed to America from Bavaria three years ago, and her Uncle Johann was gamekeeper of the studio's zoo and ranch. Universal's founder, also an émigré from Bavaria, had brought many of his family and friends to this country. Most were Jews, but Ilsa and her family were Catholics, and they revered the founder for his generosity.

People teased Ilsa that, with her braided blonde hair and pretty eyes, she should be in the Movies. She'd blush and laugh. There were many sheep on the ranch, and she was the shepherdess.

It was 2:00 A.M. Ilsa had taken some of her sheep up into the hills, across the bridge over a ravine, near the reservoir. She'd take another part of the flock up mid-morning, and the third group early evening, thereby avoiding the afternoon heat. Tonight, she stood with her flock, the stars above them, looking down at Universal City. To Ilsa, the Movies seemed a miracle—people talking on a giant screen! So did this studio. America was so modern, but Universal, nestled under the towering hills of the San Fernando Valley, looked like the mountain pass village in which Ilsa had lived in Bavaria.

So beautiful, she thought, time and again.

It amused her that, now that she was too old to believe in fairy tales, she lived in a place that *belonged* in a fairy tale. On the back lot below were castles, towers… the cathedral from *The Hunchback of Notre Dame*… .a lake, glowing in the starlight. On the front lot were the huge soundstages.

85

One night, Ilsa had dreamed that Stage 12, the largest of them all, was the sarcophagus of a giant, naked ogre, who rose up in the moonlight to haunt the mountainside.

Ilsa had suffered nightmares since arriving at Universal City.

A coyote howled in the hills. Ilsa, who carried a crook and bell by day, was armed with a shotgun by night. Her Uncle Johann had taught her to use it. She'd been with him when he'd shot a wolf in Bavaria that had come in the night for the sheep. Any night, she knew she might have to shoot a coyote.

Her fanciful mind wandered. She thought about *Frankenstein*, which the studio was now producing... the story of a man who defied God, creating his own man, actually a Monster, with no soul. Last week, they had filmed the creation of the Monster, and had proudly invited various actors, actresses and people who worked on the lot to come and watch. Ilsa's cousin, who worked as a studio seamstress, had invited Ilsa to attend with her, and she'd worn her best dress and shoes to Soundstage 12.

It had been magnificent! The tower laboratory set. The flashing electrical machinery, that for a moment made Ilsa cover her eyes. The roaring thunder, that almost made Ilsa cover her ears. And the table, bearing the Monster, rising on chains, high toward the rafters to the lightning that gave the creature life. Ilsa had felt as if she were witnessing a wicked miracle, and everyone on the stage was deathly silent as the table descended... and the Monster's hand moved.

"It's moving," said the young actor in a surgeon's gown. "It's alive... It's alive, IT's ALIVE!... In the Name of God! Now I know what it feels like to BE God!"

The episode had haunted Ilsa ever since. And tonight, she imagined she heard the "In the name of God!" the actor's voice like a pipe organ, echoing in the dark hills, and that the Monster was loose, watching her...

17 Monster In the Bungalow

TUESDAY, SEPTEMBER 8, 1931

Frankenstein's Monster lurked in the shadows of Stage 12… reclining in a red-and-white striped beach chair, smoking a cigarette.

It was the 11:00 A.M tea break, and his lizard eyes peered from his square skull, the skin a pale green-gray. There were bolts in his neck, and his stitches suggested how this creature, sewn together from rifled corpses, blasphemously came to be. He wore no mask, but a macabre makeup of putty, collodion, and mortician's wax. He stretched in his beach chair, dangled his cigarette from his lips, and sang:

"I'm just a gigolo…"

Eve Devonshire owned a copy of the popular Bing Crosby record, but enjoyed this decidedly different take on it. Stage 12 was hot under the September morning sun, its giant doors opened during tea time. A studio photographer snapped a candid shot of the singing Monster at his leisure, his giant boots crossed before him.

"You're so lovely, Evie!" said Boris Karloff, with his British accent and distinct lisp, raising his tea cup in a toast. "Such a pretty yellow dress!"

"Thank you, Boris," said Eve. "Colin bought it for me."

Eve was what the company called "utility"—sometimes a stand-in, other times a messenger, basically whatever the director required. She'd landed the job because she was dating the film's leading man, who was playing the title role mad scientist.

* * *

"Hollywood is just *too* marvelous!" crowed James Whale, director of *Frankenstein,* holding court with several reporters.

Tall, elegantly thin, his red hair streaked with silver, the sardonic Britisher was dressed in a dark suit with tie, vest and argyle socks under his knickers. He clenched a cigarette holder in his teeth and checked his gold pocket watch, attached to his vest pocket. It was a gift upon Whale's 42nd birthday in July from his lover, Davey, a young producer at Paramount.

"As for *Frankenstein,*" said Whale to the reporters, "perhaps a *true* Hollywood monster would have Jean Harlow's albino hair, Joan Crawford's smeared red mouth, Norma Shearer's crossed eyes, and Greta Garbo's size 11 feet. *There's* a creature who'd bloody well terrify the public! And don't any of you dare print a word I've just said."

* * *

Boris Karloff, 43, showed high spirits, despite the torturous makeup, costume, and his anxiety that the Monster role could make or break his career. If it did make him, what if a reporter investigated his life, and learned he'd been thrown out of England by his family? That he'd been married four times? That there'd also been a common-law marriage?

Monster, indeed! thought Karloff, with a chuckle.

Nearby was Dwight Frye, playing Fritz, the hunchbacked dwarf who tortures the Monster. Previously an acclaimed Broadway actor, Frye, 32, had recently played Renfield, the lunatic who ate flies in Universal's *Dracula.* The diminutive actor stayed in ghoulish character between scenes, scuttling like a spider inside and outside Stage 12, leering from under his giant hump.

Meanwhile, a third actor, restless in the heat, sat virtually unnoticed on a crate, deep in the soundstage shadows. He was Colin Clive, portrayer of *Frankenstein's* title role. Slender, long-legged, the 31-year-old Clive pushed back a strand of hair that had fallen over his right eye, lit a fresh cigarette, and thought of the date. It was an anniversary, really. Although liquor was easily available in Prohibition Hollywood, this was his 25th day without a drink.

He hadn't believed he could do it.

* * *

Eve brought Colin a paper cup of iced tea. "Bloody hot, isn't it?" he asked.

"Imagine how Boris is suffering," said Eve.

"I hear he hikes up 100 steps to his house every night," said Colin, "after working all day in that makeup and costume. Hope his wife has a stiff drink waiting for him."

"Places!" called the assistant. The dozens of crew technicians took their places behind the cameras and up in the catwalks, two men closed the stage doors, the trio of actors gathered on the dungeon set, and the lights came up.

"Remember, lads," said Whale. "'Insane passion' is our key. Action!"

Karloff's Monster, in chains, gave a wild, piercing scream—*Almost like a woman*, thought Eve. Frye's Fritz scampered into the dungeon and grabbed a torch, sadistically scaring the Monster, who fell to the dungeon floor, crying in terror. Colin's Henry Frankenstein feverishly entered, taking the torch from Fritz.

"Oh, leave it alone, Fritz," he said, his voice full of torment. "Leave it alone!"

Eve watched, fascinated. Colin's talent awed her. Indeed, all three actors were amazing.

"Cut!" cried Whale. "Thank you, gentlemen. We'll break it up for the camera later. Shall we have an early lunch?"

"Lunch!" shouted the assistant.

Everyone scrambled. The crew reopened the stage doors. Mustached makeup man Jack Pierce placed a scrim sack over Karloff's head and a man came forward to drive Karloff to his dressing room bungalow. The actor, due to his hideous visage, was forbidden to be seen outside the soundstage or enter the commissary. Dwight Frye, even now still in character, scurried away for points unknown.

"Probably looking forward to a tasty bowl of flies for lunch," said Clive to Eve as Frye left. "Anyway, I have a cable from London to attend to. I'll see you in the commissary." He kissed her cheek and was gone.

"Oh, Miss Devonshire," said Whale, approaching Eve. "There's no one here to take Mr. Karloff his lunch. Would you please brighten the Monster's day? It's only a short way, and he'll be ever so grateful."

* * *

The San Fernando Valley late-morning heat was soaring. Eve looked at the sheep, grazing on the hill, and the young blonde shepherdess, walking with the flock, holding a crook and bell. The studio's "Old Country" ambience always amazed Eve.

She hiked through the studio streets, holding a platter with a lettuce and tomato sandwich, an orange, and a small pitcher of iced tea she'd picked up at the commissary. A lock of her dark auburn hair fell over her eye, rather like Colin's habitually did. She tried to blow it back while juggling the tray.

It's not *a short way*, she realized. *And it's so hot...*

A biplane was flying up by the mountain. It circled twice, banked... then flew directly toward her. It came low, so low she could see the pilot's goggled face and on the side of the fuselage, a painted profile of an animal and the name *Timber Wolf.*

The pilot waved, then turned, flew beyond her, soared straight up into blue sky, and performed a dazzling loop. He was showing off, Eve figured, for her benefit.

She had to admit she was flattered.

* * *

Finally, against a foothill, there was a row of stucco bungalows, for "featured" players. Each had a striped awning over the front window, a picket fence and a small yard with flowers. She found the number.

"Don't knock," Whale had told her. "Boris runs a loud fan. Just enter."

Eve went to the door. She could hear the fan roaring away inside as she juggled the tray, eased the doorknob, kicked open the door with the toe of her white high-heeled shoe, stumbled inside with her tray... and screamed.

Standing in front of the fan was "Frankenstein's Monster... arms stretched, spread-eagled, cigarette clenched in his teeth, and stark naked.

"Oh God!" cried Eve.

"Oh Christ!" cried Karloff.

He ran into the bathroom and shut the door. Eve dropped the tray on the coffee table. She ran breathlessly out of the bungalow, out of the yard and into the street. Ahead, she saw Colin, hurrying toward her.

"I came as soon as Jimmy started crowing about the prank he played on you," he said. "You see, Evie... Boris... well, he strips every noon in his bungalow. In that Monster costume, he perspires so terribly that he'd risk pneumonia staying in that wet clothing. We've learned about how he cools off, and it's become a joke, rather."

"Why doesn't he wear a robe until someone delivers his lunch?" asked Eve.

"No one delivers his lunch," said Colin. "He keeps his lunch in his icebox."

"Really?" asked Eve, looking forward to kicking Whale right in his knickers.

* * *

As they approached the soundstage, Whale and a few of the crew were outside, standing by an old Eucalyptus tree, awaiting her return, all of them grinning.

Eve walked ahead of Colin, looking Whale directly in the eye. "Your little joke, Mr. Whale, has made me admire Frankenstein all the more," she said. "I now know that, in selecting all the most impressive parts for his Monster... he never scrimped."

The men laughed. Whale cocked an eyebrow. "*Touché,*" he said. "Forgive me?"

"No!" said Eve. "And you can all go to Hell!"

"Would you reconsider," asked Whale, unruffled, "if I offer you a term contract?"

18   Soaring

TUESDAY, SEPTEMBER 8, 1931

Outside the commissary, a small band of Bavarian émigrés, all members of Universal's Music department, sat by the screen door entranceway. They were playing *I Want to be Loved by You* in a decidedly oom-pah style.

Whale, Eve, and Colin shared a table beside the empty fireplace in the commissary's Indian Room. Native American artifacts decorated the hearth and walls. Eve could hardly believe the news she'd heard. Suddenly, for the first time, she felt that maybe her dream was coming true

It was nearly noon now and the commissary was becoming crowded. Lew Ayres, the star of *All Quiet on the Western Front*, for which Universal had won the 1930 Best Picture Academy Award, entered, sitting alone and reading a book. Then Bela Lugosi, star of *Dracula*, appeared, talking with a female reporter. He was tall, handsome, and dressed in a beige suit. Eve had heard that Lugosi was to have starred in *Frankenstein*, but Junior Laemmle had wanted him to play the Monster, Lugosi had demanded the role of Henry Frankenstein, and Whale had refused to cast him at all. Lugosi nodded to Whale and Colin, crinkled his blue eyes at Eve, and sat at a nearby table.

"They wanted *me* to play the Monster in *Frankenstein*, you know," he said loudly to the reporter, "but I told them the part did not have enough *meat*."

"Actually," said Whale *sotto voce*, "Lugosi had too much *ham*. Anyway, Eve, I want you as a bridesmaid, and to continue as 'utility' work. Every day, night, or both. If that's understood, your contract will be ready for your signature early next week."

92

"But you'll want to screen test me, won't you?" asked Eve. Whale glanced significantly at Colin. "That isn't necessary," he said.

* * *

Shooting of *Frankenstein* continued that afternoon. Whale took many shots of the torture scene, skipped a dinner break and carried on until nearly 9 P.M. Karloff had been in the makeup studio at 4:00 A.M. and had endured a 16-hour day.

Universal City took on a different reality at night. It seemed more remote, and as darkness fell, the coyotes howled in the hills. Three Canadian gray wolves in the studio zoo challenged the coyotes' howls.

"We'll celebrate, Evie," said Colin. "Supper... .and then I have a surprise for you!"

* * *

Eve had met Colin four weeks ago. There'd been a reception for him at Universal, following his ship voyage from London and flight from New York. Eve had been one of several freelance "starlets" invited to "spruce up" the party. The guest of honor was visibly shy and ill at ease, and Eve was flattered but nervous when Colin invited her to flee the party with him and drive to the ocean.

"The Pacific is one of the few niceties of 'Hellywood,'" he'd said that night, using his personal expression for the movie capital.

He'd been courteous and a gentleman. Eve had since learned that Whale had personally selected Colin, at the time a virtual unknown, to play Captain Stanhope, a young officer "doped with whiskey" in R.C. Sherriff's 1929 play *Journey's End*. Its triumph had made each of the three men an overnight London sensation. Whale, directing the film version for Tiffany Studios, had refused to cast anyone but Clive as Stanhope, and Colin had made his first trip to Hollywood in December of 1929. His harrowing performance crowned him a movie star, and Whale had insisted Universal star him in *Frankenstein*.

When Eve had first met Colin, she'd told him his performance in *Journey's End,* had made her cry. He'd become almost angry, claiming most of the credit belonged to Whale. Even after a month, Eve knew few personal facts about him. She'd learned that his father and grandfather had been soldiers, and that Colin's military dream—to become a Bengal Lancer in India—had ended after a horse fall in cavalry training at the Royal Military Academy at Sandhurst. Another horse fall might have crippled him, yet in their evening horseback rides, he rode daringly, even recklessly.

For all his restlessness, he was a consummate professional on the set—arriving ahead of his call, lines solidly learned, polite to everyone. Eve sensed he brought the same discipline to the acting craft that he would have given to his life as a soldier.

* * *

Colin and Eve dined tonight at the Brown Derby on Vine Street in Hollywood. Afterwards they headed west on Sunset Boulevard in Colin's open coupe. The "surprise" was still to come. As they drove and turned south, Eve asked a question that had been preying on her mind.

"Colin… Why isn't Mr. Whale screen-testing me?"

"Jimmy knows what he wants… and needs," said Colin. His tone seemed cryptic.

* * *

It was nearing midnight when they drove onto a private airfield in Inglewood. There sat a fleet of biplanes that had seen service in such films as *Hell's Angels* and *The Dawn Patrol*. Most were dilapidated, the airborne equivalent of automobile jalopies. Called "Flying Coffins" during the War, they were now more dangerous than ever, many of them bolted and hanging together with rivets and wire. There was even an old zeppelin, crashed on a pile at the corner of the field.

"Shall we go flying?" asked Colin. "I've taken a lesson or two this trip, secretly, of course. The owner, for a hefty fee and a signed waiver, keeps a biplane reserved for me."

He took Eve by the hand, briskly walking her toward a plane that appeared to be one of the better of the lot. "It's a JN-4 'Jenny,'" he said, "one of thousands of its kind sold off after the War to barnstormers. Keys and goggles in the barn. Shall we?"

"Colin! Does the studio know you're flying a plane?"

"The devil with the studio," laughed Colin. "Will you join me, Evie, or not?"

Eve took the dare. Fifteen minutes later, after a bouncy take-off and a too-sharp ascent, they were a thousand feet in the sky, looking down at the Pacific. Colin piloted in the rear cockpit and Eve sat in the front.

"Magnificent, isn't it?" he shouted over the roaring engine and the night wind.

"Yes!" she cried out, hardly believing where she was. Just wait, thought Eve, till she told Bonnie about this!

19   Bonnie

Eve's apartment was in a stone and timber house, owned by an MGM set designer who leased the top floor. A small fountain trickled outside the front wall. Above on Mount Lee was the HOLLYWOODLAND sign, illuminated tonight and every night with its thousands of light bulbs.

Her roommate, Bonnie Bristeaux, had been in Chicago the past week, where auditions were taking place for chorus replacements in the new Broadway edition of *Earl Carroll's Vanities*. Her train was due tonight at 11:00 P.M. The trolley took Eve to La Grande Station, south of Hollywood, on the west bank of the Los Angeles River. The distinctive station boasted a domed Moorish tower.

Los Angeles, thought Eve. *Full of architecture that belongs someplace else.*

Eve was anxious to tell Bonnie about the contract, as well as the plane ride. The train was almost a half-hour late. Bonnie exited the coach, dressed in a long blue coat and matching hat. She carried a single suitcase and, despite the long trip and the late hour, looked every inch the movie star she dreamed of becoming.

"They hired me!" said Bonnie, rushing to Eve and kissing her cheek. "I start rehearsals in a month. And they want me to dye my goddamned hair—again!"

During her three years in Hollywood, Bonnie, who no one would have guessed was a farm girl from Montana who'd changed her surname from Hockstader to Bristeaux ("rhymes with 'Hello!'" she'd flirt to casting directors), had sported three different hair colors. Currently, she was

96

a honey blonde. Eve had met Bonnie three months ago at a casting call. She occupied the Hollywood nether world between "set dressing" and bit player, and could dance, wear clothes attractively, and deliver dialogue. Paramount hired her frequently and Bonnie freely shared her good fortune with her roommate. Eve owed a great deal to Bonnie's kindness.

They were the trolley car's only two passengers. "I knew I was in the running when I auditioned—I sang *Barnacle Bill the Sailor* as a torch song." She began singing the ribald lyrics.

"Pipe down, sister," groused the uniformed conductor, passing through the car.

"Aye, aye, captain," said Bonnie, saluting. "Anyway, Evie, I'll fill you in later. Meanwhile, tell me what *you've* been up to."

Eve excitedly told Bonnie about the Universal contract as they rode toward Hollywood, the night growing cold, the wind blowing the scent of oranges and pepper trees. She also regaled her about the plane flight. As Eve concluded her account, Bonnie silently lit a cigarette. She'd previously given Eve the impression she didn't approve of Colin Clive. This was odd, as Bonnie rarely disapproved of anyone.

"Aren't you excited for me?" asked Eve.

"Eve," said Bonnie, "Jimmy Whale doesn't want you as a bridesmaid. He wants you as a *nursemaid…* to keep Clive sober."

"We've been through this before," said Eve. "I've never seen him take a drink!"

"You just proved my point," said Bonnie. "You've refused to listen to me when I've tried to warn you, but you weren't out here two years ago when Whale directed *Journey's End.* Clive could be a poster boy for Prohibition."

"I can't even imagine him drunk," said Eve.

"You wouldn't want to," said Bonnie. "He's a dangerous drunk. A belongs-locked-up drunk. Clive's on the wagon now, playing Prince Charming to impress you. Whale needs to keep him that way, so you're getting a term deal."

"Have *you* ever seen him drunk?" demanded Eve.

"Yes," said Bonnie. "A Christmas Eve party in '29. Want to hear about it?"

"No," said Eve. "And as I said, maybe he had troubles two years ago… but he's better now."

"Alcoholics never are 'better now,'" said Bonnie. "They might be recovering, but they never shake it."

Eve was silent.

"Listen, Evie. Your first option will come up in 90 days. *Frankenstein* will be finished, the studio will stick you in a bathing suit and a couple of parades, and throw you out the door. Meanwhile, Clive will be back in London... with his wife."

"He says they plan to divorce."

"Sure he does! Damnit, smarten up, Evie! I believe in letting people make their own mistakes, but I won't let that fancy-pants Whale bait this trap for you."

Bonnie tossed her cigarette. "Evie... Universal's on the verge of collapse. Say Clive hits the bottle. If Whale replaces him, they have to start shooting the movie all over again, it never recoups its cost, and the studio shuts down. And guess what? It's all *your* fault, because you didn't keep your alcoholic boyfriend balanced on the high wire he's walking every day and night."

"It can't be bad as all that," said Eve

"You and I've talked many nights," said Bonnie, taking Eve's hand, "about women getting kicked around in this town. Don't let Whale trick you, Evie... making you his insurance policy for a drunk."

They were both silent for a while. "I brought you a present from Chicago," said Bonnie, removing her hand from Eve's. "Would you like to open it tonight?"

"Tomorrow," said Eve.

Bonnie lit another cigarette. "You know, Evie, Paramount started shooting *Dr. Jekyll and Mr. Hyde* the same day Universal started *Frankenstein*. They're making up Fredric March to look like a gorilla." She paused, exhaled smoke.

"But Colin Clive's the boy for *Dr. Jekyll and Mr. Hyde*. He wouldn't need any gorilla makeup, Evie. All your dreamboat needs to turn into Mr. Hyde is a bottle."

20 Fox Eyes

It was the start of a new week. Eve arrived at Universal City this beautiful morning and saw the shepherdess up on the mountain with her flock.

Universal, always packed with showmanship, looked this morning like a circus coming to town, with its crowd and colorful billboards. There was even a man with a handlebar moustache, wearing top hat and tails and riding atop "Houdini," a camel from the studio's zoo. Draped over each side of the dromedary was a blue and gold banner, reading: *CITY OF DREAMS.*

It's so lovely here, Eve thought, trying to put Bonnie's warnings out of her mind.

* * *

Stage 12's doors were open. Colin, full of high spirits the past few days, greeted Eve, kissing her cheek. Karloff lounged in his beach chair, smoking and singing a Noel Coward song:

Mad dogs and Englishmen...

There'd been some "sniggering," as her British colleagues expressed it, about Karloff ever since Eve's trip to his bungalow, and her remark to Whale and several of his crew about the endowment of the naked Monster. She figured Boris was probably aware of it.

She wondered if he minded.

* * *

99

On Saturday, James Whale had started shooting the boudoir episode, where the Monster frightens Frankenstein's bride-to-be, Elizabeth, played by Mae Clarke. Mae was Universal's "Queen" this summer, having starred in Whale's *Waterloo Bridge*. She was hoping to erase the infamy she'd won earlier in 1931 in Warner Bros.' *The Public Enemy*, in which James Cagney had hit her in the face with a grapefruit.

For the *Frankenstein* boudoir scene, Eve had first worn her beautiful pale pink bridesmaid costume, with bonnet, exquisitely fashioned by the costume department. There were four bridesmaids on the set, and each of the silk costumes was slightly different. Eve's dress had tiny pearls sewn onto it. She loved wearing it.

There'd been trouble Saturday—Mae hadn't been able to scream to Whale's satisfaction, and he shot multiple takes of her attempts.

"That scream was more of a capon's squawk, Mae," he'd teased her after the tenth take. "Do try again, please." However, she'd never satisfied him Saturday, and today would begin with a new attempt to get an effective scream.

Mae Clarke, blonde and visibly nervous, arrived on the stage in her lovely white bridal gown. Colin appeared, dapper in his bridegroom costume. He promptly got back up on his crate in the shadows and lit a cigarette.

"Best be ready for a long, hot morning," he whispered to Eve. "And much squawking."

* * *

Mae sounded several squawks. Whale had a sly look about him, and Eve suspected another of his tricks was in the works. He chatted with his cameraman, Arthur Edeson, and two sound technicians. Then an assistant said something to him and he went outside the stage.

"What's going on?" Eve asked Colin.

Whale returned, escorting a young, very tall woman. She wore a black silk dress with a floral design, sashed at the waist, and a large dark beret, cocked over her right eye, crowning her long, loosely-worn red hair. Eve noticed her angular profile, her long sharp nose. In her black high heels, she was taller than Whale, who wasn't short. A technician positioned a microphone above the woman as Whale spoke to her softly.

"Do you think Jimmy has a protégée?" asked Eve.

"Not bloody likely," said Colin.

The woman's face suddenly turned, and she looked toward Eve and Colin, smiling shyly. Her eyes were very bright. A tendril of red hair had escaped from under her beret, hanging beside her left eye.

"She's a strange, gangly creature," Colin whispered to Eve.

Mae Clarke and Boris Karloff took their places. Whale spoke privately to Mae, who gave a reluctant nod. The woman at the microphone stood very still, her arms dangling at her sides, and Eve noticed her long fingers and red-painted nails. Whale moved beside the camera and the crew closed the soundstage doors.

"Quiet on the set!" shouted an assistant.

"Action!" cried Whale.

Mae Clarke paced in her bridal gown. Karloff, as the Monster, came creeping behind her. She turned and saw the Monster face-to-face.

"Arrgh!" growled the Monster.

Clarke opened her mouth to scream but made no sound. Nevertheless, a shriek of horror filled the soundstage, so wildly, so hysterically, that Karloff's Monster broke character and jumped.

"Merciful Jesus!" lisped Karloff.

"Cut!" cried Whale. The scream had startled everyone, the company breaking into nervous laughter. Whale took the hand of the red-haired woman by the microphone. "May I introduce our 'ghost screamer,'" he said. "Hollywood's own witch, Saint Valerie!"

Everyone applauded except Mae Clarke. Valerie grinned and took a little curtsey.

"The secrets and vanities of Hollywood, eh?" smiled Whale. "By the way, this lady's also known professionally as 'Lucifer's Archangel.' Her actual name is Valerie Le Fay."

The company applauded again. Whale invited Valerie to meet Colin first, as he was the film's star. Colin introduced her to Eve.

"I so admire you, Mr. Clive," said Valerie softly. "And you, Miss Devonshire... your dress is so pretty!"

"Thank you," said Eve.

"Saint Valerie" had a wild theatricality about her, at striking odds with her apparent shyness, and Eve noticed three things. One was the woman's eyes which, under what Eve felt must be false eyelashes, were bright, hazel, almost yellow... feral.

They're like an animal's eyes... a fox's eyes, thought Eve.

The second thing was her perfume, or scent... honeysuckle. And the third thing was the small crystal angel figure that Valerie wore, hanging from her neck on a delicate silver chain. It had tiny, pinpoint red eyes.

Colin, Eve, and Valerie stood there, almost in a circle, silently regarding each other. Valerie's hair flowed under her beret and down off her shoulders.

"It's hot... isn't it?" she said softly, as if she could think of nothing else to say.

Mae Clarke had gone to her dressing room but Karloff was still there, and Whale brought him over to Valerie to introduce him. Whale projected his voice a bit, as if to get attention, and Eve was suspicious of another trick.

"Frankenstein's Monster," said Whale, "may I introduce 'Lucifer's Archangel.' Or perhaps I should say, 'Boris Karloff, meet Miss Valerie Le Fay.'"

Valerie took Karloff's hand. "Oh, Mr. Karloff!" she said, also in a stage voice. "I've heard such *big* things about you!"

A beat... and then many of the company burst into laughter at the pre-arranged *double-entendre*. Valerie kept a straight face for a moment, then laughed too.

Karloff blushed right through his gray-green Monster makeup.

* * *

The group hobnobbed a bit longer as Whale made more introductions. Then suddenly, there was a wrenching sound from above. A large klieg light was tearing loose from the catwalk.

Colin grabbed Eve and another of the bridesmaids, yanking them toward him. As the giant light deafeningly smashed to the floor, Valerie gave a genuinely hysterical scream.

It had barely missed them.

* * *

Come lunch, Colin and Eve sat at their accustomed commissary table by the fireplace. He seemed embarrassed by her effusive thanks for having saved her life.

"Please," he said desperately. "Say nothing more about it. Change the subject."

"So," said Eve. "Do you believe in witches?"

"At the Catholic schools I attended," said Colin, "the nuns and Jesuits believed."

"Did you notice her amulet?" asked Eve. "A crystal angel with a broken wing. It had tiny red stones, maybe amethysts, for eyes."

"Well, after all, this is 'Hellywood,'" said Colin. He sipped his tea. "'Valerie Le Fay,'" he grinned. "Her real name is probably 'Aggie Jones,' or something equally prosaic."

"I can still...*smell* her," said Eve. "Her perfume... honeysuckle."

"She's spooked you, Evie," said Colin. "Hasn't she?"

Whale entered and joined them at their table. "Are you sure you're both alright?" he asked. "You appear to be eating perfectly well."

"Your 'ghost screamer,'" said Colin, "made quite an impression on Evie."

"On everyone!" said Whale, regarding his menu. "Except poor Mae. She feels hopelessly upstaged. I fear we'll have to go with Mae's barnyard screech, rather than Valerie's marvelous rafter- rattler."

"Where did you ever find her?" asked Colin.

"Oh, she's 'Lucifer's Archangel' indeed!" said Whale. "I saw her Black Mass out at Malibou Lake. Blasphemous! Barbaric! The Devil's answer to Aimee Semple McPherson! I must confess... when I told you and Boris you both must display 'insane passion?' It's how Miss Valerie describes herself and her act."

"A Black Mass?" asked Colin.

"All a hoot, of course," said Whale. "Although some of her pagan priestess histrionics might trouble a nice Catholic boy like you, Colin."

Colin didn't reply.

"I invited her to join us for lunch," said Whale, "but I fear the near-death occurrence you two just shared before her very eyes unnerved her. She preferred to go off alone and visit the back lot zoo."

"The zoo?" asked Eve.

"Yes," said Whale. "The girl loves animals."

21 An Invitation

As Eve and Colin were leaving the commissary, Johnny Johnston, the studio's genial publicity chief, was entering it. It was part of his job to know everybody on the lot.

"Listen, Eve," said Johnny. "A gal called in sick this morning for a photo session. Can I borrow you from the *Frankenstein* gang for just an hour?"

"Go ahead, Evie," said Colin. "I'll tell Jimmy."

* * *

It was only September, but the studio was already preparing Thanksgiving shots for newspapers and magazines. Within the hour, Eve was in the photography studio, wearing a blue, fur-trimmed bathing suit, a tall pilgrim hat, tights, and high heels with buckles. The photographer, Roman Freulich, handed her a long blunderbuss rifle and introduced her to the large, live turkey that joined her for this Thanksgiving cheesecake.

Freulich carefully directed Eve on just how to point the blunderbuss in the desired way. The turkey strutted and fretted, as if it were John Barrymore, concerned about his best angle.

"Now, Eve," said Freulich. "Point that rifle... keep it jaunty... and purse your lips."

The turkey suddenly lunged, nipping Eve on the thigh and tearing her tights.

* * *

104

The photos took over two hours, due mainly to the temperamental turkey. It was almost 3:30 P.M. when Eve arrived on the *Frankenstein* soundstage.

Whale was in a rage.

"I told you that you must be here *all* day, *every* day!" he shouted, almost screaming. "How dare you do this... How *dare* you!"

The company was silent. Colin looked mortified. Eve tried to keep from crying. She stayed remote the rest of the day, not joining the 4 P.M. tea break, although Colin pleaded with her to do so. Whale called on her for nothing.

After shooting wrapped, Eve quickly left the stage. She went up to the studio "Lookout," an area offering a view of the back lot, its mountain and lakes. She needed to be alone. She realized that, although she'd been away from the set that afternoon for only a couple hours, Whale presumably feared it could have been enough time for Colin to find a drink.

She thought of Bonnie's warning.

* * *

The Lookout lamppost was lit, the evening star had arisen and the night wind had a chill to it. Eve looked out at the darkening giant soundstages, the towering hills, the old sets. A light was moving along the foothill and Eve realized it was the shepherdess with a lantern, leading her flock back to the ranch. From high on the mountain, Eve heard a coyote howl... and realized she was thinking again about "Saint Valerie."

Eve had decided the woman had made so vivid an impression because her bright eyes and red hair had reminded Eve of an evil princess in the fairy tale book she'd loved as a child.

Lucifer's Archangel, thought Eve. *Hellywood.*

The coyote howled again. The night wind blew.

"So, here you are."

Colin's voice startled her. He wore a polo coat, his hat low over his eyes. "Chilly night," he said, leaning on the railing. "Wonderful view."

Eve looked at the view, not at him.

"Please don't mind Jimmy," said Colin. "He can be beastly, as you know. I'm taking you to his bungalow... he's going to apologize. I couldn't confront him in front of the company, but I bloody well will now."

"That isn't necessary," said Eve formally.

"Yes, it is," said Colin. "Oh, incidentally... Stand under the lamppost and see what I found tonight in my bungalow."

Eve had seen Colin's "bungalow," more of a country cottage, larger than Karloff's bungalow, out on the back lot. He took from his coat pocket an envelope, *Mr. Colin Clive* written on it in purple ink. Eve smelled perfume on the letter... honeysuckle.

"It's a hand-written invitation... to a Witch's Sabbath!" he laughed. "Friday night, 11:15. From our screamer friend, Saint Valerie. It's apparently the Black Mass show Jimmy described. Only in 'Hellywood,' eh?"

"How'd she get into your bungalow?" asked Eve.

"Well, Evie, I'm sure she didn't. She likely gave it to a studio messenger, who slid the invitation under the door. I imagine the cleaning girl placed it on my table."

"Why didn't she invite you when she was on the set?" asked Eve, instinctively alarmed.

"Come," said Colin, ignoring the questions. "Let's face Jimmy in his lair."

He took her arm. A coyote was howling.

* * *

James Whale's bungalow at Universal, like Colin's, was actually an English-style cottage, personally decorated by the director with fresh flowers. "I say, Jimmy," said Colin as he and Eve entered. "Oh, I beg your pardon."

Whale stood at his desk with Porter Down beside him. Porter stood at almost military attention, dressed in a sailor suit and a pea coat. He held a round white sailor's cap. Eve noticed his gray eyes, which made contact with hers. It was Colin who finally spoke.

"Eve," he said formally, "may I present Mr. Down."

"Hello," said Porter. "You look familiar."

"I do?" asked Eve, startled by the directness of his stare.

Now Whale spoke. "Despite appearances, Mr. Down is not here tonight courtesy of the United States Navy. He's working here"—he paused— "on a security matter for the studio. Right, Mr. Down?"

"That's right," said Porter, still looking at Eve.

"Shall we all sit down?" said Whale.

They did. Eve was alarmed. Something about the faces and manner of all three men made her suspect there was a secret the trio shared, and of which she knew nothing. The fact that Colin had obviously already met "Mr. Down" made her all the more suspicious.

"Mr. Down has enjoyed a colorful life," said Whale to Eve. "He was a Lafayette Escadrille pilot. And a hero, I'm told, a few years ago back east in what you Yanks call 'the beer wars.'"

The man's credentials spiked Eve's fear… someone of his caliber was apparently required for whatever mystery was at play here. "Is anything wrong?" Eve asked directly.

"No," chorused Whale and Clive. Porter looked amused.

"I don't need to tell you, Miss," he said, "that Hollywood's a strange town. You're shooting a strange movie. So, please contact me if you see or hear anything suspicious. That's all, really."

"Mr. Down," said Eve. "Colin received a letter tonight… in his bungalow." Colin appeared surprised Eve had volunteered this information, but promptly took the invitation from his pocket and handed it to Porter. The detective read it silently until he came to the signature. His face and voice hardened as he read, "Valerie Le Fay.'"

"Valerie?" asked Whale. "Well, she has my standing invitation to visit the studio."

"She does?" asked Porter coldly.

"Oh, come now," said Whale. "Valerie's an *actress*! A *showgirl*! Her 'Black Mass' is a *burlesque* show! As Colin and Eve are aware, I hired her to scream in *Frankenstein*. I say, Mr. Down… drive up to Malibou Lake. See 'Lucifer's Archangel' at her leisure. I wager you'll find her barefoot, enjoying a weenie roast."

"I've seen her show," said Porter flatly. "It's swell. Mr. Clive, may I take this letter with me?"

"Yes," said Colin. Porter stood. Whale and Colin stood too. "Anyway, thanks for your time," said Porter, looking right into Eve's eyes as he shook her hand. "By the way… Were you that girl I saw from my plane last week, carrying a tray?"

"Were you that pilot I saw," asked Eve, "flying *Timber Wolf*?"

Porter grinned and Eve laughed.

"Good night, Miss," said Porter, and left the bungalow. Whale moved to the door and watched Porter walk away into the night. "The fellow marches like a puffin," he said.

"Jimmy," said Colin. "About the way you treated Eve today…"

"I regret if I were cross," interrupted Whale, "but you hopefully do realize, Miss Devonshire, the demands of your assignment. I've spoken to Mr. Laemmle about your value to our production. You may sign your contract tomorrow." He held open the door, signaling the couple to go.

"Good night," said Whale frostily.

Neither Eve nor Colin replied as they left the bungalow.

22   Junior

The next morning, Eve and Bonnie got off the trolley and strolled through Universal's gates. The previous night, Bonnie had tried once more, futilely, to dissuade Eve from signing the contract.

"Alright," Bonnie had said finally. "If you have to make a deal with the Devil, let me help you make the *best* deal."

Eve and Bonnie approached Universal's executive building. With its Spanish architecture and stained-glass window of a globe, the studio's talisman, the building resembled a small monastery. Bonnie looked critically at Eve's plain white ensemble.

"That hat makes your face look round," said Bonnie. "Of course, your face *is* round. Are you sure you want to do this?"

"Yes," said Eve.

Bonnie sighed. "Alright. But let me talk to Junior. I've dealt with him before. Trust me, I know how far to go. With both of us in there, the runt won't dare pounce."

* * *

In the mad mountain fiefdom that was Universal, its goblin king was Carl Laemmle, Sr., a gnarled, 5'3" immigrant from Bavaria, who'd opened Universal City in Los Angeles in 1915. The "Crown Prince" was his son, Carl Laemmle, Jr., who had been the studio's General Manager since he was 20-years-old. The elder Laemmle's nepotism was infamous, so much so that Ogden Nash rhymed, "Uncle Carl Laemmle has a very large faemmle."

"Junior," as he was widely known, was now 23, and barely as tall as his father, despite his custom-made elevator shoes. His diminutive size was a torment to him.

Eve and Bonnie were now in his presence. There, behind his giant mahogany desk, was Junior Laemmle, standing very stiffly as they entered, his black hair slicked down against his oval head, his hands clasped behind his back, framed against the rich, ceiling-to-floor red velvet draperies. The "Crown Prince" smiled broadly, seemingly showing every tooth in his head.

"Mr. Laemmle," said Bonnie, her voice low and lush. "How *darling* to see you again!"

Junior said nothing. He indicated two copies of the contract on his desk and kept smiling.

"The Ruth Pruitt Agency has authorized me to assist Miss Devonshire negotiate her contract," said Bonnie, picking up the papers.

Bonnie was a client of the Ruth Pruitt Agency, Eve had no agent at all, and Bonnie's claim sounded like a load of clams to Junior, but he didn't care. He just kept smiling.

"May we sit?" asked Bonnie coyly.

Junior nodded. The ladies sat. He kept standing. Bonnie, in a carefully rehearsed gesture, crossed her legs, brushing her arm against her dress so that the hem came up to her knee. She pretended not to notice. Junior did. Eve saw him admiring the view of Bonnie's legs.

Bonnie seemed to be studying the contract, and then slowly looked up, as if sensing somebody or something of potent allure. "Oh, there it is," she said softly and sensually. "The Academy Award that Mr. Laemmle won for *All Quiet on the Western Front!*"

Indeed, the golden statue glistened, reverently ensconced in its own niche, shining like some holy relic above the Crown Prince's anointed head. Junior smiled. Actually, he hadn't stopped smiling.

"Oh, Mr. Laemmle!" sighed Bonnie. "It's so *bold* and *erect!*"

Bonnie wasn't looking anymore at the statue. Junior, perspiring, instinctively glanced down at his crotch and then raised his eyebrows. He looked at Eve. Instinctively she raised her eyebrows too, then stared at an imaginary spot on her white shoe.

"Now, Mr. Laemmle," said Bonnie. "I think $75 a week is low, considering..."

Suddenly, a strange sound came from behind the desk, like wood creaking. Junior stared straight ahead, his hands still clasped behind him. A loud crash followed, and 5'3" Junior fell through the box on which he'd been standing.

"Goddammit," he said.

Eve began to laugh. She couldn't stop. "Eve," hushed Bonnie. "Eve!"

Junior clumsily extricated himself from his broken box. The toothy grin now gone, he leaned across the desk and brusquely offered Eve a pen.

"Seventy-five a week, 90-day options, take it or leave it," he snapped.

"We'll take it," said Bonnie. Eve, still uncontrollably laughing, signed both copies.

"*Mazel tov,*" said Junior tersely. "Now… go keep your Limey boy-friend sober."

Eve stopped laughing.

* * *

The two women were outside now. "I guess I overestimated my charms, as far as Junior's concerned," said Bonnie. "The last time I was in there, he chased me around his office."

"How?" asked Eve. "With a box tied to each foot?"

Bonnie laughed. "Anyway, $75 it is. Congratulations… I guess."

Eve was thinking of Junior's final words. Bonnie had been right. Whale had talked to Junior, demanding Eve as Colin's "insurance policy."

"I'm not doing this," said Eve. "I'll be a waitress, a dishwasher… but not this."

"Sorry, honey," said Bonnie. "That contract gets Universal your 'ex-clusive services.' No waitressing or dishwashing allowed."

She kissed Eve on the cheek.

"Anyway, better hurry over to the *Frankenstein* stage. Make sure your 'mad dog and Englishman' grabs your fanny instead of his flask."

Bonnie headed for the exit gate. For a moment, Eve considered fol-lowing her. She thought again of the previous night, the impromptu visit to Whale's bungalow, the mysterious Mr. Down and his piercing eyes. Had he been enlisted too, to keep watch over Colin… and perhaps confront dangers facing the production, of which she knew nothing? Why had Mr. Down responded the way he had to the letter from Valerie Le Fay, and taken it with him? What was happening?

Then she thought of Colin. For all the mystery, all the suggestiveness of this arrangement, and all the humiliation she felt, she knew he was a kind, brilliant, and sadly ill man who needed help. Perhaps her devotion could prevent him from becoming the tragedy that Bonnie predicted he'd be. Maybe she could help him… save him… and this was what truly mattered.

Eve hesitated only a moment, and then headed for Stage 12.

23   Abyss

20-year-old Luke Foster had named his fishing trawler after his father—*The Frederick*.

Fred Foster, a decorated LAPD policeman, had been murdered three years ago. Determined not to fall under the same overwhelming grief that killed his Mom, Luke had finished school, taken the residue of insurance money, and bought this old trawler, renting a ramshackle pier at Venice Beach. It was Luke's "Marina," and his dream was to become a prosperous fisherman.

It was Porter Down who'd tracked down the man who'd killed Luke's Dad and had emptied his pistol into him.

Now, as during his past few jobs in L.A., Porter was staying on Luke's trawler, paying him the *per diem* lodging rate he demanded of his clients, that would have afforded a suite at the Ambassador Hotel. The trawler had two bunks, a shower and bathroom, and a two-way radio that could send and receive mainland messages. A shack on the pier provided other basic amenities, including a telephone. Luke had a couple of broken-down cars and a truck that, while a jalopy, was tough and spunky, and Porter used it in his travels, always keeping it filled with gas. Porter kept his biplane at a private airfield in nearby Inglewood.

Luke hero-worshiped him.

* * *

It was after 1:00 A.M. and Porter Down was flying *Timber Wolf* over the Pacific.

He enjoyed flying at night. He looked down at the ocean, the lights of the fishing trawlers, one of which might have been Luke's, and the brighter lights of the gambling ships that sailed just beyond the three-mile mark.

The investigation had been consuming his time and attention. Tonight, however, the darkness had come, as it still did, even after four years. It was merciless, but he was tough. He'd proven that to himself. Not a drop of alcohol in over three years. No lost days… lost weeks.

Sometimes on these nights, he had a ritual, although he didn't like to think of it as such. When he was in San Francisco, he'd fly his plane over the Bay. When in L.A., he'd fly over the ocean. Tonight, he looked down at the Pacific blackness. A storm was predicted this night, and there were no stars, no moon.

The abyss. Yeah, he'd been in the abyss. He'd come out. He'd do it again now.

He was almost a mile high, and now, tipping his plane, working the wings, he went into a nosedive. The plane plunged, gaining speed, whining, shrieking, and as it did, the memories of four years ago were in the darkness too, driving him back against his cockpit seat. The figure he saw in his mind seemed to be so close, so real in the blackness, that he almost felt he could touch her, grab her… but as always, not save her.

There was another figure now, and he sensed the smell of blood and feel of broken bone, and the realization that he'd caused both, and was trapped in his own violence. The plane was screaming now. He smelled the ocean. The momentary temptation came, as it always did, to release his hands and smash into the abyss, but he yanked the controls, the plane lurched, and he was so close to the ocean that water splashed against the wheels, almost overturning the plane.

Porter soared back up, almost a straight arrow, into the sky. He righted the plane. His goggles were streaked with moisture and he removed them and his flyer's cap. For a few moments he flew west over the Pacific, then banked, turned, and headed back to shore.

He'd completed his ritual.

24 "The Demonic Rites of Insane Passion, As Performed by Saint Valerie, aka Lucifer's Archangel"

I chose Colin Clive for Frankenstein *because he had exactly the right kind of tenacity to go through with anything, together with the kind of Romantic quality that makes strong men leave civilization to shoot big game...*

Jimmy Whale had said these words today to a reporter on the set during the 4:00 P.M. tea break. As shooting ended that evening around 8 o'clock, Whale approached Colin and Eve.

"Do hope you'll enjoy the Black Mass tonight," he said. "I'm sure Valerie will be at her best for both of you."

After a light supper, the couple drove in Colin's open roadster up Pacific Coast Highway, heading for Malibou Lake. Eve looked at Colin beside her, trying not to think of his wife in London or Bonnie's warnings. She thought only of how she'd fallen in love with him.

* * *

At Malibu, the coast grew wilder, the surf louder. Porter Down drove Luke Foster's pick-up truck into the canyon wilderness. A coyote ran across the road in the headlights and Porter swerved to miss him. About 10 miles from the ocean, Porter reached Malibou Lake. Across the lake on a cliff, he saw the bonfire.

115

Since arriving in L.A. to investigate the case, it was his second visit to *"The Demonic Rites of Insane Passion,"* performed by its star attraction, "Saint Valerie."

"The Abbey," he'd learned, was formerly the ranch of a now-deceased doctor from Vermont, who'd added a barn, a silo, a springhouse, and a windmill, similar to the ones on his farm back east. A bell had replaced the rotor blade on the windmill. The main house was a sharply-sloping stucco A-frame with an orange tile roof. A circus tent stood on the grounds, amidst the barns, shacks, and pens for goats and sheep. Lanterns hung from several trees.

Porter parked his truck and joined the sensation-seeking crowd. He saw Colin Clive and Eve Devonshire arrive. Some recognized Colin, despite the polo coat and slouch hat, and a few asked for autographs, which he obliged.

11:00 P.M. Someone began tolling the windmill bell, as if it were a death bell. The crowd laughed and filed into the tent to behold the attraction. Porter followed, keeping a distance from Clive and Eve, not wanting them to know he was there, at least for now.

The packed audience sat on benches on three sides of the altar. Porter saw an usher escorting Colin and Eve to the third-row center. Taking an end seat in the last row, Porter regarded the altar. Two candles lit the altar's centerpiece, a looming crucifix over 15' tall. At the altar's "downstage" foot was a large pentagram, painted red. Between it and the cross was a black, smoking cauldron. There were netting and pulleys in the crown of the tent, and in its dome was a painting: a dragon, breathing fire, threatening a woman and baby.

There's not an empty seat in the tent, Porter noticed. *Suckers.*

The bell outside stopped ringing. A middle-aged man, in cap and work clothes, emerged from the lighting booth in the rear of the tent. He looked carefully around the tent, and then went behind the altar and into the darkness. He'd been here last week, and Porter hadn't nailed down his identity yet, but presumed he headed the backstage crew. Then a tall, bearded, very heavy young man took his place at the organ stage left of the altar. Porter had learned about this man and his reputation and his eyes narrowed at the very sight of him.

Simon Bone, thought Porter. *Frisco's upper-crust all-star sex creep.*

11:15 P.M. The lights dimmed, leaving only candlelight for illumination, and Bone began playing the *Dies Irae,* the ancient "Day of Wrath" hymn from the Roman Catholic Requiem Mass. After this prelude the candles suddenly flickered and died, as if by black magic. All was darkness, and then…

"Do… what thou wilt… shall be the whole law…"

The soft, chanting female voice came from the blackness. There followed a blast of organ music, Liszt's *The Devil Sonata,* and a spotlight.

There stood "Saint Valerie," naked, a long boa constrictor entwined around her, its head resting on her shoulder. The audience screamed loudly, and then applauded. Porter had learned the inspiration for Valerie's pose: *Lilith,* a painting by John Collier, a British artist of the late 1800s who painted in the Pre-Raphaelite style. Valerie had the cascading red hair, and despite her angular face and long, thin nose, appeared to be the painting incarnate. The draped snake hid what appeared to be total nudity.

You're awfully cuddly tonight with that snake, Valerie, thought Porter.

The music started, and Valerie began to sing:

From childhood's hour, I have not been
As others were—I have not seen
As others saw…

It was Poe's poem *Alone,* set to music—Porter, a Poe aficionado, had recognized it instantly last week. Valerie's soprano voice was hauntingly lovely, and Eve saw she was wearing the crystal angel figure she'd worn that morning at Universal.

From the lightning in the sky…

The snake's tongue flickered, and Valerie touched her tongue to it. Screams. To prove the reptile was real, she crossed to a silver chalice on the altar, took off its lid, and with her long red fingernails, removed a white mouse by its tail.

When the rest of Heaven was blue,
Of a demon in my view.

She held the mouse at arm's length before her. The snake lunged, grabbing the mouse in its jaws and devouring it. Screams rose from the audience, and Valerie screamed back at them. It was a shriek, a howl, so filling the tent that many women screamed again. A 30'-tower of fire erupted from the upstage fulcrum, nearly touching the dome of the tent.

"Hail Lucifer!" screamed Valerie.

Yeah, she's hot tonight, thought Porter.

* * *

The audience, jolted by the constrictor, the scream and the fire, eventually applauded. The fire receded, the lights came up, and Valerie now wore a black, sheer negligee, draped in flowing "strips," giving ample view of her legs. She carried a pair of silk stockings, black high heels and a tall, black top hat. The crew had removed the snake and set up a small prop table and chair during the blackout, and Valerie sat on the chair.

"Tonight, my faithful," smiled Valerie, teasingly pulling on the stockings, "we focus on the celebrated sin…Carnality! Music, Simon?"

The fat, bearded young organist smiled jovially and began playing what sounded like burlesque music, shifting from the ominous mood.

"Blessed are we who live in Hollywood," said Valerie. "In proximity to the Sex Goddesses of the Silver Screen… who, in their boudoirs, sample, like mere mortals, the joys of the flesh… and their sexual climaxes."

The crowd tittered. Valerie, having hooked her stockings and put on her heels, announced: "My faithful… Miss Jean Harlow."

Valerie exaggerated the vapid expression Harlow had worn in *Hell's Angels,* sprawling stiffly on the stool, her legs spread. "Oooh," she said flatly. "Oooh-Oooh." Her eyes grew comically wide but her expression never changed, and she began blowing a gum bubble, actually a balloon, that became enormous, finally suggestively exploding.

"*Ooooooh!*" deadpanned the priestess in her toneless, Harlow-esque voice. "*Next!*"

The audience roared with laughter. Valerie stood and followed as "Norma Shearer," MGM's "American Beauty Rose," simulating a dainty orgasm while completely crossing her eyes. Then came "Jeanette MacDonald," who climaxed while sounding a piercing high "C" note. Uproarious laughter and applause. Then came Valerie's *pièce de résistance.*

"My faithful… Miss Marlene Dietrich."

Valerie cocked the top hat over her long red hair, sat, revealed her legs *a la* Dietrich in *The Blue Angel,* and began singing *Falling in Love Again,* to a hand mirror. She vainly stroked herself, the crowd loving this vulgar, outlandish lampoon:

> *Falling in love again, never wanted to.*
> *What's a girl to do? Can't help it!*

Valerie's narcissistic "Marlene" raised one leg high and suggestively. After comic primping and explicit self-love mime, she gave a low growl, hitting her climax, musically and sexually:

Can't... .hellllp... .it!

The Devil Sonata pealed at the organ and there was a blackout as a rope swing fell from the tent's dome. A spotlight caught Valerie, standing in the swing like a circus trapeze artist, riding it high into the air. She smiled radiantly in her top hat and negligee, the rope swinging her over the audience. Valerie gave a sly, lascivious wink. As if by magic, a whip appeared in her hand. In Marquis de Sade fashion, she cracked it above the heads of the faithful, almost ritualistically.

"All praise to the Brightest Angel!" cried Valerie exultantly, and winked.

* * *

Colin and Eve had regarded the comedy and acrobatics seemingly impassively. Now Valerie changed to a long red silk robe, and the Black Mass proceeded, mocking the Roman Catholic consecration of Christ's Body and Blood. In a lewd lampoon of the rite, she held up a black wafer and a crystal chalice of red wine, licking the host and consuming it, licking the rim of the chalice and drinking from it. She stripped off her robe, appearing naked in the ambiguous lighting, dancing a mournful ballet to music of only four notes, sadly ominous and haunting.

Her intensity spiked. Colin had heard of opera divas in Europe with such powerful presence that they virtually hypnotized audiences. "Saint Valerie" had this power. He was fascinated. Even in this penny-dreadful devil show, the actress clearly had a quicksilver brilliance, remarkable to behold. He'd imagined one day daring to play a season of Shakespeare in London, and now conjured up Valerie as his horrific Lady Macbeth, or his raving Ophelia.

Colin also had a rather funny thought: If anyone ever presented an all-female company of *Journey's End*, Valerie Le Fay would be tops as Stanhope.

Finally, Valerie put back on her red robe, came to the foot of the stage, and raised her arms as in prayer. She was trembling, and appeared to be chillingly losing control of her body and voice:

And we all know, my faithful... that just as God sent His only begotten Son, so has Satan sent his angel... his Archangel...And I... I am Lucifer's Archangel!

The lights blacked out, the organ pealed deliriously, the towering jet of fire roared again, and then she was rising, hooked to a wire, madly staring at the sky, creating a remarkable tableau... the pre-Raphaelite ascension of Lucifer's Archangel. The tower of fire erupted behind her, the crowd screamed, she disappeared into the darkness above...

Blackout.

* * *

The lights came back up after lengthy applause. Valerie was on the altar, wearing her robe, holding a white lily. She gave a curtsey, finally raising her arms to signal the applause to stop.

"Thank you," she said, her voice soft but carrying. "Inspiring me tonight was the presence of the celebrated actor, Mr. Colin Clive...now portraying the great blasphemer in *Frankenstein!*"

She indicated Colin, who gave a somber nod but didn't stand as the crowd applauded. Valerie, as in a take-off of the sign of the cross, touched the lily inside her robe to both her breasts, then her pubis, and tossed the lily to him. He reflexively caught it.

"In your honor, my dear sir," Valerie said, "a special benediction."

The lights went out. The death bell tolled. Bone reprised the *Dies Irae*. A shaft of light hit the stage, and there was Valerie, wearing a long purple robe and a crown of thorns... the satanic priestess, playing the Agony of Christ.

The crowd gasped.

It was sensationally profane showmanship—whore at Calvary. Valerie opened the robe, wearing under it the traditional loincloth of the suffering Christ, but it was black instead of white. Her long hair appeared to cover her breasts in the semi-darkness and a long-stemmed rose hung from the loincloth like a phallus.

She was Christ as voluptuary... and hermaphrodite.

Eve had become increasingly repulsed by the show, but was especially so by this "benediction." Beside the repellant blasphemy, there was something else at play here... sly, taunting, strangely familiar, that she couldn't quite pinpoint, as the lights went out again. The sound of driven nails echoed in the Abbey. There were more gasps, and then the lights came up suddenly to the sight of Valerie hanging on the cross, in black loincloth and crown of thorns, her head tilted, her face anguished, in the throes of agony and death:

I thirst.

It was the voice that made Eve realize… *She's imitating Colin!* Valerie's expression, her body language, her voice… it was a masterful, terrifying impression of Colin Clive, playing the tortured Christ. Eve wondered if he realized he was the subject of this horrific tribute as Valerie looked up and gasped:

It… is… finished!

And she screamed, so wildly, so piercingly that many women and a few men instinctively screamed in response. She hung there, her eyes opened, her smile a rictus. The lights went out. Everything was silence and darkness. When the candles lit again, the cross was vacant. No applause started. Several women were crying, and the "faithful," after sitting very still for a moment, silently filed out into the night.

* * *

Porter Down stood outside the tent, watching the crowd depart. He saw Colin Clive, who appeared violated, walking ahead of Eve Devonshire. Porter looked at Eve and tipped his sailor cap.

"Good evening, Miss," he said.

She was too embarrassed by what she'd just seen and by Colin's brittle response to it, to say more than "Good evening" in reply. Porter watched as Clive threw the lily onto the ground and Eve followed him to the car. Meanwhile, two men, seeing the lily and realizing where it had been, both dived for it.

Porter smirked, yet felt now what he'd sensed after his first visit to the Black Mass last week… a strange, visceral danger. He'd also learned today that the handwriting expert at LAPD had determined that the same person who'd anonymously drawn the Christ Crucified sketch sent to Clive weeks ago had handwritten Clive's invitation to the Black Mass tonight.

The person, of course, was Valerie Le Fay.

25 Apology

On Saturday morning, the *Frankenstein* company went on location to the Pasadena Gardens. The only players involved were Colin and Mae Clarke. As Eve's "duties" require she come along, Whale had her pose there in her bridesmaid costume for publicity shots.

It was a brief scene: Henry Frankenstein and Elizabeth, flanked by dogs, talking about their upcoming wedding. However, Colin, rattled by the previous night, couldn't relax into the romantic mood. Mae, in a pretty white gown and bonnet, gazed adoringly at him, to no avail. A photographer asked for a candid shot. Mae smiled charmingly but Colin, hyper-tense, glared furiously.

"Well, we sure in hell can't use *that* one," murmured the photographer.

Whale finally took Colin aside. They were gone some time. Meanwhile, Eve was delighted to wear again the beautiful silk dress and bonnet. Although it was the property of the studio, Eve felt "ownership" of the costume, and was proud that the wardrobe people had sewn a tag with her name inside it.

Eventually Whale got what he considered a satisfactory take from Colin and Mae before lunch. The company packed up to return to the studio.

"Incidentally, we won't be doing a retake on the bridesmaid scene," Whale said to Eve, curtly. "When we get back, see that you return that costume to wardrobe."

Eve was disappointed she wouldn't wear it again.

* * *

122

They worked that afternoon at Universal, a retake of the scene where Frankenstein and the hunchbacked dwarf Fritz cut down the corpse from the gibbet. Dwight Frye, who'd completed his scenes as Fritz, returned for the retake, his face leering, his hair tousled, crouching under the huge prosthetic hunchback Jack Pierce had provided him.

Colin's mood had lightened, to Eve's relief. He'd be off Monday and Tuesday. This seemed to revive his spirits, and he and Eve watched from behind the camera as Frye, clenching a knife in his teeth, crawled along the top of the gibbet to cut down the cadaver.

"They say the little fellow was a ripping Broadway actor," said Colin. "Even sang and danced."

"I hear he has a lovely wife and a baby boy," whispered Eve. "And that he lives his roles."

"Which means that tonight," said Colin, "Mrs. Frye's sleeping with a sadistic hunchbacked dwarf."

"And that during *Dracula*," Eve grinned, "she slept with a fly eater."

* * *

This night James Whale was hosting a party in his rented villa on Dundee Drive, high in the Hollywood Hills.

Colin, nervous at parties, knowing there'd be drinking, didn't want to go. Still, as a courtesy to Whale, he accepted the invitation. Inside the great house, Colin and Eve, nicely turned-out, found a female pianist and smartly dressed guests, several of them from the studio. Eve had hoped Boris Karloff would be here, for she'd never seen him without his Monster makeup. He wasn't.

"Hardly likely," whispered Colin. "Jimmy dislikes Boris. Calls him a 'truck driver'—Boris drove one during his lean times. I think it's jealousy over all the attention Boris is getting. Jimmy can be a snooty bitch, you know."

They found Whale on the patio, smoking a cheroot, entertaining his guests. "You see," said Whale, "*Frankenstein's* frightful Monster, Boris Karloff, whose real name is Billy Pratt, actually has a most definite lisp. Fortunately, the Monster only howls and screams… otherwise people might think I discovered him dancing at one of Noel Coward's pajama parties."

Laughter. *Jimmy's very open about it*, thought Eve.

Whale noticed Colin and Eve. "This is the star of *Frankenstein*," said Whale, "and he's giving a perfectly splendid performance."

The guests applauded. Colin blushed. A butler arrived and Whale took two wineglasses from the tray. "It's ginger ale," Whale said to Colin under his breath, winking as he handed the glasses to Colin and Eve. "Roberto will keep you harmlessly refreshed throughout the evening."

The butler nodded gravely. Eve was embarrassed.

"Also," said Whale, "I have a surprise for you. Up the front stairs. End of the hallway."

* * *

Nobody appeared to be on the second floor. Colin and Eve walked down the dimly-lit hallway and came to a dark bedroom. An interior door in the room was open to a balcony, affording a dazzling view of the city lights far below.

Eve smelled honeysuckle. Then a tall, willowy figure, who'd been to the side of the balcony, moved into the room. The figure stood silently for a moment, its face almost hidden in the darkness.

"I owe you an apology," said Valerie softly. "Both of you."

Colin and Eve said nothing. Valerie timidly took a step forward and a bit of light from the hallway fell on her face. She was wearing only a soft makeup, the eyes delicately ringed in mascara, the lips tastefully red. A high-crowned black hat, rather like a man's hat, was cocked over her right eye. Her red tresses fell loosely under it. Her dress was black, sashed at the waist, and she swayed nervously in her black high heels. She held a small bouquet of wildflowers.

"My repertoire is a freakish one, I admit," said Valerie shyly.

Colin and Eve were silent.

"You both are real actors. I was too, once upon a time." She recited Ophelia's lines:

Do not as some ungracious pastors do,
Show me the steep and thorny way to Heaven,
Whiles, like a puff'd and reckless libertine,
Himself the primrose path of dalliance treads...

Colin didn't respond. "You played Laertes in London last year, didn't you?" Valerie asked him. "A special royal performance?"

"Yes," said Colin. "I was quite dreadful."

"I once played Ophelia," said Valerie. "But not before royalty. And I was fucking awful."

If the profanity was meant to loosen the tension, it didn't. Silence followed. Eve noticed Valerie's crystal angel. Valerie, realizing Eve was looking at it, touched it, giving a small, self-conscious giggle.

"I… really am sorry for last night," she said.

Valerie's transformation amazed Eve. The woman, in her striking, bohemian fashion, seemed totally sincere. Yet she also was aware of how Valerie, even as "herself," had directed her own dramatic effects, standing here, mostly in darkness, the balcony view of the Los Angeles lights as her backdrop.

"I'm merely a sensationalist," said Valerie. "As was all-too-clear. You were the victim of my latest stab at sensation… and I truly beg your forgiveness."

Colin remained silent. Valerie looked embarrassed, as if almost tearful to be deprived absolution.

"Please," she said finally, "take these flowers." She handed them to Colin. "There's a brief note in them. Read it… please?"

Colin accepted the flowers without comment.

"Goodnight to you," Valerie sighed.

As she hurried to the stairs, Eve smelled her honeysuckle scent.

* * *

A few minutes later, Colin and Eve stood by the fireplace as Whale addressed him, his voice confidential and angry.

"It took me hours this morning, Colin, to get a scene you should have fired off in a single take. You were so miffed by that silly Black Mass that I telephoned Valerie late this afternoon and she sweetly offered to come all the way here, over 30 miles, eager to make amends. She admires you tremendously… and you two prigs ran her out! This is Hollywood, my good sir… not a First Holy Communion!" He returned to his guests.

The fire crackled. "I say, we've been lectured properly," said Colin. "Anyway, the devil with 'Saint Valerie.'"

"She certainly knows all about your career," said Eve. "Shall we read the note she gave you?"

"No," said Colin. "I've…I've already tossed it into the fire."

* * *

They soon left the party. Colin drove Eve directly home. "I'm afraid I'm rather all-in," he said. "Last night was late and ill-spent." He paused. "I'll need tomorrow to catch up on correspondence. I'm off Monday and Tuesday—we'll do something for sport."

"Of course, Colin," said Eve. He kissed her goodnight, Valerie's note in his coat pocket.

* * *

Colin drove to the top of Beachwood Drive. For a moment he sat in his car and looked out at the city lights. Then he read the note:

I've a message that will perhaps be of interest to you and your two sisters—Valerie.

The cryptic words frightened and angered Colin. He believed he knew to what they alluded. His Uncle Piercy had died in the early 1920s after years as a patient at Saint Saviour's Hospital on the Island of Jersey. The records there listed him as a "lunatic." Colin and his sisters were painfully aware of their uncle's illness.

Somehow, the woman had presumably learned of this tragedy. She probably suspected—correctly—that it haunted him and his unmarried sisters, who were terrified that the curse of "lunacy" might infiltrate the family. He lit a cigarette and looked down at the lights.

This ends tomorrow, he decided.

26 The Transfiguration

SUNDAY, SEPTEMBER 20, 1931

Colin arrived at Malibou Lake. It was mid-afternoon and the temperature was over 90 degrees. It was his 37th day without a drink. He sure in bloody Hell could have used one.

He was eager to find this damned "Saint Valerie," denounce her fakery, warn her against any idea of blackmail. He knocked at the door of the Abbey's main house. No response. He walked into the tent, looking at the tall cross on the altar, a shaft of sunlight playing on it.

"Hello?" Colin called. No answer.

He left the tent, and regarded the lake far below with its sailboats. He glanced at the windmill with its bell and the vegetable field with its scarecrow, dressed as a witch in a raggedy black dress and pointed hat. He passed the silo and a stable. A trio of small goats headed into a barn and Colin followed.

There were a few empty horse stalls, several pens for the animals, bales of hay, and a large cage in the corner. It held the boa constrictor from the Black Mass, torpid in the heat. Colin passed through behind the barn, where two white stallions pranced in the corral. He saw the head and shoulders of a tall female figure, her back to him. The figure wore a black scarf, rather like a Gypsy's, tied tightly around its head, a simple thin, sashed pale blue house dress, and black work boots. She was raking horse manure.

The figure, sensing someone behind her, turned quickly, looking at Colin. "Oh!" she gasped.

After a moment, Colin realized the woman was Valerie. She was still wearing her false eyelashes and faded makeup from the previous night, some of which was running as she perspired in the afternoon heat. Her crystal amulet flashed in the sun

"I look like a hag!" she laughed.

Her coyness angered him and he took a step toward her. "I've come all the way out here today to see you face-to-face and tell you simply this: I've read your note. Any more of the kind, and I'll inform Universal's lawyers and the Los Angeles police. Do you understand?"

Colin turned to leave. "Please!" she cried desperately. "I have a strange gift... .and I always offer it with compassion."

He kept walking. "You and your sisters have been deeply frightened of something for a long time," Valerie called to him. "My message is simply... don't be afraid. What you fear will happen, will not."

Colin had never believed in this sort of nonsense, yet couldn't deny the strange sensation of relief he felt at those words. He turned to look at her. She took a step toward him, and he smelled her honeysuckle scent and saw how bright her eyes were.

"Please stay for tea," she said.

* * *

Valerie removed her boots as they entered the starkly furnished house, with its stone fireplace, a few antiques, and several framed drawings and paintings. Colin sat at a pinewood dining room table. In its center was a glass vase of lilies.

She went to the kitchen icebox and poured tea. She wore her black scarf like a pirate, the knot draped over her front right shoulder. Colin had to admire her style.

"I hope you're enjoying California," Valerie said from the kitchen. "Have you spent time at the ocean?"

"Yes."

"Have you visited the mountains?"

"Yes."

"Have you seen the lesbian chorus line at the Sappho Club in West Hollywood?"

He grinned and she laughed as she came from the kitchen with two glasses of tea. She sat across from Colin, handing him a glass.

"I hope it's not bitter," said Valerie. It was bitter, but he said nothing.

There was a teakwood cigarette box on the table. She opened it toward him, and they both lit Fatima cigarettes. The black scarf accented Valerie's angular, rather androgynous face. He looked into her yellow eyes, and was aware again of her honeysuckle scent which, on this very hot day, he was embarrassed to notice, mixed with the acrid smell of her perspiration.

A black cat had strolled into the room. "This is Leah," said Valerie, picking up the cat and petting it. "I've read you love dogs and horses. Do you also like cats?"

"Yes," he said. Valerie began to pass him the cat over the table, but "Leah" hissed, nestling back against her. "Sorry," said Valerie. "She's not at her best today either." Valerie petted "Leah," then placed her on the floor. "Come back when you want to be a good girl," she said, shooing the cat away. "After all, we have a distinguished actor here. Not a freak show grotesquerie, like me."

"No more of that," said Colin.

Nothing he'd seen in the house, aside from the hissing black cat, suggested anything to do with witchcraft. Then he suddenly noticed, hanging to the side of the fireplace, a Goya-esque crucifix, with a naked Christ, with a penis. He remembered the sketch he'd received in the mail, the figure similarly endowed.

"Strange object," he said frankly, "for display in a witch's house."

"Jesus was a thrilling man," said Valerie softly, exhaling a jet of cigarette smoke. "He died for our sins. Even the sins of witches." She sipped her tea. "Calvary," she said. "So beautifully dramatic. Rather a stacked deck, though."

Colin was a long-lapsed Catholic, yet her remark startled him. "How so?" he asked.

"Jesus knew He was the Son of God, didn't He?" asked Valerie. A strand of hair had fallen from under her scarf, beside her left eye, and she toyed with it as she talked. "He knew that He'd endure three hours of passion and agony. Then, two days later... Resurrection, Ascension, eternal exaltation. Most of us endure our own Calvary far more than three hours... don't we?"

"I didn't come to discuss theology," said Colin curtly.

"Of course, not," said Valerie. "Forgive me. I'm just trying to impress you, like a silly schoolgirl, and making an ass of myself."

He sipped his tea.

"I've read you love horseback riding," said Valerie, "and that you wanted to be a Bengal Lancer, once upon a time. Would you like to go riding with me today? You saw my stallions, Romulus and Remus. There are beautiful trails to the west..."

* * *

Colin left his jacket in the house. Valerie pulled on her boots, removed her scarf and combed out her hair. She put on a black battered hat, the brim bent up on the front and left side. Her long hair flowed under it. Meanwhile, a man drove up near the barn in an old Ford. He was middle-aged, with powerful arms, and wore a cap and work clothes. Valerie introduced him to Colin as "Oscar," her stage manager and the ranch's foreman. Colin recalled seeing the man in the tent before the Black Mass had started Friday night.

Oscar, polite but taciturn, saddled up the stallions. Colin rode Romulus, and Valerie rode Remus. "I learned to ride in the circus," said Valerie. "The hat came from there too. It's shed its red plume. Maybe I'll tell you about that time in my life... one day."

They rode west, through the searing afternoon heat, Valerie leading the way over the paths she knew. They saw wildlife, including a buck deer and a soaring eagle. They rode recklessly at times and said little. Colin had to admit to himself how striking Valerie was, her angular profile, her command of Remus—she had a savagery, he thought, onstage and off. They rode for over two hours, eventually up a steep hill that, from its peak, offered a magnificent view of the Pacific and a sharp wind off the ocean.

* * *

It was twilight when they returned to the ranch. Oscar's car was gone. Valerie and Colin returned the horses to their stalls.

"You'll come in for some tea?" she asked.

"Just briefly," he said.

She removed her hat and boots, lit a gas light and Colin sat at the table. Valerie provided tea. As she sat, she spilled her glass on her dress, excused herself to change and went upstairs. Leah the cat slinked into the room, watching Colin from the hearth.

Then, upstairs, he heard a cry and a crash.

Colin hurried up the stairs and saw Valerie, on the floor in her dim-ly-lit bedroom, naked, writhing on the floor. He realized it was a seizure, probably epileptic. He knelt, grabbed her, held her, then stuck his fingers in her mouth to prevent her from swallowing her tongue. She convulsed, and he saw and felt that she was wetting herself.

"My God," he winced.

She bleated, shook, and his strong arms held her tightly. At last, the fit ended. He wiped her mouth with his handkerchief and, after a mo-ment, picked her up and placed her, limp, wet, and whimpering, on her bed. He found a sheet in her closet to cover her.

Then he saw them. There were livid purple needle tracings, streaking and scarring Valerie's upper arms and thighs.

Colin placed the sheet over her. She lay perfectly still, eyes slightly open, gasping, breathing lightly. Nothing about her suggested she was at all conscious.

"Rest," said Colin, not sure she heard him.

Some women could fake love and lust. Valerie, having bleated, writhed, and pissed herself, had just faked, in a *tour de force* performance, one of her own epileptic seizures.

She enjoyed humiliation—and she was about to seduce him.

* * *

Colin had stayed, worried about leaving until somebody else ar-rived. By 9:00 P.M., Valerie had spoken only incoherently and no one had come.

A mixed odor of honeysuckle perfume, perspiration and urine filled the room and he'd opened the window. He washed her arms and legs and sat by her bed, realizing that she must have covered her scars with make-up during her nudity at the Black Mass.

Finally, Valerie opened her eyes, sat up slightly, and sipped a glass of water Colin gave her. He placed it on her night table.

"You've washed me," she said weakly. "Thank you."

"No need to thank me," he said.

"I know how awful I must look... how terribly I must smell," sighed Valerie.

Her yellow eyes were bright in the dimly-lit room, staring at him through her tangled hair. She held her scarred arms out toward him.

"Aren't I pretty?" she giggled.

Colin looked at her. Two nights ago, he'd admired her as the most audacious actress that he'd ever seen. Now, in this pathetic condition, she fascinated him at least as powerfully. Feeling pity along with the fascination, he sat tentatively on the edge of her bed and adjusted her sheet. She looked longingly at his ascetic face.

"What a lover I'd be now," she laughed with self-mockery, reaching out, touching his hair.

He stood, moving to a chair near the foot of her bed.

"Do you need anything... before I go?" asked Colin after a moment.

"I need to show you Saint Dymphna," said Valerie softly. She sat up in bed, touching the crystal angel hanging on the thin chain around her neck. "She's my patron saint. Do you know about her?"

"No," said Colin.

"She was a martyr of the 7th century," said Valerie, "and her name means 'Little fawn.' She was born in Ireland... the daughter of a lusty pagan king, and a beautiful Christian woman whom she resembled. Dymphna was so pure...so lovely."

She drank, put the glass back on the night table, and continued.

"Dymphna's mother died when the girl was 14-years-old. Dymphna's father went mad with grief and sent his soldiers to search the world for a new wife who looked like his former one. They failed to find such a woman. In his lust and madness, he decided to marry Dymphna."

The sheet slid to her waist and up her legs. Colin sat motionless in the near-darkness.

"Protected by a priest," continued Valerie, "Dymphna fled Ireland and found sanctuary in Belgium. Her vile beast of a father followed. When the priest fought him, Dymphna's monstrous father ordered him beheaded. When Dymphna continued to refuse his incestuous desires, the stinking, perverted fucker spitefully severed his own daughter's head with his sword."

Silence descended. The room became very still. Valerie swallowed and a tear ran down her face. "She was so young... beautiful...innocent."

Colin realized he was soaked in sweat. "You need to rest," he finally managed to say.

"Dymphna is the patron saint of epileptics," said Valerie, her voice more under control. "...Also of runaways, martyrs, rape and incest victims..." She paused and looked intently into Colin's eyes. "And lunatics."

Colin paled. "Why are you telling me this?" he demanded.

"Depictions often show her holding a lily," said Valerie, her voice now soft, almost childlike. "Her feast day is May 15. A shrine in Belgium contains relics from Dymphna's body. The faithful believe she grants miracles." Her eyes were very bright. "You and I could make a pilgrimage there... together. She knows we need her. She's waiting for us there."

"Stop!" said Colin, standing abruptly.

Valerie stretched her arms at her sides *a la* Calvary, showing off her needle scars. "She wants to cure our curses... my addiction... and yours."

Colin glared at her, aware only now that she knew about his drinking.

"She's waiting for us!" said Valerie, tossing aside the sheet, kneeling on the bed, folding her hands in prayer. "Bow your head as I pray...'Saint Dymphna, young and beautiful... '"

"Stop!" ordered Colin, but she continued, her mania and the smell of her desire taking over the small room.

"'Give us strength and courage,'" she prayed, her voice rising and quavering, "'in fighting off the temptations of the world and evil desires... '"

"You're ill!" he shouted. "You should be... ."

"Where?" she shrieked, springing toward him on her hands and knees. "Patton Hospital? The asylum for 'lunatics and inebriates?' *You* weren't so keen about going there two years ago, were you?"

Colin froze, paralyzed with anger and shock.

"I'm sorry!" Valerie gasped, her arms now reaching toward him. "Please...stay. We'll hold each other, and pray to Saint Dymphna."

She suddenly lunged, wrapping her arms around his waist. "Stay... please..."

He broke through the miasma that had poisoned the room, hurrying downstairs, slamming the door as he ran to his car.

"She's waiting for us!" he heard her screaming upstairs.

Valerie heard the car driving away into the hills. She squealed, falling on her back on the bed, delighted by the emotional rape she'd just inflicted.

Saint Dymphna...she'd made her own pilgrimage to her shrine two years ago...but she wouldn't think of that now. Instead, she imagined her visitor naked, crowned by thorns, bleeding from the five wounds. Alone in the near-darkness, she fingered her crystal amulet, and in her quite beautiful voice began singing, softly, sensually, the mournful Good Friday hymn:

O Sacred Head surrounded by crown of piercing thorn...

27   San Francisco

The man pacing this morning in a private waiting room in San Francisco's courthouse stood 6'3" and weighed over 340 pounds. He was 28-years-old, with a Van Dyke beard and a sophisticated, theatrical aura.

He smoked a cigarette and glanced at his watch—9:35. His lawyer had been in conference for over half-an-hour. Then the door opened. Robert Pierpont, Esq., slender, silver-haired, Harvard-educated, entered.

"We've come to an agreement, Simon," said Pierpont. "No trial."

Simon Bone clasped his hands as if in prayer. "Thank you," he sighed.

"We've also agreed," said Pierpont, "to pay medical fees if the boy requires counseling."

"He only wanted money," Bone said wistfully.

"The plaintiff's leaving the courthouse now with his parents," said Pierpont. "It's best we not run into them. Also, it will give us time to have a chat." They sat across from each other at the waiting room's table. "Simon," said Pierpont wearily. "I represented your family's financial situation for decades. We can't afford another trial. This was the third in the past 18 months. One underage girl, two underage boys..."

"I can't believe the family fortune's in actively serious danger," interrupted Bone.

"The Depression, naturally, has taken a toll on your portfolio," said Pierpont. "Yes, you still have the townhouse here, the estate in Big Sur, various real estate holdings, and some bonds and stocks..."

"And the paintings," said Bone. "The antiques. The first editions... ."

"Simon, please. Some of your father's holdings are worth a fraction of what they were before the Crash. And cases like the one resolved this morning are terribly dangerous. I promised your late father I'd protect the family's fortune and good name. If any of these cases ever actually went to trial and became public… it would be disastrous."

"Yes," said Bone. "Father and Mother would spin in their graves. And dear sister Melanie would dance a Charleston in hers. I understand, Robert. Thank you."

"Also," said Pierpont. "I've learned that the real estate arrangement you made last December… the deed to your property down at Malibou Lake that you gave to the performer known as 'Saint Valerie'… has not proceeded in the manner I'd arranged."

At the mention of "Saint Valerie," Bone's manner became rigid.

"Miss Valerie Le Fay was to pay you a rental fee for use of the property and pay for any additions or improvements. I've examined bills for theatrical and circus equipment, costumes, livestock, including two expensive stallions, all absorbed by you, and none by her. I've even learned you attend her show and provide accompaniment on the organ."

Simon Bone reddened, nodded and lit a fresh cigarette.

"A Black Mass," Pierpont scowled. "Yes, you say it's only a show, the latest 'sensation' for crowds tired of watching young people collapsing at the Dance Marathons. But can you imagine what would happen if your personal involvement with this 'devil' nonsense ever leaked?"

Bone said nothing. "Very well," sighed Pierpont, standing. "It is my most sincere recommendation that you cancel this deed with Valerie Le Fay, due to her failure to live up to its terms, and begin confidential proceedings immediately to evict her from your property. I also strongly suggest you sever any ties with her in any capacity. Are you agreeable to all I say?"

"Yes," said Bone, almost inaudibly.

Pierpont wasn't encouraged. The man had the look of a lovesick schoolboy ever since Pierpont had mentioned that woman's name. He could well imagine how mortified Jonathan Bone would have been by the sordid excesses of his only surviving child.

"Simon," sighed Pierpont. "It's hardly too late for a turn-around in your life. You're young, and you have time and opportunity to reject these things that, unless checked immediately, surely will destroy you. Your satanic church, for one." He picked up his valise. "The boy and his family have likely left by now. Good day, Simon."

Simon Bone watched Pierpont leave and close the door. A few moments later he left the room, taking the elevator down to the main lobby. Relieved to see neither the boy nor his parents waiting for him, he briskly left the courthouse.

* * *

A half-hour later, Bone emerged from a taxi and walked up the steps to his front door, whistling *Falling in Love Again*. He entered his townhouse, went upstairs, entered his living room, and looked up at the framed painting. It was a reproduction of John Collier's *Lilith*, a beautiful demonic woman with flowing red hair and a large serpent wrapped around her. It had been the inspiration, of course, for Valerie Le Fay's "entrance" in her Black Mass.

Bone stared at the painting for a long time. Yes, she was beautiful... and he had helped nurture her, protect her, "create" her. He could never imagine forsaking her. He ran a bath, undressed, and looked forward to his afternoon ablutions.

28 Santa Monica Bay

Monday night, Luke Foster's trawler was anchored twelve miles out in Santa Monica Bay.

The large fishing rods-and-reels fit into braces on the bow. Porter and Jim O'Leary manned this station as the laconic Luke stayed aft with his net. Porter had been on the case for three weeks. Tonight, he'd deliver his progress report as he and O'Leary fished.

"Hell of a case, Doc," said Porter. "We've got a Monster who lisps, a mad doctor who drinks, and a real-life witch who shimmies naked at a Black Mass with a snake around her neck."

From aft, Luke appeared, bringing Porter and O'Leary each a bottle of Coke. Porter pointed at Luke. "Best damn fisherman on the California coast."

Luke smiled at the compliment and returned to his nets.

"All I really have so far is that 'Saint Valerie's' a viper," said Porter, re-casting his line. "We still have no evidence to make a charge stick on trafficking drugs. She's got no record, at least under her current stage name. There's no record of her prints. But I've got a bad sense about this gal."

"Tell me why," said O'Leary.

"It's all bits and pieces," said Porter. "For instance, she claims she acted for Belasco in New York '29, but Belasco died in May, his office is still mourning the old lecher, and nobody I talked to there on the phone claims to remember anyone matching Valerie's description. And with those crazy eyes, the long hair, and that witchy nose—not to mention her giraffe's body—she'd be hard to miss... or forget."

137

O'Leary caught a fish and reeled it in. "Finally got one," he chuckled. "Sorry, Porter. Keep talkin.'"

"Most of the gang working for Valerie are laid off studio people or ex-carnies," said Porter. "Drunks and dopers who come and go. Her foreman, however, is a guy named Oscar O'Neal. I traced Valerie and O'Neal back to an old carnie retired in Oregon, who'd crossed paths with both of them in the northwest… Croenjagger's Circus. He ID'd Valerie from the pictures I showed him. Her name was Valerie Ivy at that time."

Now Porter reeled in a fish.

"The carnie says Valerie could do all kinds of acts, including an 'I-Can-Read-Your-Past' act. Nobody could figure out how the hell she did it, even the circus old-timers. She learned at Croenjagger's to crack a whip, handle animals, and do acrobatics, the way she does in her Black Mass. But she was hooked on booze and dope, was considered a bad bet as any kind of headliner, and was mainly known as 'Valerie, the Snake Lady'—screaming half-naked in a pit while a bevy of snakes of all colors and sizes crawled over her. She'd apparently get real cozy with the snakes—anything for her needle. And eventually, they learned she was epileptic."

"When was this?" asked O'Leary.

"1930," said Porter. "The carnie in Oregon says she claimed she'd been a Shakespearean actress before joining the carnival. She boasted she'd acted for Belasco on Broadway. The carnie also told me one of the roustabouts used to rape her most nights after the show was over."

"What else did you learn about Oscar O'Neal?"

"A once-upon-a-time ace circus crew chief. Fell apart after a bear clawed his wife to death. Booze, sometimes drugs. This is his last stand. A good guy until the tragedy. His relationship with Valerie is apparently strictly business."

"What's Valerie's game?" asked O'Leary.

"I'm still figuring it out," said Porter, removing the fish from the hook. "It was Simon Bone, a whale-sized child-molester whose family's been bailing him out of jail for years, who financed her act at Malibou Lake. But I'll tell you this—the woman's nuts. And you smelled the rot on this one three weeks ago, Doc—it's her dream, for whatever insane reason, to destroy Hollywood. And one more thing. I checked dates for religious significance after the drawing you showed me that she'd sent to Clive. She's epileptic, and May 15th is the Feast Day of Saint Dymphna, patron saint of epileptics. Croenjagger's Circus burned down this

year on May 15th. Arson. No arrests. And one of the roustabouts—the one who used to rape Valerie—was found nearby, dead with his balls cut off."

It was growing colder and O'Leary pulled up his collar.

"You know," said Porter, "the Roman Catholic Church has a special branch that studies things of a 'demonic' nature. They call it 'The Department of Ascetic Investigations.' Top secret stuff. Nobody but church hierarchy is supposed to know the department even exists, who runs it, or where it's located."

"Something tells me you're trying to find out."

"I'm sure in hell workin' on it," said Porter, and recast his line.

Director of the Department of Ascetic Investigations

MONDAY, SEPTEMBER 21, 1931

Fr. Harry Burke followed Baseball and Football ... well, religiously.

A strapping 44-year-old with receding sandy hair and powerful arms, he had an amazing knowledge of averages, scores and statistics. A Philadelphia Athletics baseball cap hung on his office wall at Malvern, a Catholic retreat house in the countryside, about 25 miles outside of Philadelphia. The cap was a souvenir from the final game of the 1930 World Series, which Burke had attended at Philly's Shibe Park. The '31 World Series would begin on October 1. It would be the Athletics vs. the Saint Louis Cardinals, as it had been last year. The Athletics had won in four games the previous season, with Lefty Grove and George Earnshaw each pitching two victories. Burke was hoping to get tickets again this year, maybe for two games.

Baseball took his mind off his job. As far as the Malvern staff knew, Fr. Burke was one of the chaplains and counselors. Those jobs were a cover. Fr. Harry Burke's actual job was head of the Roman Catholic Church's Department of Ascetic Investigations.

Burke's secret post was investigating, documenting, and maintaining a comprehensive file of all blasphemies, desecrations, satanic rites, and Exorcisms occurring in the United States. His files also included certain cases from abroad. The staff at Malvern believed the time he spent traveling was to conduct retreats elsewhere.

Not only was Burke the head of the Department of Ascetic Investigations, he was basically its only full-time member.

The Church had appointed him to this assignment three years previously. He'd been a wounded front-line chaplain in France during the Great War, and had been a hard-working and resilient priest in various challenging circumstances. He'd never performed an Exorcism, although he'd since assisted twice at the bestowing of the rite.

Burke's job was to chronicle these cases, accurately and objectively, noting their validity or lack of it, providing the church hierarchy a full report. It was basically an undercover post, and the Church demanded total, abject secrecy.

The Bishop of Philadelphia, where Burke had grown up and served, had stationed Burke and his office at Malvern, due to its isolation. It had been a daunting three years, and what he examined was often violent, sordid, and deeply tragic. Nevertheless, Burke was a fighter, and he trusted God would continue to give him strength for his mission.

On nights like tonight, he needed it.

* * *

Late this night, Burke sat in his office, regarding a 9" by 12" envelope that had come in the morning mail. He'd been alarmed as soon as he saw it—he'd received a similar one before, also postmarked Agoura, California, with the same florid handwriting in purple ink. He'd delayed all day opening it.

Fr. Harry Burke slit the envelope with a pen knife and withdrew three 8" x 10" photos. They were all of the same woman, in poses of extreme and sacrilegious pornography. On the lewdest of the three, she'd written the song lines:

I'm just wild about Harry,
And he's just wild about me!

He'd never seen a case such as this one... a woman who, among her other neuroses, had a sadistic, fetishistic attraction to the Christ figure and other saints. His file on her contained nearly a dozen reports of severe blasphemies. He'd been on her trail since she'd returned from Europe two years ago, and she'd not only eluded his grasp, but had become an attraction known as "Lucifer's Archangel." She knew he was after her, and had taken to baiting him, even for a time going by her real name. These dreadful photographs were her most recent communique.

He knew that he needed to arrange her incarceration. He also knew that, since she'd become a celebrity, any apprehending of her in Los Angeles would cause a public spectacle that the Church, in its absolute commitment to keep all such sacrilegious matters secret, would never sanction

She obviously knew it too.

Fr. Burke placed the photographs back into the envelope and locked it in his file cabinet. He sat back at his desk and tried not to think of her or the photographs. He'd be obsessing about this topic, he knew, in the upcoming days, weeks, maybe months. For now, he turned his thoughts back to Baseball. His prediction was that the Cardinals would beat the Athletics in the Series in seven games.

Always an Athletics' fan, he hoped he was wrong.

30 The Pastorale

After a day off Monday, during which time they drove up the coast to Santa Barbara, Colin and Eve arrived at Universal City Tuesday about 10:30 A.M. Colin wasn't on call, but he wanted to get Whale aside and warn him of the situation with Valerie. He'd said nothing to Eve about his visit to Malibou Lake on Sunday.

This week, Whale had begun shooting *Frankenstein*'s Wedding episode in the back lot European Village, delighting in the Tyrolean atmospherics and the hundreds of extras. The sequence showed the jubilant villagers turning into a bloodthirsty mob after "Ludwig" walked through the streets, carrying the corpse of his daughter, "Little Maria," drowned by the Monster. The drowning scene itself was scheduled for next week.

* * *

Colin and Eve, dressed in riding clothes, planned to go horseback riding in Griffith Park after leaving the studio. Universal's band played, dancers practiced their Old-World fancy-footwork, and a Gypsy held a giant dancing bear on a chain. Jimmy Whale, looking very much the Hollywood director in his blue blazer, white puttees and black boots, was on a church set balcony, surveying camera angles. He came down when he saw Colin and Eve.

"Quite a carnival, isn't it?" asked Whale. "Even a dancing bear! Otto, direct from the Universal zoo. Although I daresay he's a bit too merry for the scene."

143

"Jimmy," said Colin, "could you and I ..."

"I say," interrupted Whale. "Are you game for an adventure? Look up there."

He pointed up a high, steep hill, where stood a strange, looming structure. "It's our windmill, without vanes," said Whale. "The Special Effects shop tells me they can add the vanes with trick photography, saving expense. I'm a bit skeptical. At any rate, I'd like to go up, take a few surveyors and discuss those blasted vanes. We'll have our tea there!"

Whale went off to arrange the "adventure," returning with a tall, slender, smiling man who wore a cricketer's uniform: white slacks and shoes, a red and white striped jacket, and a cap. He had dark skin, very dark eyes, and a strangely handsome face.

"My God... Boris!" said Colin. "We didn't know you! They're always putting you together when we arrive in the morning and taking you apart when we leave at night!"

"Came today to see the show!" said Karloff, indicating the many extras.

"Why, we'll take dear Boris along!" said Whale.

Within minutes, three pick-up trucks arrived in the village. Arthur Edeson, *Frankenstein*'s cinematographer, John Fulton, the studio's Special Effects man, and Karloff boarded one of them. A second truck, carrying the tea and snacks provided by the commissary, picked up Whale. A third had a four-man surveyor crew sitting in its bed. Colin helped Eve into the bed of the crew's truck, sat beside her on a tool chest, and held her hand as they started the drive up the hill.

* * *

The vaneless windmill stood about 30-feet-tall. A railed platform extended high off its one side. Up on the mountain, the shepherdess watched the sheep graze. Far below were the *Frankenstein* village and the old sets.

As the surveyors evaluated the site, Whale and the trio of actors sat under two tall trees. They'd spread blankets with pastries and a cooler of iced tea. Wildflowers grew abundantly around them. Karloff, who was looking forward to playing cricket this afternoon, spoke with schoolboy high spirits about the formation of a Hollywood Cricket Club.

"I'm a dreadful rotter at the sport," chuckled Karloff, "but I do have a grand time."

"I say, we're a fascinating group!" said Whale. "Rather like the true creators of *Frankenstein*. Did you ever read of the 'grand tour' of Europe that Lord Byron, Mary Shelley and Percy Shelley took in 1816, which led to Mary writing *Frankenstein*?"

"Yes," said Karloff. "Some call it 'the haunted summer.'"

"Indeed!" said Whale, lighting his cheroot. "And here, in 1931, we have our own 'haunted summer.' I fancy myself, in all modesty, as the wicked Byron... Colin, the brilliant Percy... and Eve, our Mary... creator of the tale, which now earns us our bread and butter."

Eve, who sat on the blanket with Colin, smiled.

"Incidentally," said Whale, "did you know that after poor Percy drowned and his body was cremated, his noble heart didn't burn? According to legend, Mary kept it in her drawer, wrapped in tissue ever after. Very romantic."

"Very messy," said Colin.

"To *our* haunted summer," said Karloff, raising his paper cup of tea in a toast.

"Good morning."

They turned at the shy, soft voice. It was Valerie. Eve recognized immediately the clothes she wore... the pale pink dress with its tiny pearls and the bonnet had been Eve's bridesmaid costume.

"May I be an extra too?" asked Valerie, her bright eyes looking beseechingly at Whale. "I thought I'd dress as a bridesmaid."

"How in the world did you get up here?" demanded Whale, on his feet.

"I'm a witch," she smiled. "I *flew* up."

Whale glanced at the truck he'd ridden in, suspecting she'd crept into its bed down in the village. He disliked tricks from others. "Not amusing, Valerie," he said tersely.

Valerie's long red hair hung loose, as she wore it at the Black Mass. Her eye makeup and false eyelashes were dark, her lips very red. She looked gawky, her arms and legs too long for the dress, exposing several inches of her legs. Valerie wore the bridesmaid bonnet with the brim up in the front, and her own black hosiery and high heels were incongruous with the costume.

Eve felt almost ill to see her wearing the lovely dress she'd briefly cherished. *She was on the set*, thought Eve...*She saw me in the costume...*

"That was my dress," said Eve firmly.

"I'm so sorry," laughed Valerie girlishly. "I just found it forsaken in wardrobe."

"Yes," said Whale, standing. "That was indeed Eve's dress." He pointed to a tear in the costume, where Valerie, too tall for it, had ripped it. "I say, you've ruined it, Valerie."

"I'm sorry," she said softly.

Valerie looked oddly more profane in the violated dress, thought Eve, than she had in full Black Mass attire… and of course, still wore the crystal angel. She was smiling at Colin, a faint, mysterious, almost challenging smile, as if they shared a secret.

"Well," demanded Whale, "why in bloody hell are you up here?"

"To apologize again," she said meekly. "To Colin. He knows why."

"Accept her apology, Colin," said Whale. "Before she drowns herself in your bathtub."

"May I please join your pastorale?" asked Valerie.

"I guess we can't very well throw you down the hill," said Whale. "I'll be polite, but it's only for politeness' sake. By the way, Miss Valerie, you remember Mr. Karloff."

"Oh yes!" said Valerie. Karloff nodded and said nothing.

Whale, Karloff, and Colin joined the surveyors at the windmill. This left Eve and Valerie alone, and suddenly Valerie knelt in the grass beside Eve, her lips close to her ear.

"Evie," sighed Valerie softly, teasingly, almost in a sing-song. "Do you have your 'menses'?"

The question so startled Eve that she didn't answer.

"You seem weepy… I wondered. Anyway, if you do, please stay away from that big dancing bear down in the village. He'll smell the blood and rip you to pieces."

Colin, suddenly aware they'd left Eve alone with Valerie, returned and saw Valerie whispering. "What did you say to her?" he demanded.

"Girl talk," giggled Valerie.

* * *

The "pastorale" resumed. Valerie, perfumed in honeysuckle, sat across from Eve and Colin, under a tree, curled up like a cat, her high heels beside her. She was picking violets, making a little bouquet. She lit a Fatima cigarette. Eve, in spite of herself, couldn't keep her eyes off her. Valerie noticed, pointing a long red fingernail at Eve.

"*Boo!*" smiled Valerie, giggling.

"You seem to amuse yourself, Valerie," said Whale.

"It's just that Eve looks so scared of me," grinned Valerie.

"Little wonder," said Karloff.

That the gentlemanly Karloff would make such a remark surprised the group. "Sorry," he said, aware he'd sounded rude. "But after all, aren't all witches scary?"

"A generalization," said Valerie. "Rather like saying all Englishmen lisp."

"Does everyone have tea?" asked Whale.

Karloff sipped his tea. Eve held Colin's hand. Valerie smoked her cigarette and stared at them.

"Well!" said Whale, still acting the host. "Perhaps while we relax, we'll play Boris's favorite game—'Poetry Jam.' Explain it, Boris."

"Name a poet," said Karloff enthusiastically, "and the first one to recite at least two lines from one of the poet's works wins the round. Ladies first. Eve?"

"Percy Shelley," said Eve. She looked at Colin, but it was Valerie who instantly responded:

"A lady-witch there lived on Atlas' mountain
Within a cavern, by a secret fountain."

"It's from Shelley's *The Witch of Atlas*," said Valerie, looking at Colin. "A witch after your own heart, 'Frankenstein.' She creates her own creature from fire and snow… a hermaphrodite. Far more versatile than Mr. Karloff's monster."

Karloff was silent.

"'The Witch of Atlas' creature also has wings," said Valerie. "It *flies*. And the witch never rejects or abandons her creation, like Frankenstein did, or God has done. The witch and her creature fly together, in an airship…and sail together, down the Nile."

"Well!" said Karloff. "I'd have expected a line or two from Shelley's *To a Skylark*, but *The Witch of Atlas* will do. And rather appropriate, I suppose. You score, Miss Le Fay…your turn."

"Aleister Crowley," grinned Valerie. Eve vaguely recognized the name, a priest of the Black Arts, occasionally making the tabloid news in Europe.

"No takers," said Karloff. "Give us a reading, Miss Le Fay." Valerie looked at Colin and recited:

"Stab your demoniac smile in my brain,
Soak me in cognac, cunt and cocaine."

Everyone was silent. "I believe you're hoping to shock us," said Karloff.

Valerie grinned. "Crowley wrote those words on a mural he painted in his bedroom in Sicily," she said. "It overlooks the sea. He calls the bedroom 'The Room of Nightmares,' and he calls the mural, 'Hell.'"

She stood, wandering off in her stocking feet, carrying her bouquet of violets. She entered the windmill.

"She's totally doped, the silly viper," said Whale. "Did you see her eyes? We best get back down to the village… before she tries to prove she really *can* fly."

Valerie appeared on the windmill balcony. "Hello!" she called, tossing a violet to the group.

"Get the devil down here," shouted Whale, "before you fall and break your neck!"

"One more game?" asked Valerie. "After all, witches can read pasts. May I show you?"

Colin looked sharply up at her. Valerie's wild eyes took in the group. She gave a little chant, spoofingly, it seemed, and Edeson, Fulton, and the surveyors gathered to watch the show. She threw a violet to Whale.

"I see you… dancing!" said Valerie. "A Tango… performed gracefully, with a beautiful woman."

"My God!" said Whale, amused despite himself. "Yes, I was quite the foxy Tango dancer… back in the early Twenties. Smartly done, Valerie."

Valerie threw a violet down to Karloff. "I see you… in a lady's clothes… a lady's wig… sticking out your tongue at a pretty girl."

"I say!" laughed Karloff. "That was back in my stock days. I once played one of the jealous stepsisters in *Cinderella!*"

Everyone laughed. And now Valerie threw a violet to Colin, who let it hit the ground. "Now, now, old boy," Whale said to him. "Whatever she says will just be stuff and nonsense she read in publicity pap."

"I see you," said Valerie, holding her last few violets, "and I see your sisters… ."

"Stop!" shouted Colin.

"Your fears," said Valerie. "I feel them… I *smell* them. Fear of lunacy in your family! Fear of your Uncle, who died in a Lunatic Asylum! Fear you'll go insane… and that any child of yours will go *insane!*"

"God damn you, stop!" shouted Colin.

"I told you that you and your sisters have no reason to fear lunacy," cried Valerie. "You don't. None of you will ever *have* children... and *you*, Colin, will be dead soon anyway!"

Colin ran furiously toward the mill. "Stop him before he kills her!" ordered Whale. Two surveyors caught Colin and held him tightly. Valerie, still on the parapet, laughed wildly, hysterically, throwing the remaining violets down at the struggling Colin.

"Get her down here, now!" shouted Whale shrilly. The other surveyors hurried into the mill and up to the parapet. Eve, shocked and frightened by what she'd heard, covered her face and began to cry.

"She's waiting for us in Belgium, Colin!" shrieked Valerie as the men apprehended her. "She's waiting for us!"

* * *

The surveyors took Valerie down the mountain in their truck and immediately contacted security. The studio police apprehended Valerie, allowing her time only to change her clothes before they escorted her out of the studio.

"If she ever dares to show her face here again," Whale vowed to Colin and Eve, "I'll kick the cackling bitch off the lot myself."

31

Mountain Manhunt

Wednesday night, with a nearly full moon over Universal's mountain, Ilsa the shepherdess sat on the hillside, watching the spectacle on the back lot below her.

The Tyrolean village was aglow, a light seemingly in every window. Hundreds of *Frankenstein*'s "villagers" with torches marched through the streets, and Ilsa knew they were supposed to be hunting the Monster. It was exciting, beautiful, and Ilsa felt fortunate to live here, work here, and behold all this magic.

* * *

Colin Clive as Frankenstein marched with the torch-bearing extras and packs of bloodhounds. Other extras sailed on lantern-lit boats on one of the back lot lakes. Jimmy Whale, high on a boom crane tower, directed the pageantry. Studio security and the fire department were on full alert.

There was a break near midnight. Eve found Colin at one of the bonfires aside the village set where coffee was served. He hadn't discussed with Eve what Valerie had said the previous day. She hadn't asked him to.

He was silent as he drank from a paper cup. Within a few moments, a loudspeaker called the company back to work. "Well, once more into the breach, my dear," Colin said to Eve, kissing her on the cheek.

She smelled the whiskey on his breath.

150

Of the various terrible things Eve had seen and heard the past weeks, this, in some strange way, was the worst. It made her suspect that Colin was losing control and Valerie's revelations yesterday had perhaps pushed him over the brink. Suddenly, she needed to get away. Eve turned and started running toward the front lot.

"Miss Devonshire."

The voice called from behind her. She turned and saw Porter Down. He took a few steps toward her. "Are you alright, Miss?"

She nodded, then broke down. After a moment, he led her toward a bench under a lamplight. He sat beside her and handed her his handkerchief.

"Anything you want to tell me?" he asked softly.

32

Scorching
the Snake

Porter Down, early Thursday morning, promptly began the 30-mile drive to Malibou Lake. It was time, he figured, he formally introduced himself to Saint Valerie.

He'd had a doozy of a nightmare the previous night after taking Eve Devonshire back home. He'd dreamed about "Valerie, The Voluptuous Viper." But rather than just being a circus freak, she'd become an actual snake with a woman's head. Somebody fired a shotgun—maybe himself?—and the damned head exploded all over the place! Where the hell had that come from?

* * *

It was about 9:00 A.M. The sun was bright and the day already hot. As he parked his truck, he saw only one figure out in the field, the scarecrow, in its rags and witch's hat. Beside it was a cart filled with pumpkins.

Porter got out of his truck, regarding the vista of lake and mountains before him He approached the odd, Grimm Brothers-style farmhouse and was knocking at the door when a voice called:

"Good morning, Mr. Down."

Valerie was on the hillside, by the springhouse. Porter strolled down beside the stream and stood facing her. She was wearing a sashed, pink house dress and her black circus hat, her red hair hanging in long, loose tendrils under it.

She looks like Anne Bonney, the pirate queen, thought Porter. *All she needs is a parrot on her shoulder.*

She was barefoot and held a spade, having been clearing wild plants and undergrowth from along the spring. Porter looked at her bright eyes, long pointy nose, and odd, angular face, pale, yet still with the false eyelashes. The red-eyed crystal angel hanging around her neck gave Porter the impression that two pairs of eyes were looking at him.

"You seem to know me," said Porter.

"You've attended my Black Mass," said Valerie. "I know all about you. And of course, there's your cute sailor suit." She placed the spade by a tree.

"Sit down," said Valerie. "Let's get acquainted.

* * *

The springhouse was stone and triangular, with a peaked wooden roof and broken windows. The stream ran past it and down the hillside.

Valerie sat with her back against a tree and lit a Fatima cigarette. Porter sat across the spring in the grass.

"I sense," said Valerie, her eyes bright, "that you hate me. I regard you only with love."

"I'm blushing," smirked Porter.

Valerie laughed softly, arranging her long legs so she hugged her knees to her bosom. The scent of her cigarette mixed with her honeysuckle perfume.

"You have pretty eyes," said Valerie.

Porter felt strangely disoriented, as if he'd had a drink, which he most definitely had not. Time seemed off, "out of joint," as Hamlet had said, as if what was happening and where he was had, in some way, happened before... or would happen later. Maybe to him, maybe someone else...

"You had a picnic with friends of mine on Tuesday," said Porter. "You played a little game called 'Poetry Jam.'"

"Would you like to play it with me?" asked Valerie.

"Ladies first," said Porter.

"A clue," Valerie giggled, slightly parting her legs. "It's from Shakespeare, and it's about women."

"Down from the waist they are centaurs,
Though women all above. But to the girdle do the
Gods inherit, beneath it is all the fiend's."

A gull flew over, screeching. Valerie looked up at the bird, then teasingly continued.

"*There's hell,*
There's darkness, there's the sulphurous pit; burning,
Scalding, stench, consumption. Fie, fie, fie..."

"*King Lear,*" said Porter.

Valerie, surprised, applauded. "Your turn," she said.

Porter, remembering his nightmare and what he'd learned about Valerie and the circus, recited:

"*We have scorched the snake, not killed it.*
She'll close and be herself whilst our poor malice
Remains in danger of her former tooth."

Valerie bridled, taking a deep drag on her cigarette. "*Macbeth,*" she said.

"It's a tie," said Porter.

"So it is," said Valerie. Silence. They looked intently at each other a moment. Porter realized he'd touched a nerve in Valerie's screwed-up psyche.

"Funny what ol' Will says about a snake," said Porter, turning the screw, never taking his eyes off Valerie's. "Cut off its head, chop it into pieces—and for a while, the pieces all wiggle and squirm, as if trying to put itself back together. Even the head keeps snapping away. That's why when people kill a snake, they mutilate it ... decapitate it."

Valerie gave a slight shiver. "Fuck you," she said, lushly and viciously.

"Funny, too," said Porter, "that Shakespeare refers to a snake as a 'she'—'She'll close and be herself...' But then, you know all about snakes, don't you?"

He stood. So did she.

"Leave my friends alone," warned Porter. "Quit while you're ahead... and while you *have* a head. See ya... .'Voluptuous Viper.'"

"Wait," called Valerie. She feared that somehow—instinctively—he'd tapped into her worst nightmare, just as she'd tapped into Clive's. She stepped into the spring, across it and up close to him, several inches taller than he was.

"I have a Gift," she said. "I can smell the tragedy sticking to you. The blood, the grief... the screams. To you, they're agony. To me they're like a lover... almost caressing me... almost licking me ..."

"Shut up," said Porter. Her eyes were wildly bright. His stared back.

"Your *abyss*," said Valerie. "You are I are going to dive deep down into 'your abyss' together, holding hands…"

She reached for his hands which he tightened into fists, her face so close that her lips were almost touching his.

"But after our fun and games burn out in your abyss," Valerie whispered, "I'll be the only one who's crawling back up."

They stood deathly still, looking into each other's eyes. The gull flew overhead, circling them, cawing and screeching, as if terrified by something it saw or sensed.

Then it veered away, flying west toward the Pacific.

PART THREE – LIZZIE
June 7 to June 28, 1967

All You Need Is Love

– The Beatles

33   L.A. Arrival

WEDNESDAY, JUNE 7, 1967

Tony Wyngate's flight from Baltimore had arrived in a rainy Los Angeles at precisely 6:00 P.M. He'd needed a week to wrap up various commitments before heading west.

He'd claimed his bags, rented a car, and found the hotel that Porter Down had arranged for him. It was a cluster of stucco buildings on a hillside in Brentwood, just off Sunset Boulevard and the 405 Freeway. The desk clerk, a young surfer-type named Brad, welcomed Tony and handed him a scribbled phone message: "Dinner/8:30 P.M." The address was on Pacific Coast Highway.

* * *

It had stopped raining, but the wind off the ocean was cold and misty. Tony arrived at the beach-front restaurant, on the border of Pacific Palisades and Malibu, a few minutes past the 8:30 P.M. invitation. He entered, expecting to see marble-faced Porter Down. A young woman, sitting in the waiting area, looked at Tony curiously and stood.

"Dr. Wyngate? Hi. I'm Janice Lynnbrooke."

She shook Tony's hand. The woman appeared to be in her late 20s, her dark hair tied back in a long pony tail, her eyes very blue. She wore jeans with a white jacket over her yellow blouse.

"Porter Down's up the coast tonight with a lead on the case and asked me to meet you. He said I'd recognize you because you're so tall." In her heeled sandals, she was at most 5'5". "I'm an investigator. I'll be working with you both."

159

Janice asked for a table on the veranda. No other customers were out there due to the weather, but the maître d' sportingly led them outside, assuring them of a table inside if the rain resumed or it became too windy. They each ordered a beer.

"I think the first thing any L. A. visitor should see is the Pacific Ocean," said Janice. "You're not too cold?"

"No," lied Tony.

The wind blew and he noticed her perfume or shampoo. They looked out at the night surfers. "I read your novel *Boudicca*," said Janice. "I loved it."

"Thanks," said Tony. "So, please tell me about yourself."

The waiter took their order, playfully shivered and hurried back indoors. "Actually," said Janice, "I'm what's called an 'extractor.' I infiltrate cults and free people held against their will. Not a bounty hunter... more of a social worker who carries a big stick... but there have been some dicey moments. Cults have exploded out here the last couple years, especially in San Francisco and some of the wilderness areas."

The waiter brought their beers. Janice pushed back a strand of hair that had fallen over her right eye.

"It began so promisingly," she said. "The peace movement, the songs, the poetry. But it's mutated. The drugs, the violence...fighting hate with hate. It's all become very dark. If the world's really going to change, Dr. Wyngate, the horseshit has to stop."

"I agree about the horseshit. And call me Tony."

"Call me Janice." She lit a cigarette. Her face was animated, her blue eyes striking. Tony saw the emotion in them. "Many young people get lost," she said softly. "It...can be very tragic."

"Yes," said Tony. "It certainly can." They sipped their beers and watched the surfers for a moment. "Have you known Porter Down long?" asked Tony.

"Only two weeks," said Janice. "He called me, we had lunch in Pasadena, and he gave me a file about the case. I'd just moved down from San Francisco, needed a job, and accepted his offer, weird as it was." She took a drink. "He's a cuddly old bastard, isn't he?"

"So, you know about Lizzie?" asked Tony.

"Oh, yes. *Saint* Lizzie. I'm a full-fledged member of the stage crew for her Black Mass. The gala first performance, you know, is only five nights away."

"How'd you get on the stage crew?"

"I went up to Malibou Lake last week to play would-be cultist. Somebody had just OD'd, so they hired me."

"What have you learned?"

"So far, not much. As far as Lizzie goes, she's winked at me a few times. She calls me 'Pretty Little Angel Eyes'... you know, like the Curtis Lee song."

"I can see why," said Tony.

"Thank you," said Janice. "She told me one night that she sensed a 'bond' with me. Probably just wanted to get into my pants. The word is that, sexually, she's ecumenical."

"Good way to put it," said Tony.

The waiter brought them each a salad. "Lizzie's inner circle's creepy," said Janice. "Especially her musical director... Jack. Dynamite musician and artist. You should hear him play *The House of the Rising Sun* on the organ. He's also restoring a religious—or actually, *anti*-religious—painting in the crown of the tent, and adding some demonic flourishes of his own. Then there's Lizzie's 'tech director', Margo... she's a dreamboat too. But, again, great at her job. She's rigging up the tent like the Ringling Brothers' circus. Rumor goes that Margo's collecting material for a bomb, which we all better hope isn't true."

Janice sipped her beer. "Of course, Lizzie herself is a time bomb. She might be seriously ill, or maybe was at one time—she's lost her hair and wears a wig. And I gather her use of acid is off the charts. Anyway, let's change the subject. I heard that in addition to your writing, you teach Classics?"

"Yes, at Mount Saint Mary's College in Maryland. Porter wants me to write a book about this case." Tony paused. "Did Porter tell you that he believes he *killed* Lizzie in 1931?"

"Hell no. Does he mean he *literally* killed her? That she's back from the dead?"

Tony shrugged. "He said a lot of strange things. He even paraphrased Lewis Carroll...he said, 'We'll go ask Alice, when she's ten feet tall.'"

"Actually," said Janice, "he might have been quoting Jefferson Airplane, though he hardly seems the type. Their album *Surrealistic Pillow* has a song called *White Rabbit*." Off-key but with no self-consciousness, she sang the words written by Carroll and sung by Grace Slick:

One pill makes you larger, and one pill makes you small,
And the ones that mother gives you, don't do anything at all...
Go ask Alice, when she's ten feet tall...
"Of course," said Tony. "'Feed your head.' The drug anthem."

* * *

She asked about his books. Tony paraded out a number of his favorite research adventure stories and Janice genuinely appeared to enjoy them. They talked through dessert. He'd become used to the cold or no longer noticed it. It was 10:30 P.M. now, 1:30 A.M. back east, but Tony wasn't tired. The mist had lifted and stars were appearing over the ocean.

"Porter Down wants to meet with us Saturday," said Janice as they walked to their cars. "I figure we'll drive to Twentynine Palms together?"

"Great," said Tony. "Meanwhile, are you free tomorrow?"

34

Davy Jones' Locker

Thursday, June 8, 1967

Ricky Valenti had his short affair with fame in a mid-1960's TV western called *Big Pine*—a saga of the Kincaid family, seeking fortune in California after the Civil War. Ricky had played Bobby Kincaid, the youngest brother of the clan. During the show's run, Ricky had enjoyed a series of network-arranged dates with starlets, a bundle of fan mail which he took great pride in not answering, a half-dozen custom-made pairs of cowboy boots with three-inch lifts inside them, a splendid set of capped teeth paid for by the studio, and a reputation as a stud that was more due to his publicist than his performance. Meanwhile, it had become painfully apparent within 13 weeks that *Big Pine* was no *Bonanza*, and Ricky Valenti was no Michael Landon.

From *Big Pine's* mid-season cancellation, it was a quick career trapdoor drop for Ricky: from futile auditions for feature film roles, to appearing at supermarket openings, to becoming a car salesman at Pierce's Jaguar in the Valley. It was there that Alfred Pinkerton, Esq. had met Ricky when Pinkerton purchased a red 1966 Jaguar as a 55th birthday gift to himself. They'd stayed in touch and Pinkerton, desperate for celebrities, had invited Ricky to his 1966 Christmas Eve party.

Meanwhile, Ricky's arrogance toward most of his Jaguar customers got him fired. His new gig: salesman at Otts' Oldsmobile in Ventura County.

* * *

Davy Jones' Locker was a bar and restaurant near Point Mugu up the California coast. A military base and landing field were nearby. *Davy Jones'* sat on a bluff above the ocean, and the stars were shining on the waves crashing on the rocks below.

It was almost 1:30 A.M. The place would close at 2:00 A.M. and the crowd was thinning. The lounge had a juke box and a Petula Clark fan kept popping in change. Right now, *I Know a Place* was blaring away. Ricky Valenti was at the bar, annoying the waitresses who dressed in short blue-and-white nautical-motif uniforms with matching caps and blue high heels. He was drinking too much, the waitresses were sick of his filthy mouth, and the bartender had told Ricky that if he talked dirty one more time to one of the gals, he just might knock his teeth out.

A dark-haired waitress named Rita approached Ricky. "The man at the booth by the window wants to buy you a drink," she said.

"He isn't queer, is he?" demanded Ricky.

"I really doubt it," said Rita.

Ricky slid off the stool, eager for a free drink. He walked to the table where a husky man sat in the shadow, looking out the window at the ocean. His pea coat was draped over the back of his chair and he wore an old, battered yachting cap.

"Understand you want to buy me a drink."

"Yep."

"You're not queer?"

"Nah."

"What do you want? An autograph?"

"I want to know about Alfred Pinkerton's Christmas Eve orgy."

"Where'd you hear about that?"

"Hey," said the man. "A star like you, the news gets out, right?"

"Yeah," nodded Ricky. "Damn right." He sat and looked curiously at the man's cap and pea coat. "You some kinda captain?"

"Nah. Just do some fishin'."

"I get it," Ricky smiled knowingly. "You'll be at sea, and you want a sexy story to think about while you're rockin' in your bunk... ya' dirty old man."

Rita arrived to take the order. "You got a little Italian in ya'?" Ricky asked her.

"No," she said.

"Would you *like* a little Italian in ya?" leered Ricky.

Rita sighed in disgust. "A beer," said Ricky. The figure at the window held up an empty bottle of Coke, signaling for another. Rita walked away. "See, I'm Italian," smirked Ricky.

"Yeah, and little," said the man.

Ricky let the man's joke slide. Petula Clark's *Who Am I?* began playing. "So," said Ricky, "you want a dirty story." He pointed at the man's cap. "How about it, Popeye? I'm gonna call you Popeye." Rita arrived with the drinks. "This is Popeye," said Ricky derisively.

"Hi," said Rita, smiling at the man and glaring at Ricky. "I guess that makes you Sweet Pea."

Ricky grabbed her thigh. Rita kicked him in the leg and walked away.

"Common bitch," said Ricky.

"The story?" asked the man.

"Yeah," said Ricky. "Well, Popeye...it all began when I'm sellin' Jags out in the Valley. Girls are comin' in who remember my TV show, *Big Pine*, and they can't keep the cars in stock. One day, Alfred Pinkerton, the hot-shot lawyer, strolls in with that Ubangi of his, and I sell him a red Jag. I sell it to Pinkerton, not the Ubangi."

Ricky laughed at his own joke, chugged his beer and banged his empty glass mug for another. "You don't mind, do ya'?"

"Drink up."

"Anyway, Alfie—I call Pinkerton 'Alfie'—gives me his card, and later invites me for Christmas Eve. I go stag because the word's out the party's gonna be, as you put it, Popeye, an orgy."

Rita delivered another beer, another Coke, and gave the man by the window another smile.

"Well, Popeye, I'll tell ya.' Christmas Eve, about 10 o'clock, I drive up to Alfie's in the Palisades. A candle in every window, and he's got a lot of windows. The party's out back. The palm trees have Christmas lights, all the way to the top. Some skinny creep in a Santa Claus hat is playing the piano on the patio. The pool's all lit up, but nobody's swimming 'cause it's too fuckin' cold. And there's Alfie, all dressed up like in *A Christmas Carol*. The long coat, the top hat... not like Scrooge, but the good-lookin' young guy in *Christmas Carol*, the part I'd be good for..."

"Fred. Scrooge's nephew."

"Yeah. Well... Felicia, Alfie's piece of tail... she's there, bragging to everybody how she's planning to take her BAR exam. She's wearing a bikini. Like I said, it was pretty bitchin' cold, but Felicia's prancin' around in her bikini anyway. I size up the crowd… mainly losers. Singers who can't sing, actors who can't act."

"Imagine such a thing," said the man at the window.

"Alfie's Ubangi's the bartender, and they're passing the grass. But here's the big thing. Popeye… that place is packed with prime pussy!"

"A real down-home Christmas."

"Oh yeah! I meet this blonde in a red dress—she's got tits and ass like you dream about. Her name's Laurie. Told me she'd almost made the last cut to be one of the dancers on *Hullabaloo*. She pretended she didn't know who I was, but I could tell she did." He paused to finish his beer. "Another one?"

The man signaled Rita. The juke box was now playing *Downtown*. Ricky waited for the beer before resuming.

"So," mumbled Ricky, lighting a cigarette. "Where was I?"

"Prime pussy."

"Oh yeah. Well… Everybody's drinking, smoking, dancing. Then Alfie stops the music—he has a 'Yuletide surprise,' as he says it, for all of us. He gives that gross laugh of his, then calls to the house, 'Come out, my Christmas Eve Angel,' and through the door comes this wild redhead … Wow!"

The man at the window leaned in slightly toward Ricky.

"She's got to be 6' tall," exulted Ricky. "I'm talking *Amazon*!—plus she's wearin' these black spiked heels, so she's like, over 6'3! She's got this flowing red hair, and she's wearing a black corset, with the garters and black stockings, and of course, she has a long black whip. You know, the Marquis de Sade bit. I mean, this girl was *wicked*!"

Ricky, warming even more to his topic, gulped his beer and wiped his mouth. "She had these big black angel wings, and she takes Alfie's top hat and wears it. And…you wanna know what *else* she had?"

"You know it."

"The corset ends just at her pussy, you know? You can see her red pussy hair. And you know what she's got *hanging* from the red pussy hair?"

Ricky took a suspense-building swig as his audience-of-one shook his head.

"*Mistletoe!*"

"Sounds like a festive kinda' gal."

"Oh, let me tell ya'! And she's so fuckin' tall, you could almost kiss *under* the mistletoe! It had berries in it, and all that… I mean, this gal was *wild*!"

"The wild girl have a name?" asked the man.

"Sure. She was 'Saint Lizzie'... the gal who's gonna open up her witch act in Malibu next week. Alfie introduced her, saying she'd soon be, as he put it, 'a sensation.' My guess is that she played his flute and he set her up."

The man at the window looked out at the ocean. He seemed pleased. "So," he said, looking back at Ricky. "Did she impress you as a new sensation?"

"Well... She was kinda' spooky. See... she kept talkin' how Christmas was the birthday of the Christ child. She sang *Happy Birthday, Baby Jesus*, and kept gigglin' to herself... singing snatches of Christmas carols—get it, Popeye—*snatches* of Christmas Carols? Anyway, she got the piano player to play Christmas carols. She was singin' parts of 'em—lousy voice, and she sang the carols with dirty words, like *Fuck the Herald Angels Sing*. Now and then she'd crack her whip... she was good at that."

Ricky drank, leaned confidentially forward at the table and lowered his voice. "But... the really sicko thing was... she had this crystal angel around her neck. It had little red eyes. Really creepy."

The man at the window was still.

"She was holdin' a black cat some of the time while she sang," said Ricky. "I saw her kiss it once. I figured she was probably stoned out of her goddamned mind... she was sucking a reefer. I tell ya', she was unbelievable."

"Oh, I believe it," said the man at the window.

"I bet you do!" leered Ricky. "But she was way too freaky, even for that crowd. They finally tuned her out. Meanwhile, Laurie's whispering to me, saying, 'I can sing way better than she can,' and 'I think she's wearing a wig,' shit like that. You know how nasty these bitches are about each other."

"Yeah, it's shocking."

"Anyway, Lizzie finally bombed out. She must have known it, because all of a sudden she let out this big scream—scared the living shit out of everybody—then cracked her whip one last time, went off to a corner, and started smokin' and drinkin.' A little later, the party picks up. Alfie shuts everybody up *again*. He has *another* surprise."

"'Tis the season to be jolly," said the man.

"Alfie announces, 'My friends... Father Christmas.' He motions to the house. Felicia opens the door, and out comes this big fat dude who's walkin' with a cane. He's wearing a long red robe and hood, one hell of a fancy costume, dragging a Santa Claus bag beside him. Everybody laughs and applauds. The guy's got a beard, but not a Santa beard, more a goatee, or Van Dyke..."

The man at the window grinned tightly.

"Father Christmas waves to everybody," says Ricky, "and Felicia's hanging on his arm, and he reaches in his bag. He gives Alfie a few joke gifts, you know, a packet of rubbers, that sort of shit. He's got this sweet, fruity voice—I figured he was a fag—and he's ho-ho-ho-ing all over the place."

"A right jolly old elf."

"Yeah, but he wasn't jolly for long." Ricky leaned in again. "Felicia leads him over where Lizzie is, smoking her joint, sitting alone on a bench by the pool with those black wings on and with her mistletoe hangin' out. Father Christmas sees Lizzie and looks scared shitless. Lizzie sees him and just stares at him, I swear, like a leopard..."

"And?"

"And all of a sudden, she leaps up and fuckin' *pounces* on him! She swipes at the man's face with her red, long nails, and she's screaming 'Simon, you Fat Fuck!' and he's squealing like a pig and trying to cover his face. At first, I thought Alfie was treating us all to some sado-maso Christmas pageant ... you know, *Redheaded Bitch Beats the Shit Out of Father Christmas,* or something like that."

The man at the window nodded, enjoying his Coke.

"Well, Lizzie gets her claws on Father Christmas, and Popeye—I swear to God—she slaps and kicks him right into the *fuckin' pool!* Gigantic splash, like when Bubbles the Whale does his big splash down at Marineland! Everybody's soaked, everybody's screaming... Christ, what a night!"

"What happened to Father Christmas?"

"The fucker sank like a rock!"

"Who the hell got him out?"

"Alfie's Ubangi, eventually. Lizzie nearly fell in herself—she's still screaming at him from the side of the pool, even though the old man's under water and can't hear shit. Nobody wants to get in the water because it's late and cold, and finally the Ubangi dives in, dragging up Father Christmas from the bottom. The old bastard looks dead, but the Ubangi starts giving him resuscitation and he starts puking up pool water. Meanwhile, that geeky piano player grabs Lizzie and drags her ass into the house."

He drained his beer. "A few minutes go by. We hear a siren. 'Who the hell phoned the police?' shouts Alfie, but everybody's screaming, running away, in case the cops find dope on the property. I ran too, lost Laurie in the crowd... and never saw her again."

A sitar began playing the jaunty prelude to Petula's *Color My World* on the jukebox. The man at the window was looking out again at the ocean and now finished his Coke. He stood and took out his wallet.

"Any parts you want to hear over?" offered Ricky, regarding his empty mug. "I'll tell it all again for another beer. No. For another *two* beers."

The man shook his head. "My ten-year-old sister had better Christmas Eve parties than that back on the farm in Wisconsin."

Ricky gave the man a long look. "Asshole," he murmured finally. "*You* insult *me*? You ever been on TV? You ever get fan mail?"

"Nah."

"Listen!" shouted Ricky. "I know some of these bitches in here say I'm just a has-been. Well—better a has-been than a never-was."

"Valid philosophy," said the man, throwing a fifty-dollar bill on the table. "Of course, my favorite is: 'There is a divinity that shapes our ends, rough hew them how we will.' *Hamlet*, Act Five, scene two." He put on his pea coat.

"I get it now!" Ricky shouted. "You're no fisherman!"

"I saw *Big Pine* once," said the man. "You're no actor."

"What are you, a cop?" demanded Ricky. He jumped up, lunging across the floor as if he were about to perform a saloon fight in his dead and buried TV show.

"Up yours, Popeye!" he shouted, taking a swing at him.

It was a mistake. A moment later, Ricky Valenti was on the floor of *Davy Jones' Locker*. He slowly sat up beside the overturned table, spat, and stared at the capped teeth—the most valuable souvenir of his brief fame—now broken and bloody in his hand. He realized Rita and the other waitresses were applauding the man at the door.

"I eats me spinach," said Porter Down.

35   The Lecture

The lecture hall at USC Berkeley was barely one-third full this evening. Simon Bone stood at the lectern, his silver whiskers lucent in the
spotlight, gesturing with his cane.

"So, my friends," he said, "the barriers are falling... and Satanism
has been fiercely *simpatico* to this intellectual freedom for centuries." He
glanced again at the particularly attractive and leggy young woman in the
front row. She appeared to be without an escort.

"And now, I conclude with a story that I hope you'll take home with
you tonight." He sipped his water, paused, and began. "Our sadly prosaic
culture deems various significant dates as wicked. October 31, All Hallows Eve. April 30, Walpurgis Night." He paused. "Does anyone here celebrate his or her birthday June 25th?"

Nobody admitted he or she did.

"I'm relieved," smiled Bone. "You see, June 25, first of all, is the cal-
endar opposite of December 25. On Christmas, the faithful sing *O Holy
Night*. Meanwhile, many perceive June 25 as the *Un*holy Night. June 25 of
1096 saw the First Crusade's unspeakable slaughter of Jews in Wereling-
hofen, Germany... a gruesome holocaust. In a more benign mode, June
25 of 1178 was the night five Canterbury monks reported observing an
explosion on the moon; and as for the moon, June 25 of 1638 is the date
of the first lunar eclipse recorded in North America. For those ashamed,
as I am, of America's arrogantly racist belief in Manifest Destiny...June
25, 1876 saw Custer and his soldiers die at Little Big Horn. And for those,
again like me, who revere the separation of Church and State, June 25,

1962, saw the Supreme Court rule New York school prayer was unconstitutional."

Several audience members applauded. Bone paused to encourage the applause.

"As many of you know," he continued, "the terrorist who likely caused the cataclysmic fire at Universal Studios last May 15th has promised to strike again on June 25, precisely 16 days from now. The suspect plans to incriminate the Church of the Light Bearer." He paused dramatically. "I assure you my church has no involvement in any such horror to come and will be fully cooperative in the apprehension of this monster. I can say no more at this time. So, my friends, I simply conclude… 'Be watchful.' Good night."

The small crowd applauded tepidly. Bone left the stage, returned for a nearly silent curtain call, and was hardly off the stage again when he dispatched a stage crew member to invite the attractive woman in the front row to meet him. She arrived a moment later and looked quizzically at Bone as he gallantly kissed her hand.

"My dear," he said, still clenching her hand, "I flatter myself, perhaps, but you seemed especially attentive to my speech. If you have any questions, I'd be delighted to answer them… perhaps over a late supper?"

The young woman pulled her hand away and left without a word. Bone stood alone, red with humiliation.

"Simon," said a female voice from behind him, "you couldn't get laid in a whorehouse."

Bone turned. "Why, Chelsea. You look… lovely."

She didn't really. Chelsea Kimball, San Francisco's most popular and aggressive journalist, could be semi-lovely on occasion, but generally chose not to be. Usually she looked like an angry, chunky hoyden. It was her trademark no-shit look, and it was agreed, as the old joke went, that she had a perfect face for radio. Indeed, radio was her medium—she no longer wrote for newspapers and hosted her own late night radio program.

Tonight, Chelsea was especially hoydenish, wearing a blue sweatshirt, yellow sweat pants, and orange tennis shoes. As usual, her short dark hair was tousled, her grin intimidating.

"I ran here tonight," she said. "I'm geared up to lose 40 more pounds by next summer's Democratic National Convention. Bobby Kennedy won't be able to keep his hands off me."

Bone, looking her over, deadpanned, "Yes, I see…"

"Let's go outside," said Chelsea, retreating toward the stage door. "Every time I'm near you I feel my gag reflex. We'll talk in the fresh air."

* * *

They sat on benches outside the lecture hall, facing each other, the only light above the stage door. "So," said Chelsea. "From what I can tell, you just flopped, in front of a mostly empty hall of half-asleep summer school kids who couldn't get a Friday night date. By the way, you left out that June 25, 1950 was the start of the Korean War."

"Forgive me," said Bone. "I'm just a silly old warlock. You're the journalist."

"Little me?" asked Chelsea mockingly. "So. What heaping helping of *Rosemary's Baby*-style bullshit do you want to spoon-feed me tonight?"

Bone grinned and lowered his voice confidentially. "This concerns the terrorist who set the fire at Universal Studios last month. Who has promised to strike again on the 25th of June. Who wishes to place the culpability on my Church of the Light Bearer."

"Do go on," said Chelsea. "Do."

"First, I'll wager that the police will fail to arrest this miscreant during the next two weeks. Next, I'll bet that the terrorist will indeed try to consecrate the promised 'sacrament' on June 25th. Third, I'm confident that I can anticipate the terrorist's target no later than June 24th. In fact, I'm quite certain of it now… but can't tell you."

"And what do I get out of this, precisely?" asked Chelsea.

"I'll inform you even before I call the police. You will be the first reporter at the scene. I'll share my shocking revelations about the terrorist exclusively with you. We shall both be heroes… .as we mutually save a famous and beloved piece of California history from the savagery of a lunatic."

"Will I have to get dressed up?" asked Chelsea.

"Consider it a sacrifice well worth making, Chelsea," said Bone.

"In a delicious irony," he continued, "I, the long-maligned high priest of the Church of the Light Bearer, and you, the most unorthodox media personality in California, personally bring on the ruination of the very prototype of violent, drug-crazed, Luciferian creature whose head Johnson and Reagan have long wanted to stick on a pole. My mellow brand of 'white witchcraft' Satanism is at last legitimate. You'll be a media superstar."

"Your slip is showing, Simon, dear," said Chelsea. "Where do you plan to go from there?"

"I plan to be the founder," said Bone proudly, "of a seminary for Satanists, based at my estate in Big Sur. It will provide a daringly alternative social and metaphysical approach to society, and I plan to select six candidates the first year, three men and three women."

"I can't wait to see the school uniforms," said Chelsea.

"It's not at all what you presumably expect it to be," said Bone. "In gratitude for what I'm offering you tonight, I'd expect sympathetic delineation of my disciples on your show."

"Simon," smirked Chelsea, "why not make this asshole pact with Faye MacConnell? No, wait… Faye doesn't like you anymore, does she?"

"Will you consider my offer?" asked Bone.

Chelsea laughed. "You're a hell of a hoot, Simon. I'll give you that."

Bone frowned. "My dear Miss Kimball. The whole country talks obsessively of revolution—political, social, racial—but what's more profound than *metaphysical* revolution? Didn't you see the cover of *Time* last year? The words, 'Is God Dead?'"

"I only read *Time* on the toilet," said Chelsea. "I must have been constipated that week."

"The world is embracing taboos," exulted Bone. "Can't you see we're on the eve of the acceptance of Satanism, and all it really means? It's the long-awaited battle for *Enlightenment!*"

"Sure," sneered Chelsea, who lit a cigarette. "And when we *do* accept it, you're the Light Bearer's Maharishi Mahesh Yogi….right?"

Bone sighed. His voice was tense. "The Church of the Light Bearer has fought its battles day and night," he said. "And believe me… we, like all armies, have our secret weapons, and our terrorists. Maybe even our counter-terrorists."

"Oh yeah," said Chelsea. "I'm sure you have your own castle outside Oz, covered with shit from flying monkeys." She stood, clenching her cigarette between her teeth, and limbered up to start running again. "Oh, by the way… have you heard of this 'Saint Lizzie' chick who's performing a Black Mass near L.A on Monday night?"

Bone stiffened. For a moment, he thought Chelsea was on to his secret.

"She's been getting a shitload of publicity," she continued, "and got tossed off Santa Monica Pier a couple weeks ago. Anyway, a reporter at the *Examiner* dug into our morgue files and learned there was a 'Saint

Valerie' who performed a Black Mass in L.A. way back in 1931. Based on your love affair with all things sick and satanic, and your advanced years... do you know anything about this?"

"I knew Valerie intimately," Bone said coldly. "As for that Lizzie creature, she's a clown and a cow." The mention of Lizzie had rattled him, but Bone had learned the value of holding his temper. "Let's just say," he went on, "that in time, you might realize that I'm more than a 'hoot.'"

Chelsea looked him in the eye. "Oh, I know who you are, Simon. Our morgue has quite a file on *you* too. Way back to 1929. All about your little predatory peccadilloes. Stories never published and charges never pressed because of your family fortune paying off victims and hiring lawyers who saved your obese butt from jail. If Satanism is what you claim it is, Simon, you're a disgrace to it."

Bone, perspiring heavily, had no reply.

"I know I'm a whore for even talking with you," said Chelsea. "Anyway, I admit, you've given me a tempting offer. I'll let you know, Fat Boy."

She flicked her still burning cigarette at him, turned, and jogged off into the night. Bone, almost queasy with rage, stood and brushed the ash from his jacket. Of course, he'd only told Chelsea a glimmer of the plan. Bone himself had selected the target for June 25th. Pinkerton had assured Bone that he had ways to keep Lizzie harmless and confined on the 25th— until Bone could send the police after her. Pinkerton, concealing his part in the plan, would defend her, make headlines, recapture his stature— while intentionally losing the case... and Bone would be safe from her vengeful madness forever.

The heroics. The flamboyance. The showmanship! Not the assassin he might have hired simply to shoot her one night. Certainly not detailing his and her sordid history to the police and asking for protection. This way, she'd basically be buried alive in a prison or an asylum—or go to the electric chair or gas chamber. Meanwhile, Simon Bone would become the great Messiah of 1960s Satanism.

After all his years tormented by her memory, it would be his ultimate revenge. For, after all, Saint Lizzie was Saint Valerie incarnate.

As he relished the idea, the lecture hall crew suddenly turned off the stage door light, leaving Simon Bone alone in the darkness.

36 Twentynine Palms

It was typical of Porter Down's defiantly iconoclastic life that, come dawn each day, he watched the sun rise in the west.

He'd stand on the deck of his adobe house, "Yaqui Crest," originally built in the 1920s by a rich Native American. Porter had lived here in Twentynine Palms, over 140 miles east of Los Angeles, since 1932. The restored house, with its round tower, sat atop a crag, looking like a fortress, offering a magnificent view of the desert. On the flats below, to the side of the fruit trees and vegetable garden, was an airplane hangar he'd built himself, housing his old Spad biplane, *Timber Wolf*, still in flying condition.

Wearing only his shorts and the Saint George and the Dragon amulet, he looked at the purple darkness over the desert. Then the rising sun in the east cast a tiny pinpoint of light on the tip of a towering granite mountain to the west, the point of light tracing down the mountain like a laser, spreading as it hit bottom, exploding into different colors as it brilliantly illuminated the desert floor. There'd been too many mornings over the past 35 years when he hadn't taken the time to enjoy this miracle. Now, at the age of 66, he felt he couldn't afford to miss it. He was faithfully on his deck every dawn.

An old man's rituals, he thought.

He'd had a fine, full life. A fighter pilot in the Great War, a Prohibition federal agent in the Roaring '20s, a Hollywood studio troubleshooter in the Depression '30s, an espionage agent and flight instructor during World War II, and a private investigator in the booming post-war 1940s

175

into the I-Like-Ike 1950s and JFK early 1960s.

Hell of a run, he thought.

He watched a jet, bearing north, its silver-pink vapor in the early light. Then he showered and shaved, carefully trimmed the mustache he'd worn since World War II, dressed, and prepared his usual breakfast—pancakes and a slice of homegrown cantaloupe. He went into the living room, sitting by the fireplace and under the tower ceiling where the original Yaqui owner had painted a mystical scene of eagles and spirits. He looked at the small, framed photographs on his table, and said his prayers.

The 40th anniversary of Mary's death was 18 days away.

* * *

Tony and Janice left for the desert Saturday morning, driving in Janice's Ford Falcon with a bumper sticker reading PEACE. On Thursday, they'd taken in an attraction that, considering their mission, they felt should be experienced: The Universal City Tour. They rode the "Glamor Tram," enjoyed the stuntmen and animal shows, but saw little from the Golden Age. The European village was still under reconstruction since the May 15th fire.

On Friday night, Janice had taken Tony up to her home in Laurel Canyon for dinner. She lived in the upstairs of a quirky, comfortable two-story house erected on stilts, deep in the trees. It had a large wicker peace sign hanging on the interior chimney, various candles wedged in wine bottles, and shelves of books and records. It seemed a lonely locale.

Probably no lonelier than Charnita, Tony thought to himself.

He learned that his new friend was a native of Washington State and a graduate of Stanford. She was divorced. Her father was dead, her mother remarried. She had a step-sister but they weren't close. They talked about her early career as a social worker, her anti-war activism, their mutual love of animals, their mutual mistrust of LBJ, their admiration and criticisms of *Star Trek*, their agreement that *The Girl from U.N.C.L.E* had been the past TV season's worst hour, and their favorite books, films, and music. Both were Judy Collins' devotees and Janice's favorite song was also *Suzanne*. She played Collins' *In My Life* album during dinner.

Janice had said little about her work as an extractor. However, as she drove Tony back to the motel that night, they saw a crowd of young, long-haired people, congesting traffic along Sunset Boulevard, approaching cars, trying to sell newspapers. Police were breaking up the gagged traffic and Janice maneuvered through the bottleneck.

"They're peddling 'narc lists,'" explained Janice. "Names and addresses of undercover narcotics agents. Dangerous work, being a 'narc.'" She paused. "My name ended up on a 'narc' list in San Francisco. That's why I moved to L.A."

* * *

During the three-hour plus drive to Twentynine Palms, they talked about many things.

"You teach at a Catholic college, Tony. Are you a Catholic?"

"Yes. Are you?"

"No. I have no religious faith. I see people struggling every day for a better world. I don't see what God's doing."

"Sometimes Faith comes at the right time," said Tony.

"And sometimes not at all," said Janice. "I don't disrespect your faith, Tony. Don't lecture me for not having any."

He wasn't about to do that.

* * *

They arrived at Porter's home early afternoon. He was dressed in tan slacks and shirt and, as it had been a while since he'd had company, he wore a western-style string tie. He was hospitable if taciturn, offering them the house's two bedrooms and inviting them to enjoy the pool—he'd said to bring swimsuits.

Tony and Janice swam in what Porter called his "oasis," surrounded by Joshua trees. The host barbecued steaks on the grill for dinner. The guests admired the sunset view.

"Like living on the moon," said Porter. "Not that I've ever been on the moon."

Night fell. Porter lit an old railroad car lantern that hung on the deck. The wind picked up, the tall palm tree over the house swayed, and the stars were very bright.

"Okay," said Porter. "Let's get to it."

* * *

"Once upon a time," he began, "way back in 1920, there was a satanic high priest named Aleister Crowley, aka 'the Beast of the Apocalypse.' His mantra: 'Do what thou wilt shall be the whole law.' He performed Black Masses in his abbey in Sicily with his 'scarlet woman' and a goat. You get the idea."

"Afraid so," said Janice.

"Mussolini eventually exiled Crowley and his gang," said Porter, "which was quite a distinction. Nevertheless, Crowley still attracted his acolytes. Some made pilgrimages to meet him, or to visit his abandoned abbey in Sicily. Some merely learned his history. Jump ahead to 1931. There was a witch priestess in L.A., who'd aspired to be a Crowley 'scarlet woman.' She'd taken the name Valerie Le Fay, billed herself as 'Saint Valerie' and 'Lucifer's Archangel,' and performed a Black Mass out at Malibou Lake."

"Where the Black Mass takes place now," said Tony.

"Yep," said Porter. "'Saint Valerie' was a dope addict, a 'viper,' as we called 'em in those days. She infiltrated the company of *Frankenstein* and had an affair with the film's star, Colin Clive. Valerie told her disciples she desired him because, in her words, he had 'the face of Christ.'"

They were silent for a moment. The wind blew more sharply now. "What had happened to her?" asked Janice, sympathy in her voice. "How'd she ever lose her way?"

"Who knows?" asked Porter impatiently. "Maybe she screwed too many goats."

Janice glared at him.

"Actually, Valerie Le Fay never met Crowley in her life," said Porter, "although she claimed otherwise. Anyway, the short version is that 'Saint Valerie' killed one woman, very nearly killed another, and might have killed Clive."

"And you stopped her," said Tony. "You…killed her?"

"A story for another night," grumbled Porter. "Let's jump ahead 36 years to now. 1967. There's a new 'Lucifer's Archangel' in town—same look, same act, even the same 'abbey' at Malibou Lake. Her stage name is 'Saint Lizzie,' aka Lizzie Hirsig. Leah Hirsig was Crowley's original 'Scarlet Woman' of the Roaring '20s and Lizzie presumably has taken the name in her honor."

"Lizzie's a copycat, obviously," said Janice.

"Maybe," said Porter. "The connection's Simon Bone, grand Pooh-Bah of the Church of the Light Bearer in San Francisco. It's rumored that he witnessed Crowley and Leah Hirsig in action in Sicily in the early 1920s. What's a fact is that in 1931, he was part of Valerie's original coven at Malibou Lake and could have directed Valerie how to play 'the Scarlet Woman.' All these years later, we have 'Lizzie Hirsig,' doing the same schtick. Bone has owned the 'Abbey' property since 1930. He's an heir—like Crowley, he never had to work a day in his life. He and Lizzie Hirsig have a history that goes back at least to last summer. And her name at that time was Alice Elizabeth Fawkes."

"'Alice, when she's ten feet tall!'" said Tony, snapping his fingers. "In Gettysburg, you said, 'Alice, when she's ten feet tall'... meaning high on acid, right?"

"Yeah," said Porter. He took a book from under the table and handed it to Tony. It was the Saint Joseph College Yearbook for 1955.

"Back in May," said Porter. "The pub in Gettysburg. You asked me where I'd been that night. I didn't tell you. Well, after we'd had our little run-in that morning with Sister Rod-Up-Her-Ass, I went back to the campus that evening. Broke into the archives."

Tony opened the book to a marked page, looking at a senior portrait in the upper corner.

"'Fawkes' was her original name and that was her original nose," said Porter. "She never graduated. You can see her alumni record, swiped the same night by yours truly, stuck in the back of the book. She didn't come back after Christmas, 1954... after the desecrations in the Grotto following the suicide of the seminarian whose body you discovered, Tony."

Tony nodded. "Drama Society" he said, reading her yearbook writeup. "Literary Club..."

"Yeah," said Porter. "Saint Joe's apparently didn't have a devil worshipper sorority."

"Is her family still alive?" asked Janice.

"They're dead," said Porter. "No surprise. The college has had no address for her for years. I found Alice's name among a list of creeps who made a pilgrimage to Crowley's abbey in 1962. From there I traced her back to Saint Joseph's in the early 1950s."

"So, we can assume Alice Fawkes and Jonathan Brooks had a relationship," said Tony. "Maybe he killed himself because he was ashamed of that relationship... and maybe she, unsettled by his suicide, became the Grotto's defiling ghost."

"Good guesses," said Porter.

"Have you questioned Bone?" asked Janice.

"Based on what happened in '31," Porter chuckled, "Bone considers *me* a murderer. He has a restraining order that keeps me at least 50-feet from his blubbery neck."

"He's sponsoring and protecting Lizzie?" asked Tony.

"He *was*," said Porter. "Now, Lizzie's gone rogue. On May 15th, she and her disciples set off the fire at Universal's *Frankenstein* village. Bone had originally engaged Alfie Pinkerton, sleaze ball lawyer, to keep an eye on Lizzie, but she slithered into Alfie's bed, so now *he's* sponsoring her. Alfie invited Bone to his home in the Palisades last Yuletide, apparently unaware of how deep the hatred was between Lizzie and Bone, probably hoping for a reconciliation. Instead, Lizzie nearly drowned Bone in Pinkerton's pool."

"Looks as if Bone created his own monster," said Tony.

"Maybe, said Porter. "But my hunch is that Lizzie created herself."

"You both sound awfully sure of yourselves," said Janice. "Obviously, the police don't suspect Lizzie of the fire. Otherwise, they'd arrest her."

"Bone's made attempts to throw her off his Malibou Lake property," said Porter, ignoring Janice's remark, "but Lizzie got Pinkerton to stall him. Also, if Bone *does* call the cops, she can blab all about the past they shared... and it isn't pretty." He paused and lit his pipe. "Trouble is, I can't find any record of Alice, aka Lizzie, between 1962, when she was at Crowley's abbey in Sicily, and 1966, when she made contact with Bone in California. Must be some fun stuff there."

"Where do we go from here?" asked Tony.

"The letter Lizzie wrote to police after the Universal fire gave June 25th as the date for her next 'sacrament,'" Porter replied. "I'm betting Lizzie wants to show the world that Satanism, despite the 'touchy-feely' brand that Bone preaches, is grislier than anybody ever imagined... and practiced just the way Bone's dream girl Valerie would have done it. Meanwhile, Bone's been giving talks, telling everyone to 'be watchful,' citing June 25th as the historic date of all kinds of looney stuff. But none of it has anything to do with the canon of Satanism... and Bone knows it."

"What do you mean?" asked Tony.

"Valerie-Lizzie, two-in-one, realizes all too well the true significance of June 25," said Porter. "It all has to do with Valerie's 'insane passion,' which has passed on to Lizzie... and why she plans her 'sacrament' for that date."

"What is it?" demanded Janice.

"Colin Clive!" said Porter decisively. "The 30th anniversary of his death is in 15 days… on June 25th!"

* * *

They took a break. Porter served Janice and Tony a beer and he drank a Coke. The cold wind blew and the tall palm tree swayed in the night under the stars. "Is anyone left from 1931 and *Frankenstein* who can weigh in on this?" asked Janice finally.

"Only a few people from *Frankenstein* actually knew what was happening," said Porter. "Dwight Frye, who played the hunchback, suffered a fatal heart attack on a bus in Hollywood in 1943. James Whale, the director, drowned himself ten years ago. Junior Laemmle, the producer, can't remember what he had for breakfast today. I've written to Karloff in London, care of his agency. No answer." He paused, "There is another person, but…"

"But what?" asked Tony.

"We'll talk about her some other time," said Porter. "Anyway, we'll go to the Black Mass Monday night. Janice will be with the crew. Tony and I will be in the audience. Tony, sit up front. You and she were both in the Grotto the morning that Jonathan Brooks' body was found."

"But as you know," said Tony, "I didn't see her."

"Maybe *she* saw *you*," said Porter. "She might have a good memory for men who almost found her shortly after she mutilated her dead lover's genitalia."

"Yeah," said Tony.

Porter downed his Coke and stood. "Anyway, that's all for tonight. I'm sleeping down at the pool house. The main house is yours. Both bedrooms. Behave yourselves."

"One last question," said Janice impatiently. "If you 'killed' Valerie Le Fay in 1931, how can she and Lizzie Hirsig be the same person? What is she—a vampire?"

"Ever hear this poem?" asked Porter:

"All things once are things forever,
Soul, once living, lives forever…"

"It's from *Ghazeles*," said Porter, "by Richard Monckton Milnes. As he wrote, souls live forever. Heaven, Hell, Reincarnation… whatever.

Sometimes souls move on, sometimes souls come back. In this case, the bitch came back. Good night."

"Wait," said Tony suddenly. He went into the house, emerging with the folder Porter had given him in Gettysburg. He removed the picture of the woman in the bridesmaid costume, standing on *Frankenstein's* village set. "Porter.... who is this?"

Porter looked at the picture in the lantern light. "Who do you think?" he grinned.

Tony handed the picture to Janice. "This was taken in 1931," he said.

"My God," said Janice. "That's..." She paused. "Her eyes. Those are Lizzie's eyes..."

"Sweet dreams," said Porter, and headed down the hill to the pool house.

37 "The Demonic Rites of Insane Passion, As Performed by Saint Lizzie, aka Lucifer's Archangel"

MONDAY, JUNE 12, 1967

A bonfire burned on the cliff at Malibou Lake.

Some drove out via Pacific Coast Highway and up the canyon drive. Others came out the Ventura Freeway, off Las Virgenes, over Mulholland Highway, through the mountains, up the twisting road to the driftwood sign:

The Abbey

They parked beside a cornfield with a scarecrow, away from the silo at the cliff's edge. Lanterns hung from the trees. At a small booth outside the tent, the "faithful" paid admission.

"I hear it's just a burlesque show," said a legal secretary.

"They say she looks like Vanessa Redgrave," said a DJ from the Valley. "A really tall, fucked-up Vanessa Redgrave."

The death bell rang on the windmill. "Wooo!" laughed the crowd. A few women raced each other to the porta-pots in the courtyard corner as the crowd began filing into the tent.

Porter Down, Tony, and Janice had each driven out separately. Janice was in the lighting booth, assisting Margo. Tony was near the front, as Porter had requested, in the third row of benches. Porter stood in the back.

It was opening night for *Saint Lizzie's Black Mass*.

* * *

The tent covered the three-sided amphitheater, the altar dominated by its 15'-high cross. Smoke curled from the cauldron upstage. The downstage pentagram glowed red. Above, inside the crown of the tent, was the original painting of a red-eyed dragon, snarling fire at a woman and baby... restored by the Abbey's current resident artist/musician, Mad Jack. He'd embellished it, adding all the flames, imps and flourishes of a tormented medieval artist.

"The Devil's answer to the Sistine Chapel," joked a Berkeley Art professor.

Margo brought down the lights. Mad Jack entered in candlelight, garbed in a black cassock. He bowed, received a smattering of applause, sat at the organ, and ripped into his delirious *The House of the Rising Sun* overture. The man, Tony had to admit, was a virtuoso.

Following the overture and applause, the candles flickered, and all but one, as if by magic, blew out. The full house quieted. The final candle extinguished. A woman's voice chanted:

"Do... what thou wilt... shall be the whole law..."

Mad Jack blasted Liszt's *The Devil Sonata* at the organ, a brilliant shaft of light hit the stage, and there she was, the snake draped over her shoulders.

"My faithful," she smiled.

Assholes, she thought.

* * *

It was a rattlesnake, not a boa constrictor, as in 1931... .perfectly safe if you knew where to hold its head. Lizzie gazed out into a sea of '67 fashion: the gals in their thigh-high mini-skirts, the guys in their carnival-color polyester... all those silly fuckers gawking at her.

Tis now the very witching time of night...

Rather than appearing naked, as Valerie had in 1931, Lizzie wore a black negligee, hiding from her adoring public her black girdle, her black bra with the foam rubber tits, and her scar. She gave her sly wink...her blessing. She strolled with her snake, and began her song, Poe's *Alone:*

From childhood's hour I have not been
As others were...

She couldn't sing at all like the 1931 Valerie, so she basically crooned—and the rattler was the show anyway. The reptile's tongue flickered, and she touched her tongue to it. French-kissing the rattler—true showmanship! One woman got up and hurried out, Lizzie presumed, before pissing her panties.

From the lightning in the sky...
When the rest of Heaven was blue
Of a demon in my view.

She finished the song, again touching her tongue to the snake's, then took a rat from a jar and fed it to the rattler. Big scream. Applause. A minion ran onstage, took the rattler, and ran off.

OK, Margo, let it rip.

The lights went out and the new, improved, state-of-the-art 1967 tower of fire soared volcanically, shooting up almost 20', right through the aperture in the canvas roof, into the sky. The crowd screamed, the organ pealed deliriously, and Lizzie raised her arms.

I am Lucifer's Archangel!

Applause. She had them now. The tower of fire extinguished, the lights came up again, and as a "disciple" placed a chair and a small table of props and costume pieces on the altar, she checked out the faces in the audience.

Yes, there he was, the stocky puffin bastard, standing in the back. "Pretty Little Angel Eyes" had come out of the booth and was standing beside him. And up front was a handsome man... his hair now silver, his face defined, and she almost shrieked in recognition.

Bleeding Christ Almighty, look who it is!

* * *

"Tonight, my faithful...we focus on the celebrated sin—Carnality..."
The crowd tittered. Smoke curled from the cauldron and Mad Jack began playing *Piece of My Heart*.

"My faithful—Miss Janis Joplin…"

Lizzie took a bottle of *Southern Comfort* from the table, guzzling from it as she delivered a singing, growling, and finally climaxing Joplin: "*WAAAGHHH!*"

Uproarious laughter and applause. Lizzie gave a curtsey. She put on a crystal crown, waving a wand as she imitated Billie Burke's Glinda the Good Witch from *The Wizard of Oz*, coming as Mad Jack played *Come Out, Come Out, Wherever You Are*. She followed with a soulful, show-stopping Jackie Kennedy, performed while wearing a pink pill box hat, and while Mad Jack played *Camelot*.

"Finally," she said, "an oldie but goodie. My faithful… Miss Marlene Dietrich."

Dietrich was a crone now, but the young crowd knew all about her shtick and her narcissism. Lizzie sat, put on a black silk top hat, raised her leg, stroked her stocking and sang:

Falling in love again, never wanted to.
What's a girl to do?

Suddenly she stopped singing. "I need a volunteer to do *La* Dietrich justice," she said. Mad Jack, surprised by the ad-lib, vamped at the organ. Tony suddenly realized that Lizzie was wiggling her finger at him.

"Come here, Big Boy," she purred in her Teutonic Dietrich accent.

The crowd applauded, demanding his cooperation. Lizzie came from the stage and took Tony's hand, leading him to her chair, seating him on it.

Falling in love again…

She slinked around Tony, running her hands over his shoulders, grabbing his hair, yanking back his head, singing into his face. Tony looked up into her yellow hazel eyes, the garish point-blank makeup, smelling her lush perfume as Lizzie sat, wriggling in his lap, stroking his chest, placing his hand on her thigh.

What am I to do? Can't helllp it!

Then suddenly, the lights went out. The audience laughed suggestively. It was darkness for a few moments, and by the time the lights were back up, Tony was standing and heading back to the audience. Lizzie, obviously thrown by the blackout, grabbed his arm, stood beside him and bowed, as if they were both taking a curtain call. The audience laughed and applauded.

"Come and visit me soon," she whispered in his ear during the applause.

Tony left the stage and walked directly out of the tent. By the time Lizzie performed her climactic crucifixion finale, wearing her crown of thorns at a jaunty angle and sporting a specially designed black loincloth that hid her scar and girdle, he was miles away.

* * *

When Porter Down visited Los Angeles, he stayed at Foster's Marina, between Santa Monica and Malibu. He'd known Luke Foster since 1930 and had been so generous years ago that Luke had considered him an original investor, sending him quarterly dividends. Now, 37 years later, Luke, a wealthy man, insisted Porter stay as his guest on his best yacht, *The Vessel*, whenever he required L.A. lodging.

Porter, Tony, and Janice had planned to rendezvous on *The Vessel* after the Black Mass. Tony rode alone down Pacific Coast Highway, still smelling Lizzie's perfume, still tasting her lipstick. He stopped at a drive-in and took his time drinking a milk shake. After what had happened, he was embarrassed to face Porter and Janice.

Having seen all that he'd needed to see at the Black Mass, Porter had also left early and was already at the marina when Tony arrived. Porter gave him a bottle of beer and asked him to sit.

"Thanks, Tony. You can go home now."

"You mean back to the motel?"

"No. I mean back to Maryland."

"You… you brought me all the way across the country just to see if she recognized me?"

"Sort of. And she did. Besides, I decided that book I asked you to write is beneath your dignity."

"That's not your decision to make," said Tony. "I didn't come 2,500 miles to be made a fool of… .by her or by you."

They heard footsteps. "Tony?" called Janice, boarding the yacht. "What's going on?"

"I'll stay in Los Angeles and start my own investigation," said Tony to Porter. "I'm a damn fine researcher and you know it." He turned and left the yacht.

Janice glared at Porter. "Did you just fire him?"

"I had my reasons," said Porter.

"Then I quit," said Janice. "And you're an asshole."

* * *

"Tony!" called Janice, catching up with him at his car.

"Listen. I was the one who ditched the lights at the Abbey. I figured Lizzie had put you through enough. Right after the show, Margo ratted on me. Lizzie called me a cunt and slapped my face. I called her a bitch and slapped her back. She canned me and I just told Porter I quit. Anyway, screw 'em all."

Tony was silent. "You're right," said Janice. "We'll investigate Lizzie ourselves."

She stood on her toes and gave him a lingering kiss on the lips.

"I need to be away a few days," she said softly. "I'll call you when I get back." She kissed him again and got into her car. Tony, rather stunned by the kisses, stood on the marina's lot, watching Janice drive away down Pacific Coast Highway.

Porter stood on the yacht, watching Tony.

38 The Springhouse

Tony was awake all night, watching from his balcony as dawn lit the hills. Having been fired by Porter and with Janice away, this would be his first day as a solo investigator.

Lizzie Hirsig had invited him to come see her. He'd go this morning.

* * *

It was a few minutes before 9:00 A.M and the sky was blue as Tony arrived in the mountains above Malibou Lake. A trio of gulls sailed on the Pacific wind. Smoke was still curling from the ruins of the previous night's bonfire and sheep and goats roamed the hillside. The scarecrow, wearing a few tattered shreds, stood forlornly in the cornfield.

Tony parked in a gravel drive beside the house, the side with the lake view. He got out and looked at the house, its sharply sloping roof with the heavy orange tile, tinged green with age. He knocked at the door.

"I *seeee* you," called a voice, teasingly from above.

He turned and looked up. Lizzie was at the top of the windmill/bell tower, clinging to its side. She was wearing her usual large-brimmed hat, a short, silvery chemise, was bare-footed, and held a wrench in her hand.

"A zealot rang the bell too hard last night and rolled it over," she called down to Tony. She fiddled with the wrench, pushed the bell, and it turned over and clanged. "It's fixed now," she grinned. "I'll be right down."

189

Tony averted his face so not to see up her chemise as she climbed down the tower, reaching the ground. She put on a pair of black lace-up, high-heeled boots with pointed toes. She was so tall and willowy that her boots made her the same height as Tony himself. He figured it might have been her intention. As she approached him, she looked him in the eye.

"You invited me here," said Tony stiffly.

"It's very early," she said, indicating her chemise, which Tony noticed, was torn and not entirely clean. "I'm not even dressed yet. But before I did anything else this morning, I wanted to fix that fucking bell."

She laughed. Tony noticed the spidery false eyelashes, the flowing tendrils of wig. No, she apparently hadn't washed her face or removed the wig since last night's performance, when she'd straddled his lap and recognized him from 13 years ago.

"I'll grab us a bit of breakfast," said Lizzie. "Wait for me by the spring-house."

* * *

The stone springhouse was in bleak disrepair. There were holes in the peaked wooden roof and the panes of the windows were broken. The spring ran below it and a frog sat on a rock, seemingly staring at Tony.

At length, Lizzie appeared, making her way to the springhouse. She had a lit reefer in her mouth and held a bottle. She took a drag off the reefer, then offered it to Tony.

"Mary Jane?"

"No thanks," said Tony.

She took a swig from the bottle, and offered it to Tony. "Dandelion wine?"

"No," he said.

"Please sit," she said, and they both sat in the grass, across from each other, the spring running between them. The frog dived into the water. Tony smelled Lizzie's honeysuckle perfume, which he suspected she'd just splashed on herself. "You never mentioned your name last night," she said.

"Anthony Wyngate. I'm a novelist and college professor. Classics. Drama. Ancient and Medieval Civilizations." He paused. "As for Drama, you put on quite a show last night."

"Thank you," said Lizzie. "It was my first time. I'm a highly-strung girl, so it was a relief to get through a show without pissing myself in front of 300 people."

A gull flew over, seemingly cackling at Lizzie's remark. Lizzie blew out a jet of marijuana smoke. Tony glanced at the crystal, red-eyed angel she wore.

"Isn't she pretty?" asked Lizzie.

A black cat had come close by and was sitting on the hillside, as if watching the couple's battle of wits. Lizzie stretched her arms for it to come to her. Her chemise pulled up, and Tony saw a glimpse of red pubic hair. He averted his eyes and she laughed.

"Pussies everywhere," she grinned, curling her long legs under her and petting the cat. "So... where do you teach... Anthony?"

"Mount Saint Mary's College," said Tony, looking her in the eye. "Maryland."

"Catholics," said Lizzie. "So maybe you'll like this riddle. What's the difference between a nun and a lady taking a bath?"

"I can't imagine," said Tony.

"Well... .the nun has hope in her *soul*... and the lady has soap in her *hole!*"

Lizzie shrieked with laughter. The gull flew overhead, cawing along with her.

"So, Mount Saint Mary's," Lizzie said. She began singing, softly, teasingly:

Immaculate Mary, your praises we sing...

She saw the recognition in his eyes and sang the Grotto hymn more fully now, tauntingly, sensually, her red-eyed angel throwing the sunlight back at him...

Ave, Ave, Ave Maria...

"Stop it," he said tensely.

Lizzie laughed joyously. "Anthony, darling... I know why you're here this morning. You're trying to learn all about me. So... .let's do a little play. *Naughty Lizzie Goes to Confession.* You play the priest, and I play naughty Lizzie."

"Like hell," said Tony.

"Oh, you *must!*" said Lizzie, standing. "You sit inside the springhouse, as the priest in the Confessional booth. I kneel outside by the window and tell you my sins. And that way, you learn *all* about me."

The idea repulsed Tony, but Lizzie was taking deep drags off the reefer and, in her state, might say something to incriminate herself. He needed to learn all he could, as distasteful as her proposal was. "Alright," he said reluctantly.

"Surely," asked Lizzie, "I'll get a penance? Maybe you'll spank me?"

"Penance is supposed to be something you don't enjoy," said Tony.

"Oh! *Touché*, Anthony!" said Lizzie, tossing the still-burning Mary Jane into the stream, then swigging the rest of the dandelion wine.

* * *

Tony sat on a large stone inside the springhouse. After a moment, Lizzie knelt by the broken window and made the Sign of the Cross.

"Bless me, Father, for I have sinned," she said, her voice softly taunting. "My last Confession was...Bleeding Christ Almighty! My First Holy Communion!"

"Go on," said Tony tensely. "Quickly."

"I'm just a *fiend* at sins against purity," whispered Lizzie. "Why, right this moment, as I'm whispering my secrets to a handsome man... I'm very wet."

The gull flew above, cackling. Tony began to rise to leave the springhouse. Her hand came through the broken glass pane and grabbed his arm.

"*Please!*" cried Lizzie. "I have to tell you something else... that nobody else knows... ."

Tony sat back. For a time, she was silent. When she finally spoke, her voice seemed to change, to have a different tone, a sadness... a familiarity.

"I'm lonely," she sighed. "In the graveyard... up on the hill...so lonely..."

"What graveyard?" asked Tony, feeling a chill. "What hill?"

"*You* were there," Lizzie whispered, her hand viciously tightening on his arm. "I lie up there and think of you... I rot in my *grave*... so lonely, so awful... and think of *you*..."

Tony was too shocked to move.

"I used to be pretty, Tony...You used to like me... You wouldn't like me anymore, but I think of *you*, day and night... with impure thoughts. How I still want your cock in my cunt..."

"Stop!" he cried.

"Tony, my darling," she whispered, "have you forgotten all about ... *your BRIDGET?*"

Lizzie screamed the name and her fingernails clawed his wrist. Tony emerged from the springhouse to confront her. She was still kneeling by the window, trembling, seemingly bewildered, as if lost between herself and the personality she'd affected.

"How... did I know that?" she asked, then shrieked, "What's happening to me? What the fuck's *happening* to me?"

She huddled in the grass, her face contorted, weeping. The cat watched her, and the gull, flying in circles above, seemed to caw with cruel laughter.

* * *

Tony drove along the coast aimlessly for hours, sometimes stopping to walk by the ocean. *How did she know*, he thought. He remembered the terror in her eyes.

He finally arrived back at Brentwood mid-afternoon. Porter Down was waiting for him. "Where the hell have you been?" he demanded, climbing out of his pick-up truck.

Tony told him. "Porter... she knows things... ."

"Didn't I tell you not to listen to her?" shouted Porter. "Oh, the hell with it. Scram. Fly back to Maryland... preferably tonight." He cursed and went to his truck.

"You don't even want me anymore as bait?" called Tony after him.

"I've got my own goddamn bait," said Porter, gunning the engine as he pulled away. On the seat beside him was that day's *The Hollywood Reporter*, with a news item he'd circled:

Karloff En Route

Boris Karloff arrives from England tomorrow to discuss a new TV horror pilot.

It was 12 days until June 25, Porter realized. Nevertheless, it was close enough. Karloff was coming to town.

39 Dear Boris

THURSDAY, JUNE 15 AND FRIDAY, JUNE 16, 1967

The Normandy tower of the Chateau Marmont, 8221 Sunset Boulevard, loomed over the Sunset Strip.

Once upon a time, the Chateau Marmont housed such luminaries as Garbo, Harlow, and Howard Hughes, and neighbored such legendary clubs as the Trocadero. The clubs were gone now, with West Hollywood noted for its giant billboards that hawked movies and various western state attractions. The spectacular billboard across Sunset from the Chateau Marmont, its scaffolding three stories high, its board nearly five, presently heralded Las Vegas's *Gala de Paris*, complete with a giant showgirl who raised one leg in a sort of sinuous Can-Can. At night the Kong-sized chorine lit up in gold and silver lights.

Boris Karloff and Porter Down saw the unlit billboard this morning from the Chateau Marmont's penthouse balcony.

The 79-year-old Karloff had answered the door walking with a cane. Now he sat, a serene, living legend millionaire. He looked ancient. Always dark-skinned—various rumors persisted about his actual ancestry—he was now almost a burnished gold-green, his silver hair and mustache striking against the bespectacled face. He was dressed in a dark brown suit, tie and vest. For a moment, he admired a bird singing nearby.

"That's why Garbo used to stay here," said Karloff. "She said the Chateau Marmont was the one hotel in America where birds sang on her balcony."

Karloff had arrived the previous night. He'd taken Porter's call this morning, remembered him and the events of 1931 vividly, and agreed to

194

see him immediately. He claimed his agency had never forwarded him Porter's letters. Mrs. Karloff and a personal secretary had left for an early lunch before Porter arrived. He was direct and concise with Karloff, who listened solemnly and mostly silently.

"Was there any unusual mail waiting for you here?" asked Porter.

"I always receive unusual mail," said Karloff with dark humor. "But I believe you should see this one." He picked up an envelope on the table and removed from it a small sketch of a hangman's noose, lynching Frankenstein's Monster.

Karloff, who was set to meet Friday with producers about his proposed TV series, agreed to Porter being his bodyguard for the night. Porter thanked him for his time and bravery, left his phone number, and arranged to return by 8:30 that evening.

* * *

Porter had returned to the marina for a nap—it promised to be a long night. His cabin phone rang. "This is Mr. Karloff's personal secretary," said a crisp female voice. "He doesn't require your services."

"How about putting Mr. Karloff on the phone and letting him tell me that?"

"That isn't necessary. He repeated to Mrs. Karloff and me the outrageous story you told him. I suspect you're a thief."

"I suspect you're a tight ass."

"I've assured Mr. Karloff that there will be plainclothes police in the Chateau Marmont lobby. Those same police will arrest you if you come there tonight."

"You got me all a-tremble," said Porter, and hung up. He went out on deck and saw portly Luke Foster, well fed on his 37-years of seafood success, waddling down the pier.

"Luke," Porter shouted. "You still got your gun collection?"

* * *

It was 11:30 P.M. High above the Sunset Strip, the 50' neon showgirl, now aglow, rocked her leg on the giant billboard. The smell of marijuana wafted, rising up in the night like some incense offering to the billboard beauty.

The "flower children," packed the streets. San Francisco was their city, but L.A. was their Number Two locale. It was "La-La Land," packed with studio make-believe, with Disneyland just to the south. In some ways, the town itself was hallucinogenic. The police stationed nearby did little, for this group was virtually untouchable—united against an unpopular president, an unjust war, and a dog-eat-dog lifestyle due for re-invention. Transistor radios played and Scott MacKenzie's *San Francisco* blared away:

Gentle people, with flowers in their hair...

Eight stories above, in the Chateau Marmont penthouse, Boris Karloff lay on his bed, his wheelchair in the corner, his wife Evelyn asleep in the next room. He'd removed his leg braces and wore a pale sleeping gown, selected for its ease in slipping over his now-bent body. Often his dreams went way back, pre-Hollywood, to the western America stock companies, the women he'd known, the adventures he'd had. Now and then he dreamed of the horror movies: The outlandish make-ups, the hokey lines, the challenge to give his roles at least a jot of humanity. He was grateful. *Frankenstein* had changed his life. He'd have been a fool to have turned his back on it.

Then he awoke. He sensed someone was in the dark room.

"Evie?"

No answer. He heard a soft hissing sound, coming from the foot of the bed, and he sat up painfully, looking into the darkness. The hiss sounded again. He thought he might still be dreaming as a candle rose and he saw the form of a tall woman. The candle lit her lower face and he saw, even without his glasses, the stitches on her neck.

Her mouth opened wide and she hissed again, this time loudly. He recognized the Nefertiti hairdo and its silver streaks... and now the woman screamed.

It was all so fast, her scream so harrowing, the pain so intense that he wasn't fully aware of what was happening... a gaunt man in a devil mask had pulled him from his bed, the devil's arms wrapped around him, virtually dragging him through the suite. A single light was on and he saw a glimpse of Evelyn tied in a chair, guarded by a woman in a short red dress with a rubber Bela Lugosi-as-Dracula mask over her head.

"Gee, Mr. Karloff, can I have your autograph?" mocked the woman in the Dracula mask.

Another moment, and Karloff realized he was in the night air, on the balcony. The man in the devil mask dropped him onto the floor as somebody put a rope around his neck. He glanced up at the tall Bride, who wore cut-off shorts and a black T-shirt.

"Say your line, Dear Saint Boris," said "the Bride" viciously. "Your line from *Bride of Frankenstein* … 'We belong dead!'"

The rope tightened around his neck. His crippled back and legs were in agony.

"Say it!" the voice hissed. "We… belong… DEAD!'"

He defiantly said nothing.

"*You* belong dead, Dear Saint Boris," said the Bride's voice. "YOU BELONG DEAD*!*"

She yanked the rope, as if to raise him off the floor. He winced… and then came the explosion. A piece blew away from the wall. Seconds later another followed, chipping the balcony railing.

"*Christ!*" shrieked the woman, throwing herself to the floor beside Karloff.

He fully saw her makeup and red, silver-streaked wig, now askew. He heard the crowd below, having heard the shots, in an uproar, shouting and screaming. Then came a third explosion, shattering the glass of the balcony door.

"Shooting! Shooting!" moaned the basso voice under the devil mask.

"Go!" screamed the woman, crawling on her stomach. "*Let's get the fuck out of here!*"

There was a fourth, final explosion. Karloff eventually got up on his knees. He knew instinctively he was safe, the attackers gone. Evelyn called to him. The crowd was still screaming after the sound of the gunshots, and he looked over the balcony, toward the shots' direction. He saw the 50' Las Vegas showgirl, bedecked in lights and rocking her leg.

"Thank you, my dear," said Boris Karloff with his old bravado. Then he fainted.

* * *

It was 3:30 A.M. Porter Down, after climbing down the billboard, had been arrested and now sat contentedly in a West Hollywood lockup.

It had all happened just as he'd guessed it. Karloff in Hollywood… Lizzie would try to strike before Porter arranged protection. Would she kill the old Scare-Monger quietly in his room? Hell no, not with a nightly audience of Flower Children capering below on the Strip. Throw him off the balcony? Too quick and messy. The sketch of the noose that Karloff had received in his mail had been the tip-off. How could Lizzie have resisted dangling the legendary star of *Frankenstein* over Sunset Boulevard... for all the Great Unwashed to behold?

Allowed one phone call, Porter hadn't called a lawyer. He didn't have one. The recipient of his call had just arrived, and a cop brought in a 75-year-old, still-vital man. He looked at Porter, chuckled, and shook his head.

"How ya' doin', fella?" asked Captain James J. O'Leary, LAPD, retired.

40 The Vicarage

Simon Bone believed in rituals, although rarely what they represented. The next nine days, leading up to June 25th, called for a retreat, a pilgrimage. He drove to the Vicarage.

It was a Victorian house, high and remote in the Santa Lucia mountains, just below Big Sur, looking out to the ocean. In 1910, Bone's father had purchased the Vicarage—which had never actually served as such, its name simply appealing to the original 1890 builder—as a summer home. Its property originally ran from the gardens, through the woods, all the way down the cliffs and to the high-water mark of the Pacific. The family had sold the waterfront land and part of the property east of Highway One. Otherwise, the old estate remained virtually intact.

Bone unlocked the iron gate, parked his car, and took his suitcase—he'd be staying several nights. He looked at the arched front window, the vine-covered stonework, the stained glass, the turret, the widow's walk. He'd first come here when he was ten and had hated it—uneasy in this isolation, allergic to the garden flowers, frightened of the stable horses. His eight-years-older, handsomely attractive sister Melanie, in sympathy for her shy, obese little brother, had taken him to the beach along with her friends, and the cold, pounding ocean had terrified him.

He was now sole owner of the Vicarage, still with its grand piano, 1775 grandfather clock, antiques, first editions, and even a Guttenberg Bible. Yet Bone rarely visited. He'd hosted a few parties here, using the house to impress, but primarily leased the estate to wealthy families. At the present time, without any current residents, even the phone service and electricity had been deactivated.

As Bone unlocked the door, he knew, of course, why he'd kept the Vicarage. It wasn't because of nostalgia, nor because his father had died here of a stroke almost 38 years ago, nor because Melanie had died here after a horse fall more than 40 years ago, nor the view and sound of the Pacific, nor because it could serve as his seminary.

Simon Bone cherished the Vicarage because, on several occasions in 1931, Valerie had stayed here.

* * *

There were few surviving flowers in the gardens, so there was no longer any threat to Bone's allergies. The fountain was still, with only green pools of rain water in its basin. The stable was empty, the cursed horses long gone, promptly sold after Melanie had fatally broken her neck. The empty pool, where Bone had never learned to swim, had cracks in its walls.

Bone sat on a marble bench. Yes, Valerie had stayed at this house, walked in the gardens, looked at the Pacific from the widow's walk, swam in this pool… slept in the tower room.

36 years ago, thought Bone wistfully.

The day was warm and he perspired as he looked at the pool, remembering how it had looked those nights in 1931. He recalled the Prohibition liquor and illegal drugs he'd prodigally provided, but personally was too frightened to use… the shrill laughter… the sounds of passion.

A rat suddenly ran across the decaying pool's floor, disappearing into a crevice. Bone winced, stood, leaned on his cane and walked toward the house.

* * *

He had fruit for lunch and visited the former servants' quarters in the rear of the first floor. They'd serve nicely as the rooms for his seminarians. As night fell, he lit the antique oil lamps—he didn't want to deal with the generator—and sat in the main room, with its unlit chandelier, floor-to-ceiling bookshelves, large spinning globe, and grand piano. There were paintings on the walls, including a life-size one of his sister Melanie, commissioned by the family shortly before her death. The painting was so large and hung so high above the fireplace that Melanie's face was shadowed in the dim oil lamp light. All he could see were his sister's gown and her black buckled heels. He'd never mourned her, so he didn't care.

He played the piano, then visited the library, where the Bible rested in its locked glass case, long ignored in its airless casket. Then, as the grandfather clock struck ten, Bone ascended to the "tower room," carrying a lamp. The family had graciously reserved this showplace chamber, with its view of the Pacific, for guests. He lit another lamp in the room, opened the window, and looked out at the stars over the ocean. The wind rustled the long lace curtains. He sat by the desk and looked at the bed.

Yes, Valerie had stayed in this room. She'd put on her makeup, her perfume, her stockings. She'd used its private bathroom, slept in its four-poster bed, made love in it with men and women. One night, she'd suffered a seizure here.

Once upon a time, thought Bone.

* * *

A ship sounded its horn and the bellow echoed up the cliff and hills and into the room. When they'd first come to the Vicarage, Melanie told him that sound was the cry of a sea monster that ate fat little boys. He'd never told her how that moaning sound had given him nightmares about a giant, slimy creature with many eyes and tentacles, eking its way up from the ocean, sitting on him, triumphantly sounding its roar before devouring him. He chuckled at the memory, but acknowledged he still had a primal fear of that bellowing sound in the night. The curtains stirred in the wind and his thoughts turned from Valerie to Lizzie.

The Miracle of Saint Lizzie, he grinned cynically.

She'd come to him 13 months ago—May 26, 1966, to be precise. Alice Elizabeth Fawkes had literally arrived on his doorstep in San Francisco, pursued by police, aware of Bone's distinction as high priest in the Church of the Light Bearer. She'd been haggard, nearly bald, wearing a wig that looked as if it had been stolen off a store mannequin—and probably had been. She was seeking shelter, desperately addicted. He'd almost phoned the police, but she'd shown him the angel amulet—Valerie's "Saint Dymphna."

A miracle, he'd marveled.

In time, he came to doubt her remarkable story as to how she got the angel, presuming someone from the 1931 era had fashioned this facsimile and provided her with it. Yet, somehow, she'd known about

Valerie, never explaining how. She'd vaguely *resembled* Valerie... .tall like Valerie, hazel eyes like Valerie, although not as brightly yellow... or were they?

She was terrified of being tracked down and captured, and she'd do anything—*anything*—for protection.

As a boy, Bone had always wanted a doll. When his father and mother had refused his request, he'd cut pictures of dolls from catalogs. Melanie had found where he'd hidden the pictures, laughed at him and told their parents, who'd disciplined him for such a feminine interest. Now, all these years later, he'd had an *alive* doll. A *play* doll.

A *Valerie* doll.

He'd bought Lizzie beautiful clothes, selecting dresses and lingerie for her. He purchased her a long, red wig, that instantly strengthened her resemblance to Valerie. He bought her the same honeysuckle-scented perfume Valerie had used. He even briefly admitted her to a private sanitarium for the nose alteration, to accentuate the resemblance. Lizzie, desperately needing the drugs he illegally provided her and easily obtained by several sources in and around Carmel, agreed to the operation. She defiantly rejected, however, his suggestion that the same surgeon remove or at least cosmeticize the livid scar above her pubis.

Yes, he'd promised her safety, drugs, and protection, if only she'd be *his* "Valerie," here at the Vicarage, where no one else would ever know she existed. And for all he'd provided, the Lizzie of 1966 fulfilled all his cruelest fantasies about the Valerie of 1931, as he made love to her in his limited ways... even though, all the while, she seemed on the verge of laughing at him, and maybe at herself.

He'd shown her Valerie's pictures, told her of the Black Mass, given her the old script they followed, played her the songs at his piano. She became obsessed with "becoming" Valerie, and he could see a glint of the woman he'd adored in 1931, enough that, for a brief time, he'd fallen in love with his own dangerous, addicted creation... his own Frankenstein's Monster.

She's only a street junkie, Bone thought time and again. Yet even from the first night, Bone thought he saw a spark of hatred in her eyes, directed at him, as if she knew the whole truth of what had really happened in 1931, the full story.

That, of course, was impossible.

Then came the night that he drank too much. She'd gone up to sleep in the tower room, and he sat downstairs alone, taunted by his decades of obesity and impotence, agitated by the way Valerie, the pathetic epileptic, had treated him all those years ago, despite his adoration. As he became increasingly drunk and enraged, he'd crashed into Lizzie's room, futilely trying to rape her as she screamed beneath him, fighting against his weight and his fists, escaping the room and the house, leaving him whimpering on the floor.

He knew, with her animal's sense for survival, that she'd sell herself to some other drug-providing keeper, and likely soon die. Still, he'd engaged Alfred Pinkerton to find Alice Elizabeth Fawkes… and he had, in a fetid commune near Soledad, nearly dead from an overdose. Bone had paid Pinkerton to control her, to serve as a liaison between them. The creature had seduced Pinkerton—Bone could hardly have been surprised—and the lawyer had tried to form a peace pact the previous Christmas, with disastrous results. Bone had been fortunate he hadn't drowned. And at Malibou Lake, she'd christened herself "Saint Lizzie," reviving Saint Valerie's Black Mass, compensating for her limited talent with a mad, spiteful savagery.

Nothing, he and she knew, could torment him more.

The desecrations. The fire at Universal. And now, as he looked forward to world-wide attention with his seminary, she was surely planning a new surprise… one calculated to destroy him. He had to destroy her first. His chronic nightmare was that he'd wait too long, plan too elaborately, awaken one night and find her standing beside his bed, avenging herself as she slaughtered him… and, he strangely sensed, avenging Valerie as well.

The ship, or perhaps another, roared hungrily again from the Pacific. It was strange. Shortly before Lizzie had escaped, at his fetishistic request, she had dressed up in a version of Valerie's *The Blue Angel* costume and top hat. Her resemblance to Valerie was remarkable, and for one magical night, Bone had almost believed he'd truly performed a miracle. He'd taken Lizzie up to the widow's walk, to see the full moon over the ocean. In 1931, also during a full moon night, he'd been up there with Valerie, who'd worn a similar costume, and he'd begged her to let him touch her hair.

Valerie had profanely refused. Lizzie had torn off her wig, thrown it in his face and shrieked in laughter.

Tonight, *he'd* sleep here in the tower room. Simon Bone undressed, sensually pulling back the covers and sheets. As he extinguished the lamp, the long lace curtains blew like specters in the wind, and he lie naked in the bed, fantasizing about the past, terrified of a future where his plan engaged too late—and where this time, he'd lose the game.

Far out in the ocean, the ship's horn moaned and echoed, sounding like a monster that ate fat little boys.

41 Movies In the Sky

Dr. Sam, as his patrons called him, was 5'8" tall, wall-eyed, and weighed 280-pounds. He had a florid handlebar mustache that, like the hair on his head, had endured various bleachings to become a defiantly orange color.

His chosen mission was to tend to the stoned. Here in the hills beyond Malibu Creek State Park, on what had once been a ranch, Dr. Sam served the disenfranchised, with a proud sense of heroism. Indeed, if the revolution came soon, as Dr. Sam hoped, it would need every warrior, and his personal goal was to keep the ranks full. He also vowed, despite the many peace signs on the property, to keep the proletariat armed, stocking an arsenal of rifles and shotguns.

It was Friday night, after 11 o'clock, and hot as hell. The ranch was now a psychedelic flophouse, and with the weekend here, patients recovering from bad trips would soon be thrashing in the hay in the barns and shacks. Sam, who'd actually never made it through the second year of med school, was dozing in the back of the cabin and awoke to a mad pounding.

"Here we go," he mumbled. He grabbed a shotgun and opened the door. On the ground appeared to be a body in a bed sheet. A skinny man, wild-eyed and wearing what looked to Sam like an old linen duster, knelt by the body. A small, wispy woman in a red dress stood beside him.

"Help!" moaned the man, his basso voice warped and desperate.

"Erica!" shouted Dr. Sam, and a thin young woman with long blonde hair and granny glasses emerged from the back of the cabin. She wore only a bra and panties. Erica, who served as Dr. Sam's nurse, was quite

205

pretty. In fact, Dr. Sam often visualized Erica in his intimate fantasies, although he'd actually never touched her.

"Probably another fuckin' OD," yawned Erica. Dr. Sam put down his gun and together he and Erica lugged the body through the flophouse. Mad Jack and Margo followed. In the next room, Dr. Sam and Erica slung the patient on a table and uncovered the tall, balding figure, dressed in a t-shirt and spare denim shorts.

"How long's he been under?" asked Erica.

"It's *she!*" shouted Mad Jack.

Margo gave her porcine snort.

"She got all upset," said Mad Jack, "after we tried to..." Suddenly he slapped his hand over his mouth, like a child realizing he was about to divulge a secret.

"Is she dead?" asked Margo frankly. "She stinks like she's dead."

"Yeah," said Erica. "Sam, open a goddamn window." Sam obediently obliged.

"Look," chortled Margo. "Her eyes are rolled up in her head."

"Please, Lizzie," wept Mad Jack, falling to his knees. "Please don't die..."

Dr. Sam and Erica pulled Mad Jack to his feet, shoved him and Margo into the front room and locked the door. "Get her clothes off," ordered Dr. Sam. Erica unzipped the patient's shorts and saw the scar running up from the woman's vagina.

"Oh, that is *so* gross!" sneered Erica.

* * *

Was she dead? Was the blonde bitch in her bra and panties an angel? Was the cockeyed porker with the orange mustache a devil? He and the blonde had carried her outside, carelessly rewrapped in her sheet, into a barn, laying her in the hay, leaving her alone.

Yeah, she'd OD'd, and she'd OD'd because she'd failed. Somebody had taken shots at her on the Chateau Marmont balcony, spoiling her Karloff caper. Somehow, she knew who it had been—the pig in the sailor suit. Tony Wyngate was working with him... and Pretty Little Angel Eyes. She just knew, the way she knew all kinds of strange shit. What the fuck was happening to her, ripping her head apart?

So, she'd freaked out. They were coming for her, she figured, so she'd have the last laugh, and OD. She'd fucked that up too. Or maybe not. Maybe she'd still die... maybe tonight.

There was a hole in the barn roof, and she saw the sky, and one of the stars exploded into a giant Drive-In movie screen. This happened sometimes when she was stoned, and she'd see movies, biopics, *auto*biopics, all about her life. The movie's title hit the screen:

Alice Gives Jonathan a Blow Job

Mary's mountain. Mount Saint Mary's. The stars were shining on the purple, twisted Judas trees, in Technicolor, and she was walking hand-in-hand with sad, sweet Jonathan. A Mount seminarian. So gentle. So timid. So sensitive about his receding temples and pear-shaped body and sissy voice and skinny arms. Yet none of that mattered, she told him in the flick, because he had such beautiful eyes.

Starry eyes.

She was a college girl, still with her own auburn hair that she loved to unpin, and—Jesus, just look at her old nose! Jonathan was taking her cockteasing seriously during their secret walk up on the mountain. Pretty music played on the soundtrack—*Once Upon a Time*, she recognized—as they sat beneath the Judas tree, counting all the stars on a cold, moonless December night. The music swelled… that first, wet kiss…

Oh, Alice, I love you!

The Judas tree's dead pods cascaded upon them, and there was a full, lush, movie star close-up of Jonathan's hard-on…

And from its best angle, thought Lizzie.

Fellatio, slickly done. Jonathan wept, ashamed. Shattered seminarian vows! The movie jumped to hours later… midnight… she was awaking, sensing, knowing, dressing, escaping the locked dormitory, walking the mile to the Mount. She knew where he'd be… the old, locked, off-limits Grotto, up on the mountain. And there she found him… his wrists slashed, sprawled before the altar in the votive candlelight. Beside him was the carving knife he'd stolen that evening from the cafeteria.

"OH CHRIST!" she screamed.

She looked for help, from Christ's Virgin Mother, posing prettily in the Grotto niche… but she wouldn't resurrect poor dead Jonathan. Hysterical, furious that he'd killed himself because of her, she'd grabbed Jonathan's body and, in her insanity, had taken the knife, plunging it into his groin, over and over.

And then the movie, already a soap opera/doomed love affair/suicide melodrama, warped into something else.

In Lizzie's dreams, it was always the snake. Stretched or coiled beside her, talking to her, telling jokes, singing songs… whispering secrets. Suddenly, there was a "Dissolve" on-screen and a "Flashback" in the story. Shock treatment equipment. Panels. Wires. A tub of ice water… her stretched out in it like a torpid snake. Creepy music. Then the film sped up, the music at fast speed, her hair falling out in seconds rather than the weeks that it actually had taken to fall out…

And then something crawled from the water, out of the tub. *She* was a snake, a dead, decaying snake, raised from the dead, dug up, still covered with maggots and lice, brought to life like Frankenstein's Monster, via electrical shock. She whiplashed, crawling toward the screen for a closeup, whispering, hissing, and she could actually smell the reptile as it bared its fangs to bite her.… .

Oh Christ, oh, Christ, oh Christ… she cried, watching and remembering.

The film jump-cut back to the Grotto, and via the Special Effects, she was both herself *and* the snake, changing back and forth, she plunging the knife into Jonathan's body, then the snake sinking its teeth into his corpse. As the snake, she crawled away from the bloody body, up into the trees, and there she transformed into human again, too frightened to move, hiding there all night.

A "Dissolve" in the movie… and then, down the Grotto path in the celestial morning light, came the tall, young professor…

Fade-Out. Suddenly came coming attractions for her *other* movies, her *later* movies, all running too fucking fast, the music blaring:

"See! The Old Man with the Goat Eyes… and his Knife!"

"No!" screamed Lizzie, followed by:

"WE Dare You! Behold the Dead Woman's Corpse… Covered with her Own Maggots and Lice!"

"Stop, Goddammit!" howled Lizzie

Then the drive-in-movie in-the-sky's screen exploded, the flames towering as they had on the old *Frankenstein* village, only a month ago.

* * *

The sheet had slid off and she was naked in the loft, and alone. Where the screen used to be, there was a star. Lizzie trembled, touched her angel and began her prayer:

"Saint Dymphna… Please don't let me go crazier today…"

She broke off the prayer, weeping. She thought again of the decaying creature with its maggots and lice she'd seen slithering on the screen, trying to forget whatever was ripping her to pieces, grateful for whatever time she had left still to be herself. She ran a hand over her scalp.

"No lice," Lizzie sighed to herself. "This way, Bleeding Christ Almighty.... .no lice."

42   Monterey

Saturday afternoon, Janice called Tony. She'd been away for a few days and said she'd been investigating near the Mexican border and had learned about several cults that were probably drug contacts for Lizzie and her coven. She was now back home.

"Come with me up the coast," said Janice. "We both need a break."

They left early evening, driving over 300 miles to Salinas, the birthplace of John Steinbeck, Tony's favorite novelist. Near midnight, Janice headed slightly east, past fields of barley, down a lonely road to an open wooden gate. There was a single light in the farmhouse and a pole bearing a large wicker peace sign. It was a commune.

The ranch looked like the "place" where George and Lennie might have lived, had their dream in *Of Mice and Men* not ended so tragically—ramshackle, but picturesque. A handsome woman named Ruthie, probably in her early 20s and with long brown hair, met Janice, emotionally hugged her, and the two held each other for a long time. Tony presumed she was someone Janice had helped in her extracting work. Ruthie invited Janice and Tony to stay as long as they wished.

They stayed there that night in separate rooms, and the next day, drove 20 miles southwest to attend the finale of what became known as the Monterey Pop Festival.

They were among the 90,000 attendees and the Sunday night climax presented non-stop phenomena: Janis Joplin, belting out *Ball n' Chain* while drinking from a bottle of Southern Comfort; The Who, performing its soon-to-be-legendary *My Generation*, with Pete Townshend de-

210

stroying his guitar and Keith Moon kicking over his drums; Jimi Hendrix singing *Wild Thing*, pouring lighter fluid over his guitar, setting it afire, smashing it into the stage and tossing its remains to the screaming crowd. Scott MacKenzie sang *San Francisco* and the Mamas and the Papas closed with *Monday, Monday* and *California Dreamin.'*

The volatile concert, for whatever excesses it presented, was revitalizing and unforgettable. For Tony and Janice, the horrors in Los Angeles seemed very far away.

They left Salinas Monday afternoon, June 19. Ruthie embraced Tony as well as Janice. "You see what it can be like?" asked Janice as they drove away. "*Should* be like?"

Come nightfall she pulled over near the beach. "Let's stay here tonight," said Janice. They took blankets from Janice's trunk, found a cove on the beach, built a fire with driftwood, sat on the blankets and looked at the stars and the moon which, in a week, would be full. The night grew late.

"Are you cold?" asked Tony after a moment.

She moved closer to him and in a moment, they were in each other's arms.

43

Five Nights and Days

Tuesday, June 20: Boris Karloff, shaken but pronounced fit for travel, arrived at LAX for the red-eye flight to London at 11:00 P.M., five nights after his unpublicized attack. He'd rejected the TV pilot.

Porter Down watched Mrs. Karloff push her husband's wheelchair toward first class boarding. Karloff turned, looked at Porter, and silently nodded. No secretary was in evidence.

Police had discovered that the attackers had hidden in the Chateau Marmont's Normandy-style tower, working their way to the break-in at Karloff's penthouse. They'd worn gloves, leaving no prints, and Porter figured that Margo's technical wizardry had paved the way. Authorities sought Lizzie, but she wasn't at the Abbey. The Black Mass at Malibou Lake had been inexplicably canceled until further notice.

June 25 was five days away.

* * *

Wednesday, June 21: The Thousand Islands post office delivered mail to the islands' occupants by boat on different days of the week. This morning, Eve Cromwell and Boy were sitting at the dock, Eve hoping for another letter from California.

It was after 10 A.M. when she saw the boat heading for the island. Boy saw it too and wagged his tail. The mailman waved, pulled up to the dock, petted Boy, and handed Eve a rubber-banded packet of mail. Then

212

off he went. Eve looked through the bills, catalogs, magazines… and there it was, postmarked Los Angeles. In the corner address were the initials *P.D.* Eve read the letter immediately. The danger had increased. The similarities to what had happened in 1931 had become undeniable. A murder had almost taken place.

She wrote back to Porter immediately.

* * *

Late Wednesday afternoon, Janice left L.A., telling Tony she was heading to Capistrano to investigate a drug lead. She said she'd be back within a few days.

* * *

Alfred Pinkerton returned from San Francisco that Wednesday night. "Take the car to the garage," he told Mahugu. "You're done for the evening."

"Sir," said Mahugu. "As you know, I have been studying the Law. Please, have you any books in your library I may borrow to help me in my dream?"

"None," said Pinkerton.

"Yes, sir. Good night, sir." Mahugu drove the car to the garage.

Pinkerton took a Scotch to his oak-paneled den, sat at his desk and looked up at his wall. Looking back at him was his pride-and-joy: the death masks of three men and one woman he'd defended, unsuccessfully, for murder.

"Cheers!" smiled Pinkerton, raising his glass to the masks.

He remembered every detail of each of the executions, especially the woman's. They'd allowed him to walk with her, and he'd kissed her cheek just before they took her inside the chamber. He looked at the mask, at the area of her cheek where he'd kissed her…

This was all years ago. He didn't like to think how many. He desperately needed the excitement, the fame again. The boredom, the erosion of his once-celebrated career, and the decay of his identity were strangling him. Lizzie, he'd believed, would revitalize his life. He'd no idea precisely how, but he knew his future depended on her madness. The senses came back to him. Her scent… the vicious way she kissed, tasted, clawed, fucked. He almost missed her.

Yes, Lizzie Hirsig, he'd believed, was an angel from Heaven—a crazy, bald, junkie angel with a cross-shaped pubic scar—who'd resurrect his career and lead him to redemption.

Then she'd disappeared.

He'd had no clue she was planning the Karloff execution—after all, it had been ten days earlier than her targeted June 25th date. After its failure, he'd heard nothing of her or from her. He'd planned to have some of his underworld contacts kidnap her this week, along with Mad Jack Caldwell and Margo Coventry, and release them just after Bone had framed her on the 25th. They'd be arrested. No one would believe their story of a kidnapping. Then Pinkerton would take center stage and be Lizzie's all-star lawyer.

And now it was all fucked-up.

He went into the back yard. The night was cold and a faint mist rose from the pool. Felicia Shayne was swimming in the pool in a tan bikini. Pinkerton remembered that Lizzie had swum in the pool often when she lived here, frequently at night, naked, slithering through the water like a snake, and how it had aroused him. Yes, having Lizzie in his house had been like having a pet mamba, deadly poisonous, living day and night afraid that the reptile might escape its cage.

The mamba was loose now... and he didn't know where to track it, catch it, or cage it. Maybe it was dead.

June 25, the date Bone had promised and in which he kept such stock, was only four days away. And the site of the "sacrament," which he and Bone would use to frame Lizzie, had long been selected.

It was Santa Barbara Mission.

* * *

Thursday, June 22: Tony, who'd fibbed to the Academy Research Library that he was working on a book about *Frankenstein* films, got a call: the department was granting his request for contact information for several members of the 1931 *Frankenstein* whom, for whatever reasons, Porter had not contacted. He immediately arranged to meet with Mae Clarke, *Frankenstein's* leading lady, now largely forgotten.

Tony found her that afternoon living in humble circumstances in North Hollywood, thrice divorced. Her personality was erratic, alternately sweet and antagonistic. When Tony vaguely referred to "tragic events" during *Frankenstein's* shooting, she said there'd been nothing of the kind.

Either she never knew, thought Tony, or she was still afraid to betray a studio confidence. As Tony began to leave, Clarke, suddenly strangely mellow, talked about Colin Clive.

"He was the handsomest man I ever saw," said Clarke wistfully, "and the saddest."

* * *

That Thursday evening, Lizzie Hirsig left Dr. Sam's ranch, having rallied from near-death during her six-night/five-day stay. She departed on a natural high, with a red kerchief tied around her pate like a pirate. Sam, having learned she was "Lucifer's Archangel," had regarded her as a rock star, and had treated her with sympathy for her illnesses and disfigurements. He also noticed curiously that her hazel eyes seemed brighter, wilder, and almost yellow since her recovery.

When Mad Jack and Margo arrived to drive Lizzie away, a guy called Rob-Roy was checking in at Dr. Sam's. He knew Margo from L.A.'s underground—they were both into explosives. Rob-Roy took Margo aside and told her that some creep up the coast had hired him to build a bomb, hide it in one of the bell towers at Santa Barbara Mission, and time it to blow at 11:00 A.M. Sunday morning.

"Some asshole plans to show up just in time to get the pigs to defuse the bomb," said Rob-Roy. "Probably wants to blame it on *our* kind. I was supposed to set it up tonight, but I'm fucked up really bad and need Dr. Sam. How about if I keep their money, give *you* the bomb, and you add it to that big bomb you've been building?"

He unlocked his trunk, handing Margo the bomb, inside a cardboard box. "Maybe later," Rob-Roy droned, "when I feel better, you can give *me* something?"

Margo raised her eyebrows, grinned, and nodded.

* * *

Friday, June 23: Tony visited Jack P. Pierce, *Frankenstein*'s makeup artist, at his small apartment in Encino this morning. Pierce, sour and scrappy, was loud and clear in his bitterness that Universal paid him no royalties on his monster make-ups.

"I created make-ups for all the horror pictures," snapped Pierce. "*Dracula, Frankenstein, The Mummy, The Wolf Man, The Invisible Man!*"

How do you make up the Invisible Man? wondered Tony.

Pierce nodded that he recalled Porter Down and the murder during *Frankenstein*. Yet for all his anger, he was still a company man who kept company secrets. "I ain't talkin' about any of that," said Pierce with finality.

* * *

On Friday afternoon, Tony paid a third call—to Carl Laemmle, Jr. who, in 1931 at age 23, had produced *Frankenstein*. The house sat on Tower Grove Drive at the top of Beverly Hills. Universal's once-upon-a-time "Crown Prince" had never produced a picture after 1936, when a studio takeover had dethroned him and his father. He'd never married, and was now crippled from multiple sclerosis, greeting his caller in a wheelchair. Tony noticed Junior's Academy Award for *All Quiet on the Western Front* on a bookshelf.

Junior, a wizened 59-year-old, appeared far older. He sat by the pool, with a view all the way to Catalina Island. He looked blank when Tony brought up Universal's 1931 *Frankenstein* crisis, and changed the subject to horseracing. The little man seemed almost senile but, as Tony prepared to leave, Junior suddenly made a strange, revealing remark.

"Why'd I do it?" asked Junior. "Paying off reporters… cops. Christ, it wasn't worth it."

* * *

Saturday, June 24: Janice, back from Capistrano, called Tony that morning. "Where have you been?" he demanded, angrily. "Tomorrow's the 25th."

"I know," she said, angry that he was angry. They shared the news they'd learned. She claimed she'd found more about the drug dealers who were funding Lizzie. Tony reached Porter by phone at the marina, told him about speaking with the *Frankenstein* survivors, and said Janice had news as well.

"Meet me here at noon," said Porter.

* * *

When Tony and Janice arrived at Malibu, the yacht's engine was running. Porter, on the lower deck, invited them aboard. "Go to the bar and have a drink," he said. While they were drinking, the yacht suddenly pulled away from its moorings. Tony and Janice went back on deck. Porter, on the pier, was waving to them.

"See ya' Monday," shouted Porter.

* * *

A cordial crew of three, provided by Luke Foster, was under orders to stay at sea, no matter how much hell the couple raised. There was plenty of food, drink, and amenities. By evening, their anger having subsided, Tony and Janice sat on the bow, looking at the lights along the coast and the full moon over the Pacific.

"Unless she can turn herself into an octopus, we're ridiculously safe," said Tony.

"It's a full moon," said Janice, leaning against him. "Anything's possible."

They were quiet for a moment. "Porter really believes Lizzie's a witch and that he killed her in 1931," mused Janice. "Her craziness might just be all part of her act, but with Porter, it's for real. He might be Ahab, chasing a white whale from his youth. An angry old man. Angry old men can be dangerous."

Tony didn't respond. There was something about Porter Down that, despite his scrapes with him, he respected, a depth he sensed. He'd sensed it in Emmitsburg. It was why he'd come all this way, why he was still here tonight… that, and his growing feelings for Janice.

"Anyway," said Janice, "I've been mainly thinking more about *her*. 'Lizzie'… or 'Alice'. Imagine what horrible things must have happened to her to have made her so violent, so obsessed."

Tony said nothing. Janice looked away, was quiet for several moments, and then said, "Compassion. Everyone needs, and deserves, compassion."

"Even old men who chase white whales?" asked Tony.

* * *

They'd both been asleep in his cabin. Then, shortly before midnight, Tony awoke to Janice, curled tightly beside him, whining, crying, finally screaming.

"Janice!" He grabbed her, waking her. "You've had a nightmare."

She whimpered, looking into his eyes, as if something there had frightened her. She pulled away, grabbed her clothes and, without dressing, hurried to her own cabin.

Tony went up on the deck, rattled by her hysteria. He looked at the moon, at its reflection on the ocean, at the lights along the coast. He wondered where Porter was... where Lizzie was. And he wondered why, as he'd held Janice as she cried and trembled in his cabin, he'd felt as if he were holding Bridget.

44   Little Cindy

SATURDAY, JUNE 24 AND SUNDAY, JUNE 25, 1967

The full moon was shining on the Spanish-style house high in the Los Feliz colony east of the HOLLYWOOD Sign, near the Griffith Observatory, where Colin Clive had lived in 1937, his final year.

The current owners were Dr. Robert Conliffe, a surgeon at Good Samaritan Hospital, and his wife Veronica, a real estate agent. Today, they'd celebrated the seventh birthday of their daughter Cindy at Disneyland. For Cindy, the highlight had come when Minnie Mouse hugged her and posed with her for a picture. The family had arrived at the park when it opened that morning and came home after the fireworks.

By midnight, they were soundly asleep.

* * *

Lizzie sat outside the house, huddled in shadows by the pool house. *White Rabbit* was playing in her head, over and over. Jefferson Airplane's song had become so popular on their *Surrealistic Pillow* album that RCA-Victor had officially released it as a single this weekend. DJs all over the country were giving it lots of play:

Feed your head...

Yes, June 25th had arrived, complete with a fucking full moon, and Lizzie had finally decided how to commemorate it. No burning a church. No carving up a rectory of priests with a butcher's knife. No deflowering

219

a convent of nuns with a dildo... or, to stay with her witch motif, a broom handle. No crucifixion on the HOLLYWOOD sign, no bombing a back lot ... and no hanging of a horror icon. After all, as *Frankenstein* had proven all those years ago, nothing's so horrific as the death of a child.

Maria... She's drowned...

Drownings. *Frankenstein* history was filled with them. Shelley's estranged wife Harriet had drowned herself in the Serpentine River in London. Percy Shelley himself had drowned in a storm in the Gulf of Spezia in Italy. The Monster had drowned Little Maria in the mountain lake in *Frankenstein*, and her father and mother in the windmill in *Bride of Frankenstein*. And James Whale had drowned himself in his swimming pool.

Karloff was in England. Clive and Whale were in ashes. Where the real "Little Maria" was, now a woman in her mid-40s, Lizzie didn't know. Any others alive from *Frankenstein* didn't interest her. A little girl, living in Colin Clive's old house... it was the best connection she'd get.

She crouched, trembling in the garden, near the pool, dressed in her T-shirt, cutoffs, and black leather gloves, unwigged, barefoot, sick, stoned, shaking... scared shitless. She almost sensed a Jiminy Cricket conscience, telling her to give a little whistle. Instead, she puked. She wanted to cut out but couldn't. Tonight, she was "the Monster." "Little Maria" was in the house... upstairs.

It's all part of the ritual, thought Lizzie

She'd learned the address by getting a copy of Clive's death certificate. She'd seen the little blonde-haired girl through the window when she, Mad Jack, and Margo had crept outside the house just for kicks a few weeks ago. She'd played *Frankenstein's* flower game with her cat—now it was time to play it with a real little girl.

I am Maria... .Would you like one of my flowers?

She had to do it. The Karloff caper had failed and she'd nearly had her head blown off. She'd almost OD'd in shame. Margo had told her about the bomb and Santa Barbara Mission, and she'd realized Bone had tried to set her up. She wanted to destroy him... to avenge "Saint Valerie," the witch she'd learned about five years ago in Sicily. And as for herself, she had to get even for all the shit that had happened to her. The nightmares were burning her up... time to give other people nightmares.

Tonight, Bleeding Christ Almighty, it happens, she told herself.

Margo had broken into the house, cutting off the alarm system. She now returned, having opened a downstairs window. Margo and Mad Jack hid in the shadows. Lizzie took a baby step into the moonlight. No one watching her. No Jiminy Cricket, no God. After all, wasn't God in Heaven dead, like *Time* magazine had asked?

If He wasn't, He had only a few minutes to let her know it.

* * *

At 12:15 A.M., Porter Down, all-too-aware that June 25th was officially here, was with Jim O'Leary at police headquarters in Hollywood. Taking his cue from what Tony had told him, he'd persuaded police to send guards to the addresses of Mae Clarke, Jack Pierce, and Junior Laemmle. He'd even sent security to Forest Lawn, where James Whale's ashes were entombed in the Great Mausoleum, and Dwight Frye's body was buried in a section called Graceland.

"Where the hell is she?" growled Porter.

* * *

Inside the house, Cindy awoke in her upstairs bedroom. In the glow of her nightlight—a figure of Minnie Mouse her Daddy and Mommy had bought for her today—she saw what appeared to be a tall, scary man with eye make-up and hardly any hair, wearing short pants and standing at the foot of her bed. The figure placed a black-gloved finger against its mouth, as if warning her to stay quiet.

Cindy thought she was having a nightmare. As the figure swooped down, placing a hand over her mouth, she knew she was awake.

* * *

It was almost 2:00 A.M. The trio gathered by Malibou Lake, under the full moon, almost 40-miles from Cindy's house, carrying the small, drugged figure to the hallowed site of *Frankenstein's* Flower Game. Mad Jack and Margo placed the unconscious Cindy on her side on the shore of the lake and moved away.

White Rabbit played in Lizzie's head like an organ dirge. She held a bouquet of daisies, knelt facing Cindy, and tossed them one-by-one into the moonlit lake.

All part of the ritual, she thought again, trembling. *All part of the fucking ritual...*

She gave her Monster smile and laugh and, trembling, reached for the little girl. Lizzie saw the child's eyes open.

"Where's Mommy?" Cindy whimpered. "Please... where's my Mommy...?"

Lizzie smiled comfortingly, then gasped, hearing a hiss behind her. Jesus... the Snake Lady! Lizzie looked over her shoulder, and there was the giant snake, with its long red hair, behind her, whispering to her...

It has to be right... just right... Do it now...

Lizzie, still kneeling, could smell the Snake Lady, her rot, her decay. She turned, lunging, grabbing Cindy, holding her tightly, bursting into tears, rocking the weeping child.

Now, you scaredy cat cunt! shrieked the Snake Lady. *NOW!*

Lizzie, weeping, hugged the child even more tightly. "Don't cry, darling," she said softly, although she was crying too. "Please, don't cry..."

But Cindy did keep crying, and Lizzie, hearing the Snake Lady's hissing, smelling her rot, lost control. She lifted the child, giving a moan, a bleat, that she didn't recognize as her own voice. She tossed Cindy into the lake, then screamed and fell to the ground.

From behind her, she heard the Snake Lady, hissing with joy.

45 Direct Evidence

Around 10 o'clock that morning, a boater saw the body. Police reported to the death site and found the note nailed to a tree on the lake shore:

"Maria... She's drowned."
Frankenstein, 1931
The Church of the Light Bearer

Jim O'Leary drove Porter Down to the lake. Porter, reviewing the family's missing person call, recognized the significance of the address. He'd been in Hollywood in 1937 when Colin Clive had died. He'd never imagined Clive's house playing a part in this "event." He cursed himself for not considering it.

Road blocks were up by the lake. There were more than a dozen policemen. Porter and O'Leary approached the covered body. O'Leary knew the forensics examiner. "Howard... please?" he asked. The examiner nodded and lifted the sheet. The child's blonde hair framed her delicate face. "Cover her," said O'Leary hoarsely.

The police captain showed them the notice nailed to the tree. "The lettering's in blood," said the captain. "Looks written with a makeup brush. Probably no prints."

A sergeant came to them. "The Conliffes are here," he reported. "We're bringing them through the blockades now." The captain looked at O'Leary. "You always spoke well to the families, Jim. Will you do it again today?"

223

O'Leary glanced back at the small covered body. "Yes," he said softly.

* * *

At the same time in Santa Barbara, the media stood a safe distance from the Mission, with its tall bell towers. Police were inside, searching for the bomb, allegedly in the left tower. A large crowd, many of them who'd come to worship at the Mission that morning, stood behind the police barricade praying, many of them kneeling, asking God to spare the church.

Chelsea Kimball, while not a TV reporter, had pulled some strings and was conducting a live interview with Simon Bone, at the scene. "I contacted authorities as soon as I learned what that woman had done," said Bone, himself dressed in his favorite suit. "She was going to blame the Church of the Light Bearer for this atrocity. The loss of lives and destruction of a beloved California landmark would have been a haunting, horrible atrocity."

"And you say you know who's responsible?"

"I do, and will provide the name to you and to the police within minutes," said Bone. "And please remember… the Church of the Light Bearer has been a savior this morning."

He was nervous, even though police still had almost an hour to defuse the bomb, and Rob-Roy had been ordered to make it easy to defuse. Suddenly, one of Chelsea's crew began signaling her frantically. "Excuse me just a moment," she said to her TV audience. As the cameraman panned the Mission, the crew member began telling Chelsea the news that had just come from Malibou Lake. Almost simultaneously, a policeman appeared on the roof, waving his arms like an umpire signaling "Safe."

"No bomb here!" he shouted. "False alarm!"

The crowd cheered deafeningly, and Bone, dazed by the news, found himself in the midst of a joyful mob, shouting praise and thanks to God. Chelsea Kimball was in his face, her microphone off, shrieking something about a drowned child at Malibou Lake and a letter claiming Bone's Church of the Light Bearer was responsible.

"She cut your balls off!" shouted Chelsea over the jubilant prayers and Alleluias, striking Bone across the face with her microphone. "Do you have any idea what a fucking mess you and your church are in *now*?"

Simon Bone, aware police and reporters would descend upon him any minute, felt sudden pain, dropped his cane and collapsed upon the ground.

"Call an ambulance," he moaned. "I… I'm having a heart attack."

* * *

Police kept watch at the Abbey all Sunday night. There was no sign of the trio of suspected killers.

In the early hours of Monday, authorities found what they believed to be the murderers' car, a 1962 Chevy, dumped down into a ravine. Any evidence had burned. Investigators had found "Mad Jack" Caldwell's and Margo Coventry's prints—both had a police record—on a stone wall in the Conliffes' garden. Although there was no direct evidence yet that Lizzie had been involved, Porter Down convinced police that she'd masterminded the murder.

All three suspects were now officially fugitives from justice and the resurrected Black Mass had been a one-night wonder.

* * *

Tony and Janice had returned to the mainland Monday at noon. Porter had sent word of the murder to the yacht's radio Sunday evening. Janice, who'd been distant since her nightmare, had silently gone to her cabin at the grim news. Now Tony drove her home to Laurel Canyon, where they sat silently in the car.

"We did what we could," said Tony. "So did Porter."

"I didn't," said Janice.

"You did!" said Tony. She looked away, and moments passed before she spoke.

"I don't want to see you again," she said.

"Janice… why?"

"Two nights ago," said Janice. "When you looked in my eyes… I scare you, don't I? It's alright. I scare myself."

Her voice broke for only an instant. Tony thought of telling her about Bridget, whom he'd remembered that night as he held her, but didn't.

"I didn't believe Porter," said Janice. "Not entirely. I should have believed him."

"Janice," he said softly. "Please, let me help you. Good God! We have to help each other."

"I'll help myself… again," she said darkly, and got out of the car.

"Janice!" Tony called after her. She didn't answer him and went into the house. Tony, confused and exhausted, sat for some time in his car, then slowly drove away.

* * *

Late Monday night, Eve Devonshire Cromwell sat in her living room. The past two days, she'd had a cold sensation that bad news was coming… from California.

She'd sent Porter Down her phone number in her first letter to him. She desperately wished he'd call. Midnight passed. Eve knew she wouldn't sleep and stayed in the living room.

The grandfather clock chimed 12:30 A.M. A moment later, the phone rang.

* * *

That night, Tony barely slept. The song *Suzanne* kept playing in his head. He'd associated the song with Janice since meeting her, but now, as it refrained in his mind, he saw Janice's anguished face in the yacht cabin.

Come Tuesday morning, he tried calling her several times. No answer. He had to see her.

He arrived in Laurel Canyon to find boxes on Janice's porch. Then a woman he'd never seen before came out, carrying a folded stack of Janice's clothes.

"Is Janice here?" he asked. "My name's Tony Wyngate. She and I are friends."

"I'm her step-sister, Heather," said the woman. She was blonde, about four or five years older than Janice, wore a stylish yellow pants suit, and appeared upscale and impatient as she placed clothing in a box. "Janice phoned last night that she's in trouble, again. I flew down from Seattle this morning. I'm her only family now, so I get the honor."

"Where is she?" asked Tony, half up the steps.

"She's in a hospital," said Heather tartly. "She's been in and out of hospitals for years."

"But… she's strong," said Tony defensively. "All her investigations, the risks…"

"Yes, that's our Janice," said Heather. "She decides to save herself and the whole damn world, then she falls apart, and this shit starts all over again." She went back inside, returning with a stack of record albums, Judy Collins' *In My Life* on top. "I've called storage for a truck," said Heather. "I plan to be on my way home on the six P.M. plane."

Tony was silent. Since seeing the album, the song *Suzanne* was back in his head.

"She probably told you about her father's death, years ago," said Heather. "People move on from those things. Not our Janice."

"She never told me," said Tony. "Please, what hospital?"

"None of your business," said Heather. "And by the way… If you came for what's left of her cocaine… I've already found it and flushed it."

* * *

Tony was shocked. Although he'd sensed something seriously wrong after Janice's nightmare on the yacht, he'd never suspected drugs. The overnight trips she'd recently made, supposedly for investigation… were they for cocaine? Her acute guilt about the death of Cindy Conliffe… had it pushed her last night over the brink?

Tony walked down the steps, *Suzanne* mournfully playing in his mind. He stepped outside the gate, looking down the canyon, feeling loss and finality. He couldn't help her. She wouldn't let him.

It was time to go home.

46   The Funeral

The Cindy Conliffe funeral was to take place at Forest Lawn, Glendale, at 9:00 A.M. The morning was fair and warm.

The body of the child killed in what the press called "The Light Bearer Murder" rested in Forest Lawn's Tudor-style mortuary. Robert and Veronica Conliffe had selected a white coffin. For the viewing, their child wore her favorite dress, a pink one. Veronica, blonde like her daughter, stood by the coffin, touching Cindy's hands.

Robert and Veronica had placed two sprigs of pink roses on the casket. The card read, *We'll love you always, Cindy. Mommy and Daddy.*

The funeral would be private. Several photographers had scaled the gates hours previously, near the cemetery's swan lake. Porter Down, on guard at the cemetery all through the previous night, had routed them off the grounds. Besides his guilt at having failed to prevent this horror, and his sympathy for the heartbroken family, Porter was having a very bad week.

Today was the 40th anniversary of Mary's murder.

* * *

The Church of the Recessional, built in 1941, was a replica of a Scottish kirk with a steeple. The mourners were arriving, the men in somber suits, the women in dark dresses and hats. The funeral cortege only had to drive within Forest Lawn, the hearse transporting the casket from the mortuary to the church. It was an advantage this cemetery offered for family privacy.

228

The Conliffes rode in the limousine behind the hearse. All others went directly to the church. Jim O'Leary had offered to assist in an advisory capacity, despite his retirement—he'd supervised many major Los Angeles funerals in his day, including Jean Harlow's at Forest Lawn in 1937. There were four officers present from LAPD, four members of the cemetery's security staff, and Porter, who'd volunteered his services.

Porter wore his only suit, a blue double-breasted one. O'Leary knew about his friend's grief and the day's personal significance for him. He was worried.

* * *

The church filled quickly, quietly. Reporters arrived again, having defied cemetery security at the gate. O'Leary, Porter, and security men tried to eject the reporters as quietly as possible, to no avail. They knew fighting with them at this point, as the funeral cortege arrived, would only make things worse.

The six pallbearers, doctors who worked with Robert, carried the casket with its flowers from the hearse. Robert wore a dark blue suit, Veronica a veil and a black dress. The couple held hands as they followed the coffin to the open doors of the church, which was filled with the scent of flowers.

Porter, O'Leary, and the eight guards stood outside the church. Inside, the minister, a plump, bespectacled man, took his place on the altar, and a gray-haired woman began playing the piano aside it. As the pallbearers proceeded down the aisle, the Conliffes behind them, a young soprano, whose hair was as blonde as Veronica's and Cindy's and who wore a white choir robe, stood on the edge of the altar and began singing. The hymn was one the Conliffes had requested, *What Wondrous Love Is This, O My Soul.* The sadly pretty hymn dated to the early 19th century, and was often described as a "white spiritual:"

What wondrous love is this, O my soul, O my soul...
What wondrous love is this, that caused the Lord   of bliss,
To bear the dreadful curse, for my soul, for my soul...

Her voice was beautiful and several mourners began to cry. The pallbearers placed the casket at the foot of the altar. They filed into the left front pew, the family into the right. The soprano continued the hymn's several verses, and came to the final one:

And when from Death I'm free, I'll sing on, I'll sing on... .

And when from Death I'm free, I'll sing and joyful be.
And through Eternity, I'll sing on… I'll sing on…

As the soprano began reprising the final verse, she and the minister looked curiously toward the back of the church. There was a woman, dressed all in black, from hat to stockings to spiked heels, a crystal angel hanging from a chain around her neck, and she carried a bouquet of violets as she processed slowly down the aisle. The mourners, noting the faces of the soprano and minister, turned and saw the woman, her tall, willowy figure, her long red hair, and they whispered as she neared the casket.

The minister noticed the crystal angel and its red eyes, and the woman's honeysuckle scent. The soprano stopped singing, although the pianist continued. The long-missing Lizzie Hirsig placed her violets on the head of the small white coffin. Then she looked over at the Conliffe family, her yellow eyes very bright, and a tear ran down her cheek.

Veronica, knowing who this must be, screamed hysterically and covered her face.

Suddenly down the aisle came Porter Down, grabbing Lizzie by her arm, pulling her up the aisle and outside the church. The minister hurried to the family.

"Close the doors!" he called shrilly. "Close the doors!"

* * *

Reporters shouted outside the Church of the Recessional as the man suddenly emerged, dragging the woman behind him. Porter pulled Lizzie close to him, grabbing her by the shoulders. She was several inches taller than him in her heels, and he looked up into her wet eyes.

"I'll break your goddamn neck!" said Porter.

Lizzie lowered her face so close to Porter's that her lips almost touched his mouth. "Shouldn't you be someplace else today," she whispered, "crying over your dead wife?"

He threw her with all his might into the church's courtyard, past the cops who'd moved to arrest her at O'Leary's order. Then he charged her.

"Porter!" shouted O'Leary.

Two cops restrained Porter, handcuffing him. He looked up suspiciously at the church's steeple, as if determining that's where Lizzie had been hiding, then looked again at her. She was sprawled in the church's forecourt, her hat had fallen off, and as she put it back on, two other cops, aware she was a murder suspect, pulled her to her feet, locking her in handcuffs as well.

"I swear to God," shouted Porter at Lizzie, the police still restraining him, "next time I kill you, you'll *stay* goddamn dead!"

A TV cameraman, having filmed Porter making his promise, now focused on Lizzie, cuffed and standing stiffly by the police. She looked away from Porter, staring directly into the camera, tall, trembling, her eyes wet and bright, mascara running down her face. She wore the faint smile of a martyr. And suddenly, in an off-key, chillingly quavering voice, Lizzie sang, tearfully, defiantly, almost hysterically, the words from the hymn she'd heard in the church:

"And when from Death I'm free, I'll sing and joyful be.
And through Eternity, I'll sing on…
I'LL SING ON!"

Part Four – Valerie
September 25 to December 24, 1931

For the Sacred Wound that we marked
In the right hand of Our Lord Jesus...

For the Precious Wound that we marked
In the left hand of Our Lord Jesus...

For the Immaculate Wound that we marked
In the right foot of Our Lord Jesus...

For the Glorified Wound that we marked
In the left foot of Our Lord Jesus...

For the Blessed Wound that we marked
In the side of Our Lord Jesus ...
Adonai, Eternal Father,
Reconcile us with your Glorious Kingdom,
Amen.

– Devotional Prayer to the
Five Sacred Wounds of Jesus

47 Rudi

Ilsa had led her flock up on the mountain at Universal City at 2:00 A.M. The shepherdess had continued the night schedule due to the daily soaring heat.

It was a beautiful night and a coyote was baying at the nearly full moon. Ilsa, bracing the shotgun she carried each night to protect her sheep and lambs, looked out at the back lot below her. There was a new structure atop one of the hills—a windmill, full size, but with no vanes. It loomed in the moonlight, looking eerie and forlorn in Ilsa's eyes, and she'd heard it would be burned in *Frankenstein*.

The visit to the set of *Frankenstein*, almost a month ago, had stayed with her... almost haunted her. She still frightened herself, imagining Frankenstein and his Monster were in the hills, creeping ever-closer to her.

Then she smelled fire, and in the distance, near the ranch, she saw the flames.

* * *

Ilsa ran across the bridge over the ravine, the lambs and sheep following her. On a hillside near the ranch were five fires, surrounding what seemed a little altar, crudely made of logs and wood apparently stolen from the barn. On the altar was a young lamb. It had been gutted and its carcass was soaked in blood.

"Rudi," gasped Ilsa.

235

She recognized him by his size and markings. He'd been Ilsa's pet lamb. She'd watched his birth. He stayed close to her when they walked the sheep.

Her Uncle Johann and Aunt Vilma arrived in their nightclothes. Johann brandished his shotgun, roaring in anger, bitterly vowing to shoot the blasphemer. "This is an act of sacrilege," he said, weeping in anger. "Jesus was the Lamb of God!"

The sirens of the studio's fire department sounded, and Johann and Vilma looked toward the flashing lights of the trucks across the lot. Neither noticed Ilsa, in her lingering shock, moving between two of the fires, approaching the makeshift altar, touching her slaughtered lamb. In the firelight, she saw something circling Rudi's head. She removed it and held it up—a crown of thorns. She clenched her hand around the thorns, and her hand bled.

The shepherdess dropped the crown, looked up at the moon and screamed. The coyote in the hills mournfully howled with her, then became still.

Ilsa kept screaming.

48 Fifth Street

On Saturday morning, Porter Down had quietly informed several members of the *Frankenstein* company—Whale, Clive, Karloff, Jack Pierce and, at Colin's insistence, Eve—about the slaughtered lamb.

The studio front office, of course, forbade any of the *Frankenstein* company to talk about it at all. Porter knew the satanic ritual had been Valerie's spiteful response to his visit to her Abbey. He also realized that next time, the victim might not be an animal.

* * *

As the date neared for Bonnie Bristeaux to travel east for the *Vanities*, she'd worried about leaving Eve. This Saturday afternoon, Bonnie, her concern rising, visited Eve at Universal City. She brazenly crashed the 4:00 P.M. tea break on the *Frankenstein* set, sitting on Karloff's lap as they sang "Tea for Two" to each other. Whale, a tower of doom today, eventually had an assistant order Bonnie to leave the set.

"See you back at Beachwood, Evie," said Bonnie. She was aware work would probably go late—the film had been scheduled to finish today, but probably had another week of shooting. Bonnie blew a kiss at Whale and made a flouncing exit.

Work did go late into the night. A full moon arose over Universal. Whale finally dismissed the company near midnight. Colin wasn't on call Monday and Tuesday when the company was set to shoot the Flower Game scene at Malibou Lake. Eve, realizing she wouldn't see him again until Wednesday, and having not spoken with him all day, headed for the gate, escorted by a member of studio security, all of whom were now more in evidence.

"Evie." It was Colin's voice, calling sharply to her. "Will you take a ride with me? There's something you must see."

* * *

Dinettes designed like a namesake animal were a Hollywood craze, and the Eat-at-the-Pig was a sheet-metal eyesore, erected to resemble a jolly, squatting pig. Waitresses stood in the smiling mouth as they took orders for ham sandwiches. Customers sat beside the giant pig at picnic tables under umbrellas. Colin drove up in his open coupe, Eve beside him.

"Come inside," Colin said. Eve did. He asked for the proprietor, who came to the counter. "How much," asked Colin, "for all the ham in the shop?"

"There's at least $50 of prime pig here," said the proprietor.

Clive opened his wallet. "I'll add a tenner for the bread and soda pop. Fair?"

"Hell, yeah," said the proprietor. Two waitresses immediately wrapped up the ham. Colin took the food and a case of Coca-Cola and Eve carried the accompanying bag of condiments.

"Come, Missy," said Clive to Eve. "You best escape this nasty porker's mouth before he takes a bite out of you." They placed the food and drink in the roadster's rumble seat.

"Where are we going?" demanded Eve.

"You'll see."

He put the top up on the coupe and they drove into downtown Los Angeles. Eve thought Colin might be heading toward the theatre district, with its towering, well-lit movie houses, such as the Orpheum Theatre and the United Artists Theatre, for a late showing. Why he'd bought all the food remained a mystery.

"Colin, I'm hardly in the mood for a movie," said Eve.

"No movie, my dear," said Colin tensely. "More of a play, really."

He turned east onto Fifth Street.

* * *

Within moments, it was as if they were in a different city. The sidewalks and buildings were dark and seedy. Derelicts stretched out on the streets. There was garbage on the curbs and the air was foul as Colin parked the car by a dimly lit building. Eve looked toward an alley and thought she saw small, faint lights. Then she realized they weren't lights.

They were eyes.

"Put up your window and lock your door," ordered Colin. He got out and went inside the building. Eve saw the sign above the front doors:

The Midnight Mission

A moment later a man came outside with Colin, helping him unload the food and drink, leaving the doors open. Several unshaven, shabbily dressed men gathered, drawn by the sight of the expensive car and the rich aroma of the surprise feast. More figures emerged from the darkness and a procession came from the alleys. Colin got back in the car.

"I welcome you," he said to Eve, "to what you Yanks sportingly refer to as, 'Skid Row.'"

Still, they came, some old, some surprisingly young… all ages. Their faces were gaunt and they seemed lost, almost spectral, snaking down the sidewalk. Eve saw two women, holding hands in the shadows, slowly, silently insinuating their place in the line. A wizened man, almost doubled over and leaning on a crutch, hobbled across the street and fought them for a place.

"Why are you showing me this?" asked Eve.

"It was, I believe, John Bradford, of the 16th century's Church of England," said Colin, his voice fiercely self-mocking, "who professed, 'There, but for the grace of God, go I.' He said it in the Tower of London, watching fellow prisoners go to their executions." He paused.   "Eventually, Bradford burned at the stake too."

There was a rustle from the crowd… somebody had closed the Midnight Mission doors. The feast had ended. There was a wail from those still outside and several of the unfed banged at the door, cursing and shouting.

Colin pulled away. The tail end of the crowd directed its anger at the departing car and somebody threw an empty bottle. It smashed to pieces against the still-open rumble seat.

* * *

It was only as they reached Beachwood Drive that Eve finally spoke. "Colin... .please let me help you..."

"No!" he snapped. "It was a shoddy thing Jimmy did to you, and I was a beast for letting him do it.... making you my keeper." He took an envelope from his coat pocket. "Here," he said. "Take this money, leave this wretched town, and forget you ever saw the sight of me."

She threw the envelope back at him, got out of the car and slammed the door. Colin reversed the car and sped down Beachwood. Eve sat on the rim of the small fountain by the gate. She was crying and didn't want to go inside and risk Bonnie seeing her this upset. A truck pulled up and parked on the opposite side of the street. Porter Down got out.

"Are you alright, Miss?" he asked.

"Yes," said Eve, still crying.

He approached within a few yards of her. "I've been keeping an eye on Mr. Clive," he said. "It seemed a good idea to follow as he headed with you to that not-so-nice part of town."

"Thank you," said Eve. She removed a handkerchief from her purse, wiped her eyes and tried to compose herself. "You have to understand," she said, ashamed and defensive. "Colin's had tragedy in his life. Things that haunt him... torment him. And as for his drinking... well, once someone becomes addicted, it's very hard for them to stop."

Porter was silent. "When you feel better, Miss," he said after a moment, "I'll walk you to your door."

49

A Day At the Beach

Learning how devastated Eve had been by Saturday night's drive with Colin, Bonnie took her the next day on the long trolley ride to Santa Monica Beach. They put on bathing suits, swam in the ocean, then lay on a towel together, both looking up at the cloudless blue sky.

"It's funny," said Bonnie. "Ask a girl in Montana about Hollywood, and she'll gush that it's an all-night orgy. You come here and everyone tells you it's just a factory town, nobody has time to party, the Babylon stuff is all hooey. Then you're here for a while, get around …and realize it's a lot uglier than that Montana girl could ever imagine in her wildest dreams."

Eve was silent. "I'll miss you when you go," she said finally. "I still know so little about you. Want to play '20 Questions'?"

"Make it three," said Bonnie.

"What did your family do in Montana?"

"They raised pigs and treated me like one. Next question."

"Were they excited that you went to Hollywood?"

"They didn't care, as long as I left Montana."

"Isn't Myrna Loy from Montana?"

"She's from Helena. I'm from Butte. And that was your third question."

A beach ball bounced near them. A young man ran to get it, exchanged grins with Bonnie and Eve, then strutted away. "Betcha he's fat and bald in five years," said Bonnie. "Anyway, my turn. Do you ever hear from *your* parents?"

"I'd rather not play the game," said Eve.

241

"That's not fair," chided Bonnie. "I did."

"Well," said Eve. "My father's dead. My mother's remarried."

"Your father must have died young."

"He was only 45."

Bonnie paused. "What killed him?" she asked.

Eve looked out at the ocean. "He drank," she said.

50   The Windmill

"Action!"

The *Frankenstein* company was working for the second day on the shore of Malibou Lake. James Whale, in beret and sunglasses, watched Karloff's Monster and seven-year-old Marilyn Harris, "Little Maria," play the flower game. She threw hers into the lake, and he laughed in joy, tossing his flowers, watching them float. When he was out of flowers, the Monster picked up the child and, in his bewilderment, threw *her* into the lake. Several men in row boats, outside camera range, fetched the child.

"Throw her in again!" screamed Marilyn's hysterically-excited stage mother. "*Farther!*"

"I say, Jimmy," said Karloff, lighting a cigarette, "may we *please* discuss this again?"

* * *

Eve, off Tuesday as *Frankenstein* continued shooting at the lake, stayed close to home. Late in the day, a secretary called from Universal. Eve was to report for night shooting. She was surprised, as she knew the company had been on location these past two hot days. They all must be exhausted, especially Boris.

"Shooting will be on the back lot," said the secretary cheerfully.

* * *

243

The night was cold. A bonfire was burning. The villager extras surrounded it, dipping into cauldrons of smoking hot coffee. A pack of bloodhounds stood by.

"Hi, Eve." She turned and saw Jack Pierce. She also saw Karloff sitting in his striped beach chair, the tip of his cigarette burning in the darkness. He raised his hand and nodded. Then she saw Colin, his long polo coat over his costume, his hat pulled down over one eye. He was, per the script, wearing riding boots. "Hello, Evie," he said gently, almost shyly, and passed her.

"Listen, Evie" said Pierce confidentially. "Whale's goin' crazy. Out at Malibou Lake the past two days. See, Boris fought about throwin' the little girl into the lake. Didn't wanna' do it. He felt the Monster and little girl should just be friends."

"I like the idea," said Eve.

"Everybody did! We all sided with Boris….we got really upset about it! Whale finally says, 'It's all part of the *ritual*.' What the hell does *that* mean?"

"So they did it Jimmy's way?"

"Yeah, but Whale hates to be questioned! And he's scared, too, about this film becoming a white elephant. It's burnin' him up."

Suddenly there were headlights and a limousine arrived. James Whale emerged, wearing a long waistcoat, beret and an air of icy arrogance.

"Frankenstein, Monster, and villagers!" Whale commanded, instantly taking charge. "The scene… the Monster has attacked Frankenstein and is carrying him over his shoulder up the hill to the windmill. The villagers are in pursuit with their torches and bloodhounds. All of you run as swiftly as possible… am I clear?"

The extras lit their torches. Floodlights lit up the hill. Colin tossed off his hat and polo coat. "Action!" shouted Whale.

Boris, Colin over his shoulder, ran up the steep hill to the vaneless windmill, the torch-bearing villagers and barking bloodhounds chasing him. Karloff ran in his heavy boots carrying Colin, breathlessly managing to reach the mill just before the dogs.

"Cut!" shouted Whale shrilly. "Again!"

At midnight, almost two hours later, the *Frankenstein* company was shooting the exact same scene… for the 13th time.

* * *

A full moon had risen over the windmill. A coyote howled in the hills and the bloodhounds barked and yelped, wanting to pursue it. Eve stood by the bonfire, watching Boris hoist Colin on his back again.

"Action!" cried Whale.

"So, this is the price Boris pays for challenging the almighty," said Eve.

"It was a problem already," said Pierce quietly. "Whale's a goddamn egomaniac. Boris is winning all the attention on this picture, and Whale hates Boris for it. Boris is tough, but God! I've never seen an actor suffer like this. I tell ya,' Whale's going crazy."

Karloff had again outraced the dogs. "Again!" shouted Whale into a megaphone.

The extras groaned. Colin ran down the hill ahead of Karloff. "I say, Jimmy! Can't Boris carry a dummy for these shots? You'll break his back this way!"

"Don't tell me my bloody business," snarled Whale. "Get in place again. *Now!*"

* * *

The sadism waged almost all night. As they prepared for yet another take, Eve, her tolerance exhausted, walked defiantly past the director.

"Is Miss Devonshire leaving us?" sniped Whale.

"Go to Hell," said Eve.

Suddenly, Whale's limousine revved up. The uniformed chauffeur, sitting by the fire, jumped as the car took off and stopped beside Eve. A man in a peasant hat with the brim pulled down looked at Eve from the driver's window.

"Get in!" he ordered. The man was Porter Down.

She instinctively jumped in the back and the director's limo took off, the chauffeur in futile pursuit. The extras roared with laughter. Whale watched, a hand on one hip, as the car drove away.

"Print takes 1, 5 and 12," Whale called out so all could hear him. "Good night."

* * *

They reached the area near Universal's front gate. Porter jumped out of the limo, tossed his peasant coat and hat on a bench, opened Eve's door, and walked her to his truck.

"This was kind of you," said Eve.

"I'll be even kinder," said Porter. "Wanna' go to my favorite place in L.A.?"

* * *

Eve expected a diner or speakeasy. Instead, Porter drove south to Hancock Park, arriving at dawn. She instinctively trusted him as they walked toward an area that looked foreboding and abandoned, even within its city setting. She smelled tar.

"Welcome to the Rancho La Brea Tar Pits," said Porter.

"Your favorite place in Los Angeles?" she asked, amused.

Porter nodded. Mist rose from the pools of black, gurgling tar. "Don't fall in," he said, holding her arm more tightly as they began walking over makeshift bridges. They stopped halfway across one of the bridges and he pointed down at the bubbling pools.

"They were all here," said Porter. "Wooly mammoths. Dire Wolves. And my favorite, the saber tooth tiger… or, as the scientists call him, *Smilodon Californicus*."

Eve looked down into the smoky blackness. "It's sad, isn't it?"

"Yeah," he said. "It's sad."

The early morning's purple light streaked the pools. They walked a bit more and Eve looked at the bizarre site, the smoky pits ominously fascinating, even oddly beautiful. She stood beside Porter Down, and for now, felt strangely safe.

51

Protection

Frankenstein had resumed shooting Wednesday at 5:00 P.M., following an Academy-dictated 12-hour rest period after the all-night work on the back lot.

Clive and Karloff acted on the windmill interiors, recreated on a soundstage. Undeniable tension was in the air, a residue of Whale's sadism the previous night, but the company worked quietly and professionally, defying the physical and emotional exhaustion. They'd be on call basically around the clock the next days to finish the picture, and as such, Colin and Karloff had moved into their back lot bungalows.

Eve reported on time. At 7:00 P.M. there was a break. Colin took his tea and sat alone in a corner. Whale signaled Eve that he wished to speak to her. They went outside.

"Your presence at this point is only adding to Colin's problems," he said, formally but not coldly. "Don't report for the last days of the shoot. Your salary will continue and there's no need to come to the studio at all until after the picture has wrapped."

He turned and went back inside the soundstage. Eve headed for the gate, determined not to cry, but failed. Lt. O'Leary came from around the corner.

"What's wrong, Miss Devonshire?" he asked gently.

247

"Nothing," fibbed Eve.

"May I buy you a cup of coffee?" asked O'Leary.

* * *

They drove down to Hollywood Boulevard, where O'Leary escorted Eve into a small restaurant with a European décor. The owners knew him and cordially sat him and Eve by a burning fireplace. Neither wanted food. Both ordered coffee.

Eve warmed to the man—his gentle voice, his kind, bespectacled eyes. They small-talked, sipped their coffee, and enjoyed the warmth of the fire.

"Do you have a family, Lieutenant?"

O'Leary took out his wallet, proudly displaying pictures of his wife and two daughters.

"They're all lovely," said Eve sincerely. "I'm sure they worry about you."

"They're brave," O'Leary smiled, placing the wallet back in his pocket.

"Does... Porter Down have a family?" Eve asked.

"He used to," said O'Leary.

"Mr. Down has been kind too," Eve said self-consciously. The fire crackled beside them. "Tell me more about him," said Eve.

"Quite a fella," said O'Leary. "War hero—Lafayette Escadrille—but you probably know that. I met him in Chicago... on temporary assignment in '26. The beer wars were at full blast and Porter was workin' undercover. Very dangerous. He had a wife. Mary. Lovely young lady."

"Please," asked Eve. "What happened?"

O'Leary, uncomfortable with the question, was too polite to reject it entirely. "Porter was bustin' beer and narcotics dealers. One night, while he was out, somebody got into their apartment... and killed Mary."

O'Leary didn't tell Eve that the killer had shot a narcotics needle into Mary's thigh, where a lot of addicts injected, to make it appear she was using dope.

"Did they find who killed her?" asked Eve.

"Porter did." O'Leary didn't tell her that, before Porter killed the man, he'd made him confess his crime and broken the killer's arms and legs.

"After that tragedy," said O'Leary, "Porter sunk into a deep depression. I talked him into coming to California... thinkin' the change might help, that he might do well as a Hollywood troubleshooter. He knows this is a factory town. For every star who gets in trouble, dozens of folks lose their jobs. This Depression's a bad time to find a new one. Anyway, when he gets back, please don't tell him I told you any of this. I must be bone tired, else I wouldn't be jawin' this way."

The fire in the hearth was mostly embers. Eve thought of Porter… how she'd presumed to say to him a few nights ago that he couldn't imagine the torment that Colin was suffering. Somehow, he was bearing his own tragedy and helping others, despite having been nearly destroyed by his wife Mary's murder.

"Miss Devonshire," said Lt. O'Leary softly, "If you'd like, I'll drive you home now."

"Thank you," said Eve. "And when you see Mr. Down, please tell him…"

"What, ma'am?"

"Nothing," said Eve.

52

Fire

Late Friday night at Universal City, James Whale was directing the fiery finale of *Frankenstein*, Monster and Monster Maker fighting on the parapet of the hilltop windmill.

The creature had tossed Frankenstein (a dummy) from the parapet and, as originally filmed, his death. The villagers had set the windmill afire with their torches, the Monster screamed in agony, the blazing windmill collapsed (its burning vanes to be added later by special effects), and smoke curled into the black sky.

"A wrap!" cried Jimmy Whale, almost at the stroke of midnight. The company cheered. Universal's fire engines, their red lights swirling, went into action, their hoses spraying over the burning windmill ruins. Colin sat in his canvas chair, his polo coat draped over his shoulders against the cold night, lighting a cigarette, watching the fire. Whale made a beeline to Colin and shook his hand.

"Only a few pick-up shots tomorrow, old boy," he said to Colin. "Relax now. You've been magnificent."

"Isn't Eve here?" he asked Whale.

"I've told you, Colin," said Whale. "I dismissed Eve. Remember?"

"Yes," said Colin, "But I thought, perhaps..." His voice trailed off.

Lt. O'Leary was on special assignment and had been unable to get LAPD to approve police protection tonight. Porter was elsewhere. Whale observed the two overweight emigres that studio security had assigned to

250

flank Colin until the movie's completion tomorrow.
Bavarian Keystone Kops, thought Whale.

* * *

At Malibou Lake, the Black Mass was reaching its climax, the Calvary finale.

Valerie hung on the cross in her loincloth, body makeup, and crown of thorns. She was dripping in the prop blood that had become increasingly gory in recent performances and tonight streamed down her anguished face and nearly-naked body.

"I thirst…"

A few moments later, the performance ended to gasps, screams, and finally wild applause. She took her curtain call without her usual robe and, as always, holding a lily.

"I thank you," she said breathlessly standing before the audience, looking as if she'd come from the slaughterhouse. "And I must regretfully tell you, my disciples, that this will be the final Black Mass for perhaps some time…maybe forever."

The audience groaned and Valerie raised her arms for silence.

"For reasons I can't reveal tonight, the Motion Picture Industry, the Los Angeles Catholic Diocese, and the Police Department have viciously targeted me. My friends… my life is in danger."

The audience responded in shock. She raised her arms again, her emotion rising. "They are preparing, in their own way, really and truly… to *crucify me!*"

The crowd roared in rage. "As most of you know, of course, I'm merely an actress. Meanwhile, in a horrid act of savagery and hypocrisy, there is a major Hollywood studio, protecting this very night a star who actually *is* an addict, a Satanist, and a lunatic… likely only days or nights away from committing a shocking, ritualistic murder!"

The audience, awed by her passion, shouted out for the name of this star. Valerie stood breathlessly still and raised her arms for silence. Only when it was totally still did she speak again and as she did so, she began tearing apart the lily.

"Perhaps you've heard the rumor of animal sacrifice during a full moon at a certain back lot in Hollywood. This is no rumor. This is a fact, suppressed by a Motion Picture Industry who genuflects before the demonic god of money and power!"

The crowd was nearly hysterical, and Valerie was crying now, her tears streaming down her face with the prop blood.

"They have cast me as the scapegoat in the horror to come!" she cried, shredding the remains of the lily. "So, strange as it sounds coming from me, pray. In my agony, my Gethsemane, pray for me. Please, my friends... pray for me!"

The tower of fire erupted behind her. The crowd cheered her. Valerie stood trembling, her arms stretched at her side, as if both crucified and embracing the audience. Her eyes were wild as she stared back at the entrance of the tent.

Porter Down stood there, arms folded, staring back at her.

* * *

With only pickups scheduled for tomorrow, the *Frankenstein* company informally celebrated in the Universal commissary—the official "wrap party" would come later. Those present were mostly the technical crew and the extras who'd played the posse of villagers. Colin, having changed from his costume, arrived about 12:30 A.M. and shook a few hands.

"Isn't Eve here?" he asked several people. He seemed lost.

He didn't remove his hat and polo coat and soon left the commissary, the Laemmle émigré cops tagging behind him. He promptly offered each man $50 to go away and leave him the hell alone. The money was almost double their weekly salaries. Colin paid them cash from his wallet and they instantly skedaddled.

He walked along the back lot. Smoke was still rising from the windmill ruins atop the hill. A coyote howled and another answered it. Colin Clive, Movie Star... Damn it to Hell! He was, he knew, actually just a bottle away from being a drunken, gibbering geek in a sideshow... maybe only a few years away from being locked up in an asylum, like his uncle.... .

He bloody well needed a drink. He couldn't last this night without one. He knew that Junior Laemmle lavishly indulged his little brunette paramour, actress Sidney Fox, and rumor claimed Junior stocked her studio bungalow with bootleg liquor...

He reached Miss Fox's dark bungalow, breaking a window, then smashing it. He climbed in, cutting his hand on the broken glass, fearful of turning on lights, possibly alarming security, fumbling in the darkness, finally switching on a light as he searched for bottles. There was an entire case of them.... .

* * *

An hour later, Porter Down, alarmed by Valerie's announcement at the Black Mass and figuring she'd cast Colin Clive as her monster on the loose, found him passed out in Sidney Fox's bungalow. He placed him in Miss Fox's bed, telephoned for a doctor whom he could trust to keep his mouth shut, and closed the bungalow curtains.

53 Interim

Wednesday, October 7: To Eve Devonshire, Universal City seemed a ghost town.

James Whale was sequestered in a screening room, determining if *Frankenstein* required any retakes. Boris Karloff had checked off the lot, awaiting word if Universal would sign him to a long-term contract. If *Frankenstein* proved a hit, the contract would surely follow. If the film was a disaster as some feared, his career might be in ruins.

As for Colin Clive... the actor had rallied to complete a few *Frankenstein* pickup shots on Saturday, but Porter Down had rushed him out of town immediately afterwards. It had been Porter's idea that Colin spend the next week at Lake Arrowhead and then a second week at Palm Springs, far away from L.A. and any frame-up Valerie Le Fay had planned for him. He gently explained all this to Eve and added that Colin was accompanied by a male nurse of Porter's acquaintance named Karl Stevens, a cordial, strapping young man who'd be with Colin day and night. If the studio needed Colin for any retakes, he could be back in town within several hours.

Meanwhile Eve, not assigned to another film, spent the day doing cheesecake poses for Universal Christmas publicity.

* * *

Thursday, October 8: Bonnie Bristeaux, worried about Eve and how heartbroken she'd been by the recent events, sent a telegram cancelling her contract for the *Vanities* in the east. She'd tell Eve that the management dumped her, as Eve would surely raise Cain if she knew the truth. After sending the telegram, Bonnie took the trolley to the Ruth Pruitt Agency office on Vine Street, broke the news, and tolerated the wrath of Ruth.

"Anyway, I'm available again for movie work," she said to Ruth, "and for jumping out of cakes."

* * *

Monday, October 12: Fr. Harry Burke had been busy at Malvern, sending letters and telegrams to follow up on the packet of pornographic pictures he'd received from his tormenter in California the previous month. He desperately tried to persuade his superiors in the Roman Catholic hierarchy to allow him to take all necessary action against the danger that potentially existed.

This day, a return telegram came from Geel, Belgium. Its content was both enlightening and deeply disturbing. The same day, he received a letter from Los Angeles, written by an investigator named Porter Down. Fr. Burke was surprised that the man had learned of his identity, location, and the Department of Ascetic Investigations.

* * *

Tuesday, October 13: Colin Clive was in Palm Springs, shadowed day and night by Karl Stevens, both staying in a whitewashed adobe house on a mountainside. He and Karl passed the time playing golf and tennis.

This night he sat by the pool, thinking of Eve, wanting to talk to her, to know she was well. Colin went inside, dialed the phone, then hung up before it rang, returning to his chair by the pool, looking at the stars over the desert.

* * *

Wednesday, October 14: Universal announced that *Frankenstein's* delayed "wrap party" would take place Monday night, October 19, at "Dias

Dorados," the Laemmle home in Benedict Canyon. It was one of the cinema colony's most spectacular estates, with pools, fountains, ponds and, like Universal itself, its own zoo.

Eve learned she was to be part of the entertainment.

Universal's publicity department had noted that Dwight Frye, the hunchbacked Fritz in *Frankenstein*, had performed in musical comedy on Broadway. The plan: Frye and six Universal starlets—Eve among them—would perform a song, "The Monster's Hiding Under Your Bed Tonight!" dashed off by the studio's Music department. The ladies would dance, wearing black cat costumes, complete with tails, while Frye sang the song.

The first rehearsal took place today on Universal's "Phantom Stage," built for 1925's *The Phantom of the Opera*, that had starred the late Lon Chaney. Frye showed up looking very dapper, in light suit and hair parted off-center. Eve had never seen him without his hump. He was cordial, soft-spoken, and personally introduced himself to each of the chorines. A breezy choreographer arrived and took charge, gathering the group around a piano, explaining the number.

"And get this, Dwight," he said. "You'll sing the song wearing your hunchback costume... but with a straw hat and a cane!"

Frye's face suddenly transfixed into a blend of Renfield from *Dracula* and Fritz from *Frankenstein*. "I'll do *what?*" he demanded.

* * *

Thursday, October 15: This morning, a mailman delivered a package to Luke's Marina, addressed to Porter Down.

David Belasco's office in New York City had finally sent him a program of Belasco's final production, *Mima*. Porter had surmised, based on dates, that if Valerie had actually acted for Belasco, it would have been in that extravaganza. He sat on the trawler, tore open the envelope, turned to the program's cast list. He'd expected little, since he figured Valerie had changed her name since 1928/1929, but then noticed something else in the featured players list:

Alfons, the Spider... .Dwight Frye

Frye... the hunchback in *Frankenstein*. And who, Porter knew, was working at Universal today, rehearsing for the party. Porter was aware of this because Eve was there, and he'd been keeping track of her whereabouts day and night.

Porter took the program, along with a recent publicity portrait of Valerie Le Fay, basically as herself. He jumped in a pickup truck and headed to Universal City.

* * *

The decision had been quickly made—by Frye—that he would not sing and dance as a hunchback, but as himself. He, Eve, and the other five chorines were all bucking and winging as Porter Down entered the Phantom Stage.

"Time out," Porter shouted. The pianist stopped playing. Porter asked Frye and Eve to join him outside the soundstage. "Mr. Frye," said Porter, holding up the *Mima* program, "I see you were in this play."

"Why, yes!" said Frye proudly. "For the late Mr. David Belasco. And featured with Miss Lenore Ulric."

Porter was about to ask another question, but Frye was off to the races.

"It was a racy rewrite of Molnar's *The Red Mill*. Mima, a 'synthetic she-devil,' as the script described her, was created in Hell and sent to seduce Janos, the hero of the play."

"I see," said Porter, "but what I want to ask is... ."

"Mr. Belasco was 75-years-old when he produced and directed *Mima*," said Frye. "He was called 'the Bishop of Broadway,' and dressed the role in real-life, wearing a black suit and clerical collar. Anyway, *Mima* was a *spectacular* production! It boasted a full orchestra, a huge cast, and a magnificent set that apocalyptically collapsed in fire at the climax—only to be easily reassembled, via Mr. Belasco's wizardry, for the next performance. *Mima* cost the staggering sum of $325,000!"

"Who did you play in *Mima*?" asked Eve politely.

"I played 'Alfons, the Spider,' Mima's procurer, shall we say," said Frye. He grinned as if what he was about to say was very naughty. "Mima had a wonderful line she said to me: 'Every time you kiss my hand, you bite me.'"

Eve laughed. Frye went on, thrilled that someone in Hollywood was expressing interest in his New York stage career.

"The play ran about six months," said Frye, "but could never recoup its expenses. It cost Mr. Belasco his fortune. He died last May, you know."

Now Porter held up a photo of Valerie. "Do you recognize this woman?"

Frye looked carefully at the picture. "Why, yes," he said. "She's Valerie Ivy, one of the most remarkable actresses I've ever known. She was in *Mima's* ensemble as a Tango dancer in 'The Dance of the Damned.' She was also Miss Ulric's understudy... and almost went on."

"Almost?" asked Porter.

"Miss Ulric developed laryngitis," said Frye. "Valerie was quickly fitted for all the beautiful costumes. I rehearsed with her—she was funny, harrowing, and heartbreaking, precisely what the role called for. But only moments after her entrance..."

"What, Mr. Frye?" snapped Porter. "It's very important you tell me."

"She had an epileptic seizure," said Frye reluctantly. "It was ghastly to behold, for the players and audience. Mr. Belasco cancelled the performance. Such a terrible shame. Had Miss Ivy performed that night, I believe she'd have become an overnight star."

"Belasco fired her?" asked Porter.

Frye paused. "Yes."

"You didn't see this woman visiting the *Frankenstein* set?" asked Porter.

"Mr. Frye wasn't on call the day she was there," interjected Eve.

"You haven't heard or read anything about 'Saint Valerie'?" asked Porter. "And the Black Mass she performs at Malibou Lake?"

"I have no interest in such things," said Frye. "I'm a Christian Scientist."

"That's all, Mr. Frye," said Porter. "Thank you."

"You're very welcome," said Frye. "I'm glad to have been of help."

* * *

"It all fits," said Porter to Eve. "She went from *Mima*, in late '28 or early '29, to a dope-addicted circus snake lady by the summer of '30. She's bitter about her illness and failure as an actress and hates Hollywood because she knows she'll never be anything but a freak show devil priestess. There's her motivation... or one of them. Somehow, I get the impression there's more to all of this. Something... sacrilegious. Something... ."

"Demonic?" asked Eve.

Porter looked at her, his eyes intense.

"I'll do everything I can to help you," promised Eve.

54 Relics

Two years ago, she'd traveled over 3,600 miles to steal a relic.
A tooth. Maybe a finger.
Relics. They could be, she knew, tiny splinters, such as those of the Cross. They could be skulls. Saint Agnes, like Saint Dymphna, was a beheaded teenage virgin martyr, and her skull gawked at the faithful in a church in Rome. Saint Barbara, also beheaded—and like Dymphna, by her father—had a shrine in Kiev, where a portion of Barbara's skull was on display.

Agnes and Barbara—two tortured, decapitated, teenage female virgin martyr saints, their severed skulls still packin' 'em in.

As for Dymphna… her bones were in the gold and silver reliquary she'd seen that night on the altar in Belgium, solemnly enshrined in a protective glass case, reverently flanked by votive candles. At any rate, she'd only wanted a little relic.

A bone. Maybe just a piece of one.
Tonight, she stood on a platform, jutting from the hatchway atop the Abbey's silo, watching the lightning over the hills and lake, looking up into the rain, letting it soak her face. She sat down on the platform's edge, yanking her yellow work dress almost to her hips, so the rain drenched her thighs and long, dangling legs. She wore her black circus hat, her hair flowing in wet tresses under it, and her red-eyed angel hung around her neck. Having had a severe seizure that day—they were coming more frequently now—she stank of sweat and sickness. She wore nothing under

259

her dress and could smell herself:

There's hell, there's darkness, there's the sulphurous pit, she smiled.

Valerie thought of her past as a five-act melodrama. The title of Act I: *Mima.*

Curtain up. She saw herself that snowy night in New York, alone in the backstage shadows, a 29-year-old virgin who passionately desired to be a great actress. Tonight, she had her chance to show the world her talent. As Lenore Ulric's understudy, she was going to portray the title role in place of the ailing star. Mima, the "Supreme Siren," as the script described her, created in the foundry of Hell with two hearts, "one madly loving, one cruel and cunning," and dispatched to seduce the world's most moral man.

Beauty embodied, Sin incarnate... , all-hailed the script.

Since she was much taller than Miss Ulric, Valerie had her own specially-designed costumes, and for her entrance, she wore a long, diaphanous white gown, revealing the darkness of her nipples and pubic area beneath it. Miss Ulric wore wigs throughout the performance, but Valerie flaunted her own long, red hair... and her "Mima" evoked a wanton, Pre-Raphaelite angel.

Amy, one of her fellow Tango dancers in the "Dance of the Damned," had given her a small bouquet of violets for luck before disappearing downstairs. She saw herself clutching the bouquet... whispering a prayer to Saint Dymphna. The priest and the nuns at the orphanage had told her about Dymphna when Valerie was a child, and had ordered her to pray to the Saint because of their shared illness.

Saint Dymphna...be my holy protector tonight...

She heard the orchestra tuning up... and suddenly beheld before her, in his ecclesiastical garb, the white-haired Belasco.

"Your whole life will change after this night, my child," said Belasco, as if bestowing a blessing, and she smiled shyly in his august presence, giving a small curtsey.

"Places!" came the announcement. She was terrified, but knew that in less than three hours, as the set crashed and collapsed in smoke and fire, she'd say her death scene lines:

My two hearts... how they ache... Janos... Janos.

The orchestra thundered. The curtain rose. There was the grand procession of devils and imps, to hallowed satanic hymns. Valerie, in her translucent robe, entered as Mima, atop a ramp stage center... the heavenly glow of the lights.... the deep darkness of the audience...

This is my night of nights… what I've always dreamed of…

Then the lightning struck her head. For only a moment she was aware she was falling, rolling down the ramp, hearing the audience's screams. She awoke backstage, flat on the floor, her gown torn and fetid, blood trickling from her mouth. A doctor knelt beside her. Belasco stood God-like at her feet.

"Epilepsy," said the doctor.

"Miss Ivy, you never told me," said Belasco.

She stifled a sob. Saint Dymphna had ignored her…betrayed her.

Two men in white medical uniforms hoisted her onto a canvas stretcher. Amy, who'd brought the violets, tearfully handed them back to Valerie. The men carried her to the ambulance in the alley, where snow, mixed with ice, stung her face. Everything was deathly silent.

Valerie Ivy, the violets in her folded hands, felt as if she were being borne to her grave… and wished she were.

Blackout. Curtain. Intermission. Then lights and curtain up again.

Act II: The Angel Amulet.

The time: Three months after Act I. Valerie saw herself hiding in a shrine in Belgium determined to steal a relic of Saint Dymphna. She meant it reverently. The priests taught that God sometimes punished and degraded us only to bring us closer to Him. Perhaps Saint Dymphna had done the same to her? Yes, she believed she had. Yet there was also an emotion of rage as the saint's feast arrived at midnight on May 15, 1929, and Valerie dared to approach the altar and the reliquary. The starlight through the stained-glass windows… the perfume of the burning votive candles… the night bird that suddenly cawed and had caused her to cry out. Her futile attempt to hammer to pieces the glass case that refused to shatter, the blows echoing throughout the church…

"HEXE! SAKRILEG!"

It was the priest, old, stocky, his arms strong, shoving her against the altar wall, she taller than he, instinctively grabbing at his throat, her hands entwining in the chain of an amulet he wore around his neck. The priest clutching his chest, collapsing to the floor. She running, falling in the garden, crawling toward the bushes to hide. Something was in her hand… . the chain from around the priest's neck, and it held a crystal figure…

AN ANGEL!

Barely three inches long, willowy, beautiful, seemingly glowing in the moonlight, transfiguring as she held it, so lovely, so incandescent that it made Valerie cry. There was a wing broken away, possibly during the struggle with the priest, and she gently touched the area, wishing she could heal it, talking into the angel's eyes... two tiny red pinpoints.

"*You're* my relic," she whispered, as if an epiphany, her eyes wet, her teeth bared. "My own little *Saint Dymphna!*"

Holy, triumphant, discordant music. Curtain. Intermission. Back to the present, to the storm. Valerie pulled the dress up higher, over her naked hips, letting the rain run over her, but the stinking scent was stronger, and then came...

Act III: Valerie, the Voluptuous Viper.

July, 1930. There she was, in the pit. It had been a gruesome 14 months since she'd returned from Belgium. Drugs. Alcohol. Degradation of all variety. Now she was at very bottom—a geek in the circus—where there were snakes crawling on her... there were yokels gaping at her.

Later, there'd be the roustabout raping her.

And there was her angel amulet, her Saint Dymphna, hanging on a chain around her neck through it all.

The rain... the craving for her needle... and her scream. Her wild, passionate, crazy, spine-tingling, lost soul scream. A tortured demon's howl, a wild animal's shriek, an insane whore's climax. Agony, horror... all enjoyed by the yokels, because the screamer herself was, after all, only a freak.

She'd imitated the scream as Lucifer's Archangel. Now, on this rainy night, it came out for real. She screamed as she had from the pit. She believed she heard it echoing up into the hills and out over the lake. Lightning flashed and then the thunder rolled, as if in awed applause.

The curtain fell. Intermission.

She was awake, back to the present, the storm. Valerie pulled the dress up higher, over her naked hips, letting the rain run over her, but the stinking scent was stronger, feral, and it frightened her. For years, she'd taken solace in religious icons. A sensual solace. Valerie removed her hat, pulled the Sant Dymphna amulet by its chain up over her face and through her long, wet hair, pulled down the bodice of her dress, and traced her little angel over her breasts, tenderly, teasingly, as she'd done so many nights.

I love you, Saint Dymphna, you beheaded little bitch...

Lightning, thunder, and then, curtain up:

Act IV: The Creation of Saint Valerie

When Act IV opens, it's five months since she'd beaten her addiction in what had been a five-act horror play of its own. Valerie had been appearing in the more exotic night spots in and around San Francisco, performing her lewd lampoons of Hollywood stars, making a name for herself by her racy mimicry, beautiful singing and on-stage audacity. It was in one of these clubs one night that she'd met Simon Bone… "High Priest of the Church of the Light Bearer."

Valerie had her own name for him: "The 350-pound androgynous asshole."

She'd enthralled him, and he'd begged her to be hostess at his birthday party at the Vicarage, the Bone family retreat near Big Sur. She saw the guests gathered by the pool that April night: A bevy of whores from San Francisco. A number of acolytes from the Church of the Light Bearer. A gaggle of artists and musicians. Of course, they hadn't come for Bone, whom most of them felt was a flabby, creepy pretender. No… they'd come at the promise of all-you-can drink booze, all-you-can-inject dope, and all the all-you-can-screw party favor whores that the wealthy Bone prodigally provided, but was himself, they all knew, too timid to use.

Nearly midnight. Ivy, at Bone's request, was wearing her Dietrich *The Blue Angel* costume, modified to suit the party's Luciferian atmosphere. She'd made herself up with a flair for the demonic—her long hair hanging loose, severely dark eye-makeup, black garter belt, black stockings and heels, black top hat, and a black cape, draped over her shoulders, her naked breasts peeking coyly from its folds. She'd gotten laughs by telling guests that if they believed in the expression "cold as a witch's tit," a quick squeeze of her own would disprove the simile. When anybody tried, however, she'd grin and slap away his (or her) fingers.

She sang "Happy Birthday" to Bone, *a la* Marlene. Bone beamed. Valerie nearly gagged. She saw herself leaving the festivities, going up to the widow's walk for a cigarette break, looking out at the full moon over the Pacific. Squeals and laughter were rising shrilly from the pool area… yes, the atrocities were beginning. Then Bone entered, the birthday boy behemoth shyly kneeling to her, emboldened a bit by liquor.

"May I touch your garter and stocking?" he asked timidly.

"Well, alright," she sighed. He did.

"May I kiss your shoes?" he pleaded.

Valerie exhaled a jet of smoke from her Fatima. "Go ahead, for Christ's sake." He did.

"May I finger your hair, and maybe sniff your …?"

"Fuck NO!" she cried.

He was repulsive but she had him spellbound, and their relationship, sick and symbiotic, continued after this night. He'd promised to make her a star. He'd bought her beautiful clothes. He'd provided her his family's property at Malibou Lake—rent free—and financed her Black Mass. He told her all about Crowley and the Scarlet Woman.

Valerie saw herself, standing on the Vicarage's widow's walk, spotlighted by the moon, adorned in her cape, top hat and *Blue Angel* lingerie, a bare-breasted, pointy-nosed, epileptic Lola-Lola from Hell, knowing goddamn well what she'd truly become. California's 1931 Queen of sex freaks. Part Transylvania, part Weimar Berlin. Part vamp, part vampire. Part bloodsucker, part cocksucker.

It all could have been so different, she suddenly thought, remembering that snowy New York night in 1929 ... *so very different...*

Curtain.

* * *

Composing herself, Valerie began fantasizing about the climactic act to come. *Act V: The Destroying of Colin Clive, Porter Down, and Hollywood*, in which she ravaged the actor, made up and costumed just as she'd drawn him on Calvary, bleeding from the Five Precious Wounds. Leading into her killing Porter Down... and, as the grand finale, bringing down the "Dream Factory" itself, exorcising her own bitterness and shattered dream.

Then suddenly came a giant bolt of lightning... a seizure... and she saw a *different* act.

Night, a full moon, a weeping little girl. Valerie was on the shore of Malibou Lake below, and at first barely recognized herself. She was *bald!* And dressed in what looked like rags, *nearly naked*, and looking so sick, diseased, hysterical that she almost thought she was seeing someone else. Yet the Bitch wore Valerie's own amulet, and had her nose... and had needle tracings on her arms, almost but not quite like her own... .

Then, stage left, from under the bushes, Valerie saw herself crawling... as the Snake Lady.

She was playing *both* parts! The Snake Lady *and* the Weeping Bitch! She was the giant snake, her own red hair on her head, her own tits on her underbelly, and she was thrashing, hissing, and she was also the bald Bitch, dressed in rags, crying, moaning... a virtuoso in *each* role, both of them terrifying her.

Then the Bitch, bleating in anguish, threw the child into the lake... and the Snake Lady, watching with her beady eyes, hissed with joy.

"Please!" Valerie screamed, emerging from her seizure, shrieking to the hills and the lake. "Please! Won't somebody fucking HELP ME?"

She was fully awake now. She lie there, on the silo platform, flat on her back, soaked by the rain, remembering her new dream, trembling but realizing two things always saved her... her ferocity, and her sensuality.

Saint Dymphna...

Valerie moved the angel amulet from her breasts to her hips, slowly, sinuously stroking it up her thighs. But then Act III came back into her head, and she was in the pit... but not as herself. She was the goddamned Snake Lady, her red hair flowing, flashing her fangs as a crowd watched from above.

Among them were Colin Clive, Eve Devonshire, and Porter Down.

Valerie gasped, viciously dragging the amulet up her thighs, desperately trying to escape her own horror, deciding to play it for laughs as she had in the circus, twisting and wriggling her fetid, drenched body, performing her nasty on-her-back cooch dance just as she had two years ago in the snake pit, leering up at wide-eyed persecutors.

"I'm Valerie the Voluptuous Viper," she hissed passionately, flicking her tongue. "The Snake Lady. And you can all go fuck yourselves!"

55 Dias Dorados

The final dress rehearsal for "The Monster's Hiding Under Your Bed Tonight!" song was this morning. Tonight was the *Frankenstein* party at Dias Dorados.

One of the starlets didn't show up. A rumor reached the Phantom Stage that she'd eloped the previous night. This reduced the chorines from six to five, throwing off the balance of the dance line, but it seemed too late to do anything about it.

When Eve got home that afternoon, she told Bonnie about the missing cat girl. "I'll do it!" said Bonnie. "Teach me the routine and I'll go with you."

Bonnie, of course, could easily learn the simple dance, but Eve demurred. "We all look ridiculous in those cat suits!"

"No doubt," said Bonnie "But I always wanted to see Dias Dorados." Actually, she wanted to keep an eye on Eve.

* * *

Colin Clive had returned from Palm Springs the previous night. Karl Stevens phoned Porter that Clive had been totally cooperative the past two weeks and could attend the party without the presence of a male nurse.

* * *

266

At 8:00 P.M. Tuesday, two Universal limousines drove up Benedict Canyon, carrying Eve, Bonnie, four starlets, and Dwight Frye, who sported a black tuxedo.

Although Halloween was 12 nights away, the studio decorators had adorned the house and grounds of Dias Dorados in an All Hallows Eve motif. A scarecrow, topped by one of the Monster head sculptures Jack Pierce had made, stood sentry at the gated entranceway. Candlelit Jack O'Lanterns were all over the drive and property.

The limousines drove through the gate. Dias Dorados was a magnificent, sprawling hacienda, with a wooden balcony that ran almost the width of its edifice. There were various outbuildings, including a 20-foot-tall "pigeon tower."

"Not a bad joint," deadpanned Bonnie.

* * *

The party was to begin at 9:00 P.M. Frye and his chorus were assigned rooms in the upstairs guests' wing, where each room had heavy, Spanish-style furnishings, a large Gothic bed, a bathroom, and even its own telephone. The entire house and grounds were connected by the phone system. Eve and Bonnie shared a room while maids in uniform flitted about, tending to the visiting talent.

Downstairs, the guests were arriving. Many of the company had brought their spouses or lovers, and there was the requisite pack of want-to-be starlets, who invaded such affairs like ants at a picnic. Apropos of *Frankenstein* and Halloween, it was a costume party, optional for those who wanted to play dress-up as Hollywood stars. A few men showed up wearing Dracula capes, and there were a couple Valentino sheiks, and at least a half-dozen Charlie Chaplin tramps. As for the ladies, some wore platinum blonde wigs *a la* Jean Harlow, there were a few slightly *passe* Clara Bow flappers, and there were several ladies costumed as Marlene Dietrich had been in Paramount's film *Morocco*—in a black top hat and tails. *Dias Dorados* was redolent in the scent of perfume, hairspray, and bootleg liquor.

A strange desperation had struck Universal… an apprehension that James Whale had gone too far, that *Frankenstein* might repulse audiences and sink the studio. This fear spiked the evening's atmosphere. Parties at the Laemmle estate were respectable, as long as old "Uncle Carl" was up and about, but after he retired, they often became considerably livelier. The huge grounds had various hideaways, and after several parties, servants had found drunken lovers the next day, passed out in the guest rooms, the outbuildings, and even, on one occasion, in an empty cage in the zoo.

The dancers' costumes were precisely what Bonnie had been warned they'd be: A short black dress with "cat's tail," black silk stockings, black high heels for coordinated dancing, and a hairband with cat "ears" attached. There were extra pairs of stockings in case of a run. As Eve and Bonnie dressed, they heard the crowd talking and the studio's orchestra, seated to the side of a small stage below the main staircase, tuning up their instruments. There was a full-length mirror in the room, and Eve winced at her burlesque show reflection.

"Your tail's longer than mine," said Bonnie, who filled her costume very nicely.

Eve didn't laugh. She felt ill, terrified that Colin would be here. Embarrassed that he'd see her in this silly song number, she was more frightened about his possible condition.

She was also nervous that Valerie would crash the party.

* * *

Porter arrived at Luke's Marina at 8:25 P.M. to change to a suit so to blend in at the party. O'Leary was taking plainclothesmen to Dias Dorados and Porter would join them there to keep an eye on Colin and Eve. As Porter got out of the truck, Luke approached him immediately.

"Porter, a priest called here tonight... twice."

He handed Porter a scrap of paper with a phone number scribbled on it. Porter went into the shack and immediately dialed an operator to reach the number in Malvern, Pennsylvania. It was answered on the first ring.

"Mr. Down, I'm Fr. Harry Burke, of the Roman Catholic Church's Department of Ascetic Investigations. I received your recent letter and information, but only now, after research and much prayer and consideration, feel free to respond."

"You're not a minute too soon," said Porter.

Burke, as direct as Porter, instantly began reading from his notes. "On the night of May 15, 1929, the feast day of Saint Dymphna, the patron saint of..."

"Yeah, I know who she is. Go on."

"On that night, a trespasser broke into the church of Saint Dymphna in Geel, Belgium. It's from that church that I've received this information. The trespasser tried, unsuccessfully, to break into the glass case containing the reliquary of Saint Dymphna's bones. The priest assigned there, Fr. Otto Zimmerfeld, tried to apprehend the trespasser, who fought back and fled. Fr. Zimmerfeld suffered a fatal heart attack."

"Keep going," said Porter.

"Fr. Zimmerfeld, when found the next morning, was still alive," said Fr. Burke. "He managed to tell authorities that the trespasser was a woman, a tall woman. He called her a 'hexe'—a witch—and talked incoherently about her eyes. Fr. Zimmerfeld died that day, but shortly before his death, realized the amulet he always wore was no longer around his neck. He became very agitated in his fear that the 'witch,' as he called her, had stolen it from him."

"Describe that amulet," said Porter.

"It had been a gift to Fr. Zimmerfeld from his mother, on his ordination in 1886," said Fr. Burke. "A small crystal angel. After Fr. Zimmerfeld's death, it was never found."

Porter nodded at this revelation. "What happened to the trespasser?"

"She escaped. It was determined she sailed to America. There was a considerable search for her, because Fr. Zimmerfeld's perception of her was basically demonic. That's how she first came to my attention. At any rate, based on physical description, recent photographs she herself has sent me, and your comprehensive letter, detailing her behavior and apparent fetishes and fascinations, I believe this woman in California, known as Valerie Le Fay, is the same one who desecrated the shrine in Belgium."

"You say she sent you photographs?" asked Porter.

"Never mind that," said Fr. Burke. "I've been hunting this woman for some time. On several occasions last year, I nearly apprehended her."

"Actually, Father, we might be a couple hours from apprehending her ourselves."

"If so," said Fr. Burke, "she belongs in a hospital. A Catholic asylum I know of, in Maryland. I'll be frank, Mr. Down. My church superiors did not give me permission to call you with this information and would be gravely upset if such a situation received a court trial or public attention. I'm calling you nevertheless, because…"

"She's nuts," said Porter.

"She's more than that," said Fr. Burke. "I'm convinced this woman is possessed. She's demonic. If simply arrested by conventional means, the results could be..."

"I understand," said Porter. "Well, I'll figure a quiet way to throw a net over her—even if she's the Antichrist herself. I'll mail her to you as a present. And I personally guarantee that you get the amulet."

"There's no need," said Fr. Burke. "The pastor at Saint Dymphna's Shrine in Belgium has assured me that, if this woman Fr. Zimmerfeld described indeed stole it, it's clearly profaned—and they don't want it returned."

"Understood," said Porter. "I'll be back in touch. Thank you."

"You're welcome," said Fr. Burke. "Good night. And may Jesus Christ deliver you from Evil."

"I'll be personally offended if He doesn't," said Porter.

56   Oscar O'Neal

MONDAY, OCTOBER 19, 1931

Oscar O'Neal, Valerie Le Fay's stage manager, had never stopped grieving the death of his wife, Laura.

He'd been a jack-of-all trades in the Croenjagger Circus. Laura had been an animal trainer, working with, among other acts, the Dancing Bears. One night during the 1930 season, Croenjagger had ordered Laura to perform, despite her being quite ill. One of the bears had mauled her to death. The circus paid O'Neal $300 in restitution.

Despite his shock and sorrow, Oscar O'Neal had continued working with Croenjagger's, isolated from the other workmen. In the spring of 1931, a woman formerly known as "Valerie, the Voluptuous Viper," a geek who'd left the circus before the previous season had ended, had secretly contacted him in Mendocino. Oscar had always felt sorry for her and was surprised to see how attractive and sophisticated she appeared when he visited her at her hotel room. She enlisted him in her plan of vengeance—for her horrid treatment as the "Viper," and for his wife Laura, slaughtered by the bear. Oscar had accepted the offer, as long as the fire would kill no people or animals. "Valerie Ivy," who now called herself "Valerie Le Fay," assured him she was interested in only one man's death.

Oscar turned a blind eye to her personal vendetta and the arson had been successful, although two horses had accidentally died during the pandemonium. Police questioned him, but Le Fay, as promised, had an alibi arranged for him and herself in San Francisco. And so, for the past several months, Oscar O'Neal had been Valerie Le Fay's stage manager at her Black Mass, creating, among other things, the tower of fire effect. He was also her foreman at her ranch. She'd seduced him to be her lover, but they'd been intimate only a few times. On occasion, he'd serve as her nurse after she'd suffer a seizure. Now he was an accomplice in her crimes.

What they'd done to the lamb at Universal had sickened him. What she was planning for tonight was horrific. Still, tonight, he'd again do what he was ordered to do.

After what had happened to Laura, nothing really mattered.

* * *

One of Valerie's concerns tonight was that Porter Down would be at Dias Dorados and destroy her new little melodrama before the curtain could rise on it. He needed to be delayed, for at this point, Valerie fatalistically believed he was the only person who could stop her.

She'd discussed the scenario with Oscar. He'd been uncharacteristically surly, insisting he wouldn't personally hurt anyone. Valerie insisted she didn't want Down hurt—at least not seriously.

"He has to see what I do," she said, "but not until it's all over. Later, when the time's right, I'll personally tend to him."

* * *

O'Neal had learned that Porter Down was staying at Luke's Marina at Venice Beach. He'd arrived in a truck shortly before 8:00 P.M., figuring Down would depart for the party shortly after eight. It was now almost 8:45, and there was a light on in the shack on the pier. O'Neal could see another younger man, working on the trawler.

On a lot beside the pier was a stack of fuel cans. O'Neal, with his pyrotechnic skills, had crept from the truck and quickly rigged the cans to explode. It would be a hell of a blast and, if the wind cooperated, flames would blow onto the small pier. Down and the man on the boat would have to call the fire department and there'd be damage and delay before Down could leave for the party.

The shack door opened. O'Neal saw Down come out, wearing a suit, obviously dressed to do undercover work at the Laemmle house. Starting the truck engine, and climbing down from the truck's cab, O'Neal lit the fuse he'd attached to the nest of explosives he'd wedged under the cans.

Then he hurried back into the truck, pulled out of his hiding spot, and a block away, heard the explosion.

The cans were suddenly a blazing pyre, fireballs falling onto the pier. The force was so powerful that it knocked down Luke on the trawler. He quickly got to his feet, grabbed a fire extinguisher, joined Porter, who'd turned on a hose, and the two men sprayed the fire. Then came another explosion, this one throwing a can that nearly hit Porter squarely in the head. Dodging it, he lost his balance and fell off the pier into the sooty water.

A fisherman on a nearby dock saw the flames and called the fire department. They arrived quickly, as did the police. Porter, having climbed out of the water and onto the dock, regarded his wet, torn, dirty suit.

"Tell 'em what happened Luke," he said. "I've got a date."

He ducked into the mostly undamaged shack and changed to his sailor suit, cap and pea coat. It was 9:25 P.M. He figured the explosion had been planned to delay him. The party was already started. It was a long drive to Benedict Canyon.

57 The Stigmata

The party at Dias Dorados had started promptly at 9:00 P.M. with music and dancing. Dwight Frye, standing in the hallway outside his dressing room in Dias Dorados, did some vocal exercises. The six dancers congregated with him. Bonnie playfully tugged at Eve's cat tail.

The grandfather clock in the hallway boomed out 9:30. "Places!" said Frye.

"Relax, Evie," said Bonnie. "It'll be over soon."

* * *

As if in a royal pageant, the Universal orchestra played a fanfare, and the Laemmles, Senior and Junior, came down the great stairway to reverential applause. On Junior's arm was Sidney Fox who, in her high heels, was just about his height, and was co-starring with Bela Lugosi in *Murders in the Rue Morgue,* which had started shooting today. The trio took their seats in front of the stage, Junior sitting on the right hand of his father.

A large fireplace, along with table candles, provided most of the atmospheric light. Then, come a new fanfare, large lights from the back of the room focused on the stage, and Dwight Frye led his cat-like chorines down the stairs. Everyone applauded and there were a few appreciative whistles.

The Monster's hiding under your bed tonight …!

274

Frye's tenor voice held the tune, and Eve and her cohorts pranced behind him, coyly smiling, striking poses as if clawing and hissing, eventually maneuvering into a kick line. Eve saw the audience as a dark blur, terrified of focusing on a single face, possibly seeing Colin. In a span that seemed both intolerably long and mercifully short, the song came to an end.

"*Meeeooooow!*" cooed the chorines.

Applause. Whistles. Frye and the ladies took a bow. The Laemmles, father and son, stood and shook hands with Frye and each "cat girl." Junior, recognizing Eve, said nothing but kept smiling.

As arranged, the ladies were to join the party in their cat girl costumes, and change after the show. The program followed up with a soprano and tenor singing from *Faust*. Bonnie noticed a small tear in one of Eve's stockings.

"Maybe you better change that before it runs," said Bonnie. "I'll find us seats."

Eve, heading to the stairs, noticed the profile of a woman, costumed in a Dietrich tux and top hat, standing partially in shadow to the left of the staircase, facing away from it. She was smoking a cigarette. She wore a blonde wig as part of her Dietrich costume, and black silk gloves. A tendril of red hair had escaped the wig, running down her left cheek. Eve didn't notice these details, nor the honeysuckle perfume.

Valerie Le Fay, in her Dietrich costume, turned and watched as Eve walked up the stairs.

* * *

Eve hurried to her assigned room, changed her stocking, and then promptly headed for the staircase. Down the hallway, in the shadows, Valerie was looking around the corner, noting which room was Eve's.

* * *

The soprano and tenor were still shrieking the climactic aria from *Faust* at each other, and the audience was restive. Eve saw Bonnie waving to her from near the rear of the audience. Eve sat beside her as the opera singers finished to a standing ovation from the Laemmles and tepid applause from the crowd.

Now James Whale, elegantly attired in tuxedo and carnation, coolly stepped on the stage to respectful applause. "Ladies and gentlemen, before the party resumes, we of the *Frankenstein* company wish to extend tokens of special thanks to two gentlemen."

Eve paled, expecting one of them would be Colin.

"First," said Whale, "our Monster...Mr. Boris Karloff."

The orchestra played "spooky" music and the crowd applauded warmly... the sagas of Karloff's artistry and professionalism had spread. The actor made his way to the stage, wearing a dark suit with carnation.

"For you, Boris," said Whale, presenting Karloff an ancient, high black silk top hat, the type favored by a villain of melodrama or an old-time undertaker. "Bela Lugosi, God help him, doesn't want it," laughed Whale, "so it's yours."

Karloff chuckled and put on the hat to the delight of the crowd. "Thank you, Jimmy," said Karloff. "My special thanks to Jack Pierce. And my dear old Monster... I hope I did you justice!" He tipped his top hat and returned to his table to loud applause.

"And now," resumed Whale, "our Monster Maker... Mr. Colin Clive."

There was music and applause. Then Eve saw a shadow, silhouetted against the fireplace, moving awkwardly toward the stage. It was Colin, also wearing a dark suit with a carnation. He stepped onto the stage, looking curiously at the crowd.

"Hello?" he asked.

"He's drunk!" shouted someone, to loud laughter.

"You're bloody well right I am," said Colin.

More laughter. Bonnie held Eve's hand tightly.

"Colin," said Whale crisply, "since you played the Monster's 'father,' we present you with a beautiful portrait of the Monster's 'mother,' Mary Wollstonecraft Shelley... courtesy of Universal's art department."

Applause. Colin accepted the oil painting of the Victorian lady, regarding it for a long moment. "Yes, Mary Shelley," he said. "I went on a picnic here once with Mary Shelley... up by the windmill... before it burned." He looked out into the darkness. "Is...is she here?"

The laughter increased. "I say, Mary Shelley and I had a picnic...," said Colin earnestly. "Seems very long ago..."

Eve cried silently. She knew he was remembering the "pastorale" on the mountain.

"I... I wanted to be a Bengal Lancer," said Colin, regarding himself with shame. "Imagine... me... a Bengal Lancer... ."

He turned, holding the oil painting, and walked off the stage and into the shadows.

* * *

The party slowly came back to life. The orchestra played. Couples danced. Uncle Carl retired upstairs for the night. The music became louder, the drinking heavier.

Eve was desperate to leave. She and Bonnie went upstairs to change to their street clothes. A maid joined them in their assigned room. As they finished changing, the phone rang and the maid answered it.

"Miss Devonshire. A gentleman is calling for you."

"Who is this?" asked Eve, taking the receiver.

"Evie… please," said the caller. "I need you."

"Colin?" asked Eve. Bonnie, hearing his name, stiffened.

"I'm sorry, Evie. Please help me. Meet me near the zoo, behind the house. No one must see us. I'll have my car by the far end cage. We'll leave together through the back gate. Please?"

"I'll be there," said Eve faintly. She hung up, convinced that Colin needed her.

"Wherever you're going," said Bonnie, grabbing her purse, "I'm coming too."

"Alright," said Eve, having forgotten what an expert mimic Valerie was.

* * *

The Laemmle zoo was near the back of the property, over 100 yards from the main house. Only a few chimps, two zebras and several bears resided there. The night was cold and there was thunder and lightning, although rain had yet to fall.

Valerie hid between the two far cages. She'd had a few drinks—just enough to embolden her.

No fucking snakes… No fucking pit.

She saw the bevy of headlines she'd fantasized:

Murder/Suicide at Hollywood Producer's Home

Colin Clive, Actor Who Played "Frankenstein," A Suicide by Narcotics Overdose

Satanic Ritual Suspected

Woman at Party Dead Too—Allegedly Clive's Paramour and Murder Victim

It was all coming true. Destroy the actor with the "Face of Christ" who'd filled her with passion while he responded with repulsion. Destroy Hollywood, which would never regard her as anything more than a sideshow freak. All accomplished with sex and sacrilege. At the right time, on the right night, in the right way, she'd destroy Porter Down, too.

Words, visions were darting into her mind, as they often did… like distant stations late at night on a radio, but with pictures. She saw and heard Porter Down kneeling over his dead wife. And she could see and hear Eve Devonshire, a child, crying and trembling as she looked up at a tall man… .

Daddy, I wish you wouldn't drink…

* * *

Porter Down arrived at Dias Dorados and found O'Leary. The plainclothes police reported they'd searched the house thoroughly and found nothing unusual.

"Check the outbuildings and property," said Porter. "I swear to God, she's here. I can smell her."

* * *

A bear in its cage paced restlessly. Staying in the shadows while reaching into her purse, Valerie removed a needle, lethal enough to kill a large animal. It was one of two needles she carried tonight. She placed the purse with the other needle on the ground and waited.

Bonnie Bristeaux looked ahead, past the last cage in the zoo, for Clive's car. She saw nothing. As she walked protectively several steps ahead of Eve, a shadow lunged from between two cages.

"Surprise!" cried the shadow, stabbing the needle into her neck. Bonnie fell instantly.

Eve screamed. Valerie, startled and surprised by the second woman, attacked Eve. Eve fought back, hysterically, striking at Valerie's face. The top hat and blonde wig were knocked off and Valerie's red hair fell loose as she tried to wrestle Eve to the ground. The taller woman was also the stronger and Valerie fell upon Eve with ferocity, gasping the words that had entered her mind, in a mocking, little girl's voice…

"Daddy, I wish you wouldn't drink," she hissed, her lips almost against Eve's. "It scares Mommy and me."

Eve faintly heard the words as Valerie slammed her head on the ground, gasping before losing consciousness.

The needle was nearly empty now. Valerie rolled Eve over, face-down, tearing the back of Eve's dress, exposing her thighs, and thought of Porter Down. Making little soothing sounds, she gently squeezed the skin on Eve's thigh, just above her stocking, aiming the needle.

"Just like little Mary Down," she grinned. She began the injection.

When Porter Down came investigating, and she knew he eventually would, this is what he'd find.

* * *

Ten minutes later, Porter and O'Leary came toward the zoo, having enlisted several Laemmle servants to guide and assist them. They saw the two prone figures ahead near the cages and ran to them. O'Leary examined Bonnie.

"She's dead, Porter."

Porter examined the face-down Eve, felt a pulse, then saw the blood on the back of her thigh. O'Leary saw it too, realizing its significance.

"Porter," said O'Leary softly.

* * *

Colin stood outside the great house, near the pigeon tower, holding his painting. Then suddenly, Valerie stood before him. She again wore her top hat and Dietrich wig and tightly clutched her small black purse. He recognized her primarily by her angel amulet, hanging from her torn collar.

"Come with me, Colin. Inside. Upstairs. Eve's there. She's asking for you…"

Her plan was, she believed, realistic and close to fruition. She'd get him to the upstairs bedroom where Eve had dressed. There she'd quickly, lethally inject him with the second needle in her purse. After his death, she'd get his hand prints on both needles as her hands remained gloved. She'd maneuver his body onto the bed, and stab one needle into his side, the other into the palm of his hand.

The Stigmata, she'd imagined.

A Stigmata suicide. It would appear that, having killed two women, he killed himself in this sacrilegious way. "Frankenstein," Hollywood's great blasphemer... a murderer and suicide, dead after his final blasphemy. They'd find him this way, on the Gothic-style bed, the needles jutting from his palm and side.... two of the Five Sacred Wounds.

Actor Who Played "Frankenstein" Found Dead... Satanic Ritual Suspected....

Several couples watched Colin and his "Dietrich" as she put her arms around him and whispered to him. He pushed her away, roughly. No, Eve didn't want him. Why would she? This creature was trying to trick him. Suddenly, as the storm came closer, Colin took Valerie firmly by the arm and in an almost military march, walked her away from the house.

"You come with me," he said. "I'll take you flying."

Valerie resisted only a moment. The injections and stigmata could come later tonight. Any time... any place. She'd have to improvise, but the possibilities were rich, and she had plenty of time. All night.

After all, they'd probably have to lock up Porter Down in one of the zoo cages after he found Eve's body.

58

Flying Coffin

The Jenny biplane flew above the Pacific, bobbing on the cold, violent night wind like the toy kite it virtually was. Valerie sat in the front cockpit, screaming like a child on an amusement park ride, her arms raised, laughing at the rain and lightning.

A witch, cackling on her broomstick, Colin thought.

He sat in the rear cockpit, wearing a pilot's cap and goggles. The controls seemed perverse, elusive, as if he were in a nightmare in which he couldn't quite grasp them, work them. He knew never to fly during a storm and it seemed that she, along with the wild wind, now controlled the plane, the highest he'd ever flown, going north along the coast, 1,000-feet above the ocean.

She turned now, looking at the lightning. He saw her profile, her long red hair whipped by the wind. Nothing in the night sky seemed real to him, she least of all. She was like a ghost, a banshee, and he suddenly realized how cold and wet he was, and how frightened.

Rain, lightning, thunder…her scream. She screamed, time and again, celebrating what she was about to do. Lucifer's Archangel and Frankenstein… on a mad biplane joyride in a lightning storm. As soon as they landed, she'd inject him. Claim he was obsessed with her and had wanted to kill her. When she fled on the ground, he'd overdosed, performing the ritualistic Stigmata upon himself. All more exciting and macabre than she'd originally envisioned.

281

Her purse was at her feet, containing both needles, and she still wore her black silk gloves—they'd find his prints on the murder weapons.

Colin, meanwhile, had his own plan. He was going to crash the plane. He would kill her and himself.

* * *

Suddenly there was an explosion, a blast of lightning and thunder. The plane rocked wildly, then recovered… and they both sensed it, heard it.

There was a plane behind them, approaching dangerously near, coming now almost beside them from the west, and Valerie could see a single head in its cockpit. The plane was a Spad, faster than a Jenny, and it banked, almost striking Colin's plane. Colin spitefully aimed the Jenny straight up into the sky, but the Spad circled out to sea, sweeping in again from the west, striking with its top wing, breaking one of the Jenny's wing struts.

"Christ!" shouted Valerie, sensing it was Porter Down.

A guest at Dias Dorados had told Porter that he'd heard Clive say something to a tall woman about taking her flying. In a fortunate coincidence of which he'd long been aware, Porter had kept *Timber Wolf* at the same airfield where Clive rented his Jenny. He'd therefore driven as fast as possible directly to the airfield and taken off in the Spad, navigating the attack. He'd learned in the War how to force down a plane. This one was going to have to land on the stretch of beach below.

If Clive didn't, Porter would bring the goddamn plane down himself.

The Spad struck again and both Colin and Valerie saw the words *Timber Wolf* on the side of the plane. The Jenny lurched, not so damaged that it would crash, but crippled enough that its pilot would have to land it.

No, thought Colin, now sober. *I do this my own way.*

He pulled off his pilot cap and goggles, tossing them, jerking the controls, the wings so the Jenny tipped forward, aiming at the ocean far below… nose-diving. As the plane fell and twisted, her shriek seemed to him to fill the sky.

They both sensed death approaching. Colin suddenly realized that murder and suicide were not his right. He desperately grasped the stick, trying to level off the dive, fearing it was too late…

* * *

It was after 1:30 A.M. Rain still fell heavily. Jim O'Leary had joined the Ventura County police at the accident site, north of Malibu beach. Medics had arrived in an ambulance.

The Jenny was burning in the surf, its old, overworked engine having exploded moments after its crash landing. The Spad, intact, had landed about a quarter-mile up the beach. Near the wreckage was Colin Clive, resting on the sand, his long-injured leg worsened by the crash, but otherwise he was basically unharmed. Some distance away was Valerie Le Fay, having been thrown from the plane, covered in blood. She was in the throes of a violent epileptic seizure. Medics treated them both. Porter stood on the cold, wet beach, and O'Leary approached him.

"Is Eve still alive?" Porter asked.

"Yes," said O'Leary. "But in grave condition, Porter."

Both men watched the medics load Colin and Valerie into the ambulance. O'Leary stood silently as the Ventura police took Porter Down into custody.

59

Pursuit

Tuesday, October 20 to Friday October 23, 1931

At mid-morning of Tuesday, three people came to the Hollywood Police Station—Ilsa, the shepherdess at Universal City, and her Uncle Johann and Aunt Vilma.

O'Leary took them to his office and closed the door. Ilsa told her story. Carl Laemmle, Sr. had requested she stay at the Laemmle family estate last night and tend to an aged and ailing chimp in the zoo who needed medicine every several hours. Ilsa was coming from the barn toward the cages when she saw a figure attack a woman. At first, she'd thought the figure was a man, because it was tall and dressed in a tuxedo. However, the attacked woman had fought back, knocking off her killer's top hat and blonde wig, and as the figure's red hair fell down her shoulders, Ilsa realized it was a woman.

Ilsa wept as she described what the woman had done to both her victims. She had been so shocked she'd run back to the barn and hid, afraid to move. When her uncle picked her up this morning, she told him what she had seen.

"You're a very brave girl for coming forward," O'Leary gently told her. "You've just given the evidence we need to solve this tragic case."

* * *

284

After Ilsa's visit, O'Leary drove out to the Ventura sheriff's office, explained what he'd just learned, and arranged Porter's release. Porter still faced legal troubles, but for now was a free man.

"What's Eve's condition?" asked Porter.

It was, O'Leary told him, still very serious, and that she was at Good Samaritan Hospital in L.A. He added that Colin Clive was in fair condition at Cedars of Lebanon Hospital in Hollywood. Valerie Le Fay was in critical condition at a private sanitarium near Malibu.

* * *

The L.A. press doggedly pursued the story of the death at Dias Dorados and the plane crash up the coast. As Porter Down was now a participant in the scandal, he could hardly be expected to be a spokesman for Universal. Late Tuesday morning, he showed up at Carl Laemmle, Sr.'s office, giving a final report on the case to Senior and Junior, explaining what appeared to have been Valerie Le Fay's actual plan. He asked for the balance of his salary. Laemmle, Sr. thundered that Porter had incredible nerve asking for payment, considering all that had happened, and vowed he wouldn't give him another dime. He spoke mostly in German, but Porter got the point.

After this audience with Laemmle, Sr. Junior Laemmle directly led Porter to the paymaster's office. He had the paymaster cut Porter a large check and included a bonus.

"It actually might have been a hell of a lot worse, if it weren't for you," admitted Junior.

Universal turned to its own publicity department and Laemmle, Sr. asked for emergency help from Metro-Goldwyn-Mayer, whose trouble shooters were the slickest in town. By the time payoffs were made and favors promised, the afternoon papers noted only briefly that a largely unknown actress had died suddenly at a party at Dias Dorados, probably due to an overdose, and an investigation would follow.

There were no headlines, and no words at all about Clive, Valerie, or the plane crash.

However, the situation was under grave discussion in guarded *sanctum sanctorums* in Hollywood's upper echelons. This scandal required more than a quick cover-up in today's newspapers. An emergency solution would have to be forthcoming.

* * *

It was clear to Porter and O'Leary that, in the wake of the recent tragedy, they must shut down any sources that might offer Valerie Le Fay, should she survive, any aid and support. The source with the most money and power was Valerie's accompanist, admirer, backer, and wealthy wastrel, Simon Bone. Apparently made aware of the accident, he was nowhere to be found.

* * *

On Wednesday night, Simon Bone sat in a private train compartment, perspiring heavily. Considering his girth and anxiety, he could do little to control it.

He was fleeing his most recent molestation charge. This time the victim was a 13-year-old boy, and his parents were demanding Bone's hide, despite Pierpont's offer. Bone had defied the police's mandate he not leave California.

The train had left San Francisco at 10:00 P.M. It took a southeast route, then due east, its destination New York. He'd have done better to have taken a plane, but feared flying. The train was racing through the Arizona desert now, and Bone looked out his compartment window at the starlit cacti, thinking about the snakes, the lizards, the Gila monsters… all nocturnal hunters. He winced at the thought of the slaughters taking place tonight out in that horrid terrain.

He feared that man Down was pursuing him, and was terrified of entanglement in this scandal with Clive and Valerie. It was the other reason he was fleeing the country. He wondered if he'd actually have to launch his plan to reside for a time in Paris, at least until Pierpont handled these new charges. Perhaps he'd never be able to come home. Maybe never see Valerie again. Never see her beautiful yellow eyes, her flowing red hair, her long legs… never hear her voice… never smell her scent…

Never, never again. And if she died, Bone grinned vindictively, the bitch, who'd mocked him so viciously, deserved it.

The train blew its whistle and decreased speed. Bone looked at his schedule—there was no stop listed for this time. Outside was what appeared to Bone to be some God-forsaken adobe hovel of a station. The train chugged to a stop and after a moment there were voices in the corridor, and then a knocking at his door.

"Simon Bone? Police. Open the door."

"No!" shouted Bone, standing, terrified, backing against the window.

At length they broke open the door. Bone's legs failed and he fell to the floor, nearly swooning. He refused to get up and two detectives grabbed his legs, dragging him out of the compartment on his back and into the corridor, Bone squealing like a hog going to slaughter.

"No!" he wept and screamed shrilly. "NO!"

The Arizona police, having been alerted by the San Francisco police and the boy's family's lawyer, got Simon Bone off the train. Two more police joined them, and the four men, hefting Bone like a captured animal, tossed him into a paddy wagon, locking its door.

* * *

It was crucial that the police arrest Oscar O'Neal, who'd undoubtedly assisted Valerie in her doings. O'Leary phoned the sheriff at Malibu and asked him to apprehend O'Neal at the Abbey before he fled town after Valerie's hospitalization.

However, when the sheriff and two deputies searched the Abbey, they found Oscar, in the barn, a sack tied over his head, hanging from a beam. There was a suicide note, only asking he be buried beside his wife Laura at a cemetery near Tehachapi.

* * *

During her first two nights and days at the hospital, Eve's condition had been critical. Lt. O'Leary visited her nightly. By Thursday night, October 22, she was out of danger but still weak, and deeply upset by her memories of Bonnie's murder.

That night, O'Leary told Eve the basic details of Valerie's plan, the murder of Bonnie, the attempted murder of Eve herself, and the plane crash. He related that Colin Clive would be released shortly from the hospital and that Valerie Le Fay was still in critical condition. He also gave the details of Mary Down's murder.

"Porter Down thinks it might not be a good idea for him to see you now," said O'Leary, "considering the legal situations he might be facing." He also noted that Universal and the Hollywood hierarchy had managed so far to keep the story out of the newspapers.

"What happened to me," said Eve, "also happened to Porter's wife."

"Yes," said O'Leary. "And we're not sure how the assailant knew it. Mary Down's death was reported in the papers, but not its cause."

"What's happened about Bonnie?" Eve asked.

"She's being sent to her family in Montana for burial," said O'Leary. "I'll be at the station when the train leaves tomorrow morning to take her home." He paused. "Porter will be there, too."

A tear ran down Eve's face. She saw in her mind Bonnie falling before her eyes. Then Valerie's words came back to her, as they had the past few nights:

Daddy, I wish you wouldn't drink. It scares Mommy and me... .

They'd been the last words Eve had said to her father, before his fatal heart attack.

* * *

On Friday night, October 23, Eve had a surprise visitor at the hospital—James Whale. He wore a black raincoat, formally held his hat, and stood a distance from her bed.

"The studio is covering all your hospital expenses," he said.

Eve nodded in gratitude but said nothing.

"You need to know a few things, confidentially," said Whale, "regarding remarks that were made that morning by Miss Le Fay at Universal. Colin had an uncle who died at Saint Saviour's, the Lunatic Asylum on the island of Jersey, in 1924, I believe. Unfortunately, Colin and his two younger sisters fear that the curse of lunacy might be in the family. How Miss Le Fay learned this information is a mystery."

Eve was silent.

"We preview *Frankenstein* next week in Santa Barbara," said Whale. "I've arranged for your salary, which was to terminate December 15, to continue through December 31. There's no need for you to report again to the studio. The checks will be sent to your home address."

It was, Eve realized, the closest thing to an apology Whale was going to offer for the reprehensible way he'd used her to try to control Colin's drinking.

"Good night, Mr. Whale," she said.

"Good night," said Whale, and walked out of the room.

60 Departure

On Monday, October 26, one week after her attack, Eve came home from the hospital. She sat alone in the apartment she'd shared with Bonnie, whom she missed terribly. She also remembered this was the date Colin was supposed to leave Los Angeles and begin his trip home to London. She'd heard nothing from him during her time in the hospital.

Eve had decided to leave L.A. and start a new life in Sacramento, 400 miles up the coast. She spent the evening packing her two suitcases. At about 11 P.M., as rain fell heavily, there was a knock at the door. It was Lt. O'Leary, looking very drawn.

"I'm sorry it's so late, Miss Devonshire," he said. "Will you come along with me, please? It's regarding Mr. Clive."

* * *

O'Leary drove Eve down Beachwood Drive. The Halloween decorations looked gloomy in the pouring rain. "What are your plans, ma'am?" he finally asked.

"I'm going to look for a job in Sacramento," she said. "I hope to leave tomorrow."

"That sounds fine," said O'Leary. He was quiet for a moment. "As far as the events of October 19th and 20th, there are some things you need to know."

289

Eve said nothing, looking out the car window at the rain.

"If Miss Le Fay dies," said O'Leary, "Mr. Clive and Mr. Down both face charges of manslaughter. And of course, Miss Le Fay also faces a charge of murder ... and attempted murder. You'd naturally have to appear in court."

"I understand," said Eve. She also figured this meant Colin couldn't return to London.

"This would all make a sensational court trial, Miss Devonshire—or maybe several trials. But there will never be any."

"What do you mean?" asked Eve.

O'Leary parked by the Hollywood Tower. "Please come inside, Miss Devonshire."

* * *

O'Leary escorted Eve under an umbrella into the lobby. The clerk at the desk handed O'Leary a key and he and Eve boarded the elevator. They ascended to the top floor, stepped into the hallway, and O'Leary unlocked the door.

Eve expected to see Colin, but the suite was clearly unoccupied. It had been left in fastidious condition. There was an envelope on the coffee table by the sofa and another on a desk across the room, leaning against the painting of Mary Shelley that Colin had received at the party the previous week.

"Mr. Clive," said O'Leary, "is on the New York City-bound train that left Los Angeles at 10 P.M. He was under pressure to leave."

"But ..."

"Please sit and I'll explain," said O'Leary patiently. Eve hesitantly sat on a couch but O'Leary remained standing.

"Since last week," began O'Leary, "meetings have been taking place. Universal Studios. LAPD. Powerful men in the Motion Picture Industry. A lawyer for a man who's associated with Valerie Le Fay. They've made certain... deals."

O'Leary appeared awkward, as if personally disgraced. "They've agreed this trial can never happen. The evidence and testimony would ruin Universal Studios. Probably have a devastating impact on the industry-at-large and Los Angeles itself."

"You mean... that woman will go free?" asked Eve. "After killing Bonnie?"

"No," said O'Leary, softly but firmly. "I mentioned a man associated with Miss Le Fay. He was legally listed as her Next of Kin. As such, in exchange for certain legal and morals charges against him being handled by those men I mentioned, and certain payments being made, that man agreed to sign papers to commit Miss Le Fay to a sanitarium. They sent her away on a train three nights ago to a special religious hospital... somewhere in the east."

"You mean an asylum?" asked Eve.

"Of sorts," said O'Leary. "The argument was that this hospital specializes in treatment for Miss Le Fay's mania. It's also 2,500 miles away. A nurse accompanied her on the train. A priest in the east, who Porter Down knows, has a history with Miss Le Fay. He'll be waiting for her at the hospital. And if Miss Le Fay lives, believe me... she'll never be pronounced well enough, or sane enough, to come back here for trial."

"I can't believe Bonnie's family will accept this," said Eve. "Or Porter Down."

"I called Bonnie's parents myself, in Montana," said O'Leary, his face grim. "They were obviously estranged from her. As for Porter... he says there's one consolation. Valerie Le Fay will consider incarceration at the religious asylum her own worst nightmare."

Eve resisted crying. "I shouldn't have told you all this, Ma'am," said O'Leary. "It's supposed to be a secret. But as you know, I have a hard time keeping my mouth shut... especially for a cop. And after what you've been through... well, you deserve to know." He paused. "There are some things here for you," he said, handing Eve the envelope from the table. It had a large sum of cash in it and a note in Colin's small, curved handwriting.

Use this to get away from here—and start a new and happy life.

Eve saw another note resting against the Mary Shelley portrait. She walked across the room, picked it up and read:

For my cherished Evie—a memento of our haunted summer—

Eve kept her back to O'Leary as she wept.

"I tried to prevent this from happening," said O'Leary. "So did Porter. There is little he can do right now—as I said, he might face a manslaughter charge, and it's almost certain he'll lose his investigator license. But he asked me to be sure to give you this note."

He handed Eve a folded piece of paper. It simply had a phone number on it. "Porter said you're probably better off never having to go to court and getting mixed up in so horrible a trial," said O'Leary. "But he also said that, if you want to fight what's happened... well, you only have to call him."

Eve looked at the number for a long moment, then put the paper in her purse.

"I'll drive you home now, Ma'am," said O'Leary, picking up the Mary Shelley portrait, tucking it under his arm.

* * *

It was after 3 A.M. Eve sat awake in the apartment, with Porter Down's telephone number beside her on a table. She'd decided to fight. Then her phone rang.

"A call for you from Salt Lake City," said the operator. Eve heard a cavernous, echoing sound and recognized it: a public address system, reverberating through a tunnel, or train station.

"Eve... ," said a voice faintly.

"Colin," she said.

Once again, the public address system boomed, drowning out his voice. All Eve could hear for a time was the strange, underwater sound of the station.

"They wouldn't let me see you," he said. "They forced me to leave tonight. I... I just wanted to hear your voice again."

Eve thought she could hear him weeping.

"I'm coming back," said Colin. "I'll take the next train from Salt Lake City to Los Angeles. I'll tell everything I know... for Bonnie... and for you."

Eve knew Colin could never give such an account. Bonnie's murder demanded justice, but Eve painfully realized the inevitably ravaging publicity would destroy Colin's career and life.

"Colin... don't come back. Go home to England. I'm leaving Los Angeles and I never want to see you again. You once told me to forget about you. Now I want you to forget about me."

They were, she knew, the words she needed to use, and there was silence on both ends of the telephone.

"I understand," said Colin finally, his voice strong but strained. "Truly I do. You're a grand girl, Eve. Thank you for all you did for me. But... I'll never forget you... I couldn't..."

Eve gently hung up the phone.

* * *

All Eve wanted now, back at her apartment, was to leave Los Angeles, never return, forget. She wouldn't wait until daylight. She'd go now, find a taxi, go to the station and take the first train to Sacramento.

Frantically, she put on her coat and hat, then noticed the Mary Shelley painting she'd brought back to the apartment. She considered leaving it here, but couldn't. Eve took a blanket from a suitcase, wrapping it around the painting to protect it from the rain. Then she awkwardly came down the stairs with a suitcase in each hand and the wrapped portrait wedged under her arm.

She stepped out into Beachwood Drive in the torrential rain, the illuminated HOLLYWOODLAND sign above her. All the horror of the past weeks, all the guilt of how she'd just broken Colin's heart came over her. She dropped the bags, held the painting tight against her, and began weeping in the rain.

"It's alright, Miss."

It was Porter Down, approaching her with an umbrella, holding it over both of them. She kept crying and it was a moment before he spoke. "O'Leary called me tonight. He told me what he'd told you and said you'd be leaving early in the morning." He paused. "I'm flying my plane to Twentynine Palms this morning to make a down payment on a little ranch. If you'd like to come along, stay a few days and nights to get away from everything… I can fly you to Sacramento later, when you're ready."

Eve wiped her eyes. "I'll be working on the barn day and night," said Porter. "You'll have the house to yourself."

She felt his closeness under the umbrella. "Thank you," she managed to say and then suddenly sobbed. "I can't fight what happened. I know you want me to… but I can't."

"I understand, Miss," he said. He took one of her suitcases, led her to his truck and opened its passenger door. After she was seated inside, he put both suitcases into the bed of the truck, then folded up his umbrella and opened the driver's door. He noticed she was holding the covered portrait and he knew what it was.

"Yeah," said Porter. "Better keep that in here." He got inside, and they drove down Beachwood Drive.

A moment later, lightning hit the HOLLYWOODLAND sign transformer on Mount Lee and blew out the 4,000 light bulbs.

61 Christmas Eve

The light of a full moon flowed through the bars of a fifth-floor window, and a record playing down the hall welcomed Christmas, now less than an hour away:

Gloria!
In Excelsis Deo!

Several nuns knelt in the hallway. Last night, they'd wept, shocked by the woman's screams behind the door as she'd profanely defied Fr. Burke's attempts to provide Last Rites. Tonight, they prayed, hoping that Christ still might save her soul.

Christmas Eve, after all, is a night of miracles.

* * *

Last night, she'd believed she was the Snake Lady... her reptilian body shot into pieces, agonizingly attempting to reattach itself... .

See Valerie, the Voluptuous Viper...

Tonight, however, Valerie was aware. Her tangled red hair cascaded over the pillow, and her yellow hazel eyes were bright in the semi-dark room. She'd kicked the sheet onto the floor and her long, parted legs draped the bed, her hospital gown having bunched at the hips. She smiled slyly, enjoying her coarsely seductive pose, her almost vile near-death scent. She arched her head back, looking up at the moon through the barred window:

294

She's at her most vicious on nights of the full moon, she remembered from the circus.

Would she transform again? Would she die as her nightmares had long prophesied, the Snake Lady with her head blown off by that shadowy figure… who might, or might not, have been Porter Down? Might he be on his way here tonight? Yet hadn't her agonizing, rotting-away-piece-by-piece-for-two-months death been worse? Lorded over by Fr. Burke, gawked at by sanctimonious nuns, shrieking for the dope they'd deprived her, strapped to the bed by that blonde, oval-faced bitch Dr. Arthur, hearing the hymns day and night in the chapel, the hallway, everywhere, and the giant fucking bell booming the Angelus three times a day in the tower above her?

In Excelsis Deo!

The carol ended. Another began playing—*Hark! The Herald Angels Sing*. Valerie looked across the room and saw her crystal angel, hanging from its chain, glowing in the moonlight. Dr. Arthur, had draped it there, where Valerie could see it, but couldn't hold it.

And then, the amulet began… to *change*. It grew almost to adult size, a shaft of translucent light, its only distinct features its red eyes and broken wing, and in a gentle voice, it spoke to her.

"I'm waiting for you, Valerie," softly whispered the figure.

Almost instantly, Valerie appeared awestruck, her eyes glowing as if beholding a beatific vision. "Oh, Saint Dymphna!" she cried rapturously, tears running down her face as she recited the prayer a priest had taught her when she was 12-years-old. "My beautiful Dymphna! Let thy sacred martyr's blood consecrate me! Drench me with it! Spray me with it…!"

"I love you, Valerie," sighed Saint Dymphna. "I've always been with you…"

At these words, Valerie's joy vanished, and her face filled with rage. "Liar!" she cried, and then she screamed, "*LIAR!*"

She lunged forward hysterically in the bed, straining against the ligatures, reaching out as if to grab the Vision by its neck. Her famous Voluptuous Viper scream was genuine, and it mixed with her death rattle, sounding like a monster's laughter.

Then Valerie, her yellow eyes insane with hatred, fell back onto her bed and died.

* * *

At the sound of the scream, Dr. Arthur and a small, mousy-haired nurse named Elmira hurried into the room and put on the light. Dr Arthur, pronouncing the patient dead, didn't bother to close the corpse's eyes or cover the body. The nuns outside the door heard Elmira crying, sensed the stillness of death, and made the Sign of the Cross. "The first Sorrowful Mystery, the Agony in the Garden," prayed one of the sisters, and her fellow nuns reached for their rosaries...

Dr. Arthur looked at the corpse, this dead, gangly creature on the bed, in this private Catholic hospital for aged nuns and "the religiously insane," hidden away in the Maryland countryside. The nuns had to recruit "nurses" from local farms... hence simple-minded Elmira.

"Elmira!"

"Yes, Dr. Arthur?" She was wiping her nose with a small handkerchief simply embroidered with flowers, her sole gift from the nuns the previous Christmas.

"There will be no autopsy," said Dr. Arthur. "She had no family so there will be no viewing, hence no embalming. She was in a state of mortal sin, so there will be no Mass."

Elmira squirmed, blew her nose and nodded.

"Prepare her for burial," said the doctor. "On the hill. The unsanctified lot. As soon as possible. The nuns will provide a shroud and coffin. Proceed immediately."

"Yes, Dr. Arthur. But... what about *this*?"

She stood on her toes, reaching the top of the mirror where the small crystal figure hung from its silver chain. The nurse took the figure, and her voice had a sense of child-like wonder.

"She loved this...most of all... ."

Dr. Arthur looked at the amulet. Suddenly, she yanked it from the nurse's hands and threw it into the waste can. "You fool!" jeered Dr. Arthur, and Elmira whimpered.

"I'll fill out the death certificate in my office," said Dr. Arthur. She stood at the foot of the bed, taking a long final look at the corpse's fierce eyes, her livid face, the long, parted legs.

Still trying to shock me, thought Dr. Arthur.

O Come, O Come Emmanuel was playing now, sung reverently by a soprano—*like a dirge,* thought Dr. Arthur. She'd lived for eight weeks with this mad woman's savagery. She'd told Dr. Arthur secret shameful things that she couldn't possibly have known about her. Now Dr. Arthur sensed a cold, bizarre energy in the room, almost as if there were an unseen presence. Rejecting an uncharacteristic urge to pray, Dr. Arthur composed herself, opened the door, turned out the light, and walked briskly past the kneeling nuns.

"She is at peace now," said Dr. Irene Arthur, her back to them. "Merry Christmas."

Elmira was left in the moonlit room, standing very still, listening to the nuns praying, the carol playing. She knew what she had to do before the burial. She truly believed the dead woman would haunt her forever if she didn't, for the woman had known Elmira's impure secrets, too.

She closed the door, knelt by the waste can, felt inside for the crystal figure's chain, shut her eyes as she retrieved it, afraid to see it broken. Then she opened her eyes. It hadn't shattered. It was aglow in the moonlight.

"A miracle," sighed Elmira reverently, as if it were a sacred relic.

She leaned over the bed, raising the cadaver's head, slipping the chain and figure over the tangled hair, the long thin nose, and around the neck. Now, very close to the face, she spoke to the corpse like a child talking to her doll.

"I think you're beautiful!" she sighed.

The nuns prayed outside the door, and the full moon was bright in the Christmas Eve sky.

PART FIVE – LIZZIE

September 27 to December 25, 1967

… the Lord will lay bare their secret parts…
Instead of perfume there will be rottenness…
and instead of well-set hair, baldness…
instead of beauty, shame…
ravaged, she shall sit upon the ground.

– Isaiah 3, 17–26

62 The Witch Hunt

On September 1, 1967, Pham Von Dong, Prime Minister of North Vietnam, vowed that Hanoi would "continue to fight." On September 11, the Beatles began filming their *Magical Mystery Tour* movie. On September 17, The Doors sang lyrics that they'd agreed to censor on *The Ed Sullivan Show* and were banned from appearing again on the program.

Meanwhile, the trial of Alice Elizabeth Fawkes, aka Lizzie Hirsig, for the first-degree murder of seven-year-old Cynthia Mary Conliffe, was set to begin in Los Angeles on October 10.

* * *

Alfred Pinkerton, Esq. reclined by his pool in his swim trunks, chain-smoking, watching the wind stir the palm trees, and savoring the fact that no other lawyer in L.A.—or probably anywhere else—had the style, brilliance, or balls to defend a witch for killing a little girl. It was, as he naturally called it, "a Witch Hunt."

He was at ease regarding the trial, although Lizzie'd gone off on her own insane way and murdered a child. For one thing, she was now on strict house arrest and 24-hour watch. This concession had been granted because there was little evidence against her. For another, with her on house arrest, Pinkerton had control.

In Pinkerton's eyes, this sensational trial wasn't about a dead little girl—it was about headlines, book deals, maybe film rights. He relished the glamour Felicia Shayne would provide, just as she welcomed the publicity. Each day he was increasingly relieved that no one had found "Mad Jack" Caldwell or Margo Coventry who, he'd learned, had fled to Mexico after Cindy Conliffe's murder. With luck, he figured, they'd both OD'd by now.

Indeed, as far as Pinkerton was concerned, this trial wasn't about Lizzie Hirsig or Cindy Conliffe—it was about Alfred Pinkerton. He'd be the star attraction. And he'd present his case just far enough off-kilter that Lizzie would be doomed for execution. As he always said, the public despises lawyers who get monsters free. They hero-worship the ones whose monsters go to death row.

This monster's death mask would be the prize of his collection.

* * *

In San Francisco, Simon Bone, recovering from his heart attack, had left the hospital, taking sanctuary in his townhouse. He'd given multiple depositions and interviews that he never knew Lizzie Hirsig, and that she never had any connection whatsoever to the Church of the Light Bearer, despite the message left at the murder site. He publicly theorized the killer was a Christian zealot, trying to defame modern Satanists. Still, Bone shuttered the church in San Francisco, temporarily, "for the safety of my disciples."

Today was a special day for him—he was signing a contract for his long-planned new book. A female agent from New York had flown out to seal the deal, and they sat in Bone's townhouse living room, beneath the John Collier painting of *Lilith*.

"It's quite a stunning love story, my dear," said Bone. "As the book will relate, Porter Down was Valerie Le Fay's killer, still a free man after all these years. I was Valerie's lover, still devoted after all these years. At any rate, the current trial in Los Angeles is a perfect prelude to our publication, and my manuscript will be ready in only two weeks."

The agent glanced up toward the ceiling. "I imagine Valerie used to swing on the chandelier during those long-ago nights?"

"Actually, she did her chandelier-swinging at my estate in Carmel," smiled Bone. "Perhaps you'll drive there with me tomorrow?"

The agent made a quick excuse. Something about this man made her want to get away from him as quickly as possible.

* * *

Tony Wyngate had worked the third consecutive night as a volunteer at Gettysburg Hospital. It was after 2:00 A.M., he was driving home to Charnita, and he was thinking about California and Janice Lynnbrooke.

This afternoon, after his classes had ended, he'd visited the Grotto, looking at the statute of the Blessed Virgin in the niche above the altar. It was the same statue he'd found that morning 13 years ago, days after the suicide of Jonathan Brooks, the statue's porcelain face then covered in whorish makeup, a clay phallus attached to its hips, blasphemously transformed in the night into a hermaphrodite. He'd learned since that such a desecration was not unique, but the memory still sickened him, as did the knowledge of who was likely responsible.

Arriving home tonight, he retrieved his mail, saw the Los Angeles postmark and tore open the envelope. It was a summons to appear in the trial of the State of California vs. Alice Elizabeth Fawkes, aka Lizzie Hirsig, on the charge of Murder.

To his shock, he read that he'd been called as a witness for the Defense.

63

The Defense, Day One, Morning Session

MONDAY, OCTOBER 16, 1967

The Los Angeles Courthouse Building appeared austere and monolithic in the Monday morning sunshine.

The trail accusing Lizzie Hirsig of the kidnapping and murder of Cindy Conliffe, although closed to the public, was open to press members, selected each evening by lottery. People with legal connections also managed to gain entry. It had been a packed house since the jury selection began Tuesday, October 10, without an empty seat in the courtroom.

Tony Wyngate had arrived in L.A. Sunday, October 15, the night before his scheduled testimony. He'd driven from the airport to the Brentwood Motor Inn, where Brad had cordially provided him his former room. Jim O'Leary called, arranging to drive Tony to the courthouse. He also told Tony he'd soon be seeing another Defense witness—Janice Lynnbrooke.

During Monday's drive into the city Tony, dressed in a somber blue suit and tie, listened carefully as O'Leary brought him up to date. The first two days had been spent in jury selection and the next two days had been taken up with the attorneys' opening statements and with testimony by Porter Down as star witness for the Prosecution. The Prosecutor carefully skirted his statements about "killing" Lizzie in 1931 and his belief about a resurrected or reborn witch. Still, Alfred Pinkerton's objections had riddled Porter's claims about the defendant's "inspirations and influences." The Hon. Judge George DeSylla Bacharach had sustained Pinkerton's protests, insisting this murder trial rested, as he put it, "not on spicy 1931 tales, but on irrefutable 1967 evidence."

"Old Bacharach just loves saying that," O'Leary told Tony.

With no "irrefutable 1967 evidence" physically linking Lizzie to the murder, the Prosecution's case had floundered. Pinkerton had declined to cross-examine Porter, but O'Leary was uneasy about the Defense reserving the right to cross-examine him at a later time.

He also told Tony that Universal Studios had withdrawn *Frankenstein* from its TV library, claiming they might never lease the film again.

* * *

"I haven't heard from Porter since June," Tony had said as they drove.

"He's sorry he ever got you and the lady mixed up in this," said O'Leary. "He never imagined you'd be called as Defense witnesses."

"Why were we?" asked Tony.

"I don't know," said O'Leary.

As they arrived at the courthouse, O'Leary told Tony that Janice was set to testify tomorrow. He added that Robert and Veronica Conliffe had not yet attended the trial, unwilling to confront Pinkerton's legal tricks or tolerate the very sight of the defendant.

* * *

Tony sat in the front row, where O'Leary had escorted him before hurrying off to other concerns. The retired policeman had placed his hat beside Tony, saving the seat. Tony had met neither lawyer, given no pre-trial deposition, and had come to an unnerving suspicion: The Defense knew of his scandal of 13 years ago. Porter had known of it. What prevented Alfred Pinkerton, with his legal network, from uncovering it too, to discredit him, Janice, and Porter?

Meanwhile, the prosecutor made her entrance. She was Sandra Duke, a young black woman who wore her assurance as smartly as she did her black-and-charcoal Rodeo Drive ensemble. She was a Watts to Westwood success story who'd won scholarships through the USC law school, quickly becoming a fireball L.A. courtroom star attraction. The lady had a round, softly pretty face that contrasted with her large, angry eyes, a curly Afro hairstyle, a slim but shapely figure, and a sassy mouth that had proven both a blessing and curse for her in the courtroom. Among her staff, she referred to the defendant as "that devil lovin' hippie bitch."

She nodded to Tony, as if she knew who he was, sat at her table, and examined some documents. Her secretary, a young white male, respectfully waited until her entrance had registered, then briefly conferred with her.

Now Alfred Pinkerton, attired for California fall in the light tweeds and vest of a British gentleman, entered the courtroom. If Duke gave off assurance, Pinkerton radiated arrogance, his bright cat eyes making contact, it seemed to Tony, with everyone in the room—including Tony.

The jury filed in, taking their seats to the right side as one faced the bench. The seven women and five men appeared smartly dressed and decidedly Californian.

A guarded corner door opened, a policeman appeared, followed by Felicia Shayne. She wore a sharply tailored navy-blue suit with a very short skirt, moving with the style of a fashion model, her dark brunette hair lustrous. She let her own entrance make its impact, went back into the corner room, and after a dramatic pause, re-emerged with Alice Elizabeth Fawkes, aka Lizzie Hirsig, aka Saint Lizzie, on her arm. The defendant looked strikingly attractive. Her makeup was more subtle than usual, but she still evoked a red-haired archangel in a stained-glass window, only in a short black dress and heels. She stood considerably taller than Felicia, and as she moved into the morning sunlight streaming through the large courtroom window, the transfiguration was complete.

Catching Tony staring at her, Lizzie winked at him.

* * *

"All rise."

The assemblage stood. The Hon. Judge George DeSylla Bacharach entered. He was in his early 70s, with a prominent nose, a fringe of gray hair, and a steel-trap face. The recent death of Bacharach's wife of 35 years and a minor stroke had taken their toll. O'Leary had told Tony that there'd been criticism regarding Bacharach's handling of recent cases—"loosey-goosey," in O'Leary's words—and there'd been blunt accusations of imminent senility.

"I welcome back the jury," said Bacharach, "from what I hope was a restful weekend." His large, watery eyes turned to the lawyers. "The Defense will open its case. Mr. Pinkerton, Miss Shayne... please proceed."

Lizzie sat at the Defense table on the far end from the jury, having asked the first day of the trial to move from the middle chair, telling Felicia Shayne her long legs were cramping under the table. She gave off her wildly theatrical aura, casting its spell on the crowd.

Tony felt a pang of nervousness, wondering if he might be about to testify. "Your honor," said Pinkerton, "I recall the Prosecution's witness… Mr. Porter Down."

A bailiff went to the hallway, returning with Porter, dressed this October day in a dark suit and tie, looking very uncomfortable. He marched his puffin walk to the stand, to the right as one faced the judge, half-ringed with a wooden balustrade, open in the front. Porter, reminded that he was still under oath from his previous testimony in the case, sat and sullenly crossed his arms on his barrel chest. Tony couldn't tell if Porter was aware of his presence, although he sat directly before him.

"Your Honor," said Pinkerton, "in order to spare you and the jury from the irrelevancies that Mr. Down previously attempted to present, I request only 'Yes' and 'No' responses."

"Proceed."

"Mr. Down, is it true that pursuing the defendant has been your only case in two years?"

"Yes."

"Is it true that you attended the defendant's Black Mass?"

"Yes."

"Is it true that you assaulted the defendant at Forest Lawn Memorial Park last June 28, in an attack photographed and recorded by Los Angeles media?"

"Yes."

"Is it true, Mr. Down, that in 1931, you were convicted of manslaughter…"

"Objection," said Duke. "Your Honor ruled against the Prosecution's discussion of 1931 events. The Defense should abide by the same ruling."

"Sustained."

"I ask instead… during your aforementioned attack of the defendant, did you say to her, and I quote—'I swear to God, next time I kill you, you'll *stay* goddamn dead'?"

"Yes."

"Mr. Down, do you believe that you killed the defendant while she was here in, shall we say, a previous life?"

"Objection! Irrelevant to the essence of this trial!"

"Overruled. The witness will answer."

"Yes," said Porter.

The people in the courtroom reacted. Bacharach sounded his gavel.

"Look at the defendant, Mr. Down," said Pinkerton. "In nostalgia for your irresponsibly violent past, and a sense of, shall we say, deranged *déjà vu*... Are you *obsessed* by her? *Sexually* obsessed by her?"

"No."

"You're a liar," said Pinkerton. There were gasps at the accusation.

"Objection," cried Duke. "Mr. Pinkerton has forgotten who's on trial!"

"Sustained."

"Shall we all reflect a moment," said Pinkerton, "on this professionally disgraced old man, and his outrageous, violently perverse delusion..."

"Objection!"

"Sustained!"

Pinkerton, unruffled, dramatically raised his hand toward Porter in accusation. "Witchfinder Number One!" he announced.

* * *

"Miss Duke," said Judge Bacharach, "Proceed with your redirect. And do not pursue the irrelevant line of questioning about 1931 that you favored last week."

Sandra Duke stood, realized her restrictions, looked at the sullen sourpuss in the witness box who'd just testified that he'd killed the defendant in 1931, and sighed.

"So, Mr. Down," said Duke. "Who'd you root for in the World Series... the Cardinals or the Red Sox?"

Loud laughter. Bacharach pounded his gavel. "Miss Duke!"

"Sorry, your Honor," said Duke. "No further questions."

"May I, your Honor?" asked Felicia Shayne, standing. "I'll be brief."

"Praise God," mumbled Sandra Duke.

Shayne approached Porter. "Mr. Down, as you just loosened your collar, I saw a chain around your neck, sir... possibly the chain of an *amulet* of some sort. Would you show me the amulet, sir, and describe it?"

Porter pulled the charm from his shirt. "It's Saint George slaying the Dragon," he said.

"So it is," said Shayne. "I wonder... Is that how you imagine yourself, Mr. Down? A saint, trying to slay a dragon?"

"Objection," said Duke.

"Nothing more, your honor," said Shayne. Immensely pleased with herself, she returned to her table. Lizzie grinned at the puffed-up Felicia.

She's creaming, thought Lizzie.

64

The Defense,
Day One,
Afternoon Session

Sandra Duke always remembered who was primarily responsible for her success: Her mother, who'd seen Sandra graduate from USC, but died before her first day practicing in court. "This is for you, Mama," said Sandra ritualistically before entering a courtroom.

Today she felt she was letting down both the Conliffes and Mama.

About 12:30, a half-hour before court was to resume, a legal clerk summoned Tony, who'd had a light lunch in the courthouse cafeteria, to Duke's office. Tony found Duke ensconced behind her office desk, noisily slurping a milk shake. He sat in front of her desk as paralegals darted in and out of the office.

Duke's staff alternately described her, depending on her mood, as Watts Sandra (her old neighborhood) or Westwood Sandra (her new neighborhood). Right now, she was Watts Sandra, complete with a milk-shake mustache.

"*Bullll-shit!*" she ranted. "Pinkerton... the smirking, posing, jive tur-key *bastard*! And that smug, ass-shakin' partner of his!" She gulped her milkshake, finally focusing on Tony. "You're next," she said, slam-dunking her empty cup into a waste can with her right hand, wiping away her milky mustache with her left. "Listen. They want to play 'Humiliate the witness.' Can you stay cool, no matter how hard these two crackers hit you?"

"Do you have any idea," asked Tony tentatively, "what they might ask?"

"Not a goddamn clue."

310

Tony believed her. He could only hope Pinkerton didn't have a goddamn clue, either.

"That devil-lovin' hippie bitch!" said Duke. "I'd like to rip that wig right off her head!"

Her legal secretary turned. He looked disillusioned. "Do you really think it's a wig?" he asked. "It doesn't look like a wig to me…"

"Oh, shut your damn fool mouth," said Sandra Duke.

* * *

Tony was back in the courtroom by 12:50. The jury filed in from lunch.

Just before one o'clock, Felicia Shayne entered the packed courtroom, escorting the defendant, who smiled casually. Bailiffs and the court clerk took their places. Sandra Duke turned at her desk and looked at Tony as if to remind him what they'd discussed in her office. O'Leary hurried in and took his place. Porter was nowhere to be seen.

"All rise."

As Judge Bacharach returned, Tony wondered where Porter was …

"Dr. Anthony Wyngate."

Tony rose, buttoned his jacket and walked to the stand. He was surprised how different everything appeared from the perspective of the witness box.

* * *

"Your honor," said Pinkerton, "please be aware this is a hostile witness."

"So noted," sad Bacharach. "Proceed."

"Name and profession?" asked Pinkerton.

"Anthony Wyngate. Professor of Classics at Mount Saint Mary's College, Maryland."

"Are you also a published author?"

"Yes. Books and articles on Ancient Civilizations. I recently wrote a novel."

"Congratulations. Dr. Wyngate, did you receive this past May a visit at Mount Saint Mary's College, Maryland, from Mr. Porter Down? Offering you a paid trip to Los Angeles to join his crusade?"

"I wouldn't use the word 'crusade'…"

"Yes or no?"

"Yes, Mr. Down came to Mount Saint Mary's, but…"

"Who else did you meet in Los Angeles besides Mr. Down?"

"Miss Janice Lynnbrooke."

"Is Miss Lynnbrooke young and attractive?"

"Objection."

"Sustained. Mr. Pinkerton!"

"Sorry, your Honor. Dr. Wyngate, your first and recently-published novel was titled *Boudicca,* who was a female Briton warrior fighting against the Romans. As a follow-up, have you considered a topical subject—perhaps a beautiful devil worshipper—especially if she were convicted of murder?"

"Actually, Mr. Down and I discussed such a book, but we never proceeded to a formal agreement. We dropped the idea some time ago."

"Have you pursued it with Miss Lynnbrooke? You're a writer, she's an investigator. Perhaps you both plan a collaboration, working together closely… helping each other straddle the sticky areas?"

"Objection!" shouted Duke over the suggestive laughter.

"Sustained. Mr. Pinkerton!"

"I haven't spoken to Miss Lynnbrooke since June," said Tony.

"Dr. Wyngate," asked Pinkerton, "on the night of June 12, 1967, didn't you *and* Miss Lynnbrooke *and* the redoubtable Mr. Down all go to the Black Mass at Malibou Lake?"

"Yes."

"And on that night, before a full crowd, didn't Miss Hirsig turn the tables on your spying, invite you to come to the altar, and make a fool of you by sitting on your lap and running her fingers through your hair…"

A woman on the jury laughed nervously, triggering more laughter. "Objection!" called Duke. "Mr. Pinkerton is trying to embarrass Dr. Wyngate."

"Judging by his interminable blush," said Pinkerton, "I'm succeeding."

"Overruled," decreed Bacharach.

"And," continued Pinkerton, "after your humiliation at the Black Mass that night, you went back to the Abbey the *very next morning*? Without Mr. Down or Miss Lynnbrooke?"

"Miss Hirsig invited me to come back."

"And so you did! *Eight hours later*! You're an *ardent* fellow, aren't you, Professor?"

"Objection."

"Sustained."

"Did you want more humiliation?"

"Objection!"

"Sustained."

"Did you hope to catch Miss Hirsig undressed? *Naked?*"

"Objection!"

"Sustained!"

"Dr. Wyngate… while you were visiting Miss Hirsig, did the two of you play a game?"

"Yes," said Tony, blushing again.

"Describe it, please?"

"We… we played that I was a priest, and she was telling me her Confession." He paused. "It was *her* idea."

The courtroom burst into laughter. Lizzie laughed too.

"Enough!" shouted Pinkerton. "I'm sick of looking at this man!"

"Objection!" shouted Duke, standing. "*Outrageous*, your Honor!"

"Sustained!"

Pinkerton sat down. Several members of the jury regarded him with awe.

* * *

Sandra Duke's eyes blazed righteously as she charged into battle. "Dr. Wyngate, very simply 'yes' or 'no': Are you currently pursuing a book project of your own, based on the events of this trial, or planning to profit from this tragedy in any way?"

"No."

"That be all!" said Duke, realizing how ruffled she was when she heard herself lapse back into her old neighborhood jargon. She sat as Pinkerton stood.

"May I, your Honor?" he asked.

Tony, soaking wet from the last round, had a feeling the fight was just beginning. "It's been an intense day," Pinkerton said casually. "And Miss Duke is not at her best."

"Objection!"

"Sustained."

"Just one final matter," said Pinkerton. "Your Honor, I ask this question as it's essential to consider, once again, this witness's validity: Dr

Wyngate, is it true that, in 1954, while studying for the priesthood, you pursued a relationship with a nun..."

"Objection!"

"Sustained."

"...and whose death," shouted Pinkerton, "a probable suicide, resulted in your disgrace and resignation from the seminary? *Yes or no?*"

"Objection, your honor!"

"Sustained! Mr. Pinkerton, you're risking contempt!"

Alfred Pinkerton pointed at Tony. "Witchfinder Number Two!" he shouted triumphantly.

The courtroom was in an uproar. Judge Bacharach demanded Pinkerton see him in his quarters and dismissed court for the day. Lizzie, who'd slipped off her high heels during the interrogation, casually put them on again.

* * *

"Shit! Shit and *Bull-shit!*" shouted Sandra Duke, leading Tony through the private courthouse corridors, followed by her squad of paralegals. They finally emerged by the loading dock area, where an unmarked police car awaited him.

"Get your smooth white ass in there, lover boy," said Duke. Tony obeyed. Sandra Duke watched the car drive away.

"This trial be a zoo," said Duke.

* * *

That night, Alfie Pinkerton did a live interview on the 11 P.M. news. When he arrived home, Felicia was awaiting him in a negligee in the master bedroom.

"I was wonderful when I asked Down about his amulet, wasn't I?" she gasped just before her climax.

* * *

"I spoke to Janice," O'Leary told Tony when he telephoned him late that night. "She wanted me to tell ya'...she's very sorry for what you went through today."

* * *

Just after 1 A.M., Tony's phone rang again. "You *baaad* boy," said Sandra Duke. "So, who told on you?"

"I don't know. Few things are as tough to get as sealed Church records."

"You got that right," said Duke. "*We* can't get them and we've been trying all night. *Somebody* knew. Anyway"—Tony heard her pause to yawn—"here's the deal. If you want to respond to today's situation, I can call you to the stand tomorrow…"

"That's kind of you."

"I'm just a lump of sugar."

"I don't want to respond," said Tony. "But I do want to be there tomorrow."

"Sure," said Duke sassily. "To cheer for your lady. See you then."

She'd hardly hung up when the phone rang again. "You were tough today, Tony," said Porter Down, then hung up.

* * *

Eve Devonshire Cromwell was on a red-eye flight to Los Angeles. A house sitter would take care of Boy and the Thousand Islands property until her return.

She hadn't been in Los Angeles for over 30 years.

65   The Defense, Day Two

TUESDAY, OCTOBER 17, 1967

On the Defense's second day, the courtroom and hallway were packed and noisy by 8:30 A.M.

Naturally, Alfred Pinkerton's raising the question about Porter Down's "killing" a woman in 1931 had sparked intense media curiosity. Reporters found a few eyewitnesses who'd attended the "Saint Valerie" Black Mass 36 years ago, but located neither surviving cultists, nor her death record. Nor had any overnight discoveries confirmed or denied the story of Dr. Anthony Wyngate's suicide nun.

Meanwhile, outside the courthouse, police apprehended three self-proclaimed witches, armed with glass jars of feces and urine, ready to hurl their makeshift bombs at Sandra Duke, claiming they had Lizzie's "blessing and benediction."

* * *

Tony, wearing a gray suit and driven to the courthouse by a policeman, immediately sensed a marked change from the previous day, a sense of cruel amusement among the reporters and hangers-on. The bailiffs and police clearly felt it too.

Tony sat in the seat reserved for him in the second row. The two seats beside him were also marked as reserved. Alfred Pinkerton, dressed in his finest suit, a brown, tailor-made three-piece, stood at the Defense table, casually reviewing some papers. Sandra Duke took her place, wearing a forest green business suit with a pale green chiffon blouse. She was every inch the epitome of "Westwood Sandra." The jury entered with the look of an enthused audience

There was a rustle beside Tony—O'Leary had arrived with Janice. To Tony's surprise, she wore a dark, very short dress that showed off her shapely legs, as well as stockings and black heels. Her long dark hair, usually tied in a ponytail, fell over one shoulder and she'd taken time with her makeup. Tony imagined that after seeing the newspaper pictures of Lizzie and the female lawyers, all dressed for battle, Janice had decided to show up at the arena today looking like a hosiery model.

O'Leary took the end seat. Janice sat between him and Tony. After a moment, she touched Tony's hand.

Now Felicia Shayne appeared from the corner room, wearing a very short white pleated skirt with blue jacket and red heels. She escorted Lizzie, dressed today in her black short dress, black stockings and heels, the black, wide-brimmed hat, with a veil, and as always, her red-eyed crystal angel. She looked, Tony thought, a bit like glamorous 1930s divorcees whose photographs he'd seen in old rotogravures. The room quieted and her honeysuckle scent accompanied her entrance. She sat at the end of the Defense table, raised the veil and draped it over the back of her hat.

Just before Judge Bacharach's entrance, two people entered the courtroom and took the back row seats Jim O'Leary had saved for them. They were Porter Down and Eve Devonshire Cromwell, whom Porter had welcomed and picked up at the airport. Lizzie, as if feeling a chill, turned, looked back, and saw Porter and the woman beside him. Both women looked at each other across the room in a sort of strange recognition. After a long moment, Lizzie turned, touched her amulet, and gave the impression she was praying to it.

* * *

"All rise!"

Judge Bacharach entered. He'd just begun addressing the court when bailiffs brought Veronica and Robert Conliffe, Cindy Conliffe's parents, into the courtroom. Mrs. Conliffe wore a black, tailored dress and her blonde hair reminded everyone of the pictures they'd seen of her murdered child. They sat in the row behind Tony and Janice, taking the courtroom's two remaining seats. Dr. Conliffe kissed his wife's cheek. They'd decided to come to bring gravitas to the trial and their surprise presence was almost overpowering. The room was deadly still. The jury regarded them both, especially Mrs. Conliffe, with fascination.

Bacharach allowed the moment, then spoke. "Mr. Pinkerton... proceed."

Pinkerton stood. "Your Honor, I call Miss Janice Lynnbrooke... also a hostile witness."

Pretty Little Angel Eyes, thought Lizzie, slowly rocking her leg.

* * *

Janice walked to the witness box with almost a swagger. She appeared composed, confident. Pinkerton grinned casually at her, as if oblivious to the darkness that had fallen over the courtroom since the Conliffes had entered.

"Name and profession?"

"Janice Lynnbrooke. Investigator... specifically an extractor."

"An extractor? That sounds like some sort of dentistry."

"No. As I'm sure you already know, Mr. Pinkerton, I infiltrate cults and communes..."

"To drag young people back to hearth and home?"

"No. To help young people held against their will escape dangerous situations. I have a bachelor's degree in Sociology from Stanford."

"Congratulations," Pinkerton smirked.

"Thank you," Janice smirked back.

"Miss Lynnbrooke, when did you begin your unlicensed 'extracting' career?"

"September of 1966."

"Did you infiltrate the defendant's so-called 'cult'?"

"Yes."

"And after a very brief time, did *she* 'extract' *you*?"

"Objection!"

"Overruled. The witness will answer."

"Yes, I worked on her technical crew. And yes, she fired me because one night she slapped me and I slapped her back."

"Pardon me," Pinkerton interrupted. "Miss Lynnbrooke... are you *trembling*?"

"Objection!"

"Sustained."

"No, I'm *not* trembling," said Janice.

"I remind you, Miss Lynnbrooke, you're under oath. But please... I promise you, neither I, nor Miss Shayne, nor Miss Hirsig, will bite you. Just take a deep breath, relax... and tell the court why you've been living a lie these past several years."

"I beg your pardon?"

"Miss Lynnbrooke, in 1963, did you divorce and go back to your maiden name?"

"Yes."

"In early 1966, did you move from Washington State to California?"

"Yes."

"During the two-and-a-half years between your divorce and your move to California, did you, as a single woman, work at any full-time job?"

"No."

"Why not?"

"Objection," said Duke. "Irrelevant."

"Sustained."

"I'll rephrase. Miss Lynnbrooke... are you familiar with Queens Hospital in Washington?"

"Objection! Again, relevancy."

"Relevancy, indeed, your Honor," said Pinkerton. "Miss Lynnbrooke's health history is of vital importance regarding probable prejudice toward the defendant."

Bacharach considered. "Objection overruled. Respond, Miss Lynnbrooke."

Janice paused. "I refuse to answer that question."

"Miss Lynnbrooke," said Bacharach firmly, "you're in no position to select what questions you do or do not answer. Respond!"

Janice closed her eyes, opened them. "Yes."

"Will you tell us," asked Pinkerton, "what kind of hospital Queens is?"

"No, I will not," said Janice.

The court reacted. Bacharach smacked his gavel. "Miss Lynnbrooke. You will respect this court!"

"The same way it's respecting me?" asked Janice.

Pinkerton raised his hands helplessly. "I'll try again, your Honor. Miss Lynnbrooke, what kind of hospital is Queens?"

"It's... ," began Janice, "for mental illness... . for psychiatric cases..."

"Really? And how do *you* know that, Miss Lynnbrooke?"

"Objection!"

"I'll allow it."

Tony looked over at Lizzie. Her leg was rocking.

"I...I was a patient there."

Lizzie gave a gasp of mock surprise. Janice glared at her. Bacharach hammered for the crowd's silence. Sandra Duke turned and looked questioningly at Tony. She could see in his face that he'd never known.

"According to telephone conversations we had with your ex-husband and your step-sister," said Pinkerton, "you suffered from nightmares so severe that they virtually incapacitated you, driving you into a mental hospital...for *two years*. True?"

"Objection!" cried Duke, standing. "Your Honor! I demand that Mr. Pinkerton explain this particularly brutal questioning!"

"Health issues of the witness make her hostile to the defendant," said Pinkerton.

"Proceed," said Bacharach.

"My question stands, Miss Lynnbrooke, and I require a 'Yes' or 'No' response: did your nightmares cause you to commit yourself to a mental hospital for two years?"

Janice nodded and kept her eyes down. "Yes."

Lizzie gasped again. Felicia quickly scribbled a note and passed it to her. *Stop it*, read the note.

"Did you keep this a secret," asked Pinkerton, "from your friends and associates? If I re-called your dear friend Dr. Wyngate to the stand, would that fine fellow have to testify that you kept this a secret even from *him?*"

"I never told him."

Pinkerton took a step back and looked analytically at Janice. "Are you trembling *now*, Miss Lynnbrooke?"

"Objection!"

"Sustained!"

Janice pushed back the stray hair that had fallen over her eye. Meanwhile, there was the sound of someone softly crying in the courtroom. It was Mrs. Conliffe.

"Miss Lynnbrooke," resumed Pinkerton, "is it true that, most recently, you were back in institutionalized care, here in Los Angeles, from June 29 through August 22 of this year, due to another health issue... namely, recurrent cocaine addiction?"

The crowd reacted again. "Objection!" shouted Duke.

"Credibility of witness, your Honor," said Pinkerton.

"Objection overruled," said Bacharach. "Please answer, Miss Lynnbrooke."

"Yes," said Janice quietly.

Duke snapped her pencil in half.

"And are you prepared to admit," asked Pinkerton, "that your infiltration into various cults was in fact a shameless ruse to form contacts to secure cocaine to satisfy your addiction?"

"Objection!"

"Sustained."

"How dare you!" said Janice, fighting back tears.

"Finally," asked Pinkerton, "is it true that you've had periods of incapacitation due to mental illness and recurrent substance addiction ever since you were 15-years- old… when you found the corpse of your father, moments after he had fired a shotgun into his mouth?"

Janice shuddered, Lizzie squealed, Bacharach sounded his gavel, and Sandra Duke stood, charging furiously from around her desk.

"Objection! Your honor, this is outrageous! The defense is trying to break down the witness, who surely needs an adjournment to compose herself."

"No, I don't," said Janice.

"Objection sustained," said Bacharach. "Miss Duke, sit down! Mr. Pinkerton, proceed very carefully with this line of questioning."

"A murdered child is calling out for justice," cried Duke, "and you've allowed Mr. Pinkerton to turn this trial into a circus!"

"Sit *down*, Miss Duke!" thundered Bacharach. She kept standing. Mr. Conliffe put his arm around his wife's shoulder as she wept, more loudly now.

"A mentally ill woman," said Pinkerton, raising his voice, moving aggressively toward the jury, "pathetically dependent on cocaine… a hypocritical, righteous junkie…"

"Leave her alone," Tony heard himself say.

"Dr. Wyngate!" admonished Judge Bacharach.

"I understand Dr. Wyngate's agitation, your Honor," said Pinkerton, "considering that he's a sexual predator who prefers emotionally ill young women."

"Objection!" cried Duke over the crowd. Janice looked helplessly at Tony, tears of anger and shame running down her face. Lizzie rocked her leg.

"Sustained," said Bacharach. "Mr. Pinkerton..."

"You look at Miss Hirsig, Miss Lynnbrooke," said Pinkerton, "and see a personification of all your nightmares about your father's suicide ... all the torment that led you to asylum incarceration and cocaine addiction..."

"Objection!"

"Sustained!"

"Lizzie Hirsig is all your demons incarnate, isn't she, Miss Lynnbrooke!" shouted Pinkerton. "Your *spying* on her, your *obsession* about her... She *terrifies* you, doesn't she... *Witchfinder Number Three?*"

"Objection!"

"Sustained! Mr. Pinkerton! One more inflammatory word and I'll assuredly find you in contempt! For the remainder of this trial, your questions will only focus on any evidence related to your client. Otherwise, I shall declare a mistrial!"

Bacharach loudly pounded the gavel with finality. Pinkerton milked the silence and its one anomaly, the soft weeping of Janice Lynnbrooke and of Veronica Conliffe. "No further questions," he said, and sat at the table.

Sandra Duke had never sat during Pinkerton's rant. "I have no questions for Miss Lynnbrooke," she said. "Only an apology for this total disgrace of a trial."

"Objection," said Pinkerton casually.

"Sustained. You may step down, Miss Lynnbrooke."

For a moment, Janice didn't move. She finally stood, looking for a moment at Veronica Conliffe, her face buried in her husband's arms. Janice slowly came down from the witness box, everyone watching her, the room totally, eerily silent. Then, as she reached the railing, there was a sound. It was Lizzie, crying, or pretending to cry.

"You poor little girl," wept Lizzie, her voice almost child-like. "I'm so sorry..."

Janice stopped and gripped the railing. She turned toward the taunting voice, looked at Lizzie for what seemed a very long moment, and dropped her purse to the floor.

Then she went for her.

"Bailiffs!" shouted Judge Bacharach, and the crowd screamed as Janice rushed toward the Defense table, her arms raised to strike. Pinkerton and Felicia Shayne both jumped up, cowering behind their chairs as Lizzie stood and faced Janice.

"*Bailiffs!*" shouted Bacharach again.

A husky bailiff was almost instantly upon Janice, pulling her arms behind her back. "Let me go," she cried, fighting manically to free herself. "Let me *GO!*"

Two more bailiffs moved in and reporters and photographers stood, scrambling for position to take pictures of Janice's anguished, sobbing face.

"Janice!" shouted Tony.

"*Clear this courtroom!*" Bacharach shrieked, but nobody was listening or leaving. Tony and O'Leary struggled to get to Janice through the crowd, but it was impossible.

Although the defendant had stood to face her attacker, there'd been, for a moment, fear in her eyes. Now, with Janice restrained by the bailiff, Lizzie decided to camp it. She suddenly sprang up onto the table, standing in her heels, posing timidly like a woman frightened by a mouse, coyly lifting her short dress, revealing the tops of her stockings.

Then, loudly and lushly, she screamed.

66 Adjournment

Trial had been cancelled for the day at 9:47 A.M. Over two hours later, Security escorted Tony Wyngate from a locked room at the courthouse to Sandra Duke's office.

"Sorry about the wait," Duke said, her mouth full of pastrami sandwich. "I want you to know that Bacharach will declare a mistrial. Miss Janice is fine and Lt. O'Leary is taking her to a safe place… secret even from you for now. You understand."

Tony nodded. Duke sipped her milk shake, rocked back in her swivel chair, and regarded Tony's sad expression with amusement. "Don't worry, honey," said Duke. "I don't believe that you're a…" She reached for the transcript of the morning testimony and read, "'…a sexual predator who prefers emotionally ill young women.'"

"I wasn't thinking about that," said Tony. "I'm afraid Janice will blame herself for the mistrial."

"I already assured her before she left that's not the case," said Duke. "Saint Lizzie's peep show on the table guaranteed that. No way this trial had a chance in hell of going on after she hiked up her dress and showed everybody her black garters. Of course, your spitfire lady Janice didn't help by going for her throat, but she did just what everybody else wanted to do. Especially me."

"Yeah," said Tony.

Duke shook her head. "That pumpkin head Pinkerton! The way he acted today, and with the Conliffes there in the courtroom… it was like he was *tryin'* to make the jury hate him, hate her… .as if he was *tryin'* to lose."

"Why would he try to lose?" asked Tony.

324

"These fat cat lawyers who defend creatures like Lizzie" said Duke wisely. "They all want to lose. They know the game. If they lose, the public will love 'em, and if they win, the public will hate 'em. Pinkerton could have got her off easily by playing up the limited evidence, and if Bacharach weren't already half brain-dead, he'd have shut down Pinkerton's 'witch-finder' act right away. For some reason, Pinkerton wants Lizzie Hirsig locked up or dead and buried. Maybe Lizzie realized it. Maybe that's why that screamin', wig-wearin' harpy got herself a mistrial."

"Will there be a new trial?" asked Tony.

"I don't believe it," said Duke. "Unless they find new evidence. Where it all goes from here, who knows? But I'll tell you this. That devil hippie bitch's funky ass is headin' for Hell, honey. And fast."

Tony stood. "Thank you, Miss Duke," he said. "Goodbye."

Duke stood and shook his hand. "Goodbye," she said.

He left the office. Sandra Duke finished her milk shake and stared out the window. "I'm sorry, Mama," she said softly. "Wish I'd won this one for you… and that poor little child, and her Mommy and Daddy."

After a moment, she started to cry.

* * *

The picture was perfect.

There was "Saint Lizzie," standing on the table in her large hat, short dress, and high heels, eyes wild, lifting her dress, screaming. Even her crystal angel was in perfect focus. Facing her was Janice Lynnbrooke, crying and grappled by a bailiff.

Courtroom Catfight! read the newspaper headline.

Tony held a copy of the paper as he made his way through the reporters, answering no questions. The desk had a message for him from Porter Down:

We're getting together tomorrow night—Janice, O'Leary, and a lady you need to meet. Beverly Hills Hotel at 7 P.M. Tell them at the desk you're there to see Mrs. Cromwell. P.D.

* * *

Alfie Pinkerton sipped his Scotch, sitting alone tonight by his pool. He'd invited Felicia to join him for a sunset *post-mortem* on the day's mortifying events, but she'd refused.

"You didn't have to *rape* her!" Felicia had privately sniped at him regarding his grilling of Janice Lynnbrooke.

He didn't know where Lizzie was now and didn't give a damn. Tomorrow was the official announcement of the mistrial. By her stunt in court today, Lizzie had swiped control, stolen the show... and won her freedom.

Pinkerton was seething. Of course, crazy as she was, she still might end up dead. Soon. Maybe he could help move things along before all of this boomeranged on him worse than it already had.

Owning her death mask was still a possibility.

67

Callers and Visitors

Tony had just returned from a solo dinner at the nearby restaurant when the telephone rang. "Someone says he has information for you," said Brad, who put through the call.

"Dr. Wyngate?" asked a deep voice. "My name is Edward Marsden."

* * *

Whitley Heights was a historic colony in the Hollywood Hills, developed during World War I. Legend claimed that Rudolph Valentino, Jean Harlow, and Boris Karloff had resided there during the Roaring '20s and/ or early '30s.

The address Tony sought was "Whitley Steps." It was what it said—a steep flight up a hillside past Italianate bungalows. Near the top of Whitley Steps, Tony saw the candlelit lantern sitting on the wall of a small fountain, behind a wooden fence laden with flowers and bearing the house number.

* * *

His host was very tall, dressed in shorts and a white, unbuttoned cotton shirt, barefoot, his silver hair tousled, his height and mustache at odds with his attire.

"Please, make yourself comfortable," said Edward Marsden. He indicated the dimly lit living room, sparsely furnished, the fireplace empty. Tony sat in one of the two chairs. "I hope the hour is convenient for you," said Marsden. "Unfortunately, my wife only sleeps during these hours."

"Is she ill?" asked Tony.

"Yes," Marsden said softly, looking toward the bedroom. "Terminally. Cancer. The pain killers prescribed only have any effect at this time of night."

"I'm sorry."

"Thank you," said Marsden, who'd set up a small card table and poured two glasses of wine. "Forgive my awkward amenities. It's been a while since we entertained." He reached beside his chair and handed Tony a copy of *Boudicca*. "You'll sign this for me?"

"Of course," said Tony, surprised. "But…"

"No," said Marsden. "I didn't lure you here under false pretenses for your autograph. Ancient civilizations always fascinated me. Current circumstances forced me to part with much of my library, but I couldn't resist buying this one."

"What work do you do, Mr. Marsden?"

"Oh, I'm retired, but I was a mediocrity at painting, writing, music. Earned a living, never made a mark. My wife had the true distinction. For years, Eleanor was a violinist with the Los Angeles Symphony." He took a framed picture from an end table and handed it to Tony. It showed Marsden with his wife, herself slender and attractive. Tony guessed the picture dated from the 1940s, based on their suits and hats.

"You're a striking couple," he said sincerely. "Any children?"

"No. But I'll get to the point." Marsden took the picture, placed it back on the table and sipped his wine. "Once upon a time, Dr. Wyngate, I was determined to be worldly. After Princeton, I wanted to revel in Paris, but spent most of the past 40 years in Los Angeles. The Roaring '20s had nose-dived into the Depression. Great anxiety. For a young man, it was quite…heady. But I needn't lecture you on cultural history, do I?"

He downed his wine and refilled both glasses. "Eleanor and I married in 1925. She had dreams of becoming a great violin virtuoso, and might have been, had she not compromised her career for marriage. And for a time, to get to the point of why I invited you here tonight, we were an audience for, but not actually acolytes of, Saint Valerie."

"Please tell me all you know," said Tony.

"I'm afraid we had no belief in a Divine Father or a Prince of Darkness," said Marsden. "We were simply admirers of Valerie and her mad, bitter defiance. I have to laugh at the topical flower children and their stabs at daring originality. As to true depravity and all the showmanship it offers, Valerie was beyond any of them. She could have been a sensation in Berlin, Paris… maybe even ancient Rome or Babylon, for Christ's sake. She wasn't actually attractive—a witchy nose, feral eyes, too tall, gawky. Still, believe me, my friend…she was a spellbinder."

There was a moaning from the next room and Marsden immediately excused himself. Tony looked again at the picture, the sophisticates looking back at him from the frame. The moaning stopped and Marsden returned.

"I can come back another time," said Tony.

"No. She's asleep again, but perhaps I should accelerate my story." Marsden refilled each glass again. "As you probably know, Valerie insinuated herself into the company of *Frankenstein* that summer, attracted to the actor Colin Clive. She told a few of her closer disciples she desired him, because he 'had the face of Christ'—and he did have a rather ascetic look. Anyway, the newspapers noted you and Porter Down as acquaintances, so you must know what happened?"

"He only told me that he was responsible for Valerie's death."

"Well, it was quite a show, apparently. The story we heard was that Clive, who was a pilot, flew with Valerie up the coast in a biplane. Down, a World War I pilot, as you know, followed in pursuit in another biplane. The irresistible imagery is of Clive and Down, dogfighting in the night over the Pacific, Valerie the prize in a sort-of flying circus. My guess is that Down simply forced Clive to land his plane and Clive, probably drunk, as the poor soul so often was, crashed… but survived. The Hollywood watchdogs kept the melodrama out of the news, 'Dr. Frankenstein' went safely home to jolly old England… and none of us ever saw Valerie again."

"She died in the crash?"

"Ah! That's a mystery. And here's where a prime mover enters the case… Simon Bone."

Tony nodded. "I should have known."

"You know him today as a bestselling author and head of the Church of the Light Bearer. We all knew him as something else altogether. Every group has its court jester, its toady fool. Valerie had Bone."

"I see," said Tony.

"Now, Valerie managed rather a Garbo act with her own coven. She was aloof, keeping an aura of mystery with her various echelons of admirers. Few, I gather, ever actually bought into the Devil business. Some of them had a certain degree of distinction, even if only in the way they fucked or sucked, pardon my language. Bone had none. He was a barely competent pianist who played at the Black Mass, but he let Valerie use the Malibou Lake property at no cost. Mainly, he was a simpering fool from an old-money San Francisco family. No true ability whatsoever."

"Not even the fucking or sucking?" asked Tony.

"That least of all. It was a very sexual group, or so they claimed. It didn't matter *who* you fucked, or *what* you fucked, but if you *didn't* fuck, or *couldn't,* that was unforgivable. For Valerie and her boys and girls, it was the blackest of mortal sins, although no one actually knew who Valerie's lovers were. Maybe she actually hadn't any. She kept secrets, including, for quite a while, her epilepsy. But Simon Bone... well, he was rich, even during the Depression, so she kept him around for his money and for laughs. At a party for his birthday, Valerie gave Simon both the smallest jock strap she could find, and a mammoth pink brassiere."

"Yet he stayed?"

"Oh yes! He adored her. The joke was that he drank her piss and ate her shit. Actually, it might not have been a joke."

"How did he respond to her death?"

"That's why I called you," said Marsden. "After Valerie's death, or disappearance, Simon ransacked the 'Abbey' for relics, taking the tent, Valerie's costumes, her clothes... surely her intimate apparel. She'd named him her 'Next of Kin,' probably due to his providing her the Malibou Lake property, so he had the right to go spelunking into her belongings. But a few of the coven members got in before him, largely to spite Simon, and a friend of ours took Valerie's diary."

"How did Bone react?"

"Badly. He threatened our friend. She finally asked us to keep the diary while she got Bone off her back—a nasty image—but died a short time later in a car accident. Eleanor wanted to destroy the diary, but unknown to her, I placed it in a safe deposit box as a rainy-day asset. It was there for 30 years. Then, three years ago, Eleanor learned she had cancer. She's had victories and setbacks. To pay the doctors, we sold off most of our library, our furniture... some of it custom-made and quite desirable. Eventually I bit the bullet and contacted the never-give-up Simon Bone. He bought the diary for an amount that paid for six months of cancer treatment. I never told Eleanor."

"So, Bone got the diary," said Tony, "found a mad woman, gave her the diary as a catechism, and baptized a new Valerie."

"Yes," said Marsden. "And based on the pictures I've seen, 'Saint Lizzie' is rather a striking facsimile of 'Saint Valerie.' Even the unfortunate nose."

"Bone must still have the diary," said Tony.

"And I have a copy," said Marsden. He took a packet from the hearth and handed it to Tony. "I'm not sure why I took the trouble… maybe I had an instinct it would come in handy someday. Poor quality, but you can decipher most of Valerie's writing, poetry, and her artwork. Bone's address and phone number are in the packet."

"Don't you want to give this to the police?" asked Tony. "And… sorry, but why are you only coming forward with this now?"

"I didn't want to get involved with this whole sordid mess, especially at this time in my life—and with Eleanor's being so sick…," Marden admitted somewhat shamefacedly. "It might be of help to you, however, in regard to what you—a 'witchfinder,' according to the press—do from here."

"I promise I'll return this to you as quickly as possible."

"No need," said Marsden quietly. "There's a certain justice, I suppose. After all those years, Bone and Valerie bought me more time with Eleanor."

"Thank you so much," said Tony.

"There's one more thing," said Marsden. "Conflicting, but of interest. After Valerie's disappearance, Simon told the coven that he had been Valerie's secret lover for the past months. Of course, they laughed in his face. But also… Simon drank heavily in those days, and while drunk, ran off at the mouth. On at least two occasions, he claimed that Universal, terrified by the potential publicity after the plane crash, got Valerie out of town. He claimed she was, in his words, "a basket case" and that, as her Next of Kin, he'd signed the legal papers for her incarceration. Simon even boasted that, in exchange for his signature on the commitment papers, certain charges against him were wiped clean by the powers-that-were."

"Where did Valerie go?" asked Tony.

"Bone said authorities had shipped her all the way across the country," said Marsden, "basically burying her alive in a Catholic madhouse for religious lunatics. He'd relate this with lip-smacking pride, as if delighted he'd avenged himself on the way Valerie had enjoyed eviscerating him. He inferred she died there."

A Catholic sanitarium in the east for religious lunatics, thought Tony. *My God.*

Tony, amazed by this news he'd just heard and the diary copy he now owned, let a respectful silence register, and then asked, "Mr. Marsden... do you believe there could be anything supernatural, or demonic, about the current situation?"

"Dr. Wyngate," said Marsden, "in that bedroom lies the woman I've cherished for 42 years... the most beautiful, brilliant woman I've ever known. She now weighs 85 pounds, weeps in agony 18 hours a day, and doesn't recognize me, be I changing her diapers or telling her how much I still love her. If I go to Hell, I defy Lucifer to show me anything more 'demonic' than what this life has done to my Eleanor. Now before you go, please sign my book."

* * *

Tony drove back to Brentwood and examined the photocopy of the diary—the profanity, the poetry, the drawings. The passion in the mockery chilled him.

There were various pornographic sketches of the Christ figure, and Tony recognized the face: Colin Clive's. The following pages used the same imagery, with sketches of sexual blasphemy, uglier and more extreme than Tony had ever seen. There were also sketches of a woman, clearly supposed to be Valerie, in sexual relations with the Christ figure.

The final submission was dated October 18, 1931. There was a crucifix, Clive-as-Christ nailed to it, almost mutilated, blood pouring from his hands, feet and side. Scrawled in purple ink below the sketch were the words:

The Five Sacred Wounds!

68

Night

WEDNESDAY, OCTOBER 18 TO
SUNDAY, OCTOBER 29, 1967

The next evening Eve Cromwell sat in her suite at the Beverly Hills Hotel. With her were Janice, Jim O'Leary, and directly beside her, Porter. She'd been talking about Colin Clive, Bonnie Bristeaux, and Valerie Le Fay.

"You were so kind to me, Jim," she said to O'Leary. "And I always regretted that you, Porter, took the punishment for all that happened."

"I did fine," said Porter, winking at her.

"After 1931," asked Janice, "did you ever see Colin Clive again?"

"Only in the movies," said Eve. "He went back and forth between England and the States for a time...stage and film work. In 1935, he did *Bride of Frankenstein*. I was in Sacramento then, but I'd sometimes hear stories about him...and his drinking. The last film he made was called *The Woman I Love*. Colin played a Lafayette Escadrille captain. I saw the film. He was gaunt, like a skeleton...and died shortly afterwards."

Eve became silent. She remembered the stories about that final film, how Colin had been so drunk that the crew had to hold him up for close-ups. She remembered coming down on the train for the funeral. "The Colonial Mortuary," on Venice Boulevard. ... the morbidly curious movie fans lined up that night to get into the viewing, with some of the women holding movie magazines... the funeral the next afternoon, with a crowd of 300 people, as if it were a Hollywood premiere. And she remembered her nightmare, his body in the funeral bed, Valerie coming in the night to mourn and kiss the corpse and scream. She kept these stories to herself.

What mattered was justice for Colin, Bonnie, and that poor little child and her parents.

"Incidentally," said Eve, "my husband and I were both good friends of a prominent attorney in New York. One of his specialties is libel and slander, so whatever happens, he's already agreed to defend us. Jim, you're sure you have no problem validating that the Los Angeles police concealed Bonnie's murder?"

"None," said O'Leary.

Eve was silent for a moment, and sipped her glass of white wine. "Colin always wanted to die in his movies," she said. "Strange, wasn't it?"

* * *

It was after 7:00 P.M. when Tony arrived, carrying a briefcase. Porter introduced him to Eve, and he was taken by her charm and attractiveness. Tony sat beside Janice, who told him of the group's plan to expose the true story of Valerie Le Fay.

Tony placed his briefcase on his lap, opened it, and removed the photocopy. "In that case," he said, "Christmas came early."

* * *

"The Witchfinders," who now included Eve Devonshire Cromwell, and Capt. James J. O'Leary LAPD Ret., first spoke with the press Sunday night, October 22, at the Beverly Hills Hotel.

The revelations continued for over a week. Eve gave the facts about Bonnie Bristeaux's 1931 murder. Porter, avoiding the "I was the one who killed her" remark for the time being, provided details of the 1931 plane crash and his manslaughter charge. Tony released passages and artwork from the 1931 journal, although the newspapers could use only the more restrained ones. Janice made the points that Lizzie Hirsig, in her Malibou Lake Black Mass, was clearly a copycat of Valerie Le Fay. O'Leary validated that LAPD and the studios had concealed the details of Bonnie's death. The group fired broadsides at both Simon Bone and Alfred Pinkerton.

The story was a wildfire sensation—the murder of a beautiful woman, a Golden Age Hollywood cover-up, Satanism... .all coming on the heels of a raucous mistrial that permitted the murderess of a child to escape justice.

There was no definite information given as to where and when Valerie had died, only that she had been incarcerated "on the east coast" and had died shortly thereafter. Tony realized the problem if investigative reporters suddenly descended on Villa Magdalena.

Of course, Alfred Pinkerton announced he'd file a "colossal" defamation suit, noting that Lizzie Hirsig, convicted of no crime, was a free woman. Eve replied that her own lawyer in New York City would be more than a match for Pinkerton. Simon Bone was in hiding, but released a communique through Pinkerton that he'd sue and clear his "grotesquely smeared reputation." Meanwhile, Chelsea Kimball, feeling exploited by Bone, eviscerated him on her radio show, calling him, among other things, the original Saint Valerie's "chief eunuch."

No one knew where Lizzie was. There was no word from her.

* * *

Eleanor Marsden died from her cancer on October 25. After the funeral, Edward Marsden left Los Angeles to stay indefinitely with his sister in Oregon.

* * *

On Sunday night, October 29, Janice shared a late dinner with Tony in her room at the Miramar. It was nearly midnight as they both went out on the balcony, looking at the ocean. Tony gently pushed back the strand of hair that had fallen over Janice's right eye and then they were kissing, her mouth wet and open. Hours later, as they slept in each other's arms, the news traveled throughout middle-of-the-night Los Angeles:

Lizzie Hirsig was giving a press conference in the morning to respond to the accusations against her.

The Eve of All Hallows' Eve

MONDAY, OCTOBER 30, 1967

They'd come to see the Freak.

As hurriedly arranged by Alfred Pinkerton, the press conference would take place at 10:00 A.M. on the courthouse steps. The authorities there had originally rejected Pinkerton's demand, but when he vowed that Lizzie would defiantly show up anyway, they decided permission would be the less volatile action.

The press, the police, and the morbidly curious gathered. Yes, they wanted to behold the Freak… the monster, who'd recreated herself… the synthetic reincarnation of a drug-addicted witch who'd killed a woman 36 years ago… and who, as that reincarnation, had likely, savagely and ritualistically, drowned a little girl.

A black sedan was parked at the curb, waiting to drive Lizzie and her lawyers away after the press conference. Behind the wheel was Gerald Mahugu, his impassive face masking his shame.

Watching the crowd from a window in a guarded room on the top floor was Lizzie. She wore a long, simple black dress, with small red flowers, sashed at the waist, and black stockings and heels. She appeared pale, wilted, and the darkness around her eyes was maybe makeup, maybe not. Her usual black, brim-up-in-front hat crowned her long red wig and her honeysuckle perfume was subtle.

Felicia Shayne stood near her, somber in fashion. At precisely 9:55 A.M., Pinkerton phoned from the lobby. Felicia answered it, then turned to Lizzie. "It's time," she said. She saw that Lizzie, still at the window, was smiling.

"You should look anguished," advised Felicia.
"I am anguished," Lizzie grinned. "My girdle is killing me."

* * *

Alfred Pinkerton and Felicia Shayne came outside the courthouse, taking their places on the stairs. Lizzie came between them, taller than both of them by several inches. She smiled shyly at the crowd, who beheld her in silence and fascination. The press jostled for pictures, and Lizzie's crystal, red-eyed angel, catching the sun, seemed to glow.

"My accusers," said Lizzie, her voice soft but carrying, "say that I'm a witch who flies a time machine broomstick... that I killed a young woman in 1931 and a helpless child this past summer." Her eyes took in the crowd, and her voice became louder. "I wish to stand before you today and respond to these profane allegations."

She paused, reviewing what she'd told Pinkerton and Felica she'd planned to say. She'd lied to them. They didn't know about her recent dreams... the mercilessly vivid ones of the child she'd drowned... the shadowy but frighteningly detailed ones of the woman killed with an overdose in 1931... the other woman almost killed at the same time. She'd felt the presence of that woman that day in the courtroom...had turned and seen her face. And of course, they didn't know about the lady in her nightmares... part-skeleton, part-snake, with long red hair that looked like Lizzie's wig, but grew from its skull.

I see you, the Snake Lady skeleton would hiss... *I am you... .*

Who was she? *What* was she? She no longer knew. And yet now, this morning, under a navy-blue L.A. sky, before hundreds of people, Lizzie Hirsig did know precisely what she wanted to say.

"I am Lucifer's Archangel," she shrieked, raising her arms above her head, "a witch of the almighty Light Bearer!"

She gave a piercing witch's cackle. Several women in the crowd screamed.

"Witches of the Light Bearer *always* kill pretty women and little girls!" she shrieked hysterically. "We *eat* them! Just ask that fat asshole, Simon Bone!"

Pinkerton and Felicia stood stunned.

Lizzie blessed herself, raising her quavering, pleading voice:

Saint Dymphna, keep me from going crazy today, save me from a seizure, don't let me run away scared, and please don't let anyone rape me...

Two policemen, recognizing her rising mania, moved to restrain her, but Pinkerton and Felicia grabbed her first. "I'll accept responsibility for my client!" shouted Pinkerton. Felicia, genuinely alarmed by Lizzie's ferocity, hugged her, desperately trying to calm her.

Pinkerton took Lizzie's place addressing the crowd. "Miss Hirsig is suffering a breakdown, a victim of media persecution, brought on by those cowards called the witchfinders!" shouted Pinkerton, paraphrasing the speech Lizzie was supposed to give. "You don't see *them* confronting her today, do you?"

As if on cue, from the crowd across the street, came Porter Down, Eve Cromwell, Tony Wyngate, Janice Lynnbrooke, and Jim O'Leary, all five maneuvering their way through the reporters. Pinkerton was speechless. Eve, in the middle, took a step forward.

"Stop, Ma'am!" ordered a policeman. "Please go back. Now." Eve stood defiantly, looking at Pinkerton, backed up by her four friends. Lizzie, weeping, broke away from Felicia, turned... and now she saw Eve.

She froze.

The crowd, silent, spellbound, watched Eve and Lizzie eyeing each other intently. Lizzie, nodding as if in recognition, pulled herself away from Felicia and opened her arms widely towards Eve, as if recognizing a living memory from her past that she wanted both to embrace and attack. She came down one step, trembling, then smiled, speaking in a mocking, breaking, child-like voice:

"Daddy, please don't drink. It scares Mommy and me."

Eve swallowed but didn't flinch. Then Lizzie pulled from the pocket of her dress a sharp knife.

"My beautiful Dymphna!" she cried above the crowd's screams. "Let thy sacred martyr's blood consecrate me! Drench me with it! Spray me with it...!"

She pressed the knife against her own neck and blood glistened. But a mere instant before Lizzie could complete the public suicide she'd secretly planned, and just as two policemen reached her, she gasped, dropped the knife, her legs suddenly gave way, and she fell between the two policemen, violently convulsing as each cop held her up by an arm.

"She's having an epileptic seizure!" said one of them.

"She's not an epileptic, you idiot!" shouted Pinkerton.

The crowd drowned out his words as many saw Lizzie, blood running from her neck, violently writhing between the two police, as if held up on a rack, as if her body would burst.

"Christ, *look* at her!" shrieked someone in the crowd

Policemen surrounded Lizzie, and Porter came under the rope, gently taking Eve by the arm, leading her away.

70 Halloween

TUESDAY, OCTOBER 31, 1967

Simon Bone sat before the hearth at the Vicarage, alone, staring into the fire. He wore a sashed robe and slippers. A wedge of cheese and a goblet of wine sat on the table beside him.

There'd been too many reporters nearby in San Francisco, so he'd taken refuge here in Big Sur, although the generator was broken and the house seemed a drafty tomb. He sipped his wine, and looked up at Melanie's painting above the fireplace, her face and body shrouded in the room's darkness, her shoes barely discernible in the firelight. He glanced up at the chandelier. Yes, one night in 1931, on a dare, Valerie actually had ridden the chandelier. Two guests had fetched a ladder from the barn and she'd climbed up there, somehow straddling the chandelier, coming close to falling. She might have broken her neck—like Melanie had in her fatal horse fall, thought Bone.

His seminary idea scrapped, his book contract cancelled. There was almost a romantic aspect to it all, he thought... he was a cursed mariner, washed up on Life's shore, destroyed by a singing siren... *two* singing sirens, although only one of them could actually sing. Too bad they weren't here tonight, to lounge by the fire with him, and lick his wounds...

Yet there was hope. Alfred Pinkerton had called late last night with a new plan. In all the hysteria, neither Lizzie, nor Pinkerton, nor anyone else had thought of the fact that Bone was still legally Lizzie's Next of Kin. Just as he'd been with Valerie. He had the authority to commit her, as he had with Valerie. The "witchfinders" would jump on this case of history repeating itself, but after Lizzie's fit yesterday, didn't she clearly *need* to be in an asylum? Wasn't it the only humanitarian thing to do?

340

Not a religious hospital, but a modern facility in the Sierra-Nevadas. Not indefinitely, but for only 30 days and nights. After all, she was still a free woman, had never been convicted of a crime and deserved every consideration. Bone would demand it. And Pinkerton had insisted to Bone that he could, with the underworld connections he'd made over the years, engage an assassin within those 30 days and nights to kill her upon her release and rid her forever from both their lives. No one would ever find the body.

Pinkerton, knowing Bone very well, had tossed in a bonus: He'd arrange for Bone to have the corpse.

Bone nibbled some cheese and drank some wine. It was a gamble, and the pleasure forthcoming would be limited... but what was a man without his dreams?

71 Holy War

TUESDAY, NOVEMBER 28 TO
TUESDAY, DECEMBER 5, 1967

Almost a month had passed.

"Keep up, Margo," said Mad Jack.

"Fuck you, fish-face," said Margo.

It was after 2:00 A.M. on November 28. Mad Jack and Margo walked along the dirt road, she, as usual, behind him. He still wore his slouch hat and linen duster, and smiled at the trees. She still wore her filthy red dress, and lugged the guitar sack. Again, he had bags of grass stuffed in his pockets, and she had a plastic bag of poppy weed wedged up her ass. During his time in Mexico, he'd grown a long black beard, now rather resembling a hippie Christ.

"Holy war!" roared Mad Jack, raising his fist.

"Asshole," mumbled Margo.

While hiding in the Tijuana dope dens, they'd heard the stories about the mistrial, Lizzie's violent courthouse steps seizure, and her capture and commitment to the place in the Sierra-Nevadas that Mad Jack called "the loonie bin." He told Margo that Lizzie spoke to him at night—"with the voice of an angel!" he said—pleading for his help.

They want to kill me… He wants my corpse… .

The "they" were the witchfinders, who'd gone to the press about Lizzie. The "He" was Simon Bone, who Mad Jack gathered, was the fat-fingered god who'd made Lizzie have a nose job. And Lizzie's inspiration, apparently, was a crazy cunt named Valerie, who'd died 36 years ago. Presumably Bone wanted Lizzie dead and desired to keep her body. And Si-

342

mon Bone was now claiming that both Valerie and Lizzie were loonies, and that he was a hero for denouncing them.

Lizzie was to be released on December 3. The voice in Mad Jack's head claimed it knew that Alfred Pinkerton and Simon Bone would hire an assassin to kill her. And as for that gross-out spectacle on the courthouse steps, where Lizzie went all epileptic, Mad Jack had his own take on it: It had *killed* Lizzie. God had struck her dead, but the Devil had raised her up. She really was Lucifer's Archangel now, calling him at night. *Come... help me... .*

Mad Jack told all this to Margo. She'd been hearing a voice too... or actually, a hiss. In fact, she was having nightmares, dreaming that a giant snake with Lizzie's head came a-slithering through her window. Yes, Lizzie was a Slither-ee, and with real hair, and she got Margo in her jaws, biting her, playing with her, finally swallowing her like that dinosaur swallowed the guy in *King Kong.*

For Margo, Lizzie wasn't funny anymore.

So, the duo hiked, stoned, Lucifer's Archangel's nocturnal crusaders. Sometimes they hitched a ride, and Margo now and then fucked the driver, but nobody got killed anymore. Too many cops were on their tails. They kept to back roads, sleeping by day in culverts and abandoned freight trains. Mad Jack's butcher knife was still sharp, but Margo's guitar case held no guitar. It now held what she'd been collecting for a long time: the components for a bomb. *Two* bombs.

"Holy war!" bellowed Mad Jack once more.

* * *

Saturday, November 30: Tony Wyngate was back in Emmitsburg, having resigned from Mount Saint Mary's College, working at his chalet on completing his long-delayed novel about Egypt. Janice Lynnbrooke, feeling a need to work again, had taken a job with a social agency near Bakersfield, California. She'd promised she'd come to Maryland to spend Christmas with Tony.

* * *

The same day: Eve Devonshire Cromwell was now home in the Thousand Islands, hoping Porter Down would accept her invitation to visit her for Christmas and the New Year. After leaving California for her home, she'd first flown to Butte, Montana, where the sheriff had driven her to the site of an old farm, where Bonnie Bristeaux's parents had died weeks apart in 1948. The small family cemetery was on a mountain foothill. Back in the corner was the stone that Eve was seeking:

Gladys Hockstader
1904-1931

Bonnie had never mentioned her actual first name was Gladys. Eve had placed flowers on the grave. Now back at the Sanctuary, she walked Boy, observed the approach of winter, and remembered Lizzie's words:
"Daddy, please don't drink. It scares Mommy and me."
She walked in the twilight, thinking about Porter, hoping he was safe.

* * *

Tuesday, December 3: The wind howled in the Sierra-Nevadas as a tall, female figure stood outside the hospital gates, a suitcase on either side of her. She wore a long black coat, a black wool cap, and shivered as she waited. At length a Volkswagen pulled up. Mad Jack got out and placed Lizzie's bags in the trunk before helping her into the passenger seat and driving away.

* * *

Tuesday, December 5: Alfie Pinkerton had not recovered from Lizzie Hirsig's hysterical fit at the courthouse on October 30th. The recent news that she'd left the sanitarium had him terrified.

He knew Lizzie had always desired to destroy Simon Bone, but she'd professionally ruined Pinkerton as well. As an ambulance had driven away with Lizzie, drenched in her own piss, he knew the score.

The cunt destroyed me, thought Pinkerton, over and over.

Pinkerton had originally thought the seizure on October 30th had been a performance, calculated to bring down him and Bone, and to satisfy Lizzie's own masochism, with which he was well-acquainted. Yet the doctors at the sanitarium had reported additional seizures since entering the sanitarium, some of them dangerously violent.

"Fuck you, Lizzie," he said aloud, sitting at his bar. "Fuck you, you spastic bitch."

He poured another drink. Near-bankruptcy. Hate mail. Death threats. Likely disbarment. His behavior in court, association with Lizzie, and finally his cowardly abandonment of his client to save his own skin, had made him a joke. Now she'd left the sanitarium. Those cretins Mad Jack and Margo might have rejoined her. Any day or night, the trio could come to call.

Any attempts to hire an assassin had been fruitless. Not even the lowest of the lot responded when he attempted to contact them.

Pinkerton was drunk, but his instincts nevertheless were sharp—and warned him that he best get out of California, maybe even the country. Yes... he'd leave tomorrow... perhaps go to London. Fuck Bone, the bankrupt old pervert.

Tonight, Pinkerton would get Gerald Mahugu to drive him to a hotel. As Pinkerton went outside to speak with his chauffeur, Mahugu came out of the garage, dressed in his tribal clothes and carrying a suitcase.

"I am leaving, Mr. Pinkerton. Now. I was about to tell you. After all, you have not paid me in three weeks. And I have been taking your money unfairly anyway. I do not admire you."

Pinkerton paled in fear and anger. "How *dare* you," he hissed. "You insolent, ungrateful... *nigger!*"

For a moment, Mahugu looked directly and threateningly into Pinkerton's eyes. Then suddenly a horn honked and a yellow convertible Corvette came around the side of the house, driven by a stunning blonde. She got out of the car in her blouse and shorts, opened the trunk, and Mahugu placed his suitcase there. He closed the hatch, and both he and the blonde got into the car.

The blonde who drove away with Mahugu had never once glanced at Pinkerton.

* * *

Pinkerton stood by his pool, too drunk to drive himself, afraid to re-enter the house. Eventually, he went inside and phoned Felicia, begging her to come and drive him to a hotel. Felicia, who figured Pinkerton had ruined her own career, was prompt in her response.

"Kiss my ass," said Felicia, and hung up.

It was nearly midnight. Pinkerton decided he'd call a cab to take him to a hotel tonight, and head for LAX in the morning. He went to the den, squatting by the safe, so increasingly nervous that his trembling fingers required three attempts to unlock it. He grabbed several stacks of bearer bonds and his rare stamp album, sliding them into his valise. He stood and looked at the death masks. No, Lizzie's mask had never joined them, as he'd long fantasized. He'd never kissed her cheek at the gas chamber door. The masks, he uncomfortably sensed, seemed to be smirking at him.

And then the lights went out.

Pinkerton, terrified, stumbled and fell in the pitch-black room. It was silent at first, and then he heard the soft, teasing, off-key singing:

I sit and watch, as tears go by...

He began whimpering. A flashlight shone into the room. Behind it were, as far as he could tell, three figures. The flashlight lit his face, then went up and focused on the masks, then on his face again.

As he imagined what they were planning to do, Alfred Pinkerton began screaming.

72

A Diving Board Charleston

WEDNESDAY, DECEMBER 6, AND THURSDAY, DECEMBER 7, 1967

The Big Sur surf was loud tonight, almost thunderous. The stone wall in front of the Vicarage was now splattered with graffiti from people who'd fervently followed the witch vs. witchfinders saga, and found their way to the remote house with clashing sentiments:

Ave Saint Lizzie
Burn in Hell, Witch!

Simon Bone had phoned an agent today to place his San Francisco townhouse on the market. His money was almost exhausted, and he was to meet a buyer here tomorrow morning to sell some of the family antiques. Otherwise, he'd have left tonight. Alfred Pinkerton had not answered his calls and Bone was becoming increasingly terrified. He'd been about to call a cab and take a room in one of the area's bed-and-breakfasts.

He had been too late.

Tonight, Bone lie on the cracked concrete bottom of the empty swimming pool, naked, obese, bound and trussed like a Thanksgiving turkey that still had its head.

"Please," he whimpered.

Beside him in the pool was a buck head with handsome antlers that had hung in the Vicarage's study. To his left was the rigid corpse of Alfred Pinkerton, redolent, after riding over 300 miles in the trunk of a car. It too was naked and it had no face. Mad Jack Caldwell, at Lizzie's instruction,

347

had carved the face off with a butcher knife. The pulp of his face, yet to be discovered, now hung in Pinkerton's den, nailed to the wall beside his death masks.

* * *

Bone writhed, begging for mercy, first from Mad Jack, who stood beside the pool, stripped to his shorts, holding a buzz-saw. Then he pleaded to Margo, who sat on the edge of the pool, her legs dangling over the side, casually toying with the pieces of her bomb. Mad Jack playfully revved his buzz-saw, imitating its sound.

"Rrrrr-rrrr-rrr!" he growled.

And then Lizzie came from the house, walking tentatively, as if ill and weak. She wore Melanie Bone's finest 40-year-old flapper dress, too short and tight for her. She slowly ventured out onto the diving board, step-by-step. Bone rolled on his side to look up and see her, shut his eyes, then looked up at her again.

"*I want to be loved by you...*" sang Lizzie softly and off-key and posing in her Roaring 20s togs.

"No," wept Bone. "Please..."

Lizzie ventured a Charleston kick on the diving board, but lost her balance and nearly fell into the empty pool. She landed on her ass on the board, the dress split in the back, and she straddled the board, standing again slowly.

"Tonight, Simon, we're presenting *Frankenstein*—and you're our Monster. Frankenstein created his Monster by sewing together dead bodies..."

Bone shrieked.

"You'll be our customized monster," said Lizzie, "but we're doing it differently—we're including animal parts."

Bone screamed.

"You always saw yourself as a devil," said Lizzie, "so you'll have horns—actually antlers." She pointed at the buck head on the pool's floor.

Bone gagged.

"Of course, we'll give you a few pieces of your faceless, sweet-smelling buddy Alfie," cried Lizzie. "You can have his cock—it's bigger than yours—but wouldn't it *have* to be? You and Pinky can be two-in-one, to plan your lies and your bullshit!"

Bone wailed.

"What are you waiting for?" screamed Lizzie at Mad Jack. He jumped into the pool, revved up the buzz saw, and knelt, looking into Bone's anguished face.

"Here goes!" said Mad Jack.

"Boop-boop-e-doo!" sang Lizzie.

* * *

Three hours later, Margo Coventry lounged in the Vicarage, drinking some wine she'd found in the cellar. Lizzie and Mad Jack had left two hours ago, and they expected Margo to follow after setting the bomb in the house and cramming as many pawnable antiques as she could into their second car, a decrepit station wagon.

Margo had set the bomb to blow at 3:16 A.M.—her birthday was March 16. She'd stuffed some old books, clocks, and bric-a-brac into the station wagon. Lizzie had written and mailed the note to the cops earlier that night claiming that she and her acolytes had avenged themselves on Pinkerton and Bone, then blown up the Vicarage, along with themselves and the two corpses. Of course, remains of only two people would be found, but the bomb was so powerful that the authorities might not find many bones at all.

Actually, Margo didn't give a shit anymore about Lizzie or Mad Jack. She'd secretly decided to desert them and head for Haight-Ashbury. A cute little guy named Charlie, whom she'd met in the Haight last spring, was forming "a family" and chasing his dream of becoming a rock star. Margo had a major crush, and the stuff she'd just stolen from Bone's house could go into Charlie's place on Cole Street, if he were still there.

Fuck you, Lizzie and Mad Jack. Charlie, here I come.

Margo looked at her watch—2:35. Plenty of time. Drunk on the wine, she wandered out by the pool for a last look down at the carnage. Mad Jack had basically just made a big fucking mess, although Bone was funny with those antlers sticking out his temples, looking more like a road-killed Bullwinkle than the Prince of Darkness.

"Yuck," said Margo.

She went back in the house, sprawled on a couch by the empty fireplace, and guzzled the rest of the wine. She figured she had time for another bottle—if she left by three, she'd be safely away from the blast, but close enough at 3:16 to have a great view of the explosion. As she got up, the grandfather clock in the living room chimed the quarter hour. She figured the grandfather clock was wrong. Then she looked again at her watch, and held it to her ear—it still read 2:35.

It had stopped. It was 3:15. Margo Coventry, 4.0 at M.I.T. before her expulsion, had forgotten to wind her watch.

"Oh, shit!" cried Margo.

She was running for the door when the blast erupted magnificently, spectacularly, the flames soaring 1,000-feet into the night sky, the Vicarage a fiery volcano that a ship's crew, twenty miles out in the Pacific, saw epically erupting above the Big Sur cliffs.

The ship blew its horn, which sounded like the cry of a sea monster that ate fat little boys.

73 Revelations

Monday, December 11, 1967

Tony Wyngate, home in Charnita, had just finalized a chapter for his novel. The stereo played *Nights in White Satin*, by the Moody Blues. It was a rainy night, and he'd placed another log into the fireplace and poured a glass of Sherry when the phone rang about 11:30 P.M.

It was Porter Down, calling from Twentynine Palms. Porter had previously informed Tony of last week's Vicarage explosion and the murder/suicide letter received by the police. "How's Janice?" asked Porter.

"Fine. She's in Bakersfield and plans to fly here for Christmas. How's Eve?"

"Fine. She's home in the Thousand Islands, and wants me to come there for Christmas."

"Will you?"

There was silence for a moment. "They're still excavating in Big Sur," said Porter, ignoring Tony's question. "Police have found remains, but considering what little's left, they might never identify them."

"Do you have reason to doubt Lizzie's letter?"

"Tony, there are some things about this case I never told you. In 1931, when I investigated Valerie, I met a priest named Fr. Harry Burke. He headed the Roman Catholic's Department of Ascetic Investigations. It was a secret division of the Church that examined cases of demonic possession."

Porter told Tony the story of the defiled Saint Dymphna shrine in Belgium in 1929, the death of the priest there, and the evidence that Valerie Le Fay had been responsible and stolen the amulet.

351

"Porter, why hadn't you ever told me this before?"

"I told you she was a witch," said Porter. "And that I killed her in 1931. Wasn't that enough to swallow? Listen, Tony. I'm heading to Maryland next week to meet with Fr. Burke... now Msgr. Burke. It's been many years since he was Director of Ascetic Investigations, and he's in his 80s now, but he's still got access to church records. You should meet with us, but you might not want to."

"Why not?" asked Tony.

"The meeting," said Porter, "will take place at Villa Magdalena."

74 Valley of Tears

The morning was bright as Tony drove the 60 miles from Charnita to Villa Magdalena, arriving at 10:20 A.M. Two Christmas wreathes hung on the Villa's open gates

Tony turned onto the long drive leading to the Villa, glancing at the bell tower, the weeping willows, the pond. He got out of the car and instinctively looked up at the still-barred windows of the deserted 5th floor.

The appointed meeting was for 10:30 A.M. A nun admitted Tony. Porter, whose plane had arrived in Baltimore the previous night, was already there, as was Msgr. Harry Burke, who'd driven down the previous day from Philadelphia, where he lived in semi-retirement at Saint Charles Borromeo Seminary. He'd stayed at the Villa overnight as he'd reviewed the records. The nun led Tony to a spare first-floor office.

"Top of the morning," said Porter. "Dr. Tony Wyngate—meet Msgr. Harry Burke."

Msgr. Burke, a solid 83-year-old, was wearing the black monsignor's robe with purple piping. His eyes were unblinking under an almost entirely bald head and his handshake was firm. "You may go, Sister," he said, and the nun scooted out of the room, closing the door behind her. The Sisters had provided a tray with a coffee pitcher, cups, and pastries. Msgr. Burke poured himself coffee. So did Tony. Porter took coffee and two pastries.

Msgr. Burke sat behind a desk, Porter and Tony in two chairs facing him. "We'll get right to it," said the Monsignor, sipping his coffee, the veins thick in the large, strong hands. He put on a pair of wire-rim glasses.

"I'm aware, Tony, that Porter shared with you the information I'd given him 36 years ago. I've made notes. This timeline comes from the records of the Archdiocese, the Department of Ascetic Investigations, and the Villa's records, archived here." He pushed a folder across the desk. "We'll start with this file."

Tony and Porter looked at the first item. It was a death certificate. They saw the name *Valerie Ivy* aka *Valerie Le Fay*, and the death date of *24 December 1931*. Next to "Primary Cause of Death" were the words *Accident* and *Acute Narcotics Addiction*.

"I guess I was her 'accident,'" said Porter.

In the lower corner was the signature, *Dr. Irene Arthur, M.D.*

Porter took from the file a railway bill covering Valerie Le Fay's transportation to Villa Magdalena dated *23 October 1931. Universal Studios, California* had authorized and paid the bill.

"Let's move ahead 35 years," said the Monsignor, sliding another file across the table. Typed on the front was: *Alice Elizabeth Fawkes*. Msgr. Burke read from his notes.

"January, 1966. *Ospedale Sant'Agnese*, a Catholic asylum in Italy, was caring for an American woman, Alice Elizabeth Fawkes. She was, in her own words, 'a witch' in a coven that had settled for a time in the ruins of the Abbey of Thelema, Sicily, where Aleister Crowley had conducted his Black Masses in the early 1920s. She was found a vagrant, apparently abandoned by her 'coven' and possibly abused by it. She was nearly dead from drug abuse, had been recently sexually attacked, and was so violent that authorities confined her to the asylum. While there, she'd undergone psychiatric therapy and severe shock treatments."

The Monsignor sipped his coffee, then continued. "As the woman was American, the hospital eventually arranged for her to be flown back to the U.S. No relatives were found. In February of 1966, considering the nature of her mania and evidence that the patient had been Roman Catholic, Fawkes became a charity case at Villa Magdalena, 5th floor."

Msgr. Burke picked up a separate file, looking at Tony and Porter as he opened it. "This is Alice Elizabeth Fawkes," he said. There was a photograph of a woman, wild-eyed, nearly bald from the shock treatments, tied down to a gurney to be photographed. The ferocity of her expression was so vicious that Tony could barely stand to look at it.

"Well, that's our gal," said Porter

"They really had to take her picture in that condition?" Tony asked.

"It was required," said Msgr. Burke, placing the picture back into its folder. "As for the 5th floor, it had fallen on very bad times. Doctors only came several times a week. Nuns and nurses supervised the ward. It was a shameful place." He paused. "Tony, I'm aware that you had a personal experience with the ward 13 years ago."

"Yes," said Tony.

"I'm sorry," said Msgr. Burke, then looked back at his notes.

"Alice Elizabeth Fawkes was one of three patients on the 5th floor, the other two aged nuns. Fawkes' outbursts frightened her fellow patients. One died two weeks after Fawkes' arrival. The other one was moved to a different floor."

"So the 5th floor," said Porter, "was basically Lizzie's cage."

Burke continued. "Working on the 5th floor at the time was Elmira Kelly... mentally deficient, possibly unbalanced. Began work on the 5th floor in 1925..."

Tony interrupted. "She'd served on the 5th floor for over 40 years?"

"Yes," said Msgr. Burke grimly. "Elmira Kelly was 64-years-old when Alice Fawkes came to Villa Magdalena. The supervisor had written in Kelly's 1965 evaluation that Kelly should be a patient on the 5th floor, not a nurse. In March of 1966, Kelly told the supervisor that she somehow sensed and believed Fawkes was the same woman as 'Valerie Le Fay,' the patient who'd died on the 5th floor in December, 1931, and with whom Kelly had been obsessed."

"That makes two of us who believe it," said Porter. "Why did Kelly think so?"

"Certain physical characteristics," said Burke. "Height, eye color. But Kelly also made a strange remark—she told her supervisor that she could 'see' Valerie looking at her through Alice's eyes, so she knew the two 'had the same soul.' Elmira Kelly had various problems, but this was the only time in her 40-year-record that she ever made such a bizarre claim."

Porter glanced at Tony and grimly nodded.

"Later that month," read Msgr. Burke, "the supervisor found Kelly in Fawkes' room in the middle of the night, contrary to protocol. She was talking to Fawkes about various 5th floor cases over the years, including how Valerie Le Fay, who was an epileptic, had felt betrayed by Saint Dymphna."

Kelly also might have told Fawkes about Bridget... and about me, thought Tony. *That's why Lizzie knew... maybe.*

"Though repeatedly reprimanded," read Msgr. Burke, "Kelly insisted Fawkes was Le Fay's 'reincarnation.' Kelly claimed Fawkes remembered several things on her own, which proved she was Le Fay. The supervisor noted Kelly's repeated requests that Dr. Irene Arthur examine Fawkes, since Arthur had cared for Le Fay in 1931."

"Did Dr. Arthur see Fawkes?" asked Tony anxiously.

"Yes," said Msgr. Burke. "Dr. Arthur was living in Virginia, but remembered Le Fay and visited Villa Magdalena in late March, 1966. Dr. Arthur died of cancer in August of this year. Yesterday I phoned her daughter, who's also a doctor. The daughter said she'd driven Dr. Arthur, who was ill at the time, up here for the consultation. She said her mother seemed somehow 'haunted,' as she put it, by her brief tenure at Villa Magdalena, and although she'd told her nothing about her visit with Fawkes, it had affected her deeply."

"Any record of her diagnosis?" asked Tony.

"Yes," said Msgr. Burke, "It's this March 25, 1966 letter from Dr. Arthur to the Archbishop... which said the sole treatment she suggested was the rite of Exorcism."

The Monsignor passed the letter across the desk to Tony. He saw Arthur's letterhead, the word *Exorcism,* and Arthur's signature, and handed the letter to Porter.

"Dr. Arthur," said Msgr. Burke, "had left Villa Magdalena in 1933 and had gone on to some of the east coast's most prestigious hospitals, none of them with religious affiliations. She was a worldly woman. Her request would have been taken very seriously."

"Was the Exorcism performed?" asked Tony.

"Yes," said Burke. "And I witnessed it."

He cleared his throat, then gravely resumed reading his notes. "April 5, 1966. It was Tuesday of Holy Week... and the night of a full moon. The archdiocese arranged for an Exorcism of Alice Elizabeth Fawkes at Villa Magdalena. The priest was Fr. Edgar Ligpoze, a Jesuit who'd performed several Exorcisms over the decades. At this point, Fr. Ligpoze was not well, physically or emotionally. Nevertheless, he came here to do his sacred duty. As Fawkes was the only patient at that time on the 5th floor, Fr. Ligpoze administered the rite there. He asked me to assist, despite my age, because of my experience."

Msgr. Burke put down his notes. "The Exorcism became a battle of wills. The demon in Fawkes knew and mocked Ligpoze... and it knew and mocked *me*." He looked at Porter. "It was Le Fay. Her voice, her memory.

She taunted me, cursed me about the nights leading to her death in 1931. She knew things only Le Fay would have known."

Porter met Msgr. Burke's gaze. "Dear God," said Tony.

"Those nights were gruesome beyond words," said Msgr. Burke. "By the third night, Fr. Ligpoze, exhausted and traumatized, suffered a near-breakdown. On the fourth night, Good Friday, while bestowing the rite, he suddenly announced he'd 'cut the demon' from Fawkes. With a long knife, concealed in his vestments, he attacked her genitalia. I restrained him from killing her."

Porter and Tony were silent.

"Fawkes nearly bled to death," said Msgr. Burke. "I phoned a hospital. An ambulance took her to Saint Joseph Hospital in Baltimore."

He started to pick up his coffee cup, but his hand shook and he put the cup down.

"Fr. Ligpoze died two weeks later," said Msgr. Burke. "Heart attack. He's buried in his native Austria. After Alice Fawkes returned from the hospital, Elmira Kelly tended to her."

A moment passed. "I always figured," said Porter softly, "that Lizzie's hatred for the Church was beyond anything Bone had done to her. Her vendetta was much bigger. No wonder."

Msgr. Burke picked up his notes and continued. "On May 5—a month after the Exorcism—Alice Fawkes escaped from Villa Magdalena shortly after 11 P.M. Elmira Kelly confessed to having helped her, because Fawkes had threatened to 'see her soul in Hell' if she didn't. On May 6, the staff found Valerie Le Fay's grave—shallow, with no vault, same as the other graves on the hill—opened. Kelly admitted to having put a shovel and pickaxe in the cemetery for Fawkes' use. She rambled, telling how she'd prepared Le Fay for burial in 1931, and had told Fawkes about this. Asked why Fawkes had wanted to exhume Le Fay, Kelly responded: 'She wanted to get her pretty Saint Dymphna."

The angel, thought Tony. *My God, the red-eyed angel... her "Saint Dymphna."*

"What happened to Kelly?" asked Porter.

"She's dead," said Msgr. Burke. "After all those years working on the 5th floor, she became the 5th floor's last patient. Died of heart failure two months after Fawkes' escape. Elmira Kelly made a final confession to a priest and the authorities, and is buried in holy ground in Villa Magdalena Cemetery, separate from the cemetery on the hill. One of the last things Kelly did before her final illness incapacitated her was to make and place a cross marker on Valerie Le Fay's grave."

Monsignor closed the folder with a sense of finality. "A month after Elmira Kelly's death," he said, "the Archdiocese shut down the 5th floor forever."

Tony sat very still. Porter glanced out the window at the hill near the bordering woods, and its small cemetery. "It's a lot to take in," said Burke. "Feel free to examine any of these papers. There's some unusual correspondence in the 1931 file."

Porter took the file and found numerous letters paper-clipped. The first was dated January of 1932, the most recent March of 1965. He noticed the words:

I plead with you yet again to exhume and release Miss Le Fay's body to me...

He passed the letters to Tony. "Guess who?" he asked, and pointed to the first letter's signature: *Simon Bone.* Also clipped to the letters were copies of the Archdiocese's refusals to release the body. Porter read them. "Bone betrayed her," he said, "but he never got over his obsession."

"Finally," said Msgr. Burke, "I regret that there's an additional revelation… regarding why it appears that I delayed taking action on this matter."

"Okay," said Porter.

"I provided the Archdiocese, as well as Msgr. Miles, then director of Villa Magdalena, a complete report on the Exorcism, as well as Fawkes' escape. There was no attempt made to find her."

"Why not?" demanded Porter.

"There was fear among the Church Hierarchy that news of an escaped mad woman, who had satanic beliefs and had defiled a grave, would be a throwback to the old mysticism that the post Vatican II Church was trying to avoid. They also feared that revelations about the Exorcism would come to light, resulting in a comprehensive investigation of Villa Magdalena, a closing of the home, and a disbursement of the old nuns who'd lived here for years in retirement. The police never knew about the escapee. Msgr. Miles told me he considered Fawkes 'a poor, sick soul who, by the grace of God, would probably be dead soon anyway.'"

Msgr. Burke sipped his now cold coffee. "I also sent a report on all these matters to the Department of Ascetic Investigations. I never received a detailed reply. Based on recent events, any attempt to find and apprehend Alice Fawkes was tepid at best. And at my age, and considering certain health problems... I told myself there was nothing I could do."

His craggy face was dark with guilt. "You've come through, Monsignor," said Porter. "Again." The room fell silent. Eventually Tony stood. He walked over to the casement windows and looked up the hill at the cemetery.

"Bridget's up there with Valerie Le Fay," Tony said softly, almost to himself.

* * *

It was late morning as the three men climbed the stairwell to the 5th floor, the elevator long deactivated. Msgr. Burke unlocked the iron door with a ring of keys he'd obtained from the caretaker. The old ward was simple: an open circular desk for the doctors and nurses and a wing of small rooms.

"She was in Room 510," said Msgr. Burke.

"Which 'she'?" asked Tony.

"Both," said Msgr. Burke.

Room 510 was on the front side, the number slightly faded over the door. Tony entered the room and saw the bed, sink, chest of drawers, single closet. He looked out the window and saw the pond. Porter stood just inside the door, Msgr. Burke just outside it.

"Alice Elizabeth Fawkes came here," said Tony, turning from the window, "with a history of satanic ritual. Elmira Kelly filled her with stories of Valerie Le Fay. Kelly also presumably told her about Bridget Cannady and what little she knew about me. Lizzie survived the violently botched Exorcism, escaped, found Simon Bone, and her mind cracked."

"No, her *soul*," interrupted Msgr. Burke. "I've seen Evil. I was present at seven Exorcisms. What I felt at the one last year...I sense now."

The "Joseph bell" sounded in the tower above them. The sexton was ringing the noon Angelus.

"Le Fay and Fawkes... the same woman," said Porter. "We know Lizzie's motivation was to destroy Bone—she knew he'd betrayed her in 1931. And after the Exorcism in 1966, she also wanted to avenge the suffering she'd experienced at the hands of the Church."

"'Many of those who sleep in the dust of the earth shall awake... ,'" recited Msgr. Burke, quoting the Old Testament Book of Jeremiah.

"'Some shall live forever,'" continued Porter. "'Others shall be an everlasting horror and disgrace.'"

The bell, ringing the Angelus above them, stopped. The three men moved down the hallway. "Monsignor," asked Porter, "based on what Elmira Kelly confessed… after Alice Fawkes' escape, had the Saint Dymphna amulet actually been stolen from Valerie's corpse?"

"I don't know," said Msgr. Burke. "By the time Kelly told what she knew, the body had been interred again."

"Then with the Church's permission," said Porter, "I'd like to open the grave."

75 The Exhumation

The December afternoon was fading, the clouds increasingly darkening. Tony walked the fields of Villa Magdalena. He looked at the formidable building, its bell tower, its barred 5th floor windows, set forlornly against the hills and woods. There was an almost palpable sadness about the place, as if the building were a conscious, mournful thing, ashamed of its own memories.

Msgr. Burke and Porter had driven into Baltimore to get the permit for exhumation. Tony walked, thinking about religion, of how it defined people, inspiring them, embittering them. He thought of Lizzie, shockingly abused by others, ravaged by her own demons. But if he felt a strange sympathy for her, he imagined she only felt mocking hatred for him. He sensed it again this afternoon, looking at Villa Magdalena.

Tony expected the feeling would be especially potent up on the hill in the cemetery, where, by an incredible perversity, both Valerie and his pitiful Bridget lie buried within yards of each other.

* * *

Come nightfall, Tony wanted no dinner. Nor did he want to pray in the chapel where he'd last been that dreadful morning in 1954. He went to the second-floor room that one of the nuns had formally provided him, but couldn't relax.

Msgr. Burke and Porter Down returned to Villa Magdalena about 9:00 P.M. with the permit. Tony stayed in his room, waiting for Burke and

361

Porter to call for him. The wind blew outside Tony's window. He held his rosary pouch, nodded in his chair, and he dreamed.

He was in the chapel at Villa Magdalena. Candles lit the dark altar. Tony was dressed as a priest, wearing black funeral vestments. The organ played and nuns, their faces in the shadow, mournfully sang *Immaculate Mary* as if it were a dirge. He was giving Holy Communion. The nuns filed to receive the sacrament. Then, suddenly, there she was in front of him… all in black, as she'd been in court, as tall as he, lifting the veil that hung from her hat, her yellow eyes shining, the red eyes of her crystal amulet glowing. Her hands, with their long red nails, were folded in prayer and she grinned at him, and winked.

"*The Body of Christ,*" he said, holding up the Host.

"*Amen,*" she sighed. She put out her tongue lasciviously, and he gave her the sacrament, despite himself.

She moved away. There was a woman behind her. Her head was bowed, she wore the clothes of a nun, and she wept as she approached him, slowly looking up into his eyes. He trembled as he gave her the sacrament, and she turned her back to him, walking up the aisle to the rear of the chapel, where the woman dressed in black took her hand. Tony could hear the tall woman's voice as she pointed in the direction of the hill with its unsanctified cemetery.

"*Come, Bridget. We'll go home now…*"

Tony awoke at the rapping at the door. "It's time, Tony," said Porter's voice.

* * *

A hissing, freezing rain came this December 14th, the wind blowing through the tall trees that bordered Villa Magdalena. The burly caretaker had placed a few lanterns around the grave, the light dim so if by chance a resident of the Villa looked out a back window, she'd see nothing happening on the hill. He'd placed a shovel and crowbar by the grave as the Monsignor's car, its headlights on low beams, arrived at the cemetery.

The Monsignor and Tony looked mournful in their long dark overcoats, Msgr. Burke wearing a black hat. Porter appeared incongruous in his pea coat and crumpled yachting cap. They moved among the stone markers. "Here she is," said the caretaker, shining a flashlight on the middle of the tall, crooked crosspiece and its nearly faded date:

1931

The caretaker lowered the light. He'd opened the grave but not the coffin. The marble marker was in place with the Roman numeral VII. "Damn shallow grave," he said. "Hardly two feet 'til I hit the lid. No vault. Guess nobody gave a damn up here." Tony looked at the wooden coffin, then across the yard at the small marble marker in the darkness.

"You okay, Tony?" asked Porter.

"Yes," said Tony.

The caretaker confirmed he'd return in one hour, as planned. He got into the truck and, headlights dimmed, drove down the hill. The rain now mixed with sleet and flurries of snow. Msgr. Burke moved to the head of the grave, took his rosary from his pocket and blessed himself. Porter stood to the grave's left side and hefted the crowbar. Tony moved to the grave's right side and picked up a lantern.

"Here goes," said Porter.

He circled the grave and coffin, working the crowbar, extracting the few nails. Kneeling over the grave, removing the lid, he slid it on its edge beside the coffin. At first in the wet, black night, Tony could see only darkness in the casket. Then he raised the lantern and light fell on the body. It was simply wrapped in a shroud, the cloth partially chewed away by insects that had infiltrated the wooden casket. The shroud wrapped around the skeletal corpse appeared, thought Tony, like a snakeskin.

The hands were formally placed, as if in prayer, below the chest. Tony looked at the shadowy face, surprised by the strands of red hair still on the skull.

I'm lonely. In the graveyard... up on the hill...... so lonely...

He thought he heard the words so clearly that Lizzie might have been kneeling beside him, just as she'd been that morning at the Abbey, giving her profane Confession. Then he heard murmuring and saw that Msgr. Burke was reciting his rosary.

"I'll check for the amulet," said Porter, reaching down into the coffin.

Tony looked at the corpse and held the lantern to cast more light on the face. Its structure was the same as the woman he'd known as Lizzie, and the teeth were bared, as if the body was amused by its exhumation. Tony almost fancied one of Lizzie's tricks, a macabre surprise, she awaiting him in decaying corpse makeup in this grave, about to shriek "Boo!" at him. Yet the unmistakable putrid smell of decay rose from the coffin.

I rot in my grave...so lonely, so awful... and think of you...

The softly whispered words seemed to rise up out of the ground. At the same time, Tony thought he heard a sound behind him, from near Bridget's grave…a moaning, almost a weeping.

"No," said Tony suddenly.

Msgr. Burke stopped praying. "Are you alright, Tony?"

Tony said nothing. The wind picked up in the woods and the freezing mix stung his face. "I can't find the amulet," said Porter. "Tony, hold the light closer."

Tony lowered the lantern over the grave. Monsignor resumed his rosary, but Tony heard different words and a woman's voice.

I used to be pretty, Tony…You used to like me… You wouldn't like me anymore, but I think of you, day and night… with impure thoughts…

Tony could have sworn he heard the words, and then behind him, a dreadful, mournful sound, as if it too heard the words that came from Valerie's grave, and was ashamed by them…

"No!" Tony cried again.

"Tony!" said Porter. "Kneel across from me." Tony did.

Immaculate Mary…

The singing rose up from the grave, slyly, tauntingly.

"No…No!" said Tony.

"Tony!" snapped Porter. "Listen. I'll hold her up. You feel around her neck and under her. See if you can find the amulet or its chain."

Porter slid his strong arms under the corpse, lifting and cradling the cold, brittle cadaver. Tony placed the lantern on the ground, shivering as he touched the body, sliding his fingers inside the neck of the shroud, feeling for the amulet, reaching down her neck, down to where her breasts had been. He joined the Monsignor aloud in his prayer:

Holy Mary, Mother of God, pray for us sinners, now and at the hour of our death…

Her face was only inches from his own and her mouth was almost against his ear, as it had been in Lizzie's Confession at the Abbey. The wind blew, the rain and snow were on his face and hers, and again he thought he heard her, whispering in his ear:

I think of you day and night…how I still want your cock in my cunt…

"No!" said Tony.

Tony, my darling, have you forgotten all about me… Is that why you're fucking… JANICE!

The whisper became a roar, and Tony, startled, lost his balance and slid, falling into the grave, his face against the corpse's face, his mouth against its mouth. He came up out of the grave, trembling on the ground, unaware of what he clenched in his hand. Porter came quickly around the grave, put his arm on Tony's shoulder and carefully took from his hand a thin, delicate silver chain.

It was broken.

Msgr. Burke stopped praying. Porter helped Tony to his feet and kept one arm around his shoulders. The corpse's face gazed up at the sky as if grinning at the magic it had just performed, the relic it had just provided, and the kiss it had just enjoyed.

"It's Lizzie," Tony said hoarsely. "I heard her. It's her..."

Porter and Msgr. Burke were silent. The stench of decay suddenly rose again, served up by the moaning wind. As Tony looked down into Valerie's grave once more, Porter picked up the lantern and darkness shrouded the corpse.

"The crazy bitch," said Porter, holding the chain up into the rain and snow in the lantern light. "She robbed her own grave!"

76 The HOLLYWOOD Sign

FRIDAY, DECEMBER 15, 1967

She felt like a foxy showgirl in a Warner Bros.' gold-digger epic, soaring up into the sky in a crazy Busby Berkeley choreography extravaganza... atop the HOLLYWOOD Sign... .to the first L.

Lizzie wore her black dress, the one she'd worn to the Santa Monica pier that night, ripped but still nice, and her black hat, and her wig, and of course, her Pretty Saint Dymphna. No shoes, stockings, lingerie. She hung up here, like a profane Christmas decoration, head lolling, arms at her side, bare legs dangling above Hollywood.

Oh Come, All Ye Faithful... .

She knew her face was a witch mask—the mascara too dark, the false eyelashes askew, the lipstick too red. In the misty late-night air, her pretty mask was running. And she knew she stank, despite the splashes of honeysuckle perfume.

What a lover I'd be tonight, she giggled.

She sat on the L, releasing the strap around her waist. They'd *hoisted* her up here... or was it all a dream? The final disciples had been moving her up and down the coast, and she'd been dreaming in attics, cellars, and barns...but this *felt* real. Mad Jack had cried like a baby, as he and some others had rigged up the pulley and swing, probably as well as dear, dead Margo would have done.

Yes, she was atop the HOLLYWOOD Sign, from which starlet Peg Entwistle had taken her fatal swan dive in 1932. Tonight, she'd go out like poor Peg had. She'd wanted to bring her cat up with her, to be with her at the end, but Mad Jack said the cat had run away. Or maybe died.

366

Bleeding Christ Almighty, look at the lights!

She stood, barefoot, shakily gaining her balance. She raised her hands at her sides, like the statue of Christ above Rio, an Angel of Vengeance, posing above the lights, drugs, and whores of Hollywood, U.S.A.:

Saint Lizzie, in Excelsis!

The city aglow below her. Yes, once upon a time, in the zoo and bestiary of fucked-up California girls, Lizzie had been L.A.'s Panther Woman of 1967... the she-freak Queen of the Summer of Love. The song she was la-la-la-ing, however, was about a heavenly Queen:

Immaculate Mary...

The Holy Grotto... the Witchfinders... Anthony Wyngate. Funny... she'd had a crazy dream last night, a dream about Dr. Tony, finding her as a corpse, shining a light on her, his hands feeling around her boobs ... and then giving her a wet, terrific kiss. She'd liked it... but what the fuck did it *mean*?

The Witchfinders were still after her. Valerie Le Fay was still after her. Valerie Le Fay *was here.*

Then, in the sky, the movie started. *The Exorcism of Alice Elizabeth Fawkes*. Part skin flick, part religious epic, part horror drive-in movie... slapped and spanked with a Condemned rating from the Roman Catholic Legion of Decency. The film she hated to watch.

"I can't look," she said, covering her eyes like a teenage girl watching one of Vincent Price's Poe movies. Then she raised her face, and *did* look.

There she was, strapped naked to a bed in a candlelit room, bald, wild-eyed, a sheet draped over her body. It was Good Friday... the crucifixion of Jesus. There were two priests in the room: Ligpoze, the Exorcist, adorned in black vestments and holding a crucifix, and Burke, his assistant, dressed in the robe and surplice of an altar boy, swaying a thurifer of incense. She was arching her back, looking away from the priests, up through the barred window at the moon. It was her fourth night battling the priests.

The camera kept showing extreme closeups of Ligpoze... his *eyes*. His old, gold-colored goat eyes, burning with hatred in his gaunt face. Smoke rose from the thurifer, smelling like top-priced California poppy grass.

She raised herself on the bed as best she could and spat at Ligpoze. He wiped his face, spat back at her and prayed:

Exorcizámos te, ómnis immúnde spíritus, ómnis satánic potéstas, ómnis infernális adversárii, ómnis légio, ómnis congregátio et sécta diabóli-ca, in nómine et virtúte Dómini nóstri Jésu Chrísti...

She watched herself, wriggling and kicking so the sheet uncovered her breasts and legs. She spread her thighs, laughed, showered both men with profanities, mocked their faith, their vows of abstinence. There was a familiarity about Burke, and a solid wall of Faith around him, but she sensed that Ligpoze was weakening.

And then came the Voice. Lush, hissing. That night, she sensed it was somebody else's voice, and now in the movie, it clearly was.

How many altar boys did you fuck, Ligpoze?

The old man's goat eyes glared and he reached into his vestments, withdrawing a long knife...

She'd smelled the incense, heard the Voice, and now she felt the Agony. She screamed, howled, her cries of anguish echoing in the hallway. The camera went berserk, going from a closeup of her mouth wide open and screaming to a two-shot of Burke wrestling the hysterical Ligpoze away from the bed. Above it all was a sound of soaring laughter, as her "other" self, the Voice, enjoyed every horrible sense and image...

The movie ended. There were final credits. Everyone had played themselves, of course, but at the bottom of the list was:

The Voice... .Valerie Le Fay

She knew by now. Valerie had been haunting her, long before she'd opened the grave and stolen her pretty Saint Dymphna. Nevertheless, there'd come the Night of Nights... May 5, 1966, when Valerie finally got out of the ground. The skeleton in the snake skin... The Snake Lady. With her scraggly red hair and her bared teeth. Yes, Lizzie herself, in her rob-the-grave caper, had allowed Valerie to escape. What a stupid bitch she was! She'd let the Snake Lady loose! Slithering after her, hissing at her, giving Lizzie her memories and mania... making her drown Little Cindy. And just for laughs, giving Lizzie her seizures. Between attacks, the Snake Lady presumably returned to her Villa Magdalena grave, like a vampire to its coffin of native soil. It was there tonight. Or *was* it?

Lizzie would kill herself before the Snake Lady killed her... or the witchfinders killed her.

She braced to leap ... and then she saw and heard them. They were coming for her, with torches, like the villagers in *Frankenstein*, with bloodhounds, barking and leading the way up Beachwood Drive. Yes, they'd come to burn the HOLLYWOOD sign, like the villagers had burned the windmill, to roast her like they'd roasted the Monster.

"Burn!" they roared.

There they were, brandishing their torches… Eve, Tony, Pretty Little Angel Eyes, and that bastard Porter Down, who'd killed her once already, and who knew all about her… about *both* of her.

"*Burn!*" they howled.

Rain, lightning, thunder, and the faces were from *both* her haunted summers… Jimmy Whale, in his knickers… Boris Karloff, in his Monster makeup and cricket cap… and honey blonde Bonnie… all with torches, all looking up at her on the L. Was she really remembering them… or pictures she'd *seen* of them…or stories she'd *heard* of them?

"*Burn!*" they screamed.

"Cat!" she cried, like a child wanting its teddy bear, but Cat wasn't there.

But… *He* came, as she knew he would. Colin Clive, her long-lost darling from 1931… naked, except for a loincloth, prop blood on his hands and feet and side, wearing a long wig and beard, and a crown of thorns. Just like she'd sketched him… but wait—she'd never sketched…

"*BURN!*" he cried, his voice like a pipe organ.

The torchlight parade continued. There was Jonathan, direct from Hell's suicide colony, hideously bloated, looking like Humpty Dumpty, waving his skinny Egg Man arms…but still with his beautiful starry eyes.

"*BURN!*" he squealed.

There were a few bones glued together that used to be Simon Bone, with deer antlers, and some other bones that used to be "Pinky" Pinkerton, vainly wearing his pulpy, sawed-off face like a mask…. .

And Daddy.

She gasped when she saw him. A man so awful, she'd never allowed her mind to make a movie about him. She'd exiled him from her nightmares years ago, or so she thought—he was too much a part of who she was, too responsible for what she'd become. "Daddy," who came to her room at night and got in her bed and told her he loved her… who convinced "Mommy" to go away, relax and let him watch their foster child for one rainy, never-to-be-forgotten weekend.

Yes…wiry, pockmarked Daddy, with his pudgy fingers and cigarette breath and the bathtub with its dank, cold water. Daddy… who put her in his bed and probed her and licked her ass and sat on top of her and

slapped her when she cried... and made threats that he'd lock her up with other sick girls if she dared ever tell Mommy what he'd done to her...
Please don't hurt me!

... and then, Sunday morning, Mommy got back, and the family went to church, and she was afraid the blood in her underpants and on her thighs would run down her legs, and everybody would see. He'd died early from cancer, but here he was tonight, among the torch-bearers:
"*BURN!!*" he jeered.

And then, finally, *they* came. *Both* of them. Saint Dymphna and Little Cindy. Radiant and beautiful, direct and in-person from Heaven. Cindy carried Dymphna's lily, and at the saint's command, pointed the flower at Lizzie like a weapon.

No.... *Oh, Bleeding Christ Almighty, no...!*

And Lizzie *transfigured*... into the shrouded, stinking, Snake Lady skeleton she'd seen that night at Villa Magdalena, baring its smiling teeth, wearing the pretty, red-eyed Dymphna. The scene changed—they were burying the monstrosity back in the grave at Villa Magdalena, at night so no one would see, for this was a shameful thing. For a moment, Lizzie broke free from her host creature, fighting the Snake Lady in the closed coffin, entwining around each other, and then again they were one carcass... Valerie and Lizzie, now One, the Snake Lady, Forever and Ever.

Fr. Ligpoze stood above the coffin, in his black vestments, making a Sign of the Cross with his knife:

Remember, Woman, that thou art dust, and unto dust thou shalt return...

Someone shoveled dirt over her grave, *their* grave, and she screamed.

* * *

She awoke in blackness, stripped of her clothes and wig, crying on a wet mattress in the darkness, having just come out of a seizure.

There was darkness, but no rotting shroud, no casket lid, no maggots. She wasn't the Snake Lady—she was only herself. Had she been on the HOLLYWOOD sign, and she'd been afraid to jump, and they'd brought her back here, wherever *here* was? Had she never been up on the sign at all, but only dreamed it? Did it even fucking matter?

"I'm alive!" she sighed. Naked, scarred, stinking, probably only a few hours away from another seizure... but alive. Alive to fight back. Alive to give nightmares, not suffer them. Alive, maybe, to pull off one last caper.

Saint Lizzie, Avenging Christmas Angel, she smiled.

The vision danced in her head, and she felt strangely sensual.

And then she sensed the Snake Lady was back, nearby in the shadows… watching and hissing.

"Go away!" she pleaded, curling up in a ball like a scared child. "Please, please, please—GO AWAY!"

She wept, trembling and alone, listening to the hissing in the darkness.

77 Yuletide

TUESDAY, DECEMBER 19 TO
SATURDAY, DECEMBER 23, 1967

Tuesday, December 19: Porter Down, having decided to accept Eve Devonshire Cromwell's invitation, met her in New York City. They saw the Broadway musical *Man of La Mancha* and took the ferry to see the Statue of Liberty. On the night of December 21, they arrived at Eve's house in the Thousand Islands, where Porter would stay until returning to California in the New Year.

They both enjoyed their time together thoroughly.

Friday, December 22: Janice arrived at Baltimore's Friendship Airport. Tony was waiting for her and they kissed. The previous morning, she'd picked up her mail at the Bakersfield post office and opened a Christmas card, postmarked in Solvang. It showed a Nativity scene and bore a greeting in purple fountain ink:

Looking forward to visiting you for Christmas. Love, Lizzie

When she told Tony about it, he phoned Eve and Porter. Yes, Eve had received a similar card in today's mail, and Porter expected one was awaiting him at his home in Twentynine Palms. As Porter and Eve felt decidedly safe at "The Sanctuary," and Tony and Janice were across the country from where the cards had been sent, they also felt safe.

"Forget about her," said Porter. "Jim O'Leary's keeping an eye on things. If she's still out there on the loose, I'll lasso her in the New Year."

* * *

Saturday, December 23: Tony and Janice had dinner tonight in Thurmont. On the way back to Charnita, Janice requested they visit the campus of Mount Saint Mary's. The students had gone home for Christmas, of course, and the campus was very still. They went to the college church which annually had a lovely Nativity scene near the steps. The figures of Mary, Joseph, the shepherds, the Magi, and the angel, with her *Gloria in Excelsis* banner, were all in place, as were the figures of the donkey and the sheep.

The manger, however, was empty.

A few minutes later, a priest who taught at the seminary walked by and Tony asked about the absence of the Infant Jesus. The priest replied that, the previous night, someone had stolen it.

* * *

It was about 10 P.M. in the Thousand Islands, and Porter and Eve were sitting by the fireplace. Bill McDonough had brought Eve a fresh-cut Christmas tree and she and Porter had decorated it. They'd bought each other gifts while in New York City and, having wrapped them, had placed them under the tree. A few moments later, the phone rang.

"Strange, isn't it?" asked Tony, telling Porter about the theft of the Baby Jesus figure. "I'm not sure why, but I keep thinking..."

"Does Mount Saint Mary's have a Christmas Eve Midnight Mass?" Porter interrupted.

"Yes," said Tony. "People come not only from nearby, but from Baltimore and D.C. The church is large and always full."

Porter gripped the phone. Valerie dying on Christmas Eve of 1931... Lizzie's defiling the Mount Grotto during Yuletide of 1954. Now news of the stolen Christ figure. A large crowd tomorrow night at the Mount's Midnight Mass...

The Christmas cards had been postmarked December 18. Enough time for Lizzie to get across the country. Thousands of acres of forests in the Catoctin Mountains where she could hide...

"I'll get the first plane in the morning I can schedule," said Porter. "Meanwhile, call the Maryland State Police, get Mount Saint Mary's to cancel Midnight Mass... and you and Janice get the hell out of there!"

78 A Live Nativity

The tower of Mount Saint Mary's church was adorned in light, the golden statue of the Virgin Mary aglow on the mountain, a shred of moon above it.

By 11:15 P.M. a Christmas Eve crowd was filling the church—couples young and old, families in their finest attire, all come to honor the sacred solemnity. Cars had filled the lots and were now parking on the athletic field. The choir would sing religious carols starting at 11:30 P.M. up to the start of Mass at midnight. At the Nativity scene by the steps, the manger was still empty.

"Drop us off and drive away," Porter demanded as they pulled up near the church.

"Like hell," said Janice.

Tony and Janice had picked up Porter and Eve at the airport only several hours ago, their arrival postponed by Holiday delays. Eve had insisted on accompanying Porter to Emmitsburg. Neither Tony nor Janice would agree to leave the area. The State Police, contacted by Tony, had reported to Mount Saint Mary's, finding no evidence of anything amiss other than the stolen Jesus figure. The Monsignor who was the current Mount president had decided to proceed with Midnight Mass.

"The police captain told me this happens more often than you think," said Tony. "He says it's probably not blasphemy, just mischief."

"Bullshit," said Porter.

The State Police had posted two troopers at the church, but an accident on Route 15 south of the Mount had demanded their attention. They were gone by the time Tony, Janice, Porter, and Eve arrived. Giving up on trying to order Tony and Janice to leave, Porter took his pistol from his travel bag in the back seat, concealing the gun in his peacoat.

11:30 P.M. The caroling started with *Lo, How a Rose Ere Blooming.* Porter reluctantly led Eve, Tony, and Janice into the church. The congregation sat under the beautiful stained-glass windows, below the domed ceiling's painting of the Virgin. The choir loft was also filled. The church lights were on, and four altar boys lit candles on the poinsettia-decorated altar.

"Eve," said Porter, removing his cap, "go find the Monsignor and see if you can still convince him to cancel. Stay in the sanctuary, so I know where you are if I need you. Janice, go to the choir loft. See if you see anything suspicious. Tony, you look outside around the church."

They did as he asked. Porter's guess was that if Lizzie were in the church, she'd be disguised, sitting in one of the pews. He walked down the right-side aisle, looking at the people in each pew, crossing in front of the altar and heading up the left aisle, oblivious to the stares of the people watching the man in the dark pea-coat casing the church.

In the sacristy, Eve introduced herself to the Monsignor, who was vesting in white robes for the Mass. She tried to reiterate the danger but the Monsignor insisted the Mass would go as scheduled. He was gracious and allowed Eve's request that she stay in the sanctuary, near the phone if a need came for her to call the police.

In the choir loft, Janice looked out at the crowd below. Nothing struck her as unusual. Outside, Tony walked behind the church, then along its south side, looking across Echo Field where a few cars were still parking. He noticed the sharp chill in the night wind.

11:43 P.M. The lights in the church dimmed to almost darkness. Everything was now in candlelight. Porter and Tony headed up to the choir loft to join Janice to watch for any suspicious activity.

At the top of the stairs, just outside the loft, Porter noticed a door leading to the steeple belfry. He tried its knob, relieved to find the door was locked, unaware it could be locked from both sides.

Less than thirty seconds after he'd passed the belfry door, it slowly opened a crack.

* * *

11:45 P.M. After a soft organ prelude, the choir began *Silent Night*. A moment later, two figures began a slow, quiet procession down the center aisle toward the altar. There was a tall woman in a full blue robe, its hood over her head, carrying a bundle close to her breast, clearly meant to be the infant Jesus. Beside her a man, in a tan robe with a hood, carried a tall staff.

Round yon Virgin, mother and child...

The people in the back pews whispered at the surprise sight, causing those in front of them to turn, until most of the people in the church were watching the figures of Mary the Virgin and her spouse Joseph, with the Christ Child, processing in the reverential candlelight. The dim glow allowed only a glint of their faces, shrouded by the hoods. The sacred imagery, beautifully accented by the hymn, caused several people to bless themselves at the sight.

Sleep in Heavenly Peace...

In the choir loft, Porter watched, alarmed, increasingly suspicious. The height of the woman, the cadaverousness of the man. He gripped the loft's railing, watching as the couple reached the altar. The Monsignor and the altar boys were still in the sanctuary, unaware of the quiet procession, its pageantry mystically casting its spell over the awestruck faithful. The two figures, each wearing sandals, stepped onto the altar, turning slowly, standing very still, facing the worshippers.

My God, thought Porter.

As if in a rehearsed count of three, "Mary" and "Joseph" removed their hoods. The woman's robe dropped from her body. She stood bald and naked, the stolen baby Jesus figure at her breast, and her eyes were dark with makeup and her lips red with lipstick. Strapped to her hips was a long phallus.

She was what Alice Elizabeth Fawkes had fantasized becoming: The defiled and desecrated Virgin figure of 1954, alive, incarnate.

Mad Jack Caldwell, bearded and beside her, leered at her, and there were gasps and then cries from people in the first several pews. A woman screamed, and then another, and many people stood, trying to see what was happening on the altar in the candlelight. "Mary" suddenly threw the Christ Child figure to the altar floor, to more cries and screams. Then she herself screamed, wildly, mockingly, before grabbing her robe from the floor and running off the altar, "Joseph" behind her.

The choir, not fully perceiving what had happened in the dim candlelight, had never stopped singing.

* * *

"Where'd they go?" demanded Porter, having breathlessly run to the Sanctuary.

The Monsignor, surrounded by the frightened altar boys, was too shocked to speak. It was Eve, already phoning the police, who pointed outside. Porter ran out the door, looking in every direction. To the rear of the church, he saw the steps, leading up the hillside and into the woods.

The Grotto, thought Porter. *The death there in 1954, the desecrations...*

Inside the church, the singing stopped. The Monsignor went on the altar, speaking reassuringly to the congregation. Outside, Porter hurried up the steps, under the tall oak trees with their sprawling upper branches, past the twisted Judas trees, their pods black and rotting. He moved as fast as his years allowed him, gasping for air, the blood pounding in his head as much due to emotion as to exertion.

At last, he was there. The chimes tower with the gold-leaf Mary atop it, the gates with wreathes on them. Both the entrance and exit gates were open and he knew they were a bait for him. He removed his pistol from his peacoat and hurried to the entrance gate. Then he heard the voice behind him.

"Porter... No!"

It was Tony, with Janice. Both had run up the hillside steps.

"The police are on their way, Porter," Janice said.

"I don't hear any goddamn sirens," said Porter.

"Porter," said Tony, "if you're going in there, we all are. It's our battle too. We'll need to protect each other."

"I swear," said Porter, pointing his gun at them, "follow me in there, and I'll shoot both of you in the knees."

He turned and ran into the Grotto. Tony and Janice followed to the gate, hesitated, and suddenly saw flames far down the path, as if someone had set a fire. "We can't leave him in there," said Tony. He and Janice moved to the exit gate and ran down the path toward the flames.

Hark the Herald Angels Sing!

Porter heard the hymn in the church starting again, the wind in the trees, the stream under the bridge. The fire, in a nest of leaves, hadn't spread and was already extinguishing. Porter looked at the Grotto altar, illuminated by the fading firelight and the votive candles, the Blessed Virgin statue standing in the niche in the Grotto wall, its hands clasped in prayer. The phallus Lizzie had worn in the church was now strapped to the statue, the way a phallus had been attached that morning in 1954.

Then, as Porter stood there, clenching his pistol, he heard a stirring from the shadows in the Grotto's recess, and off-key singing.

"Glory to the Newborn King..."

Emerging from the shadows, from behind the flickering votive candles, came Lizzie. She wore the blue robe over her shoulders, open in the front, revealing her nudity. Porter saw the garish makeup. She appeared whorish, diseased, and was clearly enjoying her sacrilegious masquerade. She stopped singing.

"Merry Christmas," she called out. "To all three of you."

Porter quickly glanced back and saw Tony and Janice, several yards behind him. "I knew, somehow, you'd all come," said Lizzie.

Tony took Janice's hand. They moved to the left of Porter on the altar in solidarity.

"You saw me giving suck to the Holy Babe?" asked Lizzie.

"I could snap you in half," said Porter, trembling with rage, clenching his pistol.

Suddenly, Mad Jack sprang up, standing above the Grotto wall. He held a shotgun and aimed it at Porter, who instantly sensed the danger. He pointed his pistol toward the man while trying to dodge the blast, but the shot tore through the left edge of his ribcage, knocking him flat. Mad Jack pivoted, roaring in laughter, aiming toward Tony and Janice.

"Janice!" shouted Tony, trying to shove her clear of Mad Jack's aim. Janice struck the wall of the Grotto bridge and the blast hit Tony's right arm, almost blowing it in two. He fell against Janice.

"No!" screamed Janice.

Porter, seriously wounded but alert, raised himself on one knee. The dark figure aimed at him again, but Porter fired first. The bullet ripped through Mad Jack's throat and he toppled backward, the shotgun falling over the wall, between Porter and Lizzie. Porter lunged for it and slung it behind him.

The blood poured from his left side, the pain almost overwhelming. He pressed his left hand against the wound, trying to staunch the bleeding, fighting to stay conscious.

"You're kneeling to me," said Lizzie. "So sweet. But you want to know a secret? I don't really listen to prayers…or give a shit. And Baby Jesus? He doesn't give a shit either."

Porter kept his pistol aimed at her. The singing from the church had stopped. There was a siren in the distance. Fighting for breath, Porter realized Janice was to the side of him, on the bridge, on her knees, crying, tearing her jacket, binding Tony's arm, trying to save him from bleeding to death.

"You failed, Lizzie," said Porter, gripping his pistol. "He's not dead. Neither am I."

"In time," hissed Lizzie. "And as for you, Pretty Little Angel Eyes…"

"Fuck you!" gasped Janice, barely audible.

"You ever suck Tony with that filthy mouth?" asked Lizzie. "Or your dear dead daddy?"

"*Fuck you!*" cried Janice, almost screaming.

"Your dear, dead daddy," said Lizzie. "Who used to touch you, and lick you… ."

Janice gasped. "How do you know…?"

"Don't listen to her, Janice!" said Porter.

"'I'm ashamed to be your daughter,'" said Lizzie, in a mockingly righteous voice. "'I'll tell Mommy!' Isn't that what you said… minutes before he blew his head off?"

"How do you *know* that?" cried Janice, her voice anguished.

"Don't *listen* to her, Janice!" shouted Porter again.

"We're a holy trinity, all together for Christmas!" laughed Lizzie, touching her red-eyed amulet. "Each of us a daddy-fuck. You, me… and dear Saint Dymphna."

Janice, crumpled over Tony, wept bitterly as she pressed with all her might against his bleeding arm. There were two sirens now, closer, coming up the twisting mountain road. Porter saw the fierce mockery in Lizzie's eyes as she teasingly stretched her arms out at her side.

"Here they come," said Lizzie. "Go ahead. Kill me… *again,* Porter Down. I dare you."

"No," taunted Porter. "This time, they'll lock you in a cage and you'll never get out."

"Shoot me!" Lizzie hissed desperately, her face lividly pale even under the makeup, tears in her eyes. "It's my gift to you! Merry Christmas, mother fucker! *Shoot me! Kill me again!*"

Porter kept the gun aimed at her, defiantly not firing it. Lizzie trembled, crying, but as she heard the sirens stop outside the gate, she regained control. "You're right," she said. "Since I'm going into a cage anyway... This time, *I* kill *you*. As originally planned. All three of you. Give me your gun."

She approached the kneeling Porter, trying to wrest the pistol from his hand, the muzzle pointed to the sky. Her robe slipped off. They fought and swayed, and Porter fell forward, his face brushing her pubis.

"Naughty boy," said Lizzie breathlessly.

Porter, blood soaking his left side, held on as long as he could but, weakening, lost his grip on the gun. Lizzie grasped it, knocking off Porter's cap, shoving the muzzle against the top of his head.

"Let thy blood consecrate me!" Lizzie shrieked. "Drench me with it! Spray me with it...!"

Then suddenly, she looked toward the foot of the altar, her face filling with horror and a chilling realization. "No," gasped Lizzie, then howling, "No! Bleeding Christ Almighty, NO!"

In an instant, there was a blast, a flash of fire, Lizzie's face and head exploding. The force of the shot caused Porter to fall on his back, and Lizzie's blood and bone showered his face as the echo of the shotgun ran thunderously up and down the mountain. Porter turned as best he could, wiped his eyes and looked behind him.

"Eve," he said weakly.

"I *had* to... ," wept Eve, standing at the foot of the altar, holding the shotgun that Porter had slung behind him only minutes ago. She'd obeyed a sense of destiny, following her friends up to the Grotto, approaching the altar through the trees, finding the shotgun, firing just in time to save Porter's life.

"Drop the gun!" a trooper shouted as he ran toward the scene, followed closely by another trooper and two paramedics. Eve dropped the shotgun.

The receding echo of the blast now mixed perversely with the ringing of the Grotto tower chimes, announcing the midnight arrival of Christmas. Lizzie's blood and her smell and part of her skull were on Porter, and as Eve ran to him, kneeling beside him, putting her arms around him, the blood smeared her face and hair.

"I *had* to," said Eve again, her voice more forceful now, as a trooper raised her to her feet.

Barely conscious, Porter looked up at the spattered Grotto wall, and then at the Blessed Virgin statue standing in its niche, Lizzie's splashed blood trickling down its face like tears.

Epilogue

Eve Devonshire Cromwell was home this night in the Thousand Islands, alone. Logs burned in the stone fireplace. For several days, there'd been talk of a large ice and snow storm heading for the Saint Lawrence River. It was forecast to arrive within 48 hours.

By that time, Porter would be safely here.

She always enjoyed snow. The pantry was full, and the bad weather would hold off long enough for Bill McDonough to bring her company here tomorrow night on his yacht. Nancy had returned to college, and Eve had prepared for her visitor herself.

For most of January, Eve had been in Baltimore and Gettysburg, tending to various hospital and legal matters. Tony had been in Gettysburg Hospital, his right arm saved by surgeons, but now permanently crippled. He was mending slowly at Charnita, physically and emotionally. He'd join the faculty at Saint John's College, Annapolis for the upcoming fall semester and meanwhile was tending to the final fixes, one-handed, on his new book. His doctors had told him that Janice keeping pressure against his wounded arm that night in the Grotto had saved his life. His pushing Janice out of the line of fire had saved hers.

"I'm blessed to be alive," Tony had told Eve when she'd last visited him at Charnita. "And I know it." As they sat in his living room, Eve noticed on a table a red-beaded rosary, outside of its small leather pouch.

Janice Lynnbrooke was in Baltimore's Sheppard Pratt Hospital, which specialized in psychiatric care. The sordid memories and gruesome nightmares since December 24 had seriously impacted Janice's emotional health. She was making progress, but would be at Sheppard Pratt indefinitely. Tony had visited her the past several weekends.

As for Porter, he'd been in Baltimore's Johns Hopkins Hospital, recovering from his shotgun wound. After three weeks, pronounced fit for travel, learning all was stable with Tony and Janice, he'd promptly taken a plane back to California. Jim O'Leary, by telephone, had confirmed what Eve suspected: Porter was suffering guilt about what had happened to Tony and Janice, as well as regret for having placed Eve in danger.

"Janice needs us," Eve had told Porter, finally reaching him by phone. "We need each other. Our work's not finished. We have to help each other heal." Porter had agreed, arranging to visit Eve, to plan how best to help Tony and Janice, and to resume the tragic but promising long relationship the two of them shared.

As for Eve herself... an investigation had resulted in a judge's ruling of her action on the night of December 24 as defense of her friends. No charges had been filed, but Eve had engaged a defense lawyer, just in case.

There'd been a discussion about the demonic aspect of the tragedy. Msgr. Harry Burke, with his experience in such matters, told Eve that, because Lizzie's death took place in the Grotto—"sacred ground," as he expressed it—that the Evil had been basically exorcised and had likely dissipated. "I'll pray that's the case," he promised.

In the aftermath of all this horror, Eve had anticipated problems, nightmares, perhaps guilt and regret—especially considering the part she'd played in its resolution. There had been none.

The grandfather clock chimed 10 P.M. Eve looked into the fire, and then, instinctively, across the room. There was a portrait, a painting of an early 19th century lady, given to her in Hollywood in 1931. Her husband had insisted it be on display, here at the Sanctuary, although Eve had wanted to store it in the attic. It too, was a relic, from her youth, from her time with a man she'd remember always, love always. It had taken 36 years for her to achieve a form of justice for him, and for dear Bonnie, and a redemption for herself. As she thought of how Porter, Janice, and Tony all shared in this redemption, each in his or her own way, the eyes of the lady in the portrait seemed far gentler than she remembered them.

Eve put on a coat and she and Boy went outside, down to the dock, looking at the stars and full moon. She felt the wind in her hair and smelled the smoke rising from the chimney. She thought, as she often had the past weeks, of how privileged she was to be able to help and comfort her friends. She looked at the lights in the houses of the distant neighboring islands, and at the moonlit river.

"He'll be here tomorrow night, Boy," said Eve Devonshire Cromwell.

* * *

The next morning, a solitary figure stood in the unsanctified cemetery on the hill behind Villa Magdalena.

Porter Down, *en route* to New York, had taken a side-trip to Maryland, though only for a day. The car he'd rented at the airport was parked beside the cemetery's stone wall. He wore his usual navy-blue attire, with a pea coat, his yachting cap, and a scarf. He held a wooden cane in his right hand and a long-stemmed red rose in his left.

He'd considered arranging to see Tony and Janice, but decided it was best to wait, to allow more time for healing. His visit to Villa Magdalena's cemetery would be his only mission in Maryland this sunny February day before a crab cake lunch and a return to the airport for the 4:30 P.M. flight to upper New York State. Fortunately, he'd be ahead of the snowstorm, expected to hit the eastern coast in the next 36 hours. He glanced down at the marble grave marker near his feet:

XII

"I've been thinking about you, Bridget," said Porter. Not yet able to kneel since his injury, he dropped the rose on the marker.

He looked at the grave a while, then raised his head, staring a moment at the tall wooden cross marking the grave several yards away, with marker number VII. He moved slowly toward it, reaching in his pocket, removing what was left of the crystal amulet. He'd taken it from a pool of blood in the Grotto in the early minutes of Christmas, wrapping the broken chain around his wrist before the police and medics had rushed him to the hospital. The angel figure was merely a shard of crystal now, with only one of its red eyes.

Porter, who'd repaired the broken chain, had planned to destroy the figure or dispose of it, maybe throw it tonight into the Saint Lawrence River. But there was only one place where it belonged. Without emotion, or any sense of ritual, Porter slipped the chain over the top of the wooden cross, and the broken, one-eyed figure fell to the crossbeam, dangling brightly in the sunlight. It sparkled, and to Porter it seemed for a moment to be a conscious thing, glad to be returned to where it long had been, reverently keeping watch over the remains of a lost soul. Or was it *two* lost souls? No, he thought, only one.

Porter took a final look at the amulet, then got into his car and drove down the hill.

A wind blew through the cemetery, rustling the trees nearby, and then it was still again. Moments later, the sexton at Villa Magdalena began ringing the noon Angelus. The bell tolled in the tower, as it had three times a day for nearly 60 years. Inside the Villa, the aged nuns listened, reciting the accompanying words to the Virgin Mary:

... pray for us sinners, now and at the hour of our death...

The Angelus, sounding strangely mournful, echoed up the hill, drifting over the forlorn graves, finally fading away, deep into the woods and the valley.

THE END

Author's Note

TO SPECIFY the novel's fact and fiction:

There truly is a Saint Dymphna, the patron saint of lunatics, epileptics, runaways, rape and incest victims, and mental health workers. Her feast day is May 15. As noted in the story, her shrine is in Geel, Belgium.

There actually was a major fire at Universal City, California, on May 15, 1967 (Saint Dymphna's feast day), causing major damage to the back lot and burning the *Frankenstein* village. The fire at Universal in Part One takes place on the same date. The cause of the real fire, however, was not attributed to arson.

Colin Clive suffered from chronic alcoholism, which contributed to his death from consumption in Hollywood on June 25, 1937, at the age of only 37. His cremains were possibly never claimed. In 1980, the owners of the former Edwards Brothers Colonial Mortuary, answering my inquiry, informed me that the State of California had revoked the Edwards Brothers' license in 1969. At that time there were approximately 300 unclaimed cremains in the basement. The owners wrote that Clive's were possibly among them and, if so, were eventually buried in an unmarked mass grave at the Los Angeles County Crematorium Grounds.

Colin Clive's uncle, Piercy Greig, died in Saint Saviour's Asylum on the Island of Jersey in 1924. He had been a patient there since at least 1903, listed as a "lunatic." This was a family secret, discovered by the author while writing my biography of Clive, *"One Man Crazy!" The Life and Death of Colin Clive* (2018). The stigma of "lunacy" presumably haunted Clive and two younger sisters, neither of whom ever married. Clive's obsession with the tragedy might have been among the demons that plagued him.

Clive did pilot a plane in Hollywood, but the earliest reference to it is in a late 1934 newspaper notice that Clive and his lady friend, actress Iris Lancaster, were having a row because she'd soloed shortly before he did. While it's possible he first flew in 1931, the episodes depicted here are fictitious.

James Whale, director of *Journey's End* and *Frankenstein*, also directed the Universal horror classics *The Old Dark House* (1932, with Karloff), *The Invisible Man* (1933), and *Bride of Frankenstein* (in which Karloff and Clive reprised their roles from *Frankenstein*), as well as others, notably Universal's 1936 musical *Show Boat*. Whale's sadistic treatment of Karloff on *Frankenstein*, forcing him to run up and down the back-lot hill to the windmill during the shooting with Clive on his back, is factual, and included in the 1975 book *Dear Boris*, by Cynthia Lindsay, a longtime friend of Karloff. After Karloff's death, the actor's widow, Evelyn, claimed the atrocity was responsible for Karloff's severe back trouble later in his life. Whale retired from the film industry in the early 1940s and, as noted in the novel, drowned himself in his pool on May 29, 1957.

The characterizations in the 1931 section of Clive, Whale, Karloff, Dwight Frye, Jack Pierce, and Carl Laemmle, Jr. are based on research, with an admitted nod to historical fiction. For insight into these individuals, I'm grateful to such now-deceased interviewees as Mae Clarke ("Elizabeth" in *Frankenstein*), Marilyn Harris ("Little Maria" in *Frankenstein*), Dwight David Frye (son of Dwight Frye, who played "Fritz" in Frankenstein), Katharine Hepburn (Clive's leading lady in the 1933 film *Christopher Strong* and the 1933 Broadway play *The Lake*), Elsa Lanchester ("Mary Shelley" and "The Monster's Mate" in 1935's *Bride of Frankenstein*), and Valerie Hobson ("Elizabeth" in *Bride of Frankenstein*).

All the other major characters are fictitious.

The dates of the shooting of *Frankenstein* are precise, as recorded in the Universal Collection at the University of Southern California Performing Arts Library. The events of this novel coordinate with the shooting dates. The author has visited the California locales described in this book, including studios, home addresses, mortuaries, etc., and has described them in the novel as accurately as possible

Dwight Frye did appear in the Broadway play *Mima*, which opened December 12, 1928 at the Belasco Theatre. The play did feature "Dancers of the Damned." A surviving program from the production lists no one named "Valerie Ivy" among them.

"Villa Magdalena," in "Rushford" Maryland is fictitious, but based on an actual institution whose identity, for a variety of reasons, will not be detailed here.

Simon Bone's story about Dr. Riccardo Galeazzi-Lisi and his "aromatic osmosis" process used on the corpse of Pope Pius XII is factual. Vatican City banned Galeazzi-Lisi for life, not for administering the process, but due to his indiscretion with the press regarding the Pope's death. The novel fictionalizes that Galeazzi-Lisi had an assistant who misused the process for demonic purposes. Galeazzi-Lisi died November 29, 1968.

Finally, the descriptions of the Grotto at Mount Saint Mary's College, Emmitsburg, MD are accurate... the author is a 1972 Mount graduate. Considerable rumors circulated regarding blasphemies committed at the sacred site. The chaplain at the time, a well-traveled and intellectual priest, took the topic very seriously.

"Leave those things alone," he warned us. "They're far more dangerous than you realize."

– GWM, December, 2021